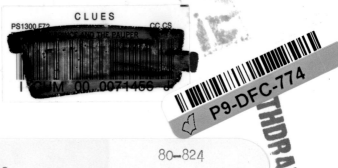

The Works of Mark Twain

VOLUME 6

THE PRINCE AND THE PAUPER

Editorial work for this volume has been made possible by a generous grant from the Editing Program of the National Endowment for the Humanities, an independent federal agency.

THE WORKS OF MARK TWAIN

The following volumes in this edition of Mark Twain's previously published works have been issued to date:

ROUGHING IT
edited by Franklin R. Rogers and Paul Baender

WHAT IS MAN? AND OTHER PHILOSOPHICAL WRITINGS
edited by Paul Baender

THE ADVENTURES OF TOM SAWYER
TOM SAWYER ABROAD
TOM SAWYER, DETECTIVE
edited by John C. Gerber, Paul Baender, and Terry Firkins

THE PRINCE AND THE PAUPER
edited by Victor Fischer and Lin Salamo,
with the assistance of Mary Jane Jones

A CONNECTICUT YANKEE IN KING ARTHUR'S COURT
edited by Bernard L. Stein
with an introduction by Henry Nash Smith

EARLY TALES & SKETCHES, VOLUME 1 (1851–1864)
edited by Edgar M. Branch and Robert H. Hirst,
with the assistance of Harriet Elinor Smith

The Works of Mark Twain

The Works of Mark Twain

THE PRINCE
AND THE PAUPER

Edited by
VICTOR FISCHER and LIN SALAMO
With the Assistance of
MARY JANE JONES

PUBLISHED FOR
THE IOWA CENTER FOR TEXTUAL STUDIES
BY THE
UNIVERSITY OF CALIFORNIA PRESS
BERKELEY, LOS ANGELES, LONDON
1979

CENTER FOR
SCHOLARLY EDITIONS
AN APPROVED EDITION
MODERN LANGUAGE
ASSOCIATION OF AMERICA

UNIVERSITY OF CALIFORNIA PRESS
BERKELEY AND LOS ANGELES, CALIFORNIA

UNIVERSITY OF CALIFORNIA PRESS, LTD.
LONDON, ENGLAND

PREVIOUSLY UNPUBLISHED MATERIAL BY MARK TWAIN
COPYRIGHT © 1979 BY THE MARK TWAIN COMPANY
ORIGINAL MATERIAL COPYRIGHT © 1979 BY
THE REGENTS OF THE UNIVERSITY OF CALIFORNIA
ISBN: 0-520-03622-0
LIBRARY OF CONGRESS CATALOG
CARD NUMBER: 77-91766

DESIGNED BY HARLEAN RICHARDSON
IN COLLABORATION WITH DAVE COMSTOCK

MANUFACTURED IN THE UNITED STATES OF AMERICA

ACKNOWLEDGMENTS

A VIRTUE of working with a staff of scholars and editors experienced in producing critical editions is that they are able to provide expert assistance, sometimes at a moment's notice, for any number of tasks—from the initial collation of texts to the final reading of printer's proofs. During the course of preparing this edition, various members of the staff of the Mark Twain Papers became available to work on it, and each brought new eyes and new insights to the problems that arose in establishing the text and developing the annotation and textual tables. When so many people perform so many tasks, it is impossible to list each of their contributions: the list that follows mentions only some. My coeditor and I would especially like to thank Kenneth M. Sanderson, who spent long hours doing original bibliographical research and such jobs as collating volumes at the Hinman machine; Harriet Elinor Smith, who copy edited much of the book and worked with the designer and typesetters; and Bernard L. Stein, whose contribution to this book is not so much particular as pervasive—his advice and consultation throughout have been invaluable. In addition, Dahlia Armon, Robert Pack Browning, Jay Gillette, Paul Machlis, and Robert Schildgen all performed such vital tasks as collation, proofreading, and what must have seemed endless checking of research and textual tables. Marie Herold patiently and accurately typed stacks of editorial material. Robert H. Hirst, a former staff member now on the faculty of the English department at UCLA, freely gave his time and expert advice and provided indispensable assistance. Frederick Anderson, the general editor, was always willing to take time from his other work to discuss editorial problems, or help with proofreading and other necessary tasks. He offered valuable counsel and much practical help.

We are grateful to Roger B. Salomon, professor of English at Case Western Reserve University, for generously sharing his research and scholarship, and for his numerous contributions to the book.

We also thank the following people and organizations: Jo Ann Boydston, general editor of the works of John Dewey at Southern Illinois University, who consulted on behalf of the Center for Editions of American Authors; George Arms, professor emeritus of English at the University of New Mexico, who inspected the volume for the Committee on Scholarly Editions and made many helpful suggestions; and the Committee on Scholarly Editions itself.

In addition, we wish to thank Mr. and Mrs. Kurt Appert, who donated to The Bancroft Library their superb collection of Mark Twain materials, some of which were immediately put to use in the preparation of this book; Theodore Koundakjian, who allowed us to roam freely through his collection of Mark Twain first editions and use several of them for collation; Charles Cornman, who also made available his collection of Mark Twain first editions for our study; William P. Barlow, Jr., chairman of the Council of the Friends of The Bancroft Library, who shared his Hinman collator with us; and Mr. and Mrs. Calvin K. Townsend, for their generous gift of funds.

Norah Smallwood of Chatto and Windus, Mark Twain's English publishers, graciously allowed us to quote from documents in the company files.

Libraries and collections of Mark Twain manuscripts across the country have made our work easier by their cooperation, and they are cited throughout this volume. But special thanks must go to the Henry E. Huntington Library and Art Gallery, which allowed us to use the manuscript in its collection as a basis for this edition. The staff extended extraordinary courtesy in taking the manuscript from its exhibition case every day for study. Mary Wright, library assistant in the Rare Book Room, was especially helpful. At the University of California, both the Interlibrary Loan Office and the Library Copy Service have responded unhesitatingly to our requests.

Editorial work for this volume has been largely supported by a generous grant from the Editing Program of the National Endowment for the Humanities. It was begun under a contract with the United States Office of Education, Department of Health, Education, and Welfare, under the provisions of the Cooperative Research Program. Financial assistance for production costs was provided by the Graduate College of the University of Iowa. We are very grateful for all of this support.

And finally, I want to thank Cheryl for her unfailing good nature and understanding when I brought work home from the office yet another night.

V.F.

CONTENTS

ABBREVIATIONS

The following abbreviations and location symbols have been used in annotations.

AD   Autobiographical Dictation

Berg   Henry W. and Albert A. Berg Collection, The New York Public Library, Astor, Lenox and Tilden Foundations

CWB   Clifton Waller Barrett Library, University of Virginia, Charlottesville

MS   Manuscript

MTP   Mark Twain Papers, The Bancroft Library, University of California, Berkeley

Yale   Collection of American Literature, Beinecke Rare Book and Manuscript Library, Yale University, New Haven, Connecticut

PUBLISHED WORKS CITED

BAL   Jacob Blanck, *Bibliography of American Literature* (New Haven: Yale University Press, 1957), vol. 2

BMT2   Merle Johnson, *A Bibliography of the Works of Mark Twain*, rev. ed. (New York: Harper and Brothers, 1935)

IE   Albert E. Stone, *The Innocent Eye* (New Haven: Yale University Press, 1961)

MT&HF   Walter Blair, *Mark Twain & Huck Finn* (Berkeley and Los Angeles: University of California Press, 1960)

MTB   Albert Bigelow Paine, *Mark Twain: A Biography*, 3 vols.
             (New York: Harper and Brothers, 1912) [*Volume num-*
             bers in citations are to this edition; page numbers are
             the same in all editions.]

MTBus   *Mark Twain, Business Man*, ed. Samuel C. Webster
             (Boston: Little, Brown, and Co., 1946)

MTCH   *Mark Twain: The Critical Heritage*, ed. Frederick Ander-
             son (New York: Barnes and Noble, 1971)

MTE   *Mark Twain in Eruption*, ed. Bernard DeVoto (New
             York: Harper and Brothers, 1940)

MTHL   *Mark Twain–Howells Letters*, ed. Henry Nash Smith
             and William M. Gibson, 2 vols. (Cambridge: Harvard
             University Press, 1960)

MTL   *Mark Twain's Letters*, ed. Albert Bigelow Paine, 2 vols.
             (New York: Harper and Brothers, 1917)

MTLP   *Mark Twain's Letters to His Publishers*, ed. Hamlin Hill
             (Berkeley and Los Angeles: University of California
             Press, 1967)

MTMF   *Mark Twain to Mrs. Fairbanks*, ed. Dixon Wecter (San
             Marino, Calif.: Huntington Library Publications, 1949)

NF   Kenneth R. Andrews, *Nook Farm: Mark Twain's Hart-
             ford Circle* (Cambridge: Harvard University Press, 1950)

N&J2   *Mark Twain's Notebooks & Journals, Volume II (1877–*
             1883), ed. Frederick Anderson, Lin Salamo, and Bernard
             L. Stein (Berkeley, Los Angeles, London: University of
             California Press, 1975)

INTRODUCTION

In THE YEARS since its publication *The Prince and the Pauper* has been read primarily as a children's story. Yet the book was not intended by its author solely for the nursery bookshelves. Indeed, Mark Twain was never strictly respectful of the distinction between juvenile and adult literature. In later life he remarked, "I have never written a book for boys; I write for grown-ups who have *been* boys."[1] *The Prince and the Pauper* was no exception. It was, as the author styled it, "a tale for young people of all ages." It was also a conscious excursion away from Mark Twain's established literary territory. He had already proved overwhelmingly successful with the public as a humorist, but he chafed at the widely accepted notion that serious novels were above his "proper level."[2] With *The Prince and the Pauper* he attempted to win a new audience, the cultivated but conventional readers epitomized by his own Nook Farm neighbors. His determination to broaden his literary reputation was fed by the comments of his family and friends even as he worked on the manuscript of *The Prince and the Pauper.* They urged him to "do some first-class serious" work and produce a book of "a sober character and a solid worth & a permanent value." His motherly advisor Mary Mason Fairbanks wrote, "The time has come for your *best book.* I do not mean your most taking book, with the most money in it, I mean your best contribution to American literature."[3]

---

[1] *IE*, p. 60.

[2] Clemens to Mary Mason Fairbanks, 5 February 1878, *MTMF*, p. 218. Clemens told a correspondent in January 1881: "I like this tale better than *Tom Sawyer*—because I haven't put any fun in it. I *think* that is why I like it better. You know a body always enjoys seeing himself attempting something out of his line" (Clemens to Annie Lucas, 31 January 1881, *Mark Twain the Letter Writer*, ed. Cyril Clemens [Boston: Meador Publishing Co., 1932], p. 37).

[3] Edwin Pond Parker to Clemens, 22 December 1880, and Mary Mason Fairbanks to Clemens, 26 July 1880, *NF*, p. 190.

The idea for *The Prince and the Pauper*, Clemens later recalled, was "suggested by that pleasant and picturesque little history-book, Charlotte M. Yonge's 'Little Duke,'" which he found in his sister-in-law's library at Quarry Farm.[4] *The Little Duke*, set in tenth-century France, follows the youthful adventures of imperious and quick-tempered Richard, duke of Normandy, who succeeds to the title when his father is treacherously murdered. After several months as a hostage at the corrupt court of King Louis IV, young Richard escapes and returns to Normandy, where he develops into a wise and gentle ruler, having learned, as a result of his experiences, Christian forgiveness, humility, and patience.

Charlotte Yonge was a fervent disciple of the Oxford Movement and intended her books to illustrate the history of Anglo-Catholic tenets while fostering Christian ideals and virtues. Clemens had no interest in the religious aspects of *The Little Duke*, but he was undoubtedly influenced by its genre, the historical romance, and by its theme, the moral education of a young boy. Most important, it showed him an orthodox literary mode, acceptable to a genteel audience, which he could employ.

There are obvious points of similarity between *The Little Duke* and *The Prince and the Pauper*. Both Richard of Normandy and Prince Edward are denied their noble birthright and, in the course of their adventures, develop a sense of justice and compassion before they regain their rightful positions. Richard, like Tom Canty, is at times delighted with the pageantry and adulation connected with his new position, but its awful isolation causes him, too, to become bored and lonely. And Prince Edward's faithful ally Miles Hendon recalls Osmond de Centeville, who is Richard's companion and protector

---

[4]Clemens to the Reverend F. V. Christ, 27 August 1908, *MTL*, 2:814. Albert Bigelow Paine quotes Clemens as saying only that he got the idea for *The Prince and the Pauper* "after reading a little book I found in my sister-in-law's library at Elmira" (Paine, " 'The Prince and the Pauper,' " *Mentor*, December 1928, p. 8). The "little book," Paine maintains, was Charlotte Yonge's *The Prince and the Page* (1865), the story of young Richard de Montfort, page to the future Edward I during the last Crusade. Paine admits, however, that "there is no point of resemblance" between the two similarly titled books (*MTB*, 2:597). Howard G. Baetzhold argues convincingly that the source was actually Yonge's *Little Duke*, published in 1854 (Baetzhold, "Mark Twain's 'The Prince and the Pauper,' " *Notes and Queries*, n.s. 1 [September 1954]: 401–403).

during his French captivity and who later rescues him from it.[5] Ultimately, however, the similarities between the two books are superficial. Yonge stayed well within a verifiable historical framework; her intention was didactic, and the simplicity and propriety of her story clearly marked it for a young audience.

The writing of *The Prince and the Pauper*, like that of many of Mark Twain's works, was accomplished over several years, interrupted by business and family affairs and other literary projects. Therefore it is not surprising that more than once he modified his concept of the book. In the earliest surviving draft of the manuscript he attempted to place the story in the nineteenth century with Victoria's heir Albert Edward, later Edward VII, as its prince. After rejecting the idea of using changelings as the central device, he wrote at least twenty pages in which Albert Edward exchanged identities with Jim Hubbard, a product of London's industrial slums. The Victorian setting proved unusable; according to Albert Bigelow Paine, the author felt that he could not plausibly depict Albert Edward's "proud estate denied and jeered at by a modern mob." So he put aside his manuscript and "followed back through history, looking along for the proper time and prince," until he found Edward Tudor. By the summer of 1876 he was "diligently" researching an English Renaissance setting, but he apparently did not then make a fresh start on the manuscript.[6] The sole fruit of that summer's historical reading seems to have been his brief scatological sketch *1601 or Conversation, As It Was by the Social Fireside, in the Time of the Tudors.*

Clemens continued his study of Tudor history in the summer of 1877 at Quarry Farm, reminding himself in his notebook to "get Froude & notes" and "Hume's Henry VIII & Henry VII" from his Hartford home. He first mentioned the narrative by name, as a possible playscript, on the same notebook page: "Write Prince & Pauper

---

[5]Baetzhold has pointed out that *The Little Duke* apparently inspired both the language and action of a scene in *The Prince and the Pauper*: when young Richard of Normandy attempts to pass King Louis' guards, he is roughly handled and turned back despite his insistent declaration, "I am the Duke!" The Prince of Wales suffers like treatment from the Westminster guard in chapter 3 of Mark Twain's book (Baetzhold, " 'Prince and the Pauper,' " p. 403).

[6]*MTB*, 2:597–598; AD, 31 July 1906, *MTE*, p. 206. It has not been possible to establish just when the early manuscript pages set in Victorian England were written.

in 4 acts & 8 changes."[7] But he probably did not begin the actual writing of the Tom Canty/Edward Tudor story until sometime after his return to Hartford in September. A notebook entry of 23 November 1877 sketched the working plan for his new project:

> Edward VI & a little pauper exchange places by accident a day or so before Henry VIII[s] death. The prince wanders in rags & hardships & the pauper suffers the (to him) horrible miseries of princedom, up to the moment of crowning, in Westminster Abbey, when proof is brought & the mistake rectified.[8]

In the course of the next three months, Mark Twain made a start on the manuscript of his novel; he revised and incorporated a few pages of his earlier draft[9] and then concentrated on describing Tom Canty's life at the palace, introducing several of the more elaborate scenes of court ceremony. For the moment, the prince's adventures "in rags & hardships" were neglected.

In February 1878, answering a query from Mrs. Fairbanks, Clemens was enthusiastic about the book: "What am I writing? A historical tale, of 300 years ago, simply for the love of it—for it will appear without my name—such grave & stately work being considered by the world to be above my proper level. I have been studying for it, off & on, for a year & a half."[10] That same month, after finishing little more than eleven chapters, the author laid the manuscript aside. Later he said he had stopped because "the tank was dry." At the time he

---

[7]N&J2, p. 39. The conception of the narrative as a drama may have been due to Clemens' current preoccupation with the theater. He had just completed one dramatization, Cap'n Simon Wheeler, The Amateur Detective, and was overseeing rehearsals of his play Ah Sin, due to open in New York on 31 July 1877. During the legal battle with Edward H. House concerning the 1889 dramatization of The Prince and the Pauper, Clemens told a Hartford Courant reporter that "the story was originally planned for a drama and not as a book. I doubted my ability to write a drama but wrote it purposely for somebody capable of doing so to turn it into a drama" (Hartford Courant, 18 January 1890). Clemens' statement, however, is qualified by the existence of the early Albert Edward/Jim Hubbard fragments—obviously drafted for a novel, not a play.

[8]N&J2, p. 49.

[9]Eight pages of the Albert Edward/Jim Hubbard manuscript were revised and incorporated into chapters 2 and 3 of The Prince and the Pauper.

[10]Clemens to Mary Mason Fairbanks, 5 February 1878, MTMF, p. 218. Clemens did not finally decide against anonymous publication until December 1880 (Clemens to Edwin Pond Parker, 24 December 1880, NF, p. 191).

told William Dean Howells that he did so to prepare for a trip to Europe.[11]

The Clemens family sailed for Europe in April 1878 and spent almost a year and a half there while Clemens gathered material for *A Tramp Abroad.* He did not add to the manuscript of *The Prince and the Pauper,* although he may have done some research for the story while in London in July and August 1879.[12] After returning to the United States in September he devoted himself chiefly to completing his travel book and almost certainly did not resume work on *The Prince and the Pauper* until after he finished *A Tramp Abroad* in January 1880.

Mark Twain probably intended at first to establish a pattern of alternating adventures of the pauper and the prince. Early in 1880, looking over the eleven chapters that he had laid aside almost two years before, he was evidently struck by his neglect of Edward's role in the plot: his first decision upon resuming work was to "put 212–13–14 [his last completed manuscript pages] further along"[13] and insert into the manuscript two new chapters (chapters 12 and 13), which dealt with the prince's adventures as an outcast in the streets of London.

By early March 1880 Mark Twain was writing chapter 15 of *The Prince and the Pauper*[14] and he had begun to modify his scheme for the book. The device of alternately presenting the adventures of Tom Canty and Edward, while it responded to the problem of narrative structure, was too restrictive. Tom's perceptions and expe-

---

[11]AD, 30 August 1906, *MTE,* p. 197; Clemens to Howells, 26 February 1878, *MTHL,* 1:219. Paine mistakenly claims that Mark Twain had completed about four hundred manuscript pages by the end of the summer of 1877 (*MTB,* 2:598). Examination of the manuscript and external evidence demonstrates that he stopped after writing three pages (212 through 214 in the original pagination) of what was then chapter 12. These three pages were later moved to the beginning of chapter 14.

[12]See the working notes in Appendix A, Group K.

[13]This comment is written in purple ink (ink 2) on an otherwise blank torn half-sheet of Crystal-Lake Mills stationery in MTP.

[14]On 5 March 1880 Clemens told Howells that he had reached page 326 since recommencing the book (*MTHL,* 1:290) and on the same day he informed his brother Orion that he had added 114 pages to the manuscript (*MTBus,* p. 145). Obviously Clemens had worked forward from the beginning of chapter 12 (manuscript page 212, original pagination) since his return from Europe.

riences, necessarily confined to the English court at Westminster, lacked interest and variety. The first eleven chapters, which dealt almost exclusively with Tom, were overburdened with long quotes from several rather tedious historical accounts. The author began to broaden the scope of his story by concentrating on Edward's adventures. In a letter of March 11 to Howells, he sketched the plot of his novel and hinted at this shift in emphasis away from Tom to Edward:

It begins at 9 a.m., Jan. 27, 1547, seventeen & a half hours before Henry VIII^s death, by the swapping of clothes *and places*, between the prince of Wales & a pauper boy of the same age & countenance (& half as much learning & still more genius & imagination) and & after that, the rightful small king has a rough time among tramps & ruffians in the country parts of Kent, whilst the small bogus king has a gilded & worshiped & dreary & restrained & cussed time of it on the throne. . . .

My idea is to afford a realizing sense of the exceeding severity of the laws of that day by inflicting some of their penalties upon the king himself & allowing him a chance to see the rest of them applied to others—all of which is to account for certain mildnesses which distinguished Edward VI^s reign from those that preceded & followed it.[15]

Mark Twain probably wrote two more chapters before abandoning the manuscript for several weeks.[16] By mid-June he was installed at Quarry Farm for the summer and he resumed work, evidently strongly under the influence of his new idea of having Edward experience, firsthand, the laws of his kingdom. From then on, the novel would focus almost exclusively on Edward's adventures.[17]

Mark Twain alternated composing his novel with writing *Huckleberry Finn*, and by August 31 he had written the "first half of the

---

[15]Clemens to Howells, 11 March 1880, *MTHL*, 1:291–292.

[16]That is, through chapter 17. Clemens wrote to Howells on 6 May 1880 that he had "knocked off" working recently and added that he didn't "intend to go to work again till we go away for the summer, 5 or 6 weeks hence" (*MTHL*, 1:306-307).

[17]The point at which Mark Twain picked up his work at Quarry Farm can be fairly safely established by ink differences. The manuscript of the first seventeen chapters was written in violet and purple inks (inks 1 and 2); thenceforth he used blue ink (ink 3). Walter Blair maintains that Mark Twain never used inks 1 and 2 (both of which he calls violet ink) at Quarry Farm and that in fact, between mid-June 1880 and the end of December 1884, "no scrap of writing in letters, datable manuscripts, or notebooks . . . is in violet ink." Moreover, the paper used in the first sixteen chapters is Crystal-Lake Mills stationery, a type Clemens did not use after mid-June 1880 (*MT&HF*, pp. 201–202).

climax chapter" (chapter 32) and anticipated only another week's work. By 14 September 1880 he had finished it.[18]

For the next four months Mark Twain revised and expanded the manuscript and sought criticisms and reactions from friends. In December he asked Howells, Edwin Pond Parker, and Joseph Hopkins Twichell to read and comment on the manuscript,[19] and some of their suggestions occasioned manuscript changes. Parker, in a 1912 letter to the Hartford *Courant*, recalled that both he and Twichell suggested striking out a certain "blot" in the manuscript, but that Mark Twain refused.[20] The author reacted more positively to comments made by Howells in a letter of 13 December 1880:

> I have read the Two Ps, and I like it immensely. It begins well, and it ends well, but there are things in the middle that are not so good. The whipping-boy's story seemed poor fun; and the accounts of the court ceremonials are too long, unless you *droll* them more than you have done. I think you might have let in a little more of your humor the whole way through, and satirized things more. This would not have hurt the story for the children, and would have helped it for the grownies. As it is, the book is marvellously good. It realizes most vividly the time. All the *picaresque* part—the tramps, outlaws, etc.,—all the infernal clumsiness and cruelties of the law—are incomparable. The whole intention, the allegory, is splendid, and powerfully enforced. The subordinate stories, like that of Hendon, are well assimilated and thoroughly interesting.[21]

Mark Twain promptly removed the "whipping-boy's story,"[22] but did nothing about the court ceremonials. Howells' praise of the book's picaresque elements may have moved Mark Twain to expand that sec-

---

[18]*MTB*, 2:683–684; Clemens to Edward H. House, 31 August 1880, quoted in the *Twainian*, March–April 1963, p. 2; Clemens to Thomas Bailey Aldrich, 15 September 1880, *MTL*, 1:386.

[19]Clemens to Parker, 24 December 1880, *NF*, pp. 191–192. Clemens also solicited, through their fathers, comments from the Twichell, Howells, and Parker children. He had previously read parts of the manuscript to his wife and children, to Lilly and Susan Warner, to Mrs. Fairbanks, and to the young ladies of Hartford's Saturday Morning Club (*NF*, pp. 191–192). Beginning with *The Prince and the Pauper*, reading manuscripts aloud became a custom in the Clemens household (*MTB*, 2:662–663).

[20]Parker to Hartford *Courant*, 21 June 1912, p. 19. Parker does not identify the objectionable passage. Kenneth R. Andrews believes that the "blot" is the passage in which Tom Canty, on being told that Henry's funeral will not take place for some time, asks, "'Will he keep?'" (*NF*, p. 266 n. 95).

[21]Howells to Clemens, 13 December 1880, *MTHL*, 1:338.

[22]See Appendix B.

tion of the book,[23] and by 21 January 1881 he had added over one
hundred thirty new pages of manuscript to the prince's adventures
in the rural districts, which pagination shows constitute the greater
part of chapters 18 through 22.[24] He then added some historical
notes—"to give it style"—and finished the book on 1 February 1881.[25]

There are numerous revisions throughout the manuscript, most of
which were made for the purpose of refining language and plot and
making the characters more believable.[26] In chapter 1, for example,
Mark Twain deleted a specific reference to the birthdate of his young
heroes. "I knew I was making them too wise & knowing for their *real*
age," he later admitted, "so I studiously avoided mentioning any dates
which would remind the reader that they were under 10 years old.
Perhaps I mention the date of Henry VIIIs death, but I don't mention
the date of Prince Edward's birth."[27] The author also carefully modified his initial portrait of Edward in chapter 3. Realizing that a
studious and sickly Edward would hardly be able to survive the rigorous adventures the plot demanded, Mark Twain sacrificed historical
accuracy in the interest of literary necessity, substituting "comely"
for "pale" in his description and adding that the prince was "tanned
and brown with sturdy out-door sports and exercises." And he was
also concerned that Tom Canty's transmutation from Offal Court
to the court at Westminster should not seem incredible, so he added
a long passage in chapter 2 describing Tom's daydreams of court life
and their effect. In chapter 3 Mark Twain inserted, for the alert
reader, the brief scene in which Edward puts away the "article of
national importance," and in chapter 10 he introduced the curious

---

[23]Mark Twain may have already contemplated such an expansion. On 31 August
1880 he told Edward H. House that he was undecided whether to "elaborate one portion" of the manuscript because he feared to impair the book's "dramatic strength"
(*Twainian*, March–April 1963, p. 2).

[24]Clemens to James R. Osgood, 21 January 1881, catalog of Parke-Bernet Galleries,
sale no. 325, 10–11 December 1941, item 114. The episode of Hugo's treachery and the
prince's arrest was originally planned for chapter 18. Mark Twain moved it, adding
to chapter 18 a preliminary incident involving Hugo and then going on to the prince's
adventures with the peasants and the hermit.

[25]Clemens to Annie Lucas, 31 January 1881, *Mark Twain the Letter Writer*, ed.
Clemens, p. 37. "I finished *once more* to-day," Clemens wrote his publisher (Clemens
to Osgood, 1 February 1881, collection of Theodore Koundakjian).

[26]Most of the revisions are in blue ink (ink 3). Since Mark Twain switched
to ink 3 in May or June 1880, the ink 3 revisions of the earlier chapters could have
been made at any time after that date.

[27]Clemens to A. V. S. Anthony, 9 March 1881, MTP.

test by which Mrs. Canty is always able to identify Tom. The author also reduced the number of archaic constructions and spellings, and tempered some of the language.

Plans for publication of the book concerned Clemens for several months before he actually finished it. In November 1880 he offered the opening chapters of *The Prince and the Pauper* to Mary Mapes Dodge, editor of the prestigious young people's magazine *St. Nicholas*. Mrs. Dodge replied that the magazine already had enough contributions for 1881, but she agreed to read the proffered chapters, saying that if "the story should prove to be one that St. Nicholas *must* have (crowded or not) I do not doubt that the publishers and yourself would agree, as to terms." After consultation with his publisher, Clemens decided against submitting the chapters for fear that serial publication might reduce sales of the printed volume.[28]

Apparently Clemens had already chosen his publisher by this time. For financial reasons he had long been dissatisfied with the American Publishing Company, the subscription-book firm he had dealt with since 1868, and he was, by 1880, confident that he could publish on a more lucrative basis. The death of Elisha Bliss, president of the American Publishing Company, in September 1880, provided him an excuse for ending his connection with that house and he entered into negotiations with James R. Osgood, a well-known Boston trade publisher. Osgood, who had published Mark Twain's *A True Story, and the Recent Carnival of Crime* in 1877 as a trade book, had no experience in subscription publishing and no network of door-to-door canvassers to reach the subscription public, but he was understandably eager to add Mark Twain to his list of authors. Clemens, on the other hand, realized the advantages of publishing his first "grave & stately work" under the aegis of a genteel and respected Boston publisher. Nevertheless he had no intention of sacrificing the vast subscription market—and its accompanying huge profits—for the relatively small and elite trade publication readership.[29] Therefore in

---

[28]Mary Mapes Dodge to Clemens, 17 November 1880, *IE*, p. 97; Clemens to Mary Mapes Dodge, 19 November 1880, *IE*, pp. 97–98.

[29]Trade publishers scoffed at the lucrative subscription method and warned authors "of established reputation" not to sacrifice "caste" for the sake of big profits (see Hamlin Hill's *Mark Twain and Elisha Bliss* [Columbia: University of Missouri Press, 1964], pp. 6–10). Clemens' view of the matter was more practical. "Mighty few books that come strictly under the head of *literature* will sell by subscription," he advised

November 1880 he made a preliminary informal agreement with
Osgood for the publication, by subscription, of *The Prince and the
Pauper*. He signed the final contract on 9 February 1881.[30]

According to the provisions of the contract for *The Prince and the
Pauper*, Osgood, subject to Clemens' approval, would provide the illustrations, pay all advertising costs, and manufacture the book, which
was to be issued by 15 November 1881. Clemens agreed to deliver the
manuscript by April 1 of that year, to pay all bills incurred in producing the volume, and to determine its retail price and the discounts
to agents and canvassers. He would own "all illustrations, plates and
stock belonging to said work." Perhaps the two most important stipu-
lations were that Clemens would retain copyright, which had not been
the case when he was dealing with the American Publishing Company, and that he would receive all funds collected except for a
$7\frac{1}{2}$ percent commission, which was to go to the Osgood company.[31]

Production began on schedule: by 16 March 1881 "high-priced
artists & engravers"[32] were at work on the book and on April 22
Clemens reported that it was "in press."[33] Over the next few months,
Clemens was consulted about a variety of production and promotional
matters, including manufacturing costs.[34] He was able to draw upon
his long association with the American Publishing Company to offset
Osgood's inexperience in the field of subscription publishing. In fact,

Joel Chandler Harris on 10 August 1881. But "when a book *will* sell by subscription,
it will sell two or three times as many copies as it would in the trade; and the profit
is bulkier" (*MTL*, 1:402).

[30]Clemens refers to the preliminary agreement in his letter to Orion Clemens of
27 November 1880 (*MTBus*, pp. 147–148). The February contract, in MTP, is reprinted
in Frederick Anderson and Hamlin Hill, "How Samuel Clemens Became Mark Twain's
Publisher: A Study of the James R. Osgood Contracts," *Proof* 2 (1972): 121–124.

[31]Anderson and Hill, "Osgood Contracts," pp. 120–125.

[32]Clemens to Pamela Moffett, 16 March 1881, *MTBus*, p. 150. Clemens agreed to
$2,800 as the limit on the cost of the illustrations (Clemens to Osgood, 30 March 1881,
MTLP, p. 135).

[33]Clemens to F. A. Teall, 22 April 1881, CWB. Clemens may have been referring only
to the printing of the illustrations for the volume (see the discussion in the textual
introduction).

[34]Clemens secured from the American Publishing Company production figures for
A Tramp Abroad, which he and Osgood then used to project costs on *The Prince and
the Pauper*. They were hopeful of reducing manufacturing costs considerably below
the subscription company's figures—from sixty-seven cents to about fifty cents a book
(Clemens to Osgood, 7 March 1881, *MTLP*, p. 134). According to Clemens, however,
his manufacturing cost on the initial 25,000 volumes of *The Prince and the Pauper*
amounted to $17,500—an average of seventy cents for each book (Clemens to H. H.
Boyesen, 11 January 1882, *MTLP*, p. 152 n. 1).

Osgood used the American Publishing Company's subscription network to some extent to market the new book.[35]

Mark Twain approved, but did not suggest, particular illustrations, allowing his publishers to select captions for them[36] and stipulating only that "the artist always picture the Prince & Tom Canty as lads of 13 or 14 years old."[37] More than half of the illustrations were the work of Frank T. Merrill, with the remainder contributed by John J. Harley (who would later work on *Life on the Mississippi*); the half-titles were designed by L. S. Ipsen.[38] The author repeatedly expressed delight with the illustrations, singling out Merrill's delicate figures rather than Harley's more robust delineations. "Merrill probably thinks he *originated* his exquisite boys himself," Clemens wrote to his publisher, "but I was ahead of him there!—in these pictures they look and dress exactly as I used to see them in my mind two years ago. It is a vast pleasure to see them cast in the flesh, so to speak—they were of but perishable dream-stuff, before." Clemens' experience of subscription publishing had convinced him of the importance of illustrations to the volume: he urged his publisher to "glorify" them in the advertising circulars and to "call attention to the historical accuracy of the costumes."[39] The publisher's announcement in the canvassing prospectus would conclude with the statement: "No pains have been spared to make the representation of the characters, costumes, buildings, and scenery historically accurate, as well as artistically correct and attractive."

Mark Twain began receiving proof sheets of the book in August 1881; by September 18 he had read two-thirds of them and was expect-

---

[35]Osgood to Clemens, 2 April 1881, MTP; Clemens to Osgood, 31 December 1881, *MTLP*, p. 149.

[36]"I'll alter [the captions] in proof if any alteration shall seem necessary," the author wrote to Osgood's partner, Benjamin H. Ticknor, on 1 August 1881 (*MTLP*, p. 139).

[37]Clemens to A. V. S. Anthony, 9 March 1881, MTP. Mark Twain later questioned the content of one of the illustrations. He was surprised to find that the illustrations included an engraving of the Great Seal, which he apparently felt would blunt the impact of the coronation scene. "I'm afraid to put it in," he explained to Ticknor on 14 August 1881 (*MTLP*, p. 140); nonetheless the engraving of the Great Seal appeared in both the American and English editions.

[38]A. V. S. Anthony to Charles L. Webster and Co., 20 March 1889, MTP.

[39]Clemens to Ticknor, 14 August 1881, *MTLP*, pp. 139–140. Clemens was so taken with the "dainty and rich" illustrations that he contemplated having a dozen or more sets bound as gifts (Clemens to Ticknor, 1 August 1881, *MTLP*, p. 138). He later decided on a small private edition of the entire book, printed and bound by the Franklin Press, which he distributed as gifts to family and friends (*BMT2*, p. 40).

ing to publish the book on December 1.[40] The November publication
date originally projected for the book could not be met because of the
necessity of coordinating printing schedules with the English and
Canadian editions. In addition, the November schedule was com-
promised by last-minute revisions in the text and by difficulties with
the impractical Kaolatype process being used to produce the volume's cover.[41]

Copyright for the first American edition was granted on 13 October
1881. Clemens was more concerned, however, with the problem of
securing clear and exclusive Canadian copyright in order to forestall
pirated editions. He journeyed to Montreal on November 26 and
remained there until December 9 in an attempt to ensure copyright
by establishing residence while a small Canadian edition was printed.
But Clemens learned even before he left Montreal that Canadian
copyright had not been granted. His maneuver was not entirely worthless: his temporary residence in Canada satisfied the requirements of
the Imperial Copyright Law of 1842 and effectively protected him from
Canadian reprints, but having failed to satisfy more recent Canadian
statutes, Clemens was powerless to prevent the importation into
Canada of foreign reprints. Two determined Canadian publishers,
the Rose-Belford Publishing Company and John Ross Robertson, found
a way to circumvent these copyright restrictions—they protected their
pirated editions of *The Prince and the Pauper* by the simple expedient
of printing the books in the United States and importing them
into Canada.

---

[40]Clemens to Mary Mason Fairbanks, 18 September 1881, *MTMF*, p. 245.

[41]Kaolatype was a process by which matrices for stereotype plates were formed by
engraving down to a steel plate through a layer of china clay or kaolin. Clemens bought
the patent in February 1880 and organized the Kaolatype Company, hiring his nephew
Charles L. Webster to manage the business and to perfect the process for use in the
production of brass dies for stamping book covers. At the beginning of September 1881
Clemens sent Webster the cover design for *The Prince and the Pauper* and told him
to set his best engraver to do the job quickly, so as not to delay the issue of the canvassing books (which would include samples of the book's binding). Nonetheless there
were delays in September and again in October. On October 19 Clemens expressed to
Osgood his pleasure with the appearance of the canvassing book and the Kaolatype-
stamped jacket and added that he believed that the illustrations also could have been
engraved "to perfection in Kaolatype . . . and about as cheaply and quickly, and a
dern sight deeper and stronger" (*MTLP*, p. 141 n. 3). Clemens also offered to send the
Kaolatype dies to Chatto and Windus for the covers of the English edition, but the
close production schedule made this impossible (Clemens to Chatto and Windus,
7 October 1881, *N&J2*, p. 401 n. 154).

Chatto and Windus' English edition appeared as planned on 1 December 1881, and the authorized Canadian edition, consisting of 275 copies issued by Dawson Brothers of Montreal merely as a concession to copyright law, probably appeared immediately thereafter. Baron Tauchnitz's Continental edition was also scheduled to appear on December 1.[42] Osgood's American edition was available on December 3 in Boston, and by the end of December, four impressions, totaling over 25,000 copies, had been prepared.[43]

The response to *The Prince and the Pauper*—especially among Clemens' friends—was enthusiastic. As Edwin Pond Parker put it in a Hartford *Courant* editorial: "Mark Twain has finally fulfilled the earnest hope of many of his best friends, in writing a book which has other and higher merits than can possibly belong to the most artistic expression of mere humor."[44] Mrs. Fairbanks was equally pleased: "It is just a lovely book, and I am as happy as if I had written it myself. . . . The book is your masterpiece in fineness—'The Innocents' was your bulletin—'The Prince & the Pauper' your specimen." Thomas Bailey Aldrich expressed his delight with the theme of the book—"a charming conception and charmingly worked out."[45] The one dissenting voice was Joseph T. Goodman, Clemens' old Nevada friend and editor. He had commented even before he saw the book—"I have been anxious that you should try your hand at another novel. But what could have sent you groping among the driftwood of the Deluge for a topic when you would have been so much more at home in the wash of today?" His disappointment became even more acute after he read the novel:

---

[42]Clemens to Orion Clemens, 26 October 1881, *MTBus*, p. 174. The German publisher Christian Bernhard, Baron von Tauchnitz, secured the rights to the Continental edition from Clemens for seventy-five pounds (Tauchnitz, Jr., to Clemens, 7 November 1881, MTP).

[43]"The book was published in London, to-day, as we know by cablegram, & will be published here pretty soon & in Boston day after to-morrow" (Clemens to Olivia Clemens, 1 December 1881, typescript in MTP). The title page of the American edition bears the date 1882. Clemens mentioned the size of the first American printing in a letter of 11 January 1882 to H. H. Boyesen (*MTLP*, p. 152 n. 1).

[44]Hartford *Courant*, 28 December 1881, quoted in *NF*, p. 193. Clemens identified Parker as the author of the anonymous editorial when he sent a copy to his publisher among material "from which to select plums for a new and powerful circular—that is if any more powerful one than the last is needful or possible" (Clemens to Osgood, 29 December 1881, *MTLP*, p. 148).

[45]Mary Mason Fairbanks to Clemens, 4 January 1882, *MTMF*, p. 245 n. 1; Aldrich to Clemens, 11 January 1882, MTP.

It might have been written by anybody else—by a far less masterly hand, in fact. You went entirely out of your sphere. The laboriousness is apparent everywhere by which you endeavor to harmonize irreconcilable improbabilities, to manage the obsolete customs and parlance of the times, and to wrestle generally with a condition of things to which you feel yourself alien and unsuited. And after all you don't succeed.[46]

In the American press, the keynote of critical reaction to the book was set by Howells, writing anonymously in the New York *Daily Tribune* in October 1881. He predicted that the book would "surprise those who have found nothing but drollery in Mark Twain's books, and have not perceived the artistic sense and the strain of deep earnestness underlying his humor." In Howells' judgment *The Prince and the Pauper* showed "interesting evidence of growth in a man who ought still to have his best work before him."[47] The reviewer in the *Critic* suggested that the "finer element in Mark Twain's nature, which has been more or less distinctly traceable in all his books, has been growing more predominant in his more recent writings."[48]

While the critics were unanimous in applauding the refinement of literary taste and the strong and pure morality evident in *The Prince and the Pauper*, they did not all agree that Mark Twain's previous publications had prepared his readers for such a work. Joel Chandler Harris, writing for the Atlanta *Constitution*, thought the new book a "wide departure from his old methods—so much so that the contrast presents a phase of literary development unique in its proportions and suggestions," and he welcomed the emergence of Mark Twain as a "true literary artist."[49]

H. H. Boyesen's long unsigned review in the *Atlantic Monthly* praised *The Prince and the Pauper* in terms characteristic of Victorian standards of literary art—"a tale ingenious in conception, pure and humane in purpose, artistic in method, and, with barely a flaw, refined in execution"—and he viewed the volume as a radically "new departure" for Mark Twain,

---

[46]Goodman to Clemens, 24 October 1881, quoted in *NF*, p. 192, corrected from original in MTP; Goodman to Clemens, 29 January 1882, MTP.

[47]New York *Daily Tribune*, 25 October 1881, p. 6.

[48]*Critic*, 31 December 1881, p. 368.

[49]Atlanta *Constitution*, 25 December 1881, quoted in *Emory University Publications: Sources & Reprints*, series 7, no. 3 (1953), p. 21.

so much so as to make it appear inappropriate to reckon it among that writer's works. It is indisputably by Clemens; it does not seem to be by Twain. . . . The book is not only a novelty of Mark Twain's handiwork; it is in some respects a novelty in romance. It is not easy to place it in any distinct classification. It lacks the essential features of a novel, and while principally about children, is by no means a tale exclusively for children. . . . That it will be accorded a rank far above any of the author's previous productions is a matter of course.[50]

Harper's magazine found nothing to criticize: the author was a "veracious chronicler, the recital being interspersed with sparkles of dry humor and covert satire yet observing a careful regard to the historical accessories," and the book was "rich in historical facts and teachings" and "charged with a generous and ennobling moral."[51]

The *Century* reserved its comments until March 1882 and was more judicious in its criticism. The reviewer found *The Prince and the Pauper* in some ways a "remarkable" book—pointing out the "quiet satire, the ingenuity of the plot, and the clever development of the thoughts and motives" of Tom and Edward. But he also expressed serious reservations about the book's "curious"—and sometimes infelicitous—"mixture of fact and fancy."

So far as it was the author's purpose to produce a work of art after the old models, and to prove that the humorous story-teller and ingenious homely philosopher, Mark Twain, can be a literary purist, a scholar, and an antiquary, we do not think his 'new departure' is a conspicuous success. It was not necessary for the author to prop his literary reputation with archaic English and a somewhat conventional manner.[52]

Clemens, with the almost unanimous commendations of the critics before him, was undisturbed by the *Century's* quibbles. "It amused me a good deal," he wrote to Edward H. House on 23 February 1882, "to observe the struggle going on in the writer's mind, to find something to find fault with, and I thought that if I could have been at his elbow, I could have saved him the humiliation of discovering such infinitesimal defects, by pointing out colossal ones."[53]

---

[50]*Atlantic Monthly*, December 1881, reprinted in *MTCH*, pp. 85–89.
[51]*Harper's*, March 1882, p. 635.
[52]*Century*, March 1882, reprinted in *MTCH*, pp. 92–94.
[53]Clemens to House, 23 February 1882, CWB.

Clemens was surprised to find the English reviews on the whole "profoundly complimentary."[54] The London *Times* praised the "remarkably ingenious and sensible story" and, while suggesting that it was perhaps too long for a young audience, concluded that it was "capitally told, in an easy and picturesque style, and imparts in a natural manner a good deal of historic information."[55] There was some adverse criticism in the English press: the book was accused of dullness, and the author's historical accuracy was questioned. The *Saturday Review* praised the illustrations, but beyond pointing out a minor inaccuracy made no attempt at a literary evaluation of the book.[56] E. Purcell's brief review in the *Academy* dismissed the new book as a "libel on the English Court," monotonous and "singularly deficient in literary merit."[57] The *Athenaeum's* remarks about "Mr. Clements's" new effort were equally ruthless and considerably longer:

The author, a noted representative of American humour, has essayed to achieve a serious book. The consequences are at once disastrous and amazing. The volume . . . is only to be described as some four hundred pages of careful tediousness, mitigated by occasional flashes of unintentional and unconscious fun. Thus Mr. Clements, who has evidently been reading history, and is anxious about local colour, not only makes a point of quoting documents, and parading authorities, and being fearfully in earnest, but does so with a look of gravity and an evident sense of responsibility that are really delicious. On the whole, however, of Mr. Clements's many jokes, *The Prince and the Pauper* is incomparably the flattest and worst. To this, as a general reflection, it may be added that if to convert a brilliant and engaging humourist into a dull and painful romancer be necessarily a function of the study of history, it cannot be too steadily discouraged.[58]

Clemens read the *Saturday Review* and *Athenaeum* notices and was philosophical. "It gave me no dis-comfort," he wrote Andrew Chatto, "because here we consider that neither of those papers,

---

[54]Clemens to House, 23 February 1882, CWB.

[55]London *Times,* 20 December 1881, p. 3.

[56]*Saturday Review*, 24 December 1881, p. 801.

[57]*Academy*, 24 December 1881, reprinted in *MTCH*, pp. 90–91.

[58]*Athenaeum*, 24 December 1881, reprinted in *MTCH*, pp. 91–92. Clemens called this reviewer "an enraged idiot" (Clemens to Howells, 28 January 1882, *MTHL*, 1:388).

would compliment the holy scriptures, if an American had written them."[59]

Clemens professed to be pleased with the book's reception and the early English and American sales.[60] "I find myself a fine success, as a publisher," he told H. H. Boyesen in January 1882, "and literarily the new departure is a great deal better received than I had any right to hope for."[61] Apparently the author, knowing that his "new departure" might puzzle his established audience, did not hope to equal the astonishing success of such previous books as *The Innocents Abroad, Roughing It, A Tramp Abroad,* or even *The Gilded Age.* During the writing of *The Prince and the Pauper* he had insisted, "If I knew it would never sell a copy my jubilant delight in writing it would not suffer any diminution."[62] Olivia Clemens too was delighted with the story, and according to Clemens was particularly anxious that the volume "be elegantly gotten up, even if the elegance of it eats up the publisher's profits and mine too."[63] Nonetheless, Clemens kept a careful eye on sales. Subscription orders dropped off sharply in the first quarter after publication. "Too brief a pre-canvass" and the poor performance of the "gang of general agents" whom Osgood had borrowed from the American Publishing Company were the problems, in Clemens' opinion.[64] He was soon disappointed enough to consider "dumping" the book into the trade market. He was only persuaded to delay this maneuver by Osgood's assurance that "the responses we receive from the agents seem to indicate a good sale for 'P & P' for the rest of the year."[65] But as the months passed sales still did not meet Clemens' expectations. In December 1883 he would describe *The Prince and the Pauper* and *Life on the Mississippi,* rather inaccurately, as "the only books of mine which have ever

---

[59]Clemens to Chatto, 3 March 1882, Yale.

[60]On 6 February 1882 Chatto reported that the sale of *The Prince and the Pauper* had reached 6,500 copies in England, a "very handsome figure" in Clemens' estimation (Clemens to Chatto, 3 March 1882, Yale). The "English sale is one third as great as the American," Clemens told House on 23 February 1882 (CWB).

[61]Clemens to Boyesen, 11 January 1882, *MTLP,* p. 152 n. 1.

[62]Clemens to Howells, 5 March 1880, *MTHL,* 1:290.

[63]Carl J. Weber, *The Rise and Fall of James Ripley Osgood* (Waterville, Maine: Colby College Press, 1959), p. 181.

[64]Clemens to Osgood, 12 February 1882, *MTLP,* p. 151.

[65]Osgood to Clemens, 31 July 1882, *MTLP,* p. 154 n. 1.

failed," admitting, however, that the failure of his historical tale was "not unbearable."[66] Years later he recalled: "[Osgood] made a beautiful book of it but all the profit I got out of it was seventeen thousand dollars."[67]

Clemens' family was especially fond of *The Prince and the Pauper*. "It is unquestionably the best book he has ever written," Susy Clemens commented in her biography of her father. "The book is full of lovely charming ideas, and oh the language! It is *perfect*."[68] Olivia Clemens, with the help of her daughters and the neighborhood children, presented her dramatization of the book, the first of several family productions, as a surprise for the author early in 1885.[69] Clemens himself would enliven later performances with his impersonation of Miles Hendon.

Seemingly, *The Prince and the Pauper* constitutes a digression in Mark Twain's literary evolution. He momentarily abandoned his most successful vein, autobiographical and purely American, and chose instead to work in an impersonal mode within the convention of the historical romance. Yet *The Prince and the Pauper* is related not only chronologically but also thematically to *Tom Sawyer* and *Huckleberry Finn*. It began to take literary shape in 1877, just two years after the completion of *Tom Sawyer*, and it was in part written concurrently with *Huckleberry Finn*. All three books feature child-heroes at the turning point—at first self-absorbed and somewhat alienated from a world that is at times confining and cruel, they learn in the course of many experiences to judge soundly and compassionately. Specific situations and even characters in the Mississippi River

---

[66]Clemens to Osgood, 21 December 1883, *MTLP*, p. 164. The first year's sale of both these books was respectable by most standards and in fact surpassed that of *Tom Sawyer*. Although Clemens overlooked the poor showing of *Tom Sawyer* when he made this statement, he had felt the failure of that book keenly at the time and it influenced his decision to break with the American Publishing Company.

[67]AD, 24 May 1906, *MTE*, p. 158.

[68]AD, 9 February 1906, *Mark Twain's Autobiography*, ed. Albert Bigelow Paine, 2 vols. (New York: Harper and Brothers, 1924), 2:88. *The Prince and the Pauper* was later supplanted in Susy's estimation by *Joan of Arc*, a book she found "even more sweet and beautiful" (Edith Colgate Salsbury, *Susy and Mark Twain* [New York: Harper and Row, 1965], p. 318).

[69]Paine mistakenly states that Olivia Clemens first produced the play during the Christmas season of 1884 (*MTB*, 2:787–789); actually, the play was first presented on the evening of 14 March 1885 (Clemens to James B. Pond, 14 March 1885, Berg).

books find their counterparts in *The Prince and the Pauper*.[70] Moreover, Mark Twain discovered in the historical perspective an effective solution to the problem of narrative structure and a medium for his social and political ideas; he returned to this device in such later works as *A Connecticut Yankee, Joan of Arc*, and *The Mysterious Stranger*. Thus *The Prince and the Pauper* helped to shape and clarify certain aspects of Mark Twain's artistic vision. At the same time its publication marked a new direction in critical appraisal of Mark Twain's work and heralded the author's growing commitment to the business of publishing his own books.

HISTORICAL SOURCES

Mark Twain's desire to be taken seriously, coupled with his theory of fiction—that literature based on fact is superior to imaginative writing—explains his extensive research for *The Prince and the Pauper*.[71] He displayed much of this research in the printed volume by quoting from his sources directly or referring to them in footnotes appended to the text in the manner of Sir Walter Scott and Charlotte Yonge. Mark Twain, however, did not hesitate to revise quoted sources for literary convenience, to obscure some facts and overemphasize others; and his disregard for exact dates necessitated more than one awkward explanatory note. The result—regardless of what the author intended—was to impart to the romance a slight and "stylish" historical gloss and to open the book to the attack of more scrupulous historians.

Between 1876 and 1881 Clemens compiled over fifty-five pages of study notes based on his reading in English history and literature. His notes include long lists of words and phrases, the result of reading, as he later said, undertaken "with the purpose of saturating myself with archaic English to a degree which would enable me to do plausible

---

[70]See *MT&HF*, chapter 13, where Walter Blair discusses at length the thematic and structural parallels, as well as some incidental similarities, between *The Prince and the Pauper* and other books written by Mark Twain between 1874 and 1884.

[71]See Leon T. Dickinson, "The Sources of *The Prince and the Pauper*," *Modern Language Notes* 64 (February 1949): 105–106.

imitations of it in a fairly easy and unlabored way."[72] These vocabulary lists are, in the main, drawn from Shakespeare's *King Henry IV, Part 1* and from Sir Walter Scott's *Kenilworth, Quentin Durward, Ivanhoe,* and *The Fortunes of Nigel.* His reliance on Scott's romances, which are set in France and England from the twelfth to the seventeenth centuries, for an approximation of Tudor speech is a curious instance of the author's slapdash historical scholarship. From Scott he also gleaned one or two details of period costume.

More important for details of pageantry and costume were the English chroniclers Raphael Holinshed and Edward Hall,[73] whose works Mark Twain quoted with rather cavalier disregard for their chronology and little or no acknowledgment. His most extensive (and unacknowledged) appropriation was Holinshed's description of the passage of Elizabeth toward Westminster before her coronation (see the explanatory note at 301.37).

For information on the streets, landmarks, and customs of London, he consulted John Timbs's *Curiosities of London,* Leigh Hunt's *The Town,* and J. Heneage Jesse's *London: Its Celebrated Characters and Remarkable Places.*[74] He may have referred to John Stow's sixteenth-century *Survey of London* and his old favorite, Pepys's *Diary.* He even studied a pocket map of the city.[75]

Another unacknowledged source for the book was George L. Craik and Charles MacFarlane's multivolume *Pictorial History of England,* first published from 1837 to 1844. The Great Seal of Henry VIII and the king's autograph, pictured facing the title page of *The Prince and the Pauper,* were reproduced from engravings in the *Pictorial History.* The *History's* numerous illustrations may also have been the source for the costumes and settings sketched by Merrill and Harley. Several references in his working notes show Mark Twain carefully read

---

[72]AD, 31 July 1906, *MTE,* p. 206.

[73]Clemens probably used the following editions, which were the only ones readily available: Raphael Holinshed, *Chronicles of England, Scotland, and Ireland,* 6 vols. (London: J. Johnson, 1807–1808) and Edward Hall, *Chronicle* (London: J. Johnson, 1809).

[74]Clemens owned and used the 1867 edition of Timbs's *Curiosities of London,* published by Virtue and Company of London. Examination of the Hunt and Jesse extracts quoted in *The Prince and the Pauper* indicates that the editions used were: Leigh Hunt, *The Town: Its Memorable Characters and Events* (London: Smith, Elder and Co., 1859) and J. Heneage Jesse, *London: Its Celebrated Characters and Remarkable Places,* 3 vols. (London: Richard Bentley, 1871).

[75]*MTB,* 2:598.

the chapters in the *Pictorial History* dealing with the "history of manners and customs," the "history of the condition of the people," and the "history of the constitution, government, and laws." There is also evidence that the coronation scene in *The Prince and the Pauper* was strongly influenced by Harriet Martineau's description of Victoria's coronation in the final volume of the *Pictorial History*.[76]

The facsimile and transcript of the Latimer letter of 19 October 1537 which appear at the front of *The Prince and the Pauper* were reproduced from a volume that Clemens owned—the second part of the *Facsimiles of National Manuscripts from William the Conqueror to Queen Anne*, "photozincographed . . . by Colonel Sir Henry James."[77]

Mark Twain got most of his historical information—names, dates, places, events, personality sketches, and social and parliamentary history—from David Hume's and James Anthony Froude's histories of England.[78] The short reign of Edward VI, in contrast to the flamboyant absolutism of Henry VIII, had a certain appeal for liberal historians such as Hume. For Hume, Edward possessed "mildness of disposition, application to study and business, a capacity to learn and judge, and an attachment to equity and justice"[79]—the very qualities that Mark Twain's young king finally develops. His portrait of Edward VI, however, was necessarily colored by the demands of plot and theme; it lacked the historical balance and perspective of Hume's sketch. Hume was careful to emphasize Edward's youth and to admit that his early death rendered any assessment of his character and

---

[76]George L. Craik and Charles MacFarlane, *The Pictorial History of England*, 7 vols. (London and Edinburgh: W. and R. Chambers, 1855–1858), 7:854–858. See the working notes in Appendix A, I-5.

[77]Southampton: Ordnance Survey Office, 1865, p. 60. According to Clemens' inscription in his copy of volume 2 of *Facsimiles*, the book was given to him in 1874 by Sir Thomas Duffus Hardy. Hardy, who was responsible for the selection of documents in the four-volume *Facsimiles* series, was deputy keeper of records from 1861 to 1876 and had become well acquainted with Clemens during the latter's trips to London in 1873 and 1874.

[78]David Hume, *The History of England from the Invasion of Julius Caesar to the Abdication of James the Second, 1688*, 6 vols. (New York: Harper and Brothers, [1854]); Clemens owned at least three volumes of this edition. James Anthony Froude, *The History of England from the Fall of Wolsey to the Defeat of the Spanish Armada*, 12 vols. (New York: Charles Scribner and Co., 1865–1870); Clemens owned ten volumes of this edition.

[79]Hume, *History of England*, 3:383.

ability to some extent presumptive. According to Hume, the young
monarch evidenced "too much of a narrow prepossession in matters
of religion, which made him incline somewhat to bigotry and persecution."[80] Mark Twain, on the other hand, suggests a degree of religious tolerance in Edward which history belies.

Froude, who as a disciple of Carlyle found much to admire in the
dominant personality of Henry VIII, was less interested in Edward's
character. His analysis of the early years of Edward's reign concentrated instead on the powerful figure of the earl of Hertford, later
the duke of Somerset and lord protector of England. The portrait
of Hertford suggested guidelines to Mark Twain for developing
young Edward's sense of justice and humanity. Hertford, wrote
Froude, "saw England . . . ripe for mighty changes. . . . He saw in
imagination the yet imperfect revolution carried out to completion.
. . . He had lived in a reign in which the laws had been severe beyond precedent, and when even speech was criminal. He was himself
a believer in liberty; he imagined that the strong hand could now be
dispensed with, that an age of enlightenment was at hand when severity could be superseded with gentleness and force by persuasion."[81]
But Mark Twain made little use of Hertford himself. In fact, in
chapters 5 and 6 of the manuscript of *The Prince and the Pauper*
he several times wrote "Herbert" (that is, Sir William Herbert, one
of the chief gentlemen of the privy chamber) and then altered the
reading to "Hertford," a revision due either to confusion over the
two names or to indecision about what degree of prominence to accord Hertford in the book. A reference in the working notes (Appendix A, F-4) and a deleted passage at the end of chapter 6 indicate that
Mark Twain considered—and rejected—the idea of having Hertford
secretly employ spies to discover the truth of the prince's identity.
Ultimately Hertford's "virtual sovereignty"[82] during the early years of

---

[80]Hume went on to say that "the bigotry of Protestants, less governed by priests,
lies under more restraints than that of Catholics," a view apparently shared by Clemens
(Hume, *History of England*, 3:384). One English reviewer of *The Prince and the Pauper*
commented on the "general Protestant tone" of the book (*Academy*, 24 December
1881, reprinted in *MTCH*, p. 91). Mark Twain dealt more directly with the issue of religious intolerance and persecution in *A Connecticut Yankee*.

[81]Froude, *History of England*, 5:16–17. Clemens briefly summarized this passage in
his working notes (see Appendix A, C-1).

[82]Froude, *History of England*, 5:26.

Edward's minority was minimized: the author hardly differentiated Hertford from the mass of royal advisers and courtiers.

Mark Twain was also indebted to historians for the social setting of *The Prince and the Pauper.* Froude, and to a lesser extent Hume, in discussing the rise in prices, enclosure, and the conversion of arable land to pasturage with the consequent displacement and impoverishment of the provincial population, sketched the economic and social conditions that the homeless prince was to experience in the second half of the book.

While Hume and Froude provided a kind of overview, Mark Twain relied on more specialized works to authenticate his picture of sixteenth-century England. Such a book was the one edited by his Hartford friend and neighbor J. Hammond Trumbull, *The True-Blue Laws of Connecticut and New Haven and the False Blue-Laws Invented by the Rev. Samuel Peters,*[83] a book which also influenced *A Connecticut Yankee.* In exposing and refuting Samuel Peters' spurious Connecticut history of 1781,[84] Trumbull showed that the laws of colonial New England were considerably milder than English laws of the same period. In his working notes Mark Twain listed some more unusual "Crimes & Penalties" mentioned by Trumbull (Appendix A, H-1, H-2). And he was so impressed by Trumbull's book that he appended to *The Prince and the Pauper* a "General Note" (whose vehemence mystified more than one reviewer) in which he feelingly urged his readers to consider and compare the "humane and kindly Blue-Law code" with the instances of "judicial atrocity" perpetuated by English law. Moreover, in Trumbull's final chapter on the "Blue Laws of England, in the Reign of James the First," Clemens found an account of punishments inflicted upon gamblers, beggars, and vagrants which suggested a number of possible adventures for his young hero in the clutches of a "gang of tramps who rove like gypsies (evicted to make sheep farms)" (Appendix A, I-1). The roving band's adventures became an ideal vehicle for the education of the prince: "With this gang he in time sees all the punishments inflicted. Sometimes he

---

[83]Hartford: American Publishing Company, 1876. Clemens' marked copy is in the Detroit Public Library.

[84]Samuel Peters, *A General History of Connecticut* (London, 1781). Trumbull reprinted much of Peters' material on the Blue-Laws.

exercises the pardoning power and is laughed at. Gets cuffs" (Appendix A, I-2). The notes even consider involving Hendon in the band's adventures (Appendix A, I-3).

Clemens found a less scholarly view of England's laws in a seventeenth-century work by Richard Head and Francis Kirkman, *The English Rogue . . . Being a Compleat History of the Most Eminent Cheats of Both Sexes.*[85] While purporting to inspire its readers with a "loathing" for "Villany" and "Vice," the book furnished a lively account of the lawless and immoral escapades of one Meriton Latroon and, incidentally, served as a complete guide to seventeenth-century "cony-catching" practices. In his footnotes to *The Prince and the Pauper* Mark Twain acknowledged only a part of his debt to *The English Rogue*. In fact, the book not only provided details concerning confidence games and argot for the chapters dealing with Edward's captivity among the vagabonds, it inspired dialogue, descriptions, and several specific incidents.[86]

In addition to *The English Rogue*, Clemens apparently consulted Francis Grose's *Classical Dictionary of the Vulgar Tongue* for cant terminology.[87]

Undoubtedly, one of the formative influences on the moral and political atmosphere of *The Prince and the Pauper* was William Lecky's *History of European Morals from Augustus to Charlemagne*, a book that Clemens discovered perhaps as early as the summer of 1874. Lecky explored the cultural basis of law and morality and theorized a direct relationship between education and compassion, showing that society's progress from barbarism to civilization was

---

[85]Head wrote part one, which was published in London in 1665 by Henry Marsh. When he declined to write a sequel, Kirkman added parts two through four during the next six years. A facsimile edition of all four parts was printed in 1874 by an unidentified publisher.

[86]For a discussion of the novel's debt to *The English Rogue*, see Dickinson, "The Sources of *The Prince and the Pauper*," pp. 104–105.

[87]London: S. Hooper, 1785. Clemens inscribed his first edition of Grose's dictionary "Saml. L. Clemens/Hartford, 1875" and annotated it fairly extensively. He probably used both the sample glossary in *The English Rogue* and Grose's more complete dictionary in researching cant terminology, but at least one character in chapter 17 of *The Prince and the Pauper* owes his name solely to Grose's dictionary: the wooden-legged beggar "Dick Dot-and-go-One." According to Grose, "Dot and go one" means "to waddle, generally applied to persons who have one leg shorter than the other, and who as the sea phrase is, go upon an uneven keel."

accomplished in part by the strengthening, through education and experience, of the individual's "power of realisation."[88] Thus, after suffering abuse at the hands of the Christ's Hospital charity boys, young Prince Edward vows to provide them with a free education, "for learning softeneth the heart and breedeth gentleness and charity" (chapter 4). Edward's journey, during which the plight of his subjects is made painfully real to him, can be seen as an illustration of Lecky's civilizing process, a moral education on the road. "Kings should go to school to their own laws, at times," concludes Edward, "and so learn mercy" (chapter 27).

L.S.

---

[88]William Edward Hartpole Lecky, *History of European Morals from Augustus to Charlemagne*, 2 vols. (New York: D. Appleton and Co., 1877), 1:132–133. Both Walter Blair (in *MT&HF*) and Howard G. Baetzhold (in *Mark Twain and John Bull: The British Connection* [Bloomington: Indiana University Press, 1970]) discuss Lecky's influence on *The Prince and the Pauper*. Clemens owned Appleton's 1874 edition, which he apparently obtained from his brother-in-law Theodore W. Crane.

THE PRINCE
AND THE PAUPER

HUGH LATIMER, *Bishop of Worcester, to* LORD CROMWELL, *on the birth of the* PRINCE OF WALES *(afterward* EDWARD VI.*).*

Hugh Latimer, *Bishop of Worcester, to* Lord Cromwell, *on the birth of the* Prince of Wales *(afterward* Edward VI.*)*.

FROM THE NATIONAL MANUSCRIPTS PRESERVED BY THE
BRITISH GOVERNMENT.

Ryght honorable. *Salutem in Christo Jesu.* And Syr here ys no lesse joynge and rejossynge in thes partees for the byrth of our prynce, hoom we hungurde for so longe, then ther was, (I trow) *inter vicinos* att the byrth of S. I. Baptyste, as thys berer Master Evance can telle you. Gode gyffe us alle grace, to yelde dew thankes to our Lorde Gode, Gode of Inglonde, for verely He hathe shoyd Hym selff Gode of Inglonde, or rather an Inglyssh Gode, yf we consydyr and pondyr welle alle Hys procedynges with us from tyme to tyme. He hath over-cumme alle our yllnesse with Hys excedynge goodnesse, so that we ar now moor then compellyd to serve Hym, seke Hys glory, promott Hys wurde, yf the Devylle of alle Devylles be natt in us. We have now the stooppe of vayne trustes ande the stey of vayne expectations; lett us alle pray for hys preservatione. Ande I for my partt wylle wyssh that hys Grace allways have, and evyn now from the begynynge, Gover-nares, Instructores and offyceres of ryght jugmente, *ne optimum ingenium non optimâ educatione depravetur.* Butt whatt a grett fowlle am I! So, whatt devotione shoyth many tymys butt lytelle dyscretione! Ande thus the Gode of Inglonde be ever with you in alle your procedynges.

The 19 of October.

youres H. L. B. of Wurcestere
now att Hartlebury.

Yf you wolde excytt thys berere to be moore hartye ayen the abuse of ymagry or mor forwarde to promotte the veryte, ytt myght doo goode. Natt that ytt came of me, butt of your selffe, &c.

(*Addressed*)   To the Ryght Honorable Loorde P. Sealle hys synguler
gode Lorde.

The Prince
and the Pauper

A TALE

FOR YOUNG PEOPLE OF ALL AGES

BY

MARK TWAIN

TO

THOSE GOOD-MANNERED AND AGREEABLE CHILDREN,

Susie and Clara Clemens,

THIS BOOK

IS AFFECTIONATELY INSCRIBED

BY THEIR FATHER.

THE quality of mercy . . .
              is twice bless'd;
It blesseth him that gives and him that takes;
'Tis mightiest in the mightiest: it becomes
The thronèd monarch better than his crown.
                        Merchant of Venice.

CONTENTS

List of Illustrations

I WILL set down a tale as it was told to me by one who had it of his father, which latter had it of *his* father, this last having in like manner had it of *his* father—and so on, back and still back, three hundred years and more, the fathers transmitting it to the sons and so preserving it. It may be history, it may be only a legend, a tradition. It may have happened, it may not have happened: but it *could* have happened. It may be that the wise and the learned believed it in the old days; it may be that only the unlearned and the simple loved it and credited it.

CHAPTER 1

The Birth of the Prince and the Pauper

IN THE ANCIENT CITY of London, on a certain autumn day in the second quarter of the sixteenth century, a boy was born to a poor family of the name of Canty, who did not want him. On the same day another English child was born to a rich family of the name of Tudor, who did want him. All England wanted him, too. England had so longed for him, and hoped for him, and prayed God for him, that now that he was really come, the people went nearly mad for joy. Mere acquaintances hugged and kissed each other and cried; everybody took a holiday, and high and low, rich and poor, feasted and danced, and sang, and got very mellow—and they kept this up for days and nights together. By day, London was a sight to see, with gay banners waving from every balcony and house-top, and splendid pageants marching along. By night it was again a sight to see, with its great bonfires at every corner and its troops of revelers making merry around them. There was no talk in all England but of the new baby,

Edward Tudor, Prince of Wales, who lay lapped in silks and satins, unconscious of all this fuss, and not knowing that great lords and ladies were tending him and watching over him—and not caring, either. But there was no talk about the other baby, Tom Canty, lapped in his poor rags, except among the family of paupers whom he had just come to trouble with his presence.

"SPLENDID PAGEANTS AND GREAT BONFIRES."

CHAPTER 2

TOM'S EARLY LIFE

L ET US SKIP a number of years.

London was fifteen hundred years old, and was a great town—for that day. It had a hundred thousand inhabitants—some think double as many. The streets were very narrow, and crooked, and dirty, especially in the part where Tom Canty lived, which was not far from London Bridge. The houses were of wood, with the second story projecting over the first, and the third sticking its elbows out beyond the second. The higher the houses grew, the broader they grew. They were skeletons of strong criss-cross beams, with solid material between, coated with plaster. The beams were painted red or blue or black, according to the owner's taste, and this gave the houses a very picturesque look. The windows were small, glazed with little diamond-shaped panes, and they opened outward, on hinges, like doors.

The house which Tom's father lived in was up a foul little pocket called Offal Court, out of Pudding Lane. It was small, decayed, and ricketty, but it was packed full of wretchedly poor families. Canty's tribe occupied a room on the third floor. The mother and father had a sort of bedstead in the corner, but Tom, his grandmother, and his two sisters, Bet and Nan, were not restricted—they had all the floor to themselves, and might sleep where they chose. There were the remains of a blanket or two and some bundles of ancient and dirty straw, but these could not rightly be called beds, for they were not organized; they were kicked into a general pile, mornings, and selections made from the mass at night, for service.

OFFAL COURT.

Bet and Nan were fifteen years old—twins. They were good-hearted girls, unclean, clothed in rags, and profoundly ignorant. Their mother was like them. But the father and the grandmother were a couple of fiends. They got drunk whenever they could; then they fought each other or anybody else who came in the way; they cursed and swore always, drunk or sober; John Canty was a thief, and his mother a beggar. They made beggars of the children, but failed to make thieves of them. Among, but not of, the dreadful rabble that inhabited the house, was a good old priest whom the king had turned out of house and home with a pension of a few farthings, and he used to get the children aside and teach them right ways secretly. Father Andrew also taught Tom a little Latin, and how to read and write; and would have done the same with the girls, but they were afraid of the jeers of their friends, who could not have endured such a queer accomplishment in them.

All Offal Court was just such another hive as Canty's house. Drunkenness, riot and brawling were the order, there, every night and nearly all night long. Broken heads were as common as hunger in that place. Yet little Tom was not unhappy. He had a hard time of it, but did not know it. It was the sort of time that all the Offal Court boys had, therefore he supposed it was the correct and comfortable thing. When he came home empty handed at night, he knew his father would curse him and thrash him first, and that when he was done the awful grandmother would do it all over again and improve on it; and that away in the night his starving mother would slip to him stealthily with any miserable scrap or crust she had been able to save for him by going hungry herself, notwithstanding she was often caught in that sort of treason and soundly beaten for it by her husband.

"WITH ANY MISERABLE CRUST."

No, Tom's life went along well enough, especially in summer. He only begged just enough to save himself, for the laws against mendicancy were stringent, and the penalties heavy; so he put in a good deal of his time listening to good Father Andrew's charming old tales and legends about giants and fairies, dwarfs and genii, and enchanted castles, and gorgeous kings and princes. His head grew to be full of

these wonderful things, and many a night as he lay in the dark on his
scant and offensive straw, tired, hungry, and smarting from a thrash-
ing, he unleashed his imagination and soon forgot his aches and pains
in delicious picturings to himself of the charmed life of a petted prince
in a regal palace. One desire came in time to haunt him day and night:
it was, to see a real prince, with his own eyes. He spoke of it once to
some of his Offal Court comrades; but they jeered him and scoffed
him so unmercifully that he was glad to keep his dream to himself
after that.

He often read the priest's old books and got him to explain and
enlarge upon them. His dreamings and readings worked certain
changes in him, by and by. His dream-people were so fine that he grew

"HE OFTEN READ THE PRIEST'S BOOKS."

"SAW POOR ANNE ASKEW BURNED."

to lament his shabby clothing and his dirt, and to wish to be clean and better clad. He went on playing in the mud just the same, and enjoying it, too; but instead of splashing around in the Thames solely for the fun of it, he began to find an added value in it because of the washings and cleansings it afforded.

Tom could always find something going on around the May-pole in Cheapside, and at the fairs, and now and then he and the rest of London had a chance to see a military parade when some famous unfortunate was carried prisoner to the Tower, by land or boat. One summer's day he saw poor Anne Askew and three men burned at the stake in Smithfield, and heard an ex-Bishop preach a sermon to them which did not interest him. Yes, Tom's life was varied and pleasant enough, on the whole.

By and by Tom's reading and dreaming about princely life wrought such a strong effect upon him that he began to *act* the prince, unconsciously. His speech and manners became curiously ceremonious and courtly, to the vast admiration and amusement of his intimates. But Tom's influence among these young people began to grow, now,

"BROUGHT THEIR PERPLEXITIES TO TOM."

day by day; and in time he came to be looked up to, by them, with a sort of wondering awe, as a superior being. He seemed to know so much! and he could do and say such marvelous things! and withal, he was so deep and wise! Tom's remarks, and Tom's performances, were reported by the boys to their elders, and these also presently began to discuss Tom Canty, and to regard him as a most gifted and extraordinary creature. Full grown people brought their perplexities to Tom for solution, and were often astonished at the wit and wisdom of his decisions. In fact he was become a hero to all who knew him except his own family—these, only, saw nothing in him.

Privately, after a while, Tom organized a royal court! He was the prince; his special comrades were guards, chamberlains, equerries, lords and ladies in waiting, and the royal family. Daily the mock prince was received with elaborate ceremonials borrowed by Tom from his romantic readings; daily the great affairs of the mimic kingdom were discussed in the royal council, and daily his mimic highness issued decrees to his imaginary armies, navies, and viceroyalties.

After which, he would go forth in his rags and beg a few farthings, eat his poor crust, take his customary cuffs and abuse, and then stretch himself upon his handful of foul straw, and resume his empty grandeurs in his dreams.

And still his desire to look just once upon a real prince, in the flesh, grew upon him, day by day, and week by week, until at last it absorbed all other desires, and became the one passion of his life.

"LONGING FOR THE PORK-PIES."

One January day, on his usual begging tour, he tramped despondently up and down the region round about Mincing Lane and Little East Cheap, hour after hour, barefooted and cold, looking in at cookshop windows and longing for the dreadful pork-pies and other deadly inventions displayed there—for to him these were dainties fit for the angels; that is, judging by the smell, they were—for it had never been his good luck to own and eat one. There was a cold drizzle of rain; the atmosphere was murky; it was a melancholy day. At night Tom reached home so wet and tired and hungry that it was not possible for his father and grandmother to observe his forlorn condition and not be moved—after their fashion; wherefore they gave him a brisk cuffing at once and sent him to bed. For a long time his pain and hunger, and the swearing and fighting going on in the building kept him awake; but at last his thoughts drifted away to far, romantic lands, and he fell asleep in the company of jeweled and gilded princelings who lived in vast palaces, and had servants salaaming before them or flying to execute their orders. And then, as usual, he dreamed that *he* was a princeling himself.

All night long the glories of his royal estate shone upon him; he moved among great lords and ladies, in a blaze of light, breathing perfumes, drinking in delicious music, and answering the reverent obeisances of the glittering throng as it parted to make way for him, with here a smile, and there a nod of his princely head.

And when he awoke in the morning and looked upon the wretchedness about him, his dream had had its usual effect—it had intensified the sordidness of his surroundings a thousand fold. Then came bitterness, and heartbreak, and tears.

CHAPTER 3

Tom's Meeting with the Prince

Tom got up hungry and sauntered hungry away but with his thoughts busy with the shadowy splendors of his night's dreams. He wandered here and there in the city, hardly noticing where he was going or what was happening around him. People jostled him, and some gave him rough speech, but it was all lost on the musing boy. By and by he found himself at Temple Bar—the furthest from home he had ever traveled in that direction. He stopped and considered a moment, then fell into his imaginings again and passed on, outside the walls of London. The Strand had ceased to be a country road then, and regarded itself as a street—but by a strained construction, for though there was a tolerably compact row of houses on one side of it, there were only some scattering great buildings on the other, these being palaces of rich nobles, with ample and beautiful grounds stretching to the river—grounds that are now closely packed with grim acres of brick and stone.

"AT TEMPLE BAR."

Tom discovered Charing village, presently, and rested himself at the beautiful cross built there by a bereaved king of earlier days; then idled down a quiet, lovely road, past the great cardinal's stately palace, toward a far more mighty and majestic palace beyond—Westminster. Tom stared in glad wonder at the vast pile of masonry, the wide-spreading wings, the frowning bastions and turrets, the huge stone gateway with its gilded bars and its magnificent array of colossal granite lions and other the signs and symbols of English royalty. Was the desire of his soul to be satisfied at last? Here, indeed, was a king's palace—might he not hope to see a prince, now, a prince of flesh and blood, if heaven were willing?

At each side of the gilded gate stood a living statue—that is to say, an erect and stately and motionless man-at-arms, clad from head to heel in shining steel armor. At a respectful distance were many country folk, and people from the city waiting for any chance glimpse of royalty that might offer. Splendid carriages with splendid people in them and splendid servants outside were arriving and departing by several other noble gateways that pierced the royal enclosure.

Poor little Tom, in his rags, approached, and was moving slow and timidly past the sentinels, with a beating heart and a rising hope, when all at once he caught sight, through the golden bars, of a spectacle that almost made him shout for joy. Within was a comely boy, tanned and brown with sturdy out-door sports and exercises, whose clothing was all of lovely silks and satins, shining with jewels; at his hip a little jeweled sword and dagger; dainty buskins on his feet, with red heels, and on his head a jaunty crimson cap with drooping plumes fastened with a great sparkling gem. Several gorgeous gentlemen stood near— his servants, without a doubt. O, he was a prince! a prince! a living

"LET HIM IN!"

prince, a real prince, without the shadow of a question, and the prayer of the pauper-boy's heart was answered at last!

Tom's breath came quick and short with excitement, and his eyes grew big with wonder and delight. Everything gave way in his mind, instantly, to one desire; that was, to get close to the prince and have a good, devouring look at him. Before he knew what he was about, he had his face against the gate-bars. The next instant one of the soldiers snatched him rudely away and sent him spinning among the gaping crowd of country gawks and London idlers. The soldier said:

"Mind thy manners thou young beggar!"

The crowd jeered and laughed; but the young prince sprang to the gate with his face flushed and his eyes flashing with indignation, and cried out:

"How dar'st thou use a poor lad like that! How dar'st thou use the king my father's meanest subject so! Open the gates and let him in!"

You should have seen that fickle crowd snatch off their hats, then. You should have heard them cheer and shout "Long live the Prince of Wales!"

The soldiers presented arms, with their halberds, opened the gates, and presented again as the little Prince of Poverty passed in, in his fluttering rags, to join hands with the Prince of Limitless Plenty.

Edward Tudor said:

"Thou lookest tired and hungry; thou'st been treated ill. Come with me."

Half a dozen attendants sprang forward to—I don't know what; interfere, no doubt. But they were waved aside with a right royal gesture, and they stopped stock still where they were, like so many statues. Edward took Tom to a rich apartment in the palace which he called his cabinet. By his command, a repast was brought such as Tom had never encountered before except in books; the prince, with princely delicacy and breeding, sent away the servants, so that his humble guest might not be embarrassed by their critical presence; then he sat near by and asked questions while Tom ate.

"What is thy name, lad?"

"Tom Canty, an' it please thee, sir."

" 'Tis an odd one. Where dost live?"

"In the city, please thee, sir—Offal Court, out of Pudding Lane."

"Offal Court! Truly 'tis another odd one. Hast parents?"

"Parents have I, sir, and a grandam likewise that is but indifferently precious to me, God forgive me if it be offense to say it. Also twin sisters—Nan and Bet."

"Then is thy grandam not over kind to thee, I take it."

"Neither to any other is she, so please your worship. She hath a wicked heart, and worketh evil all her days."

"Doth she mistreat thee?"

"There be times that she stayeth her hand, being asleep or overcome with drink; but when she hath her judgment clear again, she maketh it up to me with goodly beatings."

A fierce look came into the little prince's eyes, and he cried out—

"What! Beatings?"

"O, indeed, yes, please you, sir."

"HOW OLD BE THESE?"

"*Beatings!* And thou so frail and little. Harkye; before the night come, she shall hie her to the Tower! The king my father—"

"In sooth you forget, sir, her low degree. The Tower is for the great alone."

"True, indeed. I had not thought of that. I will consider of her punishment. Is thy father kind to thee?"

"Not more than Gammer Canty, sir."

"Fathers be alike, mayhap. Mine hath not a doll's temper. He smiteth with a heavy hand, yet spareth me; he spareth me not always with his tongue, though, sooth to say. How doth thy mother use thee?"

"She is good, sir, and giveth me neither sorrow nor pain of any sort. And Nan and Bet are like to her in this."

"How old be these?"

"Fifteen, an' it please you, sir."

"The lady Elizabeth my sister is fourteen, and the lady Jane Grey my cousin is of mine own age, and comely and gracious withal; but my sister the lady Mary, with her gloomy mien and—look you, do thy sisters forbid their servants to smile, lest the sin destroy their souls?"

"They? O, dost think, sir, that *they* have servants?"

The little prince contemplated the little pauper gravely a moment, then said—

"And prithee, why not? Who helpeth them undress at night? who attireth them when they rise?"

"None, sir. Wouldst have them take off their garment and sleep without—like the beasts?"

"Their garment! Have they but one?"

"Ah, good your worship, what would they do with more? Truly they have not two bodies each."

"It is a quaint and marvelous thought! Thy pardon—I had not meant to laugh. But thy good Nan and thy Bet shall have raiment and lackeys enow—and that soon, too—my cofferer shall look to it. No, thank me not—'tis nothing. Thou speakest well; thou hast an easy grace in it. Art learned?"

"I know not if I am or not, sir. The good priest that is called Father Andrew, taught me, of his kindness, from his books."

"Know'st thou the Latin?"

"But scantly, sir, I doubt."

"Learn it, lad; 'tis hard only at first. The Greek is harder; but neither these nor any tongues else, I think, are hard to the lady Elizabeth and my cousin. Thou shouldst hear those damsels at it! But tell me of thy Offal Court. Hast thou a pleasant life there?"

"In truth, yes, so please you, sir, save when one is hungry. There be Punch and Judy shows; and monkeys—oh, such antic creatures and so bravely dressed!—and there be plays, wherein they that play do shout and fight till all are slain, and 'tis so fine to see, and costeth but a farthing—albeit 'tis main hard to get the farthing, please your worship."

"DOFF THY RAGS AND DON THESE SPLENDORS."

"Tell me more."

"We lads of Offal Court do strive against each other with the cudgel, like to the fashion of the 'prentices, sometimes."

The prince's eyes flashed. Said he—

"Marry, that would not I mislike! Tell me more."

"We strive in races, sir, to see who of us shall be fleetest—"

"That would I like, also! Speak on!"

"In summer, sir, we wade and swim in the canals and in the river, and each doth duck his neighbor, and spatter him with water, and dive and shout and tumble and—"

" 'Twould be worth my father's kingdom but to enjoy it once! Prithee go on."

"We dance and sing about the May-pole in Cheapside, we play in the sand, each covering his neighbor up; and times we make mud pastry—oh, the lovely mud, it hath not its like for delightfulness in all the world—we do fairly wallow in the mud, sir, saving your worship's presence!"

"O, prithee, say no more, 'tis glorious! If that I could but clothe me in raiment like to thine, and strip my feet, and revel in the mud once, just once, with none to rebuke me or forbid, meseemeth I could forego the crown!"

"And if that I could clothe me once, sweet sir, as thou art clad— just once—"

"Oho, wouldst like it? Then so shall it be! Doff thy rags and don these splendors, lad! It is a brief happiness, but will be not less keen for that. We will have it while we may, and change again before any come to molest."

A few minutes later, the little Prince of Wales was garlanded with Tom's fluttering odds and ends, and the little Prince of Pauperdom was tricked out in the gaudy plumage of royalty. The two went and stood side by side before a great mirror, and lo, a miracle: there did not seem to have been any change made! They stared at each other, then at the glass, then at each other again. At last the puzzled prince-ling said—

"What dost thou make of this?"

"Ah, good your worship, require me not to answer. It is not meet that one of my degree should utter the thing."

"Then will *I* utter it. Thou hast the same hair, the same eyes, the same voice and manner, the same form and stature, the same face and countenance, that I bear. Fared we forth naked, there is none could say which was you and which the Prince of Wales. And now that I am clothed as thou wert clothed, it seemeth I should be able the more nearly to feel as thou didst when the brute soldier—harkye, is not this a bruise upon your hand?"

"Yes, but it is a slight thing, and your worship knoweth that the poor man-at-arms—"

"Peace! It was a shameful thing and a cruel!" cried the little prince, stamping his bare foot. "If the king—stir not a step till I come again! It is a command!"

In a moment he had snatched up and put away an article of

national importance that lay upon a table, and was out at the door and flying through the palace grounds in his bannered rags, with a hot face and glowing eyes. As soon as he reached the great gate he seized the bars and tried to shake them, shouting:

"Open! Unbar the gates!"

The soldier that had maltreated Tom, obeyed promptly; and as the prince burst through the portal,

"I SALUTE YOUR GRACIOUS HIGHNESS."

half smothered with royal wrath, the soldier fetched him a sounding box on the ear that sent him whirling to the roadway, and said:

"Take that, thou beggar's spawn, for what thou got'st me from his highness!"

The crowd roared with laughter. The prince picked himself out of the mud and made fiercely at the sentry, shouting:

"I am the Prince of Wales, my person is sacred; and thou shalt hang for laying thy hand upon me!"

The soldier brought his halberd to a present-arms and said, mockingly:

"I salute your gracious highness." Then angrily: "Be off, thou crazy rubbish!"

Here the jeering crowd closed around the poor little prince and hustled him far down the road, hooting him, and shouting "Way for his royal highness! way for the Prince of Wales!"

CHAPTER 4

The Prince's Troubles Begin.

Afrer Hours of persistent pursuit and persecution, the little prince was at last deserted by the rabble and left to himself. As long as he had been able to rage against the mob, and threaten it royally, and royally utter commands that were good stuff to laugh at, he was very entertaining; but when weariness finally forced him to be silent, he was no longer of use to his tormentors, and they sought amusement elsewhere. He looked about him, now, but could not recognize the locality. He was within the city of London—that was all he knew. He moved on, aimlessly, and in a little while the houses thinned, and the passers-by were infrequent. He bathed his bleeding feet in the brook which flowed then where Farringdon street now is; rested a few moments, then passed on, and presently came upon a great space with only a few scattered houses in it, and a prodigious church. He recognized this church. Scaffoldings were about, everywhere, and swarms of workmen; for it was undergoing elaborate repairs. The prince took heart at once—he felt that his troubles were at an end, now. He said to himself, "It is the ancient Grey Friars' church, which the king my father hath taken from the monks and given for a home for-

ever for poor and forsaken children, and new-named it Christ's
Church. Right gladly will they serve the son of him who hath done so
generously by them—and the more that that son is himself as poor
and as forlorn as any that be sheltered here this day, or ever shall be."

He was soon in the midst of a crowd of boys who were running,
jumping, playing at ball and leap-frog, and otherwise disporting themselves, and right noisily, too. They were all dressed alike, and in the
fashion which in that day prevailed among serving-men and 'prentices*—that is to say, each had on the crown of his head a flat black
cap about the size of a saucer, which was not useful as a covering, it
being of such scanty dimensions, neither was it ornamental; from

"SET UPON BY DOGS."

beneath it the hair fell, unparted, to the middle of the forehead, and
was cropped straight around; a clerical band at the neck; a blue gown
that fitted closely and hung as low as the knees or lower; full sleeves;
a broad red belt; bright yellow stockings, gartered above the knees;
low shoes with large metal buckles. It was a sufficiently ugly costume.

*See Note 1, at end of the volume.

The boys stopped their play and flocked about the prince, who said with native dignity—

"Good lads, say to your master that Edward Prince of Wales desireth speech with him."

A great shout went up, at this, and one rude fellow said—

"Marry, art thou his grace's messenger, beggar?"

The Prince's face flushed with anger, and his ready hand flew to his hip, but there was nothing there. There was a storm of laughter, and one boy said—

"Didst mark that? He fancied he had a sword—belike he is the prince himself."

This sally brought more laughter. Poor Edward drew himself up proudly and said—

"I am the prince; and it ill beseemeth you that feed upon the king my father's bounty to use me so."

This was vastly enjoyed, as the laughter testified. The youth who had first spoken, shouted to his comrades—

"Ho, swine, slaves, pensioners of his grace's princely father, where be your manners? Down on your marrow bones, all of ye, and do reverence to his kingly port and royal rags!"

With boisterous mirth they dropped upon their knees in a body and did mock homage to their prey. The prince spurned the nearest boy with his foot, and said fiercely—

"Take thou that, till the morrow come and I build thee a gibbet!"

Ah, but this was not a joke—this was going beyond fun. The laughter ceased on the instant, and fury took its place. A dozen shouted—

"Hale him forth! To the horse-pond, to the horse-pond! Where be the dogs? Ho, there, Lion! ho, Fangs!"

Then followed such a thing as England had never seen before— the sacred person of the heir to the throne rudely buffeted by plebeian hands, and set upon and torn by dogs.

As night drew to a close that day, the prince found himself far down in the close-built portion of the city. His body was bruised, his hands were bleeding, and his rags were all besmirched with mud. He wandered on and on, and grew more and more bewildered, and so tired and faint he could hardly drag one foot after the other. He had ceased to ask questions of any one, since they brought him only insult instead of information. He kept muttering to himself, "Offal Court—that is the name; if I can but find it, before my strength is wholly spent and I drop, then am I saved—for his people will take me to the palace and prove that I am none of theirs, but the true prince, and I shall have mine own again." And now and then his mind reverted to his treatment by those rude Christ's Hospital boys, and he said, "When I am king, they shall not have bread and shelter only, but also teachings out of books; for a full belly is little worth where the mind is starved, and the heart. I will keep this diligently in my remembrance, that this day's lesson be not lost upon me, and my people suffer thereby; for learning softeneth the heart and breedeth gentleness and charity."*

The lights began to twinkle, it came on to rain, the wind rose, and a raw and gusty night set in. The houseless prince, the homeless heir to the throne of England, still moved on, drifting deeper into the maze of squalid alleys where the swarming hives of poverty and misery were massed together.

Suddenly a great drunken ruffian collared him and said—

"Out to this time of night again, and hast not brought a farthing home, I warrant me! If it be so, an' I do not break all the bones in thy lean body, then am I not John Canty, but some other."

The prince twisted himself loose, unconsciously brushed his profaned shoulder, and eagerly said—

"O, art *his* father, truly? Sweet heaven grant it be so—then wilt thou fetch him away and restore me!"

"*His* father? I know not what thou mean'st; I but know I am *thy* father, as thou shalt soon have cause to—"

"O, jest not, palter not, delay not!—I am worn, I am wounded, I can bear no more. Take me to the king my father, and he will make thee rich beyond thy wildest dreams. Believe me, man, believe me!—I speak no lie, but only the truth!—put forth thy hand and save me!—I am indeed the Prince of Wales!"

The man stared down, stupefied, upon the lad, then shook his head and muttered—

"Gone stark mad as any Tom o' Bedlam!"—then collared him once more, and said with a coarse laugh and an oath, "But mad or no

---

*See Note 2, at end of the volume.

mad, I and thy Gammer Canty will soon find where the soft places in thy bones lie, or I'm no true man!"

With this he dragged the frantic and struggling prince away, and disappeared up a foul court followed by a delighted and noisy swarm of human vermin.

"A DRUNKEN RUFFIAN COLLARED HIM."

CHAPTER 5

TOM AS A PATRICIAN

Tom Canty, left alone in the prince's cabinet, made good use of his opportunity. He turned himself this way and that, before the great mirror, admiring his finery; then walked away, imitating the prince's high-bred carriage, and still observing results in the glass. Next he drew the beautiful sword, and bowed, kissing the blade and laying it across his breast, as he had seen a noble knight do, by way of salute to the Lieutenant of the Tower, five or six weeks before, when delivering the great lords of Norfolk and Surrey into his hands for captivity. Tom played with the jeweled dagger that hung upon his thigh; he examined the costly and exquisite ornaments of the room; he tried each of the sumptuous chairs, and thought how proud he would be if the Offal Court herd could only peep in and see him in his grandeur. He wondered if they would believe the marvelous tale he should tell when he got home, or if they would shake their heads and say his overtaxed imagination had at last upset his reason.

"NEXT HE DREW THE SWORD."

At the end of half an hour it suddenly occurred to him that the prince was gone a long time; then right away he began to feel lonely; very soon he fell to listening and longing, and ceased to toy with the pretty things about him; he grew uneasy, then restless, then distressed. Suppose some one should come, and catch him in the prince's clothes, and the prince not there to explain! Might they not hang him at once, and inquire into his case afterward? He had heard that the great were prompt about small matters. His fears rose higher and higher; and trembling he softly opened the door to the ante-chamber, resolved to fly and seek the prince, and through him protection and release. Six gorgeous gentlemen-servants and two young pages of high degree, clothed like butterflies, sprung to their feet and bowed low before him. He stepped quickly back and shut the door. He said—

"O, they mock at me! They will go and tell! O, why came I here to cast away my life!"

He walked up and down the floor, filled with nameless fears, listening, starting at every trifling sound. Presently the door swung open and a silken page said—

"RESOLVED TO FLY."

"The lady Jane Grey!"

The door closed, and a sweet young girl, richly clad, bounded toward him. But she stopped suddenly, and said in a distressed voice—

"O, what aileth thee, my lord?"

Tom's breath was nearly failing him, but he made shift to stammer out—

"Ah, be merciful, thou! In sooth I am no lord, but only poor Tom Canty of Offal Court in the City. Prithee let me see the prince, and he will of his grace restore to me my rags and let me hence unhurt. O, be thou merciful and save me!"

"THE BOY WAS ON HIS KNEES."

By this time the boy was on his knees and supplicating with his eyes and uplifted hands as well as with his tongue. The young girl seemed horror-stricken. She cried out—

"O, my lord, on thy knees?—and to *me!*"

Then she fled away in fright, and Tom, smitten with despair, sank down, murmuring—

"There is no help, there is no hope. Now will they come and take me!"

Whilst he lay there benumbed with terror, dreadful tidings were speeding through the palace. The whisper—for it was whispered always—flew from menial to menial, from lord to lady, down all the long corridors, from story to story, from saloon to saloon: "The prince hath gone mad, the prince hath gone mad!" Soon every saloon, every marble hall, had its groups of glittering lords and ladies, and other groups of dazzling lesser folk, talking earnestly together, in whispers, and every face had in it dismay. Presently a splendid official came marching by these groups, making solemn proclamation—

"IN THE NAME OF THE KING! Let none list to this false and foolish matter, upon pain of death; nor discuss the same nor carry it abroad. In the name of the king!"

The whisperings ceased as suddenly as if the whisperers had been stricken dumb.

Soon there was a general buzz along the corridors, of "The prince! See—the prince comes!"

Poor Tom came slowly walking past the low-bowing groups, trying to bow in return, and meekly gazing upon his strange surroundings with bewildered and pathetic eyes. Great nobles walked upon each side of him, making him lean upon them, and so steady his steps. Behind him followed the court physicians and some servants.

Presently Tom found himself in a noble apartment of the palace, and heard the door close behind him. Around him stood those who had come with him. Before him, at a little distance, reclined a very large and very fat man, with a wide, pulpy face, and a stern expression. His large head was very gray, and his whiskers, which he wore only around his face,—like a frame,—were gray also. His clothing was

"GREAT NOBLES WALKED UPON EACH SIDE OF HIM."

of rich stuff, but old, and slightly frayed in places. One of his swollen legs had a pillow under it and was wrapped in bandages. There was silence now; and there was no head there but was bent in reverence, except this man's. This stern-countenanced invalid was the dread Henry VIII. He said—and his face grew gentle as he began to speak,—

"How now, my lord Edward, my prince?—Hast been minded to cozen me, the good king thy father, who loveth thee and kindly useth thee, with a sorry jest?"

Poor Tom was listening as well as his dazed faculties would let him, to the beginning of this speech; but when the words "me, the good king" fell upon his ear, his face blanched and he dropped as

"HE DROPPED UPON HIS KNEES."

instantly upon his knees, as if a shot had brought him there. Lifting up his hands, he exclaimed,—

"Thou the *king?* Then am I undone indeed!"

This speech seemed to stun the king. His eyes wandered from face to face, aimlessly, then rested, bewildered, upon the boy before him. Then he said in a tone of deep disappointment—

"Alack, I had believed the rumor disproportioned to the truth, but I fear me 'tis not so." He breathed a heavy sigh, and said in a gentle voice—"Come to thy father, child, thou art not well."

Tom was assisted to his feet, and approached the majesty of England, humble and trembling. The king took the frightened face between his hands, and gazed earnestly and lovingly into it a while, as if seeking some grateful sign of returning reason there, then pressed the curly head against his breast and patted it tenderly. Presently he said—

"Dost not know thy father, child? Break not mine old heart—say thou know'st me. Thou *dost* know me, dost thou not?"

"Yea, thou art my dread lord the king, whom God preserve!"

"True, true—that is well—be comforted, tremble not so; there is none here would hurt thee; there is none here but loves thee. Thou art better, now; thy ill dream passeth—is't not so? And thou knowest thyself now, also—is't not so? Thou wilt not miscall thyself again, as they say thou didst a little while agone?"

"I pray thee of thy grace believe me, I did but speak the truth, most dread lord, for I am the meanest among thy subjects, being a pauper born, and 'tis by a sore mischance and accident I am here, albeit I was therein nothing blameful. I am but young to die—and thou canst save me with one little word—O speak it, sir!"

"Die? Talk not so, sweet prince—peace, peace to thy troubled heart—thou shalt not die!"

Tom dropped upon his knees, with a glad cry,—

"God requite thy mercy, oh, my king, and save thee long to bless thy land!" Then springing up, he turned a joyful face toward the two lords in waiting and exclaimed, "Thou heard'st it! I am not to die— the king hath said it!" There was no movement, save that all bowed, with grave respect—but no one spoke. He hesitated, a little confused, then turned timidly toward the king, saying, "I may go now?"

"Go? Surely—if thou desirest. But why not tarry yet a little? Whither wouldst go?"

Tom dropped his eyes and answered humbly—

"Peradventure I mistook, but I did think me free—and so was I moved to seek again the kennel where I was born and bred to misery, yet which harboreth my mother and my sisters, and so is home to me, whereas these pomps and splendors whereunto I am not used,— oh, please you sir, to let me go!"

The king was silent and thoughtful a while, and his face betrayed a growing distress and uneasiness. Presently he said, with something of hope in his voice—

"HE TURNED A JOYFUL FACE."

"Perchance he is but mad upon this one strain, and hath his wits unmarred as toucheth other matters. God send it may be so! We will make trial."

Then he asked Tom a question in Latin, and Tom answered him lamely in the same tongue. The king was delighted, and showed it. The lords and doctors manifested their gratification also. The king said—

" 'Twas not according to his schooling and ability, but sheweth that his mind is but diseased, not stricken fatally. How say you, sir?"

The physician addressed bowed low and replied—

"It jumpeth with mine own conviction, sire, that thou hast divined aright."

The king looked pleased with this encouragement, coming as it did from so excellent authority, and continued with good heart—

"Now mark ye all—we will try him further."

He put a question to Tom in French. Tom stood silent a moment, embarrassed by having so many eyes centred upon him, then said, diffidently—

"I have no knowledge of this tongue, so please your majesty."

"THE PHYSICIAN BOWED LOW."

The king fell back upon his couch; the attendants flew to his assistance. But he put them aside and said—

"Trouble me not—it is nothing but a scurvy faintness. Raise me!— there, 'tis sufficient. Come hither, child; there, rest thy poor troubled head upon thy father's heart and be at peace. Thou'lt soon be well— 'tis but a passing fantasy—fear thou not; thou'lt soon be well." Then

"THE KING FELL BACK
UPON HIS COUCH."

he turned toward the company; his gentle manner changed, and baleful lightnings began to play from his eyes. He said—

"List ye all! This my son is mad—but it is not permanent. Over-study hath done this, and somewhat too much of confinement. Away with his books and teachers—see ye to it! Pleasure him with sports, beguile him in wholesome ways, so that his health come again." He raised himself higher still, and went on, with energy: "He is mad, but he is my son and England's heir—and mad or sane, still shall he reign! And hear ye further and proclaim it—whoso speaketh of this his distemper, worketh against the peace and order of these realms, and shall to the gallows! . . . . . . Give me to drink—I burn; this sorrow sappeth my strength. . . . . . . There, take away the cup. . . . . . Support me—there, that is well. Mad, is he? Were he a thousand times mad, yet is he Prince of Wales, and I the king will confirm it. This very morrow shall he be installed in his princely dignity, in due and ancient form. Take instant order for it, my lord Hertford."

One of the nobles knelt at the royal couch and said—

"The king's majesty knoweth that the Hereditary Great Marshal of England lieth attainted in the Tower. It were not meet that one attainted—"

"Peace! Insult not mine ears with his hated name! Is this man to live forever? Am I to be balked of my will? is the prince to tarry uninstalled because, forsooth, the realm lacketh an earl marshal free of treasonable taint to invest him with his honors? No, by the splendor of God! Warn my parliament to bring me Norfolk's doom before the sun rise again, else shall they answer for it grievously!"*

Lord Hertford said—

"The king's will is law;" and rising, returned to his former place.

"IS THIS MAN TO LIVE FOREVER?"

Gradually the wrath faded out of the old king's face, and he said—

"Kiss me, my prince. There . . . . what fearest thou? Am I not thy loving father?"

"Thou art good to me, that am unworthy, oh, mighty and gracious lord—that in truth I know. But—but—it grieveth me to think of him that is to die, and—"

"Ah, 'tis like thee, 'tis like thee!—I know thy heart is still the same, even though thy mind hath suffered hurt—for thou wert ever of a gentle spirit. But this duke standeth between thee and thine honors;

---

*See Note 3 at end of volume.

I will have another in his stead, that shall bring no taint to his great office. Comfort thee, my prince—trouble not thy poor head with this matter."

"But is it not I that speed him hence, my liege? How long might he not live, but for me?"

"Take no thought of him, my prince, he is not worthy. Kiss me once again and go to thy trifles and amusements, for my malady distresseth me, I am aweary and would rest. Go with thine uncle Hertford and thy people, and come again when my body is refreshed."

Tom, heavy-hearted, was conducted from the presence, for this last sentence was a death-blow to the hope he had cherished that now he would be set free. Once more he heard the buzz of low voices exclaiming, "The prince!—the prince comes!"

His spirits sank lower and lower as he moved between the glittering files of bowing courtiers, for he recognized that he was indeed a captive, now, and might remain forever shut up in this gilded cage, a forlorn and friendless prince, except God in his mercy take pity on him and set him free.

And turn where he would, he seemed to see, floating in the air, the severed head and the remembered face of the great Duke of Norfolk, the eyes fixed on him reproachfully.

His old dreams had been so pleasant; but this reality was so dreary!

CHAPTER 6

Tom receives instructions

Tom was conducted to the principal apartment of a noble suite, and made to sit down—a thing which he was loth to do, since there were elderly men and men of high degree about him. He begged them to be seated, also, but they only bowed their thanks or murmured them, and remained standing. He would have insisted, but his "uncle" the Earl of Hertford whispered in his ear—

"Prithee, insist not, my lord; it is not meet that they sit in thy presence."

The lord St. John was announced, and after making obeisance to Tom, he said—

"I come upon the king's errand, concerning a matter which requireth privacy. Will it please your royal highness to dismiss all that attend you here, save my lord the Earl of Hertford?"

Observing that Tom did not seem to know how to proceed, Hertford whispered him to make a sign with his hand and not trouble himself to speak unless he chose. When the waiting gentlemen had retired, lord St. John said—

"His majesty commandeth, that for due and weighty reasons of state, the prince's grace shall hide his infirmity in all ways that be within his power, till it be passed and he be as he was before. To wit, that he shall deny to none that he is the true prince, and heir to

"PRITHEE, INSIST NOT."

England's greatness; that he shall uphold his princely dignity, and shall receive, without word or sign of protest, that reverence and observance which unto it do appertain of right and ancient usage; that he shall cease to speak to any of that lowly birth and life his malady hath conjured out of the unwholesome imaginings of o'er-wrought fancy; that he shall strive with diligence to bring unto his memory again those faces which he was wont to know—and where he faileth, he shall hold his peace, neither betraying by semblance of surprise, or other sign, that he hath forgot; that upon occasions of state, whensoever any matter shall perplex him as to the thing he should do or the utterance he should make, he shall show naught of unrest to the curious that look on, but take advice in that matter of the lord Hertford or my humble self, which are commanded of the king to be upon this service and close at call, till this commandment be dissolved. Thus saith the king's majesty, who sendeth greeting to your royal highness and prayeth that God will of His mercy quickly heal you and have you now and ever in His holy keeping."

The lord St. John made reverence and stood aside. Tom replied, resignedly—

"THE LORD ST. JOHN MADE REVERENCE."

"The king hath said it. None may palter with the king's command, or fit it to his ease, where it doth chafe, with deft evasions. The king shall be obeyed."

Lord Hertford said—

"Touching the king's majesty's ordainment concerning books and such like serious matters, it may peradventure please your highness to ease your time with lightsome entertainment, lest you go wearied to the banquet and suffer harm thereby."

Tom's face showed inquiring surprise; and a blush followed when he saw lord St. John's eyes bent sorrowfully upon him. His lordship said—

"Thy memory still wrongeth thee, and thou hast shown surprise— but suffer it not to trouble thee, for 'tis a matter that will not bide, but depart with thy mending malady. My lord of Hertford speaketh of the city's banquet which the king's majesty did promise, some two months flown, your highness should attend. Thou recallest it now?"

"It grieves me to confess it had indeed escaped me," said Tom, in a hesitating voice; and blushed again.

At this moment the lady Elizabeth and the lady Jane Grey were announced. The two lords exchanged significant glances, and Hertford stepped quickly toward the door. As the young girls passed him, he said in a low voice—

"I pray ye, ladies, seem not to observe his humors, nor show surprise when his memory doth lapse—it will grieve you to note how it doth stick at every trifle."

Meantime lord St. John was saying in Tom's ear—

"Please you sir, keep diligently in mind his majesty's desire. Remember all thou canst—*seem* to remember all else. Let them not perceive that thou art much changed from thy wont, for thou knowest how tenderly thy old playfellows bear thee in their hearts and how 'twould grieve them. Art willing, sir, that I remain?—and thine uncle?"

Tom signified assent with a gesture and a murmured word, for he was already learning, and in his simple heart was resolved to acquit himself as best he might, according to the king's command.

In spite of every precaution, the conversation among the young people became a little embarrassing, at times. More than once, in truth, Tom was near to breaking down and confessing himself unequal to his tremendous part; but the tact of the princess Elizabeth saved him, or a word from one or the other of the vigilant lords, thrown in apparently by chance, had the same happy effect. Once the little lady Jane turned to Tom and dismayed him with this question,—

"Hast paid thy duty to the queen's majesty to-day, my lord?"

Tom hesitated, looked distressed, and was about to stammer out something at hazard, when lord St. John took the word and answered for him with the easy grace of a courtier accustomed to encounter delicate difficulties and to be ready for them—

"He hath indeed, madam, and she did greatly hearten him, as touching his majesty's condition, is it not so, your highness?"

HERTFORD AND THE PRINCESSES.

Tom mumbled something that stood for assent, but felt that he was getting upon dangerous ground. Somewhat later it was mentioned that Tom was to study no more at present, whereupon her little ladyship exclaimed—

"'Tis a pity, 'tis such a pity! Thou wert proceeding bravely. But bide thy time in patience; it will not be for long. Thou'lt yet be graced with learning like thy father, and make thy tongue master of as many languages as his, good my prince."

"My father!" cried Tom, off his guard for the moment. "I trow he cannot speak his own so that any but the swine that wallow in the styes may tell his meaning; and as for learning of any sort soever—" He looked up and encountered a solemn warning in my lord St. John's eyes. He stopped, blushed, then continued low and sadly: "Ah, my malady persecuteth me again, and my mind wandereth. I meant the king's grace no irreverence."

"We know it, sir," said the princess Elizabeth, taking her "brother's" hand between her two palms, respectfully but caressingly; "trouble not thyself as to that. The fault is none of thine, but thy distemper's."

"Thou'rt a gentle comforter, sweet lady," said Tom, gratefully, "and my heart moveth me to thank thee for't, an' I may be so bold."

Once the giddy little lady Jane fired a simple Greek phrase at Tom. The princess Elizabeth's quick eye saw by the serene blankness of the target's front that the shaft was overshot; so she tranquilly delivered a return volley of sounding Greek on Tom's behalf, and then straightway changed the talk to other matters.

Time wore on pleasantly, and likewise smoothly, on the whole. Snags and sandbars grew less and less frequent, and Tom grew more and more at his ease, seeing that all were so lovingly bent upon helping him and overlooking his mistakes. When it came out that the little ladies were to accompany him to the Lord Mayor's banquet in the evening, his heart gave a bound of relief and delight, for he felt that he should not be friendless, now, among that multitude of strangers; whereas, an hour earlier, the idea of their going with him would have been an insupportable terror to him.

Tom's guardian angels, the two lords, had had less comfort in the interview than the other parties to it. They felt much as if they were piloting a great ship through a dangerous channel; they were on the alert, constantly, and found their office no child's play. Wherefore, at last, when the ladies' visit was drawing to a close and the lord Guilford Dudley was announced, they not only felt that their charge had been sufficiently taxed for the present, but also that they themselves were not in the best condition to take their ship back and make that anxious voyage all over again. So they respectfully advised Tom to excuse himself, which he was very glad to do, although a slight shade of disappointment might have been observed upon my lady Jane's face when she heard the splendid stripling denied admittance.

There was a pause, now, a sort of waiting silence which Tom could not understand. He glanced at lord Hertford, who gave him a sign—but he failed to understand that, also. The ready Elizabeth came to the rescue with her usual easy grace. She made reverence and said—

"Have we leave of the prince's grace my brother to go?"

Tom said—

"Indeed your ladyships can have whatsoever of me they will, for the asking; yet would I rather give them any other thing that in my poor power lieth, than leave to take the light and blessing of their presence hence. Give ye good den, and God be with ye!" Then he

"SHE MADE REVERENCE."

smiled inwardly at the thought, "'Tis not for naught I have dwelt but among princes in my reading, and taught my tongue some slight trick of their broidered and gracious speech withal!"

When the illustrious maidens were gone, Tom turned wearily to his keepers and said—

"May it please your lordships to grant me leave to go into some corner and rest me?"

Lord Hertford said—

"So please your highness, it is for you to command, it is for us to

"OFFERED IT TO HIM ON A GOLDEN SALVER."

obey. That thou shouldst rest, is indeed a needful thing, since thou must journey to the city presently."

He touched a bell, and a page appeared, who was ordered to desire the presence of Sir William Herbert. This gentleman came straightway, and conducted Tom to an inner apartment. Tom's first movement, there, was to reach for a cup of water; but a silk-and-velvet servitor seized it, dropped upon one knee, and offered it to him on a golden salver. Next the tired captive sat down and was going to take off his buskins, timidly asking leave with his eye, but another silk-and-velvet discomforter went down upon his knees and took the office from him. He made two or three further efforts to help himself, but being promptly forestalled each time, he finally gave up, with a sigh of resignation and a murmured "Beshrew me but I marvel they do not require to breathe for me, also!" Slippered, and wrapped in a sumptuous robe, he laid himself down at last to rest, but not to sleep, for his head was too full of thoughts and the room too full of people. He could not dismiss the former, so they staid; he did not know enough to dismiss the latter, so they staid also, to his vast regret,—and theirs.

Tom's departure had left his two noble guardians alone. They mused a while, with much head-shaking and walking the floor, then lord St. John said—

"Plainly, what dost thou think?"

"THEY MUSED A WHILE."

"Plainly, then, this. The king is near his end, my nephew is mad, mad will mount the throne, and mad remain. God protect England, since she will need it!"

"Verily it promiseth so, indeed. But . . . . have you no misgivings as to . . . . as to . . . ."

The speaker hesitated, and finally stopped. He evidently felt that he was upon delicate ground. Lord Hertford stopped before him, looked into his face with a clear, frank eye, and said—

"Speak on—there is none to hear but me. Misgivings as to what?"

"I am full loth to word the thing that is in my mind, and thou so near to him in blood, my lord. But craving pardon if I do offend, seemeth it not strange that madness could so change his port and manner!—not but that his port and speech are princely still, but that they *differ*, in one unweighty trifle or another, from what his custom was aforetime. Seemeth it not strange that madness should filch from his memory his father's very lineaments, the customs and observances that are his due from such as be about him, and leaving him his Latin strip him of his Greek and French? My lord, be not offended, but ease my mind of its disquiet and receive my grateful thanks. It haunteth me, his saying he was not the prince, and so—"

"Peace, my lord, thou utterest treason! Hast forgot the king's command? Remember I am party to thy crime, if I but listen."

St. John paled, and hastened to say—

"I was in fault. I do confess it. Betray me not, grant me this grace out of thy courtesy, and I will neither think nor speak of this thing more. Deal not hardly with me, sir, else am I ruined."

"PEACE, MY LORD, THOU UTTEREST TREASON!"

"HE BEGAN TO PACE THE FLOOR."

"I am content, my lord. So thou offend not again, here or in the ear of others, it shall be as though thou hadst not spoken. But thou needst not have misgivings. He is my sister's son; are not his voice, his face, his form, familiar to me from his cradle? Madness can do all the odd conflicting things thou seest in him, and more. Dost not recal how that the old Baron Marley, being mad, forgot the favor of his own countenance that he had known for sixty years, and held it was another's; nay, even claimed he was the son of Mary Magdalene, and that his head was made of Spanish glass; and sooth to say, he suffered none to touch it, lest by mischance some heedless hand might shiver it. Give thy misgivings easement, good my lord. This is the very prince, I know him well—and soon will be thy king; it may advantage thee to bear this in mind and more dwell upon it than the other."

After some further talk, in which the lord St. John covered up his mistake as well as he could by repeated protests that his faith was thoroughly grounded, now, and could not be assailed by doubts again, the lord Hertford relieved his fellow keeper and sat down to keep watch and ward alone. He was soon deep in meditation. And evidently, the longer he thought, the more he was bothered. By and by he began to pace the floor and mutter.

"Tush, he *must* be the prince! Will any he in all the land maintain there can be two, not of one blood and birth, so marvelously twinned? And even were it so, 'twere yet a stranger miracle that chance should cast the one into the other's place. Nay, 'tis folly, folly, folly!"

Presently he said:

"Now were he impostor and called himself prince, look you *that* would be natural; that would be reasonable. But lived ever an impostor yet, who, being called prince by the king, prince by the court, prince by all, *denied* his dignity and pleaded against his exaltation?— *No!* By the soul of St. Swithin, no! This is the true prince, gone mad!"

CHAPTER 7

TOM'S FIRST ROYAL DINNER

SOMEWHAT AFTER ONE in the afternoon, Tom resignedly under-
went the ordeal of being dressed for dinner. He found himself as
finely clothed as before, but everything different, everything changed,
from his ruff to his stockings. He was presently conducted with much
state to a spacious and ornate apartment where a table was already
set—for one. Its furniture was all of massy gold, and beautified with
designs which well nigh made it priceless, since they were the work
of Benvenuto. The room was half filled with noble servitors. A chaplain said grace, and Tom was about to fall to, for hunger had long
been constitutional with him, but was interrupted by my lord the
Earl of Berkeley, who fastened a napkin about his neck—for the great

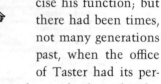

post of Diaperers to the Princes of Wales was hereditary in this nobleman's family. Tom's cup-bearer was present and forestalled all his attempts to help himself to wine. The Taster to his highness the Prince of Wales was there, also, prepared to taste any suspicious dish upon requirement, and run the risk of being poisoned. He was only an ornamental appendage, at this time, and was seldom called upon to exercise his function; but there had been times, not many generations past, when the office of Taster had its perils, and was not a grandeur to be desired. Why they did not use a dog or a plumber seems strange; but all the ways of royalty are strange. My lord d'Arcy, First Groom of the Chamber, was there, to do goodness knows what—but there he was—let that suffice. The Lord Chief Butler was there, and stood behind Tom's chair, overseeing the solemnities, under command of the Lord Great Steward and the Lord Head Cook, who stood near. Tom had three hundred and eighty-four servants beside these, but they were not all in that room, of course, nor the quarter of them; neither was Tom aware, yet, that they existed.

"FASTENED A NAPKIN ABOUT HIS NECK."

All those that were present had been well drilled, within the hour, to remember that the prince was temporarily out of his head, and to be careful to show no surprise at his vagaries. These "vagaries" were soon on exhibition before them; but they only moved their compassion and their sorrow, not their mirth. It was a heavy affliction to them to see the beloved prince so stricken.

Poor Tom ate with his fingers, mainly; but no one smiled at it, or even seemed to observe it. He inspected his napkin curiously, and with deep interest, for it was of a very dainty and beautiful fabric—then said, with simplicity—

"Prithee take it away, lest in mine unheedfulness it be soiled."

The Hereditary Diaperer took it away, with reverent manner, and without word or protest of any sort.

Tom examined the turnips and the lettuce with interest, and asked what they were, and if they were to be eaten; for it was only recently that men had begun to raise these things in England, in place of importing them as luxuries from Holland.* His question was answered with grave respect, and no surprise manifested. When he had finished his dessert, he

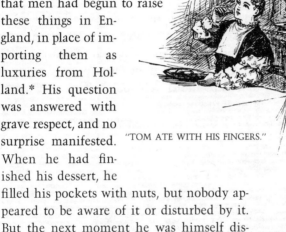

"TOM ATE WITH HIS FINGERS."

filled his pockets with nuts, but nobody appeared to be aware of it or disturbed by it. But the next moment he was himself disturbed by it and showed discomposure; for this was the only service he had been permitted to do with his own hands during the meal, and he did not doubt that he had done a most improper and unprincely thing. At that moment the muscles of his nose began to twitch and the end of that organ to lift and wrinkle. This continued, and Tom began to evince a growing distress. He looked appealingly, first at one and then another of the lords about him, and tears came into his eyes. They sprang forward with dismay in their faces, and begged to know his trouble. Tom said with genuine anguish—

"I crave your indulgence—my nose itcheth cruelly! What is the custom and usage in this emergence? Prithee speed, for 'tis but a little time that I can bear it."

*See Note 4, at end of volume.

None smiled, but all were sore perplexed, and looked one to the other in deep tribulation for counsel. But behold, here was a dead wall, and nothing in English history to tell how to get over it. The Master of Ceremonies was not present; there was no one who felt safe to venture upon this uncharted sea, or risk the attempt to solve this solemn problem. Alas, there was no Hereditary Scratcher! Meantime the tears had overflowed their banks and begun to trickle down Tom's cheeks. His twitching nose was pleading more urgently than ever for relief. At last nature broke down the barriers of etiquette— Tom lifted up an inward prayer for pardon if he was doing wrong, and brought relief to the burdened hearts of his court by scratching his nose himself.

His meal being ended, a lord came and held before him a broad shallow golden dish with fragrant rose-water in it, to cleanse his mouth and fingers with, and my lord the Hereditary Diaperer stood by with a napkin for his use. Tom gazed at the dish a puzzled moment or two, then raised it to his lips and gravely took a draught. Then he returned it to the waiting lord and said—

"Nay, it likes me not, my lord; it hath a pretty flavor, but it wanteth strength."

"HE GRAVELY TOOK A DRAUGHT."

"TOM PUT ON THE GREAVES."

This new eccentricity of the prince's ruined mind made all the hearts about him ache, but the sad sight moved none to merriment.

Tom's next unconscious blunder was to get up and leave the table just when the chaplain had taken his stand behind his chair, and with uplifted hands, and closed, uplifted eyes, was in the act of beginning the blessing. Still nobody seemed to perceive that the prince had done a thing unusual.

By his own request, our small friend was now conducted to his private cabinet and left there alone, to his own devices. Hanging upon hooks in the oaken wainscoting, were the several pieces of a suit of shining steel armor, covered all over with beautiful designs, exquisitely inlaid in gold. This martial panoply belonged to the true prince—a recent present from Madam Parr the queen. Tom put on the greaves, the gauntlets, the plumed helmet, and such other pieces as he could don without assistance; and for a while was minded to call for help and complete the matter, but bethought him of the nuts he had brought away from dinner and the joy it would be to eat them with no crowd to eye him and no Grand Hereditaries to pester him with undesired services; so he restored the pretty things to their several places, and soon was cracking nuts and feeling almost naturally happy, for the first time since God for his sins had made him a prince. When the nuts were all gone, he stumbled upon some inviting books in a closet—among them one about the etiquette of the English court. This was a prize. He lay down upon a sumptuous divan and proceeded to instruct himself, with honest zeal. Let us leave him there, for the present.

CHAPTER 8

ABOUT FIVE o'clock Henry VIII awoke out of an unrefreshing nap, and muttered to himself, "Troublous dreams, troublous dreams! Mine end is now at hand—so say these warnings, and my failing pulses do confirm it." Presently a wicked light flamed up in his eye, and he muttered, "Yet will not I die till *he* go before!"

His attendants perceiving that he was awake, one of them asked his pleasure concerning the Lord Chancellor, who was waiting without.

"Admit him! admit him!" exclaimed the king, eagerly.

The Lord Chancellor entered and knelt by the king's couch, saying—

"I have given order, and according to the king's command, the peers of the realm, in their robes, do now stand at the bar of the House; where, having confirmed the Duke of Norfolk's doom, they humbly wait his majesty's further pleasure in the matter."

The king's face lit up with a fierce joy. Said he—

"Lift me up! In mine own person will I go before my parliament, and with mine own hand will I seal the warrant that rids me of—"

His voice failed, an ashen pallor swept the flush from his cheeks, and the attendants eased him back upon his pillows and hurriedly assisted him with restoratives. Presently he said, sorrowfully—

"Alack, how have I longed for this sweet hour, and lo, too late it cometh and I am robbed of this so coveted chance! But speed ye, speed ye, let others do this happy office sith 'tis denied to me. I put my Great Seal in commission—choose thou the lords that shall compose it—and get ye to your work. Speed ye, man! Before the sun shall rise and set again, bring me his head that I may see it!"

"According to the king's command, so shall it be. Will't please your majesty to order that the Seal be now restored to me, so that I may forth upon the business?"

"The Seal? Who keepeth the Seal but thou?"

"THE ATTENDANTS EASED HIM BACK UPON HIS PILLOWS."

"Please your majesty, you did take it from me two days since, saying it should no more do its office till your own royal hand should use it upon the Duke of Norfolk's warrant."

"Why so in sooth I did; I do remember it. . . . . . . What did I with it? . . . . I am very feeble. . . . . So oft, these days, doth my memory play the traitor with me. . . . . 'Tis strange—strange—"

The king dropped into inarticulate mumblings, shaking his gray head weakly, from time to time, and gropingly trying to recollect what he had done with the Seal. At last my lord Hertford ventured to kneel and offer information,—

"Sire, if that I may be so bold, here be several that do remember, with me, how that you gave the Great Seal into the hands of his highness the Prince of Wales to keep against the day that—"

"True, most true!" interrupted the king. "Fetch it! Go—time flieth!"

Lord Hertford flew to Tom; but returned to the king before very long, troubled and empty handed. He delivered himself to this effect—

"It grieveth me, my lord the king, to bear so heavy and unwelcome tidings, but it is the will of God that the prince's affliction abideth still, and he cannot recal to mind that he received the Seal. So came I quickly to report, thinking it were waste of precious time, and little worth, withal, that any should attempt to search the long array of chambers and saloons that belong unto his royal high—"

A groan from the king interrupted my lord at this point. After a little while his majesty said, with a deep sadness in his tone—

"Trouble him no more, poor child. The hand of God lieth heavy upon him, and my heart goeth out in loving compassion for him and sorrow that I may not bear his burden on mine own old trouble-weighted shoulders and so bring him peace."

He closed his eyes, fell to mumbling, and presently was silent. After a time he opened his eyes again, and gazed vacantly around until his glance rested upon the kneeling Lord Chancellor. Instantly his face flushed with wrath,—

"What, thou here yet! By the glory of God, an' thou gettest not about that traitor's business, thy mitre shall have holiday the morrow, for lack of a head to grace, withal!"

The trembling Chancellor answered—

"Good your majesty, I cry you mercy! I but waited for the Seal."

"Man, hast lost thy wits? The small Seal which aforetime I was wont to take with me abroad, lieth in my treasury. And since the Great Seal hath flown away, shall not it suffice? Hast lost thy wits? Begone! And harkye—come no more till thou do bring his head!"

The poor Chancellor was not long in removing himself from this dangerous vicinity; nor did the Commission waste time in giving the royal assent to the work of the slavish parliament and appointing the morrow for the beheading of the premier peer of England, the luckless Duke of Norfolk.*

---

*See Note 5 at end of volume.

CHAPTER 9

THE RIVER PAGEANT

AT NINE in the evening the whole vast river-front of the palace was blazing with light. The river itself, as far as the eye could reach, citywards, was so thickly covered with watermen's boats and with pleasure-barges, all fringed with colored lanterns, and gently agitated by the waves, that it resembled a glowing and limitless garden of flowers stirred to soft motion by summer winds. The grand terrace of stone steps leading down to the water—spacious enough to mass the army of a German principality upon—was a picture to see, with its ranks of royal halberdiers in polished armor, and its troops of brilliantly costumed servitors flitting up and down and to and fro in the hurry of preparation.

Presently a command was given, and immediately all living creatures vanished from the steps. Now the air was heavy with the hush of suspense and expectancy. As far as one's vision could carry, he might see the myriads of people in the boats rise up and shade their eyes from the glare of lanterns and torches, and gaze toward the palace.

A file of forty or fifty state barges drew up to the steps. They were richly gilt, and their lofty prows and sterns were elaborately carved.

Some of them were decorated with banners and streamers; some with cloth of gold and arras, embroidered with coats of arms; others with silken flags that had numberless little silver bells fastened to them which shook out tiny showers of joyous music whenever the breezes fluttered them; others, of yet higher pretensions, since they belonged to nobles in the prince's immediate service, had their sides picturesquely fenced with shields gorgeously emblazoned with armorial bearings. Each state barge was towed by a tender; besides the rowers, these tenders carried each a number of men-at-arms in glossy helmet and breast-plate, and a company of musicians.

The advance-guard of the expected procession now appeared in the great gateway, a troop of halberdiers. "They were dressed in striped hose of black and tawny, velvet caps graced at the sides with silver roses, and doublets of murrey and blue cloth, embroidered on the front and back with the Three Feathers, the prince's blazon, woven in gold. Their halberd staves were covered with crimson velvet, fastened with gilt nails and ornamented with gold tassels. Filing off on the right and left, they formed two long lines, extending from the gateway of the palace to the water's edge. A thick rayed cloth or carpet was then unfolded and laid down between them by attendants in the gold and crimson liveries of the prince. This done, a flourish of trumpets resounded from within; a lively prelude arose from the musicians on the water; and two ushers with white wands marched with a slow and stately pace from the portal. They were followed by an officer bearing the civic mace; after whom came another, carrying the City's Sword; then several sergeants of the city guard, in their full accoutrements and with badges on their sleeves; then the Garter King-at-Arms in his tabard; then several knights of the Bath, each with a white lace on his sleeve; then their esquires; then the judges, in their robes of scarlet and coifs; then the lord high chancellor of England, in a robe of scarlet open before and purfled with minever; then a deputation of aldermen, in their scarlet cloaks; and then the heads of the different civic companies, in their robes of state. Now came twelve French gentlemen, in splendid habiliments, consisting of pourpoints of white damask, barred with gold, short mantles of crimson velvet, lined with violet taffeta, and carnation-colored hauts-de-chausses, and took their way down the steps. They were of the suite of the French ambassador, and were followed by twelve cavaliers of the suite of the Spanish

"A TROOP OF HALBERDIERS
APPEARED IN THE GATEWAY."

ambassador, clothed in black velvet, unrelieved by any ornament. Following these came several great English nobles, with their attendants."

There was a flourish of trumpets within, and the prince's uncle the future great Duke of Somerset, emerged from the gateway, arrayed in a "doublet of black cloth of gold, and a cloak of crimson satin flowered with gold and ribanded with nets of silver." He turned, doffed his plumed cap, bent his body in a low reverence, and began to step backward, bowing at each step. A prolonged trumpet-blast followed, and a proclamation, "Way for the high and mighty, the lord

Edward, Prince of Wales!"—high aloft on the palace walls a long line of red tongues of flame leaped forth, with a thunder-crash; the massed world on the river burst into a mighty roar of welcome, and Tom Canty, the cause and hero of it all, stepped into view and slightly bowed his princely head!

He was "magnificently habited in a doublet of white satin, with a front-piece of purple cloth of tissue, powdered with diamonds and edged with ermine. Over this he wore a mantle of white cloth of gold, pounced with the triple-feather crest, lined with blue satin, set with pearls and precious stones, and fastened with a clasp of brilliants. About his neck hung the order of the Garter and several princely foreign orders," and wherever light fell upon him, jewels responded with a blinding flash. O, Tom Canty, born in a hovel, bred in the gutters of London, familiar with rags and dirt and misery, what a spectacle is this!

"TOM CANTY STEPPED INTO VIEW."

CHAPTER 10

THE PRINCE IN THE TOILS

W<small>E LEFT</small> John Canty dragging the rightful prince into Offal Court, with a noisy and delighted mob at his heels. There was but one person in it who offered a pleading word for the captive, and he was not heeded; he was hardly even heard, so great was the turmoil. The prince continued to struggle for freedom and to rage against the treatment he was suffering, until John Canty lost what little patience was left in him, and raised his oaken cudgel in a sudden fury over the prince's head. The single pleader for the lad sprang to stop the man's arm, and the blow descended upon his own wrist. Canty roared out—

"Thou'lt meddle, wilt thou? Then have thy reward!"

His cudgel crashed down upon the meddler's head; there was a groan, a dim form sank to the ground among the feet of the crowd, and the next moment it lay there in the dark, alone. The mob pressed on, their enjoyment nothing disturbed by this episode.

Presently the prince found himself in John Canty's abode, with the door closed against the outsiders. By the vague light of a tallow candle which was thrust into a bottle, he made out the main features of the loathsome den, and also the occupants of it. Two frowsy girls and a middle-aged woman cowered against the wall, in one corner, with the aspect of animals habituated to harsh usage and expecting and dreading it now. From another corner stole a withered hag with streaming gray hair and malignant eyes. John Canty said to this one—

"A DIM FORM SANK TO THE GROUND."

"Tarry! There's fine mummeries here. Mar them not till thou'st
enjoyed them; then let thy hand be heavy as thou wilt. Stand forth
lad. Now say thy foolery again an' thou'st not forgot it. Name thy
name. Who art thou?"

The insulted blood mounted to the little prince's cheek once more,
and he lifted a steady and indignant gaze to the man's face and said—

"'Tis but ill breeding in such as thou to command me to speak.
I tell thee now, as I told thee before, I am Edward Prince of Wales,
and none other."

The stunning surprise of this reply nailed the hag's feet to the floor
where she stood, and almost took her breath. She stared at the prince
in stupid amazement, which so amused her ruffianly son that he burst
into a roar of laughter. But the effect upon Tom Canty's mother and
sisters was different. Their dread of bodily injury gave way at once to
distress of a different sort. They ran forward with woe and dismay in
their faces, exclaiming—

"O, poor Tom, poor lad!"

The mother fell on her knees before the prince, put her hands upon his shoulders, and gazed yearningly into his face through her rising tears. Then she said—

"O, my poor boy, thy foolish reading hath wrought its woful work at last and ta'en thy wit away! Ah, why didst thou cleave to it, when I so warned thee 'gainst it? Thou'st broke thy mother's heart!"

The prince looked into her face and said gently—

"Thy son is well, and hath not lost his wits, good dame. Comfort thee; let me to the palace where he is, and straightway will the king my father restore him to thee."

"The king thy father! O, my child, unsay these words, that be freighted with death for thee, and ruin for all that be near to thee. Shake off this grewsome dream. Call back thy poor wandering memory. Look upon me. Am not I thy mother that bore thee and loveth thee?"

The prince shook his head, and reluctantly said—

"God knoweth I am loth to grieve thy heart, but truly have I never looked upon thy face before."

"WHO ART THOU?"

The woman sank back to a sitting posture on the floor, and covering her eyes with her hands, gave way to heart-broken sobs and wailings.

"Let the show go on!" shouted Canty. "What, Nan! what, Bet! Mannerless wenches, will ye stand in the prince's presence? Upon your knees, ye pauper scum, and do him reverence!"

"SENT HIM STAGGERING INTO GOODWIFE CANTY'S ARMS."

He followed this with another horse-laugh. The girls began to plead timidly for their brother, and Nan said—

"An' thou wilt but let him to bed, father, rest and sleep will heal his madness —prithee, do!"

"Do, father," said Bet, "he is more worn than is his wont. Tomorrow will he be himself again, and will beg with diligence and come not empty home again."

This remark sobered the father's joviality and brought his mind to business. He turned angrily upon the prince and said—

"The morrow must we pay two pennies to him that owns this hole—two pennies, mark ye—all this money for a half-year's rent, else out of this we go. Show what thou'st gathered, with thy lazy begging!"

The prince said—

"Offend me not with thy sordid matters. I tell thee again I am the king's son."

A sounding blow upon the prince's shoulder from Canty's broad palm, sent him staggering into Goodwife Canty's arms, who clasped him to her breast and sheltered him from a pelting rain of cuffs and slaps by interposing her own person. The frightened girls retreated to their corner, but the grandmother stepped eagerly forward to assist her son. The prince sprang away from Mrs. Canty, exclaiming—

"Thou shalt not suffer for me, madam. Let these swine do their will upon me alone!"

This speech infuriated the swine to such a degree that they set about their work without waste of time. Between them they belabored the boy right soundly, and then gave the girls and their mother a beating for showing sympathy for the victim.

"Now," said Canty, "to bed, all of ye. The entertainment has tired me."

The light was put out, and the family retired. As soon as the snorings of the head of the house and his mother showed that they were asleep, the young girls crept to where the prince lay and covered him tenderly from the cold with straw and rags, and their mother crept to him also, and stroked his hair and cried over him, whispering broken words of comfort and compassion in his ear the while. She had saved a morsel for him to eat, also, but the boy's pains had swept away all appetite,—at least for black and tasteless crusts. He was touched by her brave and costly defense of him, and by her commiseration; and he thanked her in very noble and princely words, and begged her to go to her sleep and try to forget her sorrows. And he added that the king his father would not let her loyal kindness and devotion go unrewarded. This return to his "madness" broke her heart anew, and she strained him to her breast again and again and then went back, drowned in tears, to her bed.

As she lay thinking and mourning, the suggestion began to creep into her mind that there was an undefinable something about this boy that was lacking in Tom Canty, mad or sane. She could not describe it, she could not tell just what it was, and yet her sharp mother-instinct seemed to detect it and perceive it. What if the boy were really not her son, after all? O, absurd! She almost smiled at the idea, spite of her griefs and troubles. No matter, she found that it was an idea that would not "down," but persisted in haunting her. It pursued her, it harassed her, it clung to her, and refused to be put away or ignored. At last she perceived that there was not going to be any peace for her until she should devise a test that should prove, clearly and without question, whether this lad was her son or not, and so banish these wearing and worrying doubts. Ah yes, this was plainly the right way out of the difficulty; therefore she set her wits to work at once to contrive that test. But it was an easier thing to propose than to accomplish. She turned over in her mind one promising test after another, but was obliged to relinquish them all—none of them were absolutely sure, absolutely perfect; and an imperfect one could not satisfy her. Evidently she was racking her head in vain—it seemed manifest that she must give the matter up. While this depressing thought was passing through her mind, her ear caught the regular breathing of the boy, and she knew he had fallen asleep. And while she listened, the measured breathing was broken by a soft, startled cry, such as one utters in a troubled dream. This chance occurrence furnished her instantly with a plan worth all her labored tests combined. She at once set herself feverishly, but noiselessly, to work, to relight her candle, muttering to herself, "Had I but seen him *then*, I should have known! Since that day, when he was little, that the powder burst in his face, he hath never been startled of a sudden out of his dreams or out of his thinkings, but he hath cast his hand before his eyes, even as he did that day; and not as others would do it, with the palm inward, but always with the palm turned outward—I have seen it a hundred times, and it hath never varied nor ever failed. Yes, I shall soon know, now!"

By this time she had crept to the slumbering boy's side, with the candle, shaded, in her hand. She bent heedfully and warily over him, scarcely breathing, in her suppressed excitement, and suddenly

"SHE BENT HEEDFULLY AND WARILY OVER HIM."

flashed the light in his face and struck the floor by his ear with her knuckles. The sleeper's eyes sprung wide open, and he cast a startled stare about him—but he made no special movement with his hands.

The poor woman was smitten almost helpless with surprise and grief; but she contrived to hide her emotions, and to soothe the boy to sleep again; then she crept apart and communed miserably with herself upon the disastrous result of her experiment. She tried to believe that her Tom's madness had banished this habitual gesture of his; but she could not do it. "No," she said, "his *hands* are not mad, they could not unlearn so old a habit in so brief a time. O, this is a heavy day for me!"

Still, hope was as stubborn, now, as doubt had been before; she could not bring herself to accept the verdict of the test; she must try the thing again—the failure must have been only an accident; so she startled the boy out of his sleep a second and a third time, at intervals—with the same result which had marked the first test—then she dragged herself to bed, and fell sorrowfully asleep, saying, "But I cannot give him up—O, no, I cannot, I cannot—he *must* be my boy!"

The poor mother's interruptions having ceased, and the prince's pains having gradually lost their power to disturb him, utter weariness at last sealed his eyes in a profound and restful sleep. Hour after hour slipped away, and still he slept like the dead. Thus four or five hours passed. Then his stupor began to lighten. Presently while half asleep and half awake, he murmured—

"Sir William!"

After a moment—

"Ho, Sir William Herbert! Hie thee hither, and list to the strangest dream that ever . . . . Sir William! dost hear? Man, I did think me changed to a pauper, and . . . . . . Ho there! Guards! Sir William! What! is there no groom of the chamber in waiting? Alack it shall go hard with—"

"What aileth thee?" asked a whisper near him. "Who art thou calling?"

"Sir William Herbert. Who art thou?"

"I? Who should I be, but thy sister Nan? O, Tom, I had forgot!—Thou'rt mad yet—poor lad thou'rt mad yet, would I had never woke to know it again! But prithee master thy tongue, lest we be all beaten till we die!"

The startled prince sprang partly up, but a sharp reminder from
his stiffened bruises brought him to himself, and he sunk back among
his foul straw with a moan and the ejaculation—

"Alas, it was no dream, then!"

"THE PRINCE SPRANG UP."

In a moment all the heavy sorrow and misery which sleep had
banished were upon him again, and he realized that he was no longer
a petted prince in a palace, with the adoring eyes of a nation upon
him, but a pauper, an outcast, clothed in rags, prisoner in a den fit
only for beasts, and consorting with beggars and thieves.

In the midst of his grief he began to be conscious of hilarious noises
and shoutings, apparently but a block or two away. The next moment
there were several sharp raps at the door, John Canty ceased from
snoring and said—

"Who knocketh? What wilt thou?"

A voice answered—

"Know'st thou who it was thou laid thy cudgel on?"

"No. Neither know I, nor care."

"Belike thou'lt change thy note eftsoons. An' thou would save
thy neck, nothing but flight may stead thee. The man is this moment
delivering up the ghost. 'Tis the priest, Father Andrew!"

"God-a-mercy!" exclaimed Canty. He roused his family, and hoarsely commanded, "Up with ye all and fly—or bide where ye are and perish!"

Scarcely five minutes later the Canty household were in the street and flying for their lives. John Canty held the prince by the wrist, and hurried him along the dark way, giving him this caution in a low voice—

"HURRIED HIM ALONG
THE DARK WAY."

"Mind thy tongue, thou mad fool, and speak not our name. I will choose me a new name, speedily, to throw the law's dogs off the scent. Mind thy tongue, I tell thee!"

He growled these words to the rest of the family—

"If it so chance that we be separated, let each make for London Bridge; whoso findeth himself as far as the last linen-draper's shop on the Bridge, let him tarry there till the others be come, then will we flee into Southwark together."

At this moment the party burst suddenly out of darkness into light; and not only into light but into the midst of a multitude of singing,

dancing, and shouting people, massed together on the river frontage.
There was a line of bonfires stretching as far as one could see, up and
down the Thames; London Bridge was illuminated; Southwark Bridge,
likewise; the entire river was aglow with the flash and sheen of
colored lights; and constant explosions of fireworks filled the skies
with an intricate commingling of shooting splendors and a thick rain
of dazzling sparks that almost turned night into day; everywhere were
crowds of revelers; all London seemed to be at large.

John Canty delivered himself of a furious curse and commanded a
retreat; but it was too late. He and his tribe were swallowed up in
that swarming hive of humanity and hopelessly separated from each
other in an instant. We are not considering that the prince was one
of his tribe; Canty still kept his grip upon him. The prince's heart
was beating high with hopes of escape, now. A burly waterman, considerably exalted with liquor, found himself rudely shoved by Canty
in his efforts to plow through the crowd; he laid his great hand on
Canty's shoulder and said—

"Nay, whither so fast, friend? Dost canker thy soul with sordid
business when all that be leal men and true make holiday?"

"Mine affairs are mine own, they concern thee not," answered
Canty, roughly, "take away thy hand and let me pass."

"Sith that is thy humor, thou'lt *not* pass, till thou'st drunk to the
Prince of Wales, I tell thee that," said the waterman, barring the way
resolutely.

"Give me the cup, then, and make speed, make speed!"

Other revelers were interested by this time. They cried out—

"The loving-cup, the loving-cup! make the sour knave drink the
loving-cup, else will we feed him to the fishes."

So a huge loving-cup was brought; the waterman, grasping it by one
of its handles, and with his other hand bearing up the end of an
imaginary napkin, presented it in due and ancient form to Canty, who
had to grasp the opposite handle with one of his hands and take off the
lid with the other, according to ancient custom.* This left the prince
hand-free for a second, of course. He wasted no time, but dived among
the forest of legs about him and disappeared. In another moment he
could not have been harder to find, under that tossing sea of life, if its
billows had been the Atlantic's and he a lost sixpence.

---

*See Note 6, at end of volume.

"HE WASTED NO TIME."

He very soon realized this fact, and straightway busied himself about his own affairs without further thought of John Canty. He quickly realized another thing, too. To wit, that a spurious Prince of Wales was being feasted by the city in his stead. He easily concluded that the pauper lad, Tom Canty, had deliberately taken advantage of his stupendous opportunity and become a usurper. Therefore there was but one course to pursue— find his way to the Guildhall, make himself known, and denounce the impostor. He also made up his mind that Tom should be allowed a reasonable time for spiritual preparation and then be hanged, drawn and quartered, according to the law and usage of the day, in cases of high treason.

CHAPTER 11

AT GUILDHALL

THE ROYAL BARGE, attended by its gorgeous fleet, took its stately way down the Thames through the wilderness of illuminated boats. The air was laden with music; the river banks were beruffled with joy-flames; the distant city lay in a soft luminous glow from its countless invisible bonfires; above it rose many a slender spire into the sky, encrusted with sparkling lights, wherefore in their remoteness they seemed like jeweled lances thrust aloft; as the fleet swept along, it was greeted from the banks with a continuous hoarse roar of cheers and the ceaseless flash and boom of artillery.

To Tom Canty, half buried in his silken cushions, these sounds and this spectacle were a wonder unspeakably sublime and astonishing. To his little friends at his side, the princess Elizabeth and the lady Jane Grey, they were nothing.

Arrived at the Dowgate, the fleet was towed up the limpid Walbrook (whose channel has now been for two centuries buried out of sight under acres of buildings,) to Bucklersbury, past houses and under bridges populous with merry-makers and brilliantly lighted, and at last came to a halt in a basin where now is Barge Yard, in the centre of the ancient city of London. Tom disembarked, and he and his gallant

"A RICH CANOPY OF STATE."

procession crossed Cheapside and made a short march through the Old Jewry and Basinghall street to the Guildhall.

Tom and his little ladies were received with due ceremony by the Lord Mayor and the Fathers of the City, in their gold chains and scarlet robes of state, and conducted to a rich canopy of state at the head of the great hall, preceded by heralds making proclamation, and by the Mace and the City Sword. The lords and ladies who were to attend upon Tom and his two small friends took their places behind their chairs.

At a lower table the court grandees and other guests of noble degree were seated, with the magnates of the city; the commoners took places at a multitude of tables on the main floor of the hall. From their lofty vantage-ground, the giants Gog and Magog, the ancient guardians of the city, contemplated the spectacle below them with eyes grown familiar to it in forgotten generations. There was a bugle-blast and a proclamation, and a fat butler appeared in a high perch in the leftward wall, followed by his servitors bearing with impressive solemnity a royal Baron of Beef, smoking hot and ready for the knife.

After grace, Tom (being instructed,) rose—and the whole house with him—and drank from a portly golden loving-cup with the princess Elizabeth; from her it passed to the lady Jane, and then traversed the general assemblage. So the banquet began.

By midnight the revelry was at its height. Now came one of those picturesque spectacles so admired in that old day. A description of it is still extant in the quaint wording of a chronicler who witnessed it:

"Space being made, presently entered a baron and an earl appareled after the Turkish fashion in long robes of bawdkin powdered with gold; hats on their heads of crimson velvet, with great rolls of gold, girded with two swords, called scimitars, hanging by great bawdricks of gold. Next came yet another baron and another earl, in two long gowns of yellow satin, traversed with white satin, and in every bend of white was a bend of crimson satin, after the fashion of Russia, with furred hats of gray on their heads; either of them having an hatchet in their hands, and boots with *pykes*" (points a foot long), "turned up. And after them came a knight, then the Lord High Admiral, and with him five nobles, in doublets of crimson velvet, voyded low on the back and before to the cannell-bone, laced on the breasts with chains of silver; and, over that, short cloaks of crimson satin, and on their heads hats after the dancers' fashion, with pheasants' feathers in them. These were appareled after the fashion of Prussia. The torch-bearers, which were about an hundred, were appareled in crimson satin and green, like Moors, their faces black. Next came in a *mommarye*. Then the minstrels, which were disguised, danced; and the lords and ladies did wildly dance also, that it was a pleasure to behold."

And while Tom, in his high seat, was gazing upon this "wild" dancing, lost in admiration of the dazzling commingling of kaleidoscopic colors which the whirling turmoil of gaudy figures below him presented, the ragged but real little Prince of Wales was proclaiming his rights and his wrongs, denouncing the impostor, and clamoring for admission at the gates of Guildhall! The crowd enjoyed this episode prodigiously, and pressed forward and craned their necks to see the small rioter. Presently they began to taunt him and mock at him, purposely to goad him into a higher and still more entertaining fury. Tears of mortification sprung to his eyes, but he stood his ground and defied the mob right royally. Other taunts followed, added mockings stung him, and he exclaimed—

"I tell ye again, you pack of unmannerly curs, I am the Prince of Wales! And all forlorn and friendless as I be, with none to give me word of grace or help me in my need, yet will not I be driven from my ground, but will maintain it!"

"Though thou be prince or no prince, 'tis all one, thou be'st a gallant lad, and not friendless neither! Here stand I by thy side to prove it; and mind I tell thee thou might'st have a worser friend than Miles Hendon and yet not tire thy legs with seeking. Rest thy small jaw, my child, I talk the language of these base kennel-rats like to a very native."

The speaker was a sort of Don Caesar de Bazan in dress, aspect, and bearing. He was tall, trim-built, muscular. His doublet and trunks were of rich material, but faded and threadbare, and their gold-lace adornments were sadly tarnished; his ruff was rumpled and damaged; the plume in his slouched hat was broken and had a bedraggled and disreputable look; at his side he wore a long rapier in a rusty iron sheath; his swaggering carriage marked him at once as a ruffler of the camp. The speech of this fantastic figure was received with an explosion of jeers and laughter. Some cried, " 'Tis another prince in disguise!" " 'Ware thy tongue, friend, belike he is dangerous!" "Marry, he looketh it—mark his eye!" "Pluck the lad from him—to the horse-pond wi' the cub!"

Instantly a hand was laid upon the prince, under the impulse of this happy thought; as instantly the stranger's long sword was out and the meddler went to the earth under a sounding thump with the flat of it. The next moment a score of voices shouted "Kill the dog! kill him! kill him!" and the mob closed in on the warrior, who backed himself against a wall and began to lay about him with his long weapon like a madman. His victims sprawled this way and that, but the mob-tide poured over their prostrate forms and dashed itself against the champion with undiminished fury. His moments seemed numbered, his destruction certain, when suddenly a trumpet-blast sounded, a voice shouted, "Way for the king's messenger!" and a troop of horsemen came charging down upon the mob, who fled out of harm's reach as fast as their legs could carry them. The bold stranger caught up the prince in his arms, and was soon far away from danger and the multitude.

Return we within the Guildhall. Suddenly, high above the jubilant roar and thunder of the revel, broke the clear peal of a bugle-note.

"BEGAN TO LAY ABOUT HIM."

There was instant silence, a deep hush; then a single voice rose—that of the messenger from the palace—and began to pipe forth a proclamation, the whole multitude standing, listening. The closing words, solemnly pronounced, were—

"The king is dead!"

The great assemblage bent their heads upon their breasts with one accord; remained so, in profound silence, a few moments; then all sunk upon their knees in a body, stretched out their hands toward Tom, and a mighty shout burst forth that seemed to shake the building—

"Long live the king!"

"LONG LIVE THE KING!"

Poor Tom's dazed eyes wandered abroad over this stupefying spectacle, and finally rested dreamily upon the kneeling princesses beside him, a moment, then upon the Earl of Hertford. A sudden purpose dawned in his face. He said, in a low tone, at lord Hertford's ear—

"Answer me truly, on thy faith and honor! Uttered I here a command, the which none but a king might hold privilege and prerogative to utter, would such commandment be obeyed, and none rise up to say me nay?"

"None, my liege, in all these realms. In thy person bides the majesty of England. Thou art the king—thy word is law."

Tom responded, in a strong, earnest voice, and with great animation—

"Then shall the king's law be law of mercy, from this day, and never more be law of blood! Up from thy knees and away! To the Tower and say the king decrees the Duke of Norfolk shall not die!"*

The words were caught up and carried eagerly from lip to lip far and wide over the hall, and as Hertford hurried from the presence, another prodigious shout burst forth—

"The reign of blood is ended! Long live Edward, king of England!"

---

*See Note 7, at end of volume.

CHAPTER 12

THE PRINCE AND HIS DELIVERER

As soon as Miles Hendon and the little prince were clear of the mob, they struck down through back lanes and alleys toward the river. Their way was unobstructed until they approached London Bridge; then they plowed into the multitude again, Hendon keeping a fast grip upon the prince's—no, the king's—wrist. The tremendous news was already abroad, and the boy learned it from a thousand voices at once—"The king is dead!" The tidings struck a chill to the heart of the poor little waif and sent a shudder through his frame. He realized the greatness of his loss, and was filled with a bitter grief; for the grim tyrant who had been such a terror to others had always been gentle with him. The tears sprung to his eyes and blurred all objects. For an instant he felt himself the most forlorn, outcast, and forsaken of God's creatures—then another cry shook the night with its far-reaching thunders: "Long live King Edward the Sixth!" and this made his eyes kindle, and thrilled him with pride to his fingers' ends. "Ah," he thought, "how grand and strange it seems—I AM KING!"

Our friends threaded their way slowly through the throngs upon the Bridge. This structure, which had stood for six hundred years, and had been a noisy and populous thoroughfare all that time, was a curious affair, for a closely packed rank of stores and shops, with family quarters overhead, stretched along both sides of it, from one bank of

"OUR FRIENDS THREADED THEIR WAY."

the river to the other. The Bridge was a sort of town to itself; it had its inn, its beer houses, its bakeries, its haberdasheries, its food markets, its manufacturing industries, and even its church. It looked upon the two neighbors which it linked together,—London and Southwark—as being well enough, as suburbs, but not otherwise particularly important. It was a close corporation, so to speak; it was a narrow town, of a

single street a fifth of a mile long, its population was but a village
population, and everybody in it knew all his fellow townsmen in-
timately, and had known their fathers and mothers before them—and
all their little family affairs into the bargain. It had its aristocracy, of
course—its fine old families of butchers, and bakers, and what-not,
who had occupied the same old premises for five or six hundred years,
and knew the great history of the Bridge from beginning to end, and all
its strange legends; and who always talked bridgy talk, and thought
bridgy thoughts, and lied in a long, level, direct, substantial bridgy
way. It was just the sort of population to be narrow and ignorant

and self-conceited. Children
were born on the Bridge,
were reared there, grew to
old age and finally died
without ever having set a
foot upon any part of the
world but London Bridge
alone. Such people would
naturally imagine that the
mighty and interminable
procession which moved
through its street night and
day, with its confused roar
of shouts and cries, its neigh-
ings and bellowings and
bleatings and its muffled
thunder-tramp, was the one

"OBJECT-LESSONS" IN ENGLISH HISTORY.

great thing in this world, and themselves somehow the proprietors
of it. And so they were, in effect—at least they could exhibit it from
their windows, and did—for a consideration—whenever a returning
king or hero gave it a fleeting splendor, for there was no place like it
for affording a long, straight, uninterrupted view of marching columns.

Men born and reared upon the Bridge found life unendurably dull
and inane, elsewhere. History tells of one of these who left the Bridge
at the age of seventy-one and retired to the country. But he could only
fret and toss in his bed; he could not go to sleep, the deep stillness was
so painful, so awful, so oppressive. When he was worn out with it, at
last, he fled back to his old home, a lean and haggard spectre, and fell

peacefully to rest and pleasant dreams under the lulling music of the lashing waters and the boom and crash and thunder of London Bridge.

In the times of which we are writing, the Bridge furnished "object-lessons" in English history, for its children—namely, the livid and decaying heads of renowned men impaled upon iron spikes atop of its gateways. But we digress.

Hendon's lodgings were in the little inn on the Bridge. As he neared the door with his small friend, a rough voice said—

"So, thou'rt come at last! Thou'lt not escape again, I warrant thee; and if pounding thy bones to a pudding can teach thee somewhat, thou'lt not keep us waiting another time, mayhap"—and John Canty put out his hand to seize the boy.

Miles Hendon stepped in the way and said—

"Not too fast, friend. Thou art needlessly rough, methinks. What is the lad to thee?"

"If it be any business of thine to make and meddle in others' affairs, he is my son."

"'Tis a lie!" cried the little king, hotly.

"Boldly said, and I believe thee, whether thy small head-piece be sound or cracked, my boy. But whether this scurvy ruffian be thy father or no, 'tis all one, he shall not have thee to beat thee and abuse, according to his threat, so thou prefer to bide with me."

"I do, I do—I know him not, I loathe him, and will die before I will go with him."

"Then 'tis settled, and there is naught more to say."

"We will see, as to that!" exclaimed John Canty, striding past Hendon to get at the boy; "by force shall he—"

"If thou do but touch him, thou animated offal, I will spit thee like a goose!" said Hendon, barring the way and laying his hand upon his sword hilt. Canty drew back. "Now mark ye," continued Hendon, "I took this lad under my protection when a mob of such as thou would have mishandled him, mayhap killed him; dost imagine I will desert him now to a worser fate?—for whether thou art his father or no,—and sooth to say, I think it is a lie—a decent swift death were better for such a lad than life in such brute hands as thine. So go thy ways, and set quick about it, for I like not much bandying of words, being not over-patient in my nature."

John Canty moved off, muttering threats and curses, and was swal-

lowed from sight in the crowd. Hendon ascended three flights of stairs
to his room, with his charge, after ordering a meal to be sent thither. It
was a poor apartment, with a shabby bed and some odds and ends of
old furniture in it, and was vaguely lighted by a couple of sickly
candles. The little king dragged himself to the bed and lay down upon
it, almost exhausted with hunger and fatigue. He had been on his feet

"JOHN CANTY MOVED OFF."

a good part of a day and a night, for it was now two or three o'clock in
the morning, and had eaten nothing meantime. He murmured
drowsily—

"Prithee call me when the table is spread," and sunk into a deep
sleep immediately.

A smile twinkled in Hendon's eye, and he said to himself—

"By the mass, the little beggar takes to one's quarters and usurps one's bed with as natural and easy a grace as if he owned them—with never a by-your-leave or so-please-it-you, or anything of the sort. In his diseased ravings he called himself the Prince of Wales, and bravely doth he keep up the character. Poor little friendless rat, doubtless his mind has been disordered with ill usage. Well, I will be his friend; I have saved him, and it draweth me strongly to him; already I love the bold-tongued little rascal. How soldier-like he faced the smutty rabble and flung back his high defiance! And what a comely, sweet and gentle face he hath, now that sleep hath conjured away its troubles and its griefs. I will teach him, I will cure his malady; yea, I will be his elder brother, and care for him and watch over him; and whoso would shame him or do him hurt, may order his shroud, for though I be burnt for it he shall need it!"

He bent over the boy and contemplated him with kind and pitying interest, tapping the young cheek tenderly and smoothing back the tangled curls with his great brown hand. A slight shiver passed over the boy's form. Hendon muttered—

"See, now, how like a man it was, to let him lie here uncovered and fill his body with deadly rheums. Now what shall I do? 'twill wake him

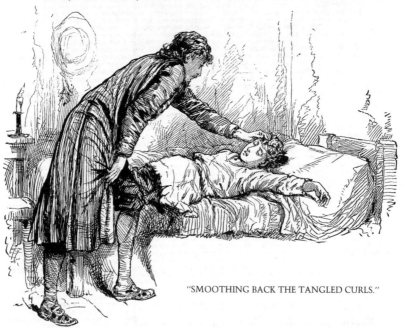

"SMOOTHING BACK THE TANGLED CURLS."

to take him up and put him within the bed, and he sorely needeth sleep."

He looked about for extra covering, but finding none, doffed his doublet and wrapped the lad in it, saying, "I am used to nipping air and scant apparel, 'tis little I shall mind the cold"—then walked up and down the room to keep his blood in motion, soliloquizing, as before.

"His injured mind persuades him he is Prince of Wales; 'twill be odd to have a Prince of Wales still with us, now that he that *was* the prince is prince no more, but king,—for this poor mind is set upon the one fantasy, and will not reason out that now it should cast by the prince and call itself the king. . . . . If my father liveth still, after these seven years that I have heard naught from home in my foreign dungeon, he will welcome the poor lad and give him generous shelter for my sake; so will my good elder brother, Arthur; my other brother, Hugh—but I will crack his crown, an' *he* interfere, the fox-hearted, ill-conditioned animal! Yes, thither will we fare—and straightway, too."

A servant entered with a smoking meal, disposed it upon a small deal table, placed the chairs, and took his departure, leaving such cheap lodgers as these to wait upon themselves. The door slammed after him, and the noise woke the boy, who sprung to a sitting posture, and shot a glad glance about him; then a grieved look came into his face and he murmured, to himself, with a deep sigh, "Alack, it was but a dream, woe is me." Next he noticed Miles Hendon's doublet— glanced from that to Hendon, comprehended the sacrifice that had been made for him, and said, gently—

"Thou art good to me, yes, thou art very good to me. Take it and put it on—I shall not need it more."

Then he got up and walked to the washstand in the corner, and stood there, waiting. Hendon said in a cheery voice—

"We'll have a right hearty sup and bite, now, for everything is savory and smoking hot, and that and thy nap together will make thee a little man again, never fear!"

The boy made no answer, but bent a steady look, that was filled with grave surprise, and also somewhat touched with impatience, upon the tall knight of the sword. Hendon was puzzled, and said—

"What's amiss?"

"Good sir, I would wash me."

"O, is that all! Ask no permission of Miles Hendon for aught thou cravest. Make thyself perfectly free here, and welcome, with all that are his belongings."

Still the boy stood, and moved not; more, he tapped the floor once or twice with his small impatient foot. Hendon was wholly perplexed. Said he—

"Bless us, what is it?"

"Prithee pour the water, and make not so many words!"

"PRITHEE POUR THE WATER."

Hendon, suppressing a horse-laugh, and saying to himself, "By all the saints, but this is admirable!" stepped briskly forward and did the small insolent's bidding, then stood by, in a sort of stupefaction until the command, "Come—the towel!" woke him sharply up. He took up a towel, from under the boy's nose, and handed it to him, without comment. He now proceeded to comfort his own face with a wash, and while he was at it his adopted child seated himself at the table and prepared to fall to. Hendon dispatched his ablutions with alacrity, then drew back the other chair and was about to place himself at table, when the boy said, indignantly—

"Forbear! Wouldst sit in the presence of the king?"

This blow staggered Hendon to his foundations. He muttered to himself, "Lo, the poor thing's madness is up with the time! it hath changed with the great change that is come to the realm, and now in fancy is he *king!* Good lack, I must humor the conceit, too—there is no other way—faith, he would order me to the Tower, else!"

And pleased with this jest, he removed the chair from the table, took his stand behind the king, and proceeded to wait upon him in the courtliest way he was capable of.

While the king ate, a grateful sense of refreshment, both of body and spirit, began to steal over him; the rigor of his royal dignity relaxed a little, and with his growing contentment came a desire to talk. He said—

"I think thou callest thyself Miles Hendon, if I heard thee aright?"

"Yes, sire," Miles replied; then observed to himself, "If I *must* humor the poor lad's madness, I must sire him, I must majesty him, I must not go by halves, I must stick at nothing that belongeth to the part I play, else shall I play it ill and work evil to this charitable and kindly cause."

The king warmed his heart with a second glass of wine, and said—

"I would know thee—tell me thy story. Thou hast a gallant way with thee, and a noble—art nobly born?"

"We are of the tail of the nobility, good your majesty. My father is a baronet—one of the smaller lords, by knight service*—Sir Richard Hendon, of Hendon Hall, by Monk's Holm in Kent."

"The name has escaped my memory. Go on—tell me thy story."

" 'Tis not much, your majesty, yet perchance it may beguile a short half hour for want of a better. My father, Sir Richard, is very rich, and of a most generous nature. My mother died whilst I was yet a boy. I have two brothers; Arthur, my elder, with a soul like to his father's; and Hugh, younger than I, a mean spirit, covetous, treacherous, vicious, underhanded—a reptile. Such was he from the cradle; such was he ten years past, when I last saw him—a ripe rascal at nineteen, I being twenty, then, and Arthur twenty-two. There is none other of us but the lady Edith, my cousin—she was sixteen, then—beautiful,

---

*He refers to the order of baronets, or baronettes,—the *barones minores,* as distinct from the parliamentary barons;—not, it need hardly be said, the baronets of later creation.

"GO ON—TELL ME THY STORY."

gentle, good, the daughter of an earl, the last of her race, heiress of a great fortune and a lapsed title. My father was her guardian. I loved her and she loved me; but she was betrothed to Arthur from the cradle, and Sir Richard would not suffer the contract to be broken. Arthur loved another maid, and bade us be of good cheer and hold fast to the hope that delay and luck together would some day give success to our several causes. Hugh loved the lady Edith's fortune, though in truth he said it was herself he loved—but then 'twas his way, alway, to say the one thing and mean the other. But he lost his arts upon the girl; he could deceive my father, but none else. My father loved him best of us all, and trusted and believed him; for he was the youngest child and others hated him—these qualities being in all ages sufficient to win a parent's dearest love; and he had a smooth persuasive tongue, with an admirable gift of lying—and these be qualities which do mightily assist a blind affection to cozen itself. I was wild—in truth I might go yet farther and say *very* wild, though 'twas a wildness of an innocent sort, since it hurt none but me, brought shame to none, nor loss, nor had in it any taint of crime or baseness, or what might not beseem mine honorable degree.

"Yet did my brother Hugh turn these faults to good account—he seeing that our brother Arthur's health was but indifferent, and hoping the worst might work him profit were I swept out of the path—so,—but 'twere a long tale, good my liege, and little worth the telling. Briefly, then, this brother did deftly magnify my faults and make them crimes; ending his base work with finding a silken ladder in mine apartments—conveyed thither by his own means—and did convince my father by this, and suborned evidence of servants and other lying knaves, that I was minded to carry off my Edith and marry with her, in rank defiance of his will.

"Three years of banishment from home and England might make a soldier and a man of me, my father said, and teach me some degree of wisdom. I fought out my long probation in the continental wars, tasting sumptuously of hard knocks, privation and adventure; but in my last battle I was taken captive, and during the seven years that have waxed and waned since then, a foreign dungeon hath harbored me. Through wit and courage I won to the free air at last, and fled hither

"THOU HAST BEEN SHAMEFULLY ABUSED!"

straight; and am but just arrived, right poor in purse and raiment, and poorer still in knowledge of what these dull seven years have wrought at Hendon Hall, its people and belongings. So please you, sir, my meagre tale is told."

"Thou hast been shamefully abused!" said the little king, with a flashing eye. "But I will right thee—by the cross will I! The king hath said it."

Then, fired by the story of Miles's wrongs, he loosed his tongue and poured the history of his own recent misfortunes into the ears of his astonished listener. When he had finished, Miles said to himself—

"Lo, what an imagination he hath! Verily this is no common mind; else, crazed or sane, it could not weave so straight and gaudy a tale as this out of the airy nothings wherewith it hath wrought this curious romaunt. Poor ruined little head, it shall not lack friend or shelter whilst I bide with the living. He shall never leave my side; he shall be my pet, my little comrade. And he shall be cured!—aye, made whole and sound—then will he make himself a name—and proud shall I be to say, 'Yes, he is mine—I took him, a homeless little ragamuffin, but I saw what was in him, and I said his name would be heard some day—behold him, observe him—was I right?' "

The king spoke—in a thoughtful, measured voice—

"Thou didst save me injury and shame, perchance my life, and so my crown. Such service demandeth rich reward. Name thy desire, and so it be within the compass of my royal power, it is thine."

This fantastic suggestion startled Hendon out of his reverie. He was about to thank the king and put the matter aside with saying he had only done his duty and desired no reward, but a wiser thought came into his head, and he asked leave to be silent a few moments and consider the gracious offer—an idea which the king gravely approved, remarking that it was best to be not too hasty with a thing of such great import.

Miles reflected during some moments, then said to himself, "Yes, that is the thing to do—by any other means it were impossible to get at it—and certes, this hour's experience has taught me 'twould be most wearing and inconvenient to continue it as it is. Yes, I will propose it; 'twas a happy accident that I did not throw the chance away." Then he dropped upon one knee and said—

"My poor service went not beyond the limit of a subject's simple duty, and therefore hath no merit; but since your majesty is pleased to hold it worthy some reward, I take heart of grace to make petition to this effect. Near four hundred years ago, as your grace knoweth, there being ill blood betwixt John, king of England, and the king of France, it was decreed that two champions should fight together in the lists, and so settle the dispute by what is called the arbitrament of God. These two kings, and the Spanish king, being assembled to witness and judge the conflict, the French champion appeared; but so redoubtable was he that our English knights refused to measure weapons with him. So the

"HE DROPPED UPON ONE KNEE."

matter, which was a weighty one, was like to go against the English monarch by default. Now in the Tower lay the lord de Courcy, the mightiest arm in England, stripped of his honors and possessions, and wasting with long captivity. Appeal was made to him; he gave assent, and came forth arrayed for battle; but no sooner did the Frenchman glimpse his huge frame and hear his famous name but he fled away and the French king's cause was lost. King John restored de Courcy's titles and possessions, and said, 'Name thy wish and thou shalt have it, though it cost me half my kingdom;' whereat de Courcy, kneeling, as I

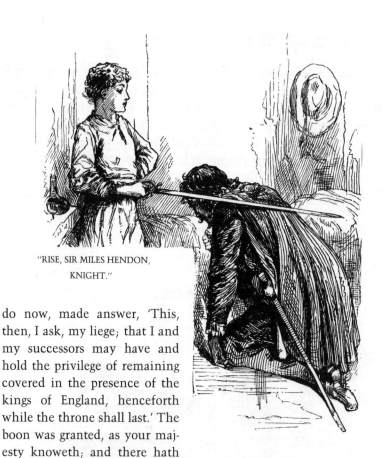

"RISE, SIR MILES HENDON,
KNIGHT."

do now, made answer, 'This,
then, I ask, my liege; that I and
my successors may have and
hold the privilege of remaining
covered in the presence of the
kings of England, henceforth
while the throne shall last.' The
boon was granted, as your majesty knoweth; and there hath
been no time, these four hundred years, that that line has failed of an
heir; and so, even unto this day, the head of that ancient house still
weareth his hat or helm before the king's majesty, without let or
hindrance, and this none other may do.* Invoking this precedent in
aid of my prayer, I beseech the king to grant to me but this one grace
and privilege—to my more than sufficient reward—and none other, to
wit: that I and my heirs, forever, may *sit* in the presence of the majesty
of England!"

"Rise, Sir Miles Hendon, Knight," said the king, gravely—giving the
accolade with Hendon's sword—"rise, and seat thyself. Thy petition is
granted. Whilst England remains, and the crown continues, the
privilege shall not lapse."

His majesty walked apart, musing, and Hendon dropped into a chair

---

*The lords of Kingsale, descendants of de Courcy, still enjoy this curious privilege.

at table, observing to himself, "'Twas a brave thought, and hath wrought me a mighty deliverance; my legs are grievously wearied. An' I had not thought of that, I must have had to stand for weeks, till my poor lad's wits are cured." After a little, he went on, "And so I am become a knight of the Kingdom of Dreams and Shadows! A most odd and strange position, truly, for one so matter-of-fact as I. I will not laugh—no, God forbid, for this thing which is so substanceless to me is *real* to him. And to me, also, in one way, it is not a falsity, for it reflects with truth the sweet and generous spirit that is in him." After a pause: "Ah, what if he should call me by my fine title before folk!—there'd be a merry contrast betwixt my glory and my raiment! But no matter: let him call me what he will, so it please him; I shall be content."

CHAPTER 13

THE DISAPPEARANCE OF THE PRINCE

A HEAVY drowsiness presently fell upon the two comrades. The king said—

"Remove these rags"—meaning his clothing.

Hendon disappareled the boy without dissent or remark, tucked him up in bed, then glanced about the room, saying to himself, ruefully, "He hath taken my bed again, as before—marry, what shall *I* do?" The little king observed his perplexity, and dissipated it with a word. He said, sleepily—

"Thou wilt sleep athwart the door, and guard it." In a moment more he was out of his troubles, in a deep slumber.

"Dear heart, he should have been born a king!" muttered Hendon, admiringly; "he playeth the part to a marvel."

Then he stretched himself across the door, on the floor, saying, contentedly—

"I have lodged worse for seven years; 'twould be but ill gratitude to Him above to find fault with this."

He dropped asleep as the dawn appeared. Toward noon he rose, uncovered his unconscious ward—a section at a time,—and took his measure with a string. The king awoke, just as he had completed his work, complained of the cold, and asked what he was doing.

"'Tis done, now, my liege," said Hendon; "I have a bit of business outside, but will presently return; sleep thou again—thou needest it. There—let me cover thy head also—thou'lt be warm the sooner."

The king was back in dreamland before this speech was ended.

"HE DROPPED ASLEEP."

Miles slipped softly out, and slipped as softly in again, in the course of thirty or forty minutes, with a complete second-hand suit of boy's clothing, of cheap material, and showing signs of wear; but tidy, and suited to the season of the year. He seated himself, and began to overhaul his purchase, mumbling to himself—

"A longer purse would have got a better sort, but when one has not the long purse one must be content with what a short one may do—

" 'There was a woman in our town,
        In our town did dwell—'

"He stirred, methinks—I must sing in a less thunderous key; 'tis not good to mar his sleep, with this journey before him and he so wearied out, poor chap. . . . . . . This garment—'tis well enough—a stitch here and another one there will set it aright. This other is better, albeit a stitch or two will not come amiss in it, likewise. . . . . . . *These* be very good and sound, and will keep his small feet warm and dry—an odd new thing to him, belike, since he has doubtless been used to foot it bare, winters and summers the same. . . . . . . Would thread were bread, seeing one getteth a year's sufficiency for a farthing, and such a brave big needle without cost, for mere love. Now shall I have the demon's own time to thread it!"

And so he had. He did as men have always done, and probably always will do, to the end of time—held the needle still, and tried to thrust the thread through the eye, which is the opposite of a woman's way. Time and time again the thread missed the mark, going some-times on one side of the needle, sometimes on the other, sometimes doubling up against the shaft; but he was patient, having been through these experiences before, when he was soldiering. He succeeded at last, and took up the garment that had lain waiting, meantime, across his lap, and began his work.

"The inn is paid—the breakfast that is to come, included—and there is wherewithal left to buy a couple of donkeys and meet our little costs for the two or three days betwixt this and the plenty that awaits us at Hendon Hall—

" 'She loved her hus—'

"Body o' me! I have driven the needle under my nail! . . . . . It

"THESE BE VERY GOOD AND SOUND."

matters little—'tis not a novelty—yet 'tis not a convenience, neither. . . . . . We shall be merry there, little one, never doubt it! Thy troubles will vanish, there, and likewise thy sad distemper—

> " 'She loved her husband dearilee,
> But another man—'

"These be noble large stitches!"—holding the garment up and viewing it admiringly—"they have a grandeur and a majesty that do cause these small stingy ones of the tailor-man to look mightily paltry and plebeian—

> " 'She loved her husband dearilee,
> But another man he loved she,—'

"Marry, 'tis done—a goodly piece of work, too, and wrought with expedition. Now will I wake him, apparel him, pour for him, feed him, and then will we hie us to the mart by the Tabard inn in Southwark and—be pleased to rise, my liege!—he answereth not—what ho, my liege!—of a truth must I profane his sacred person with a touch, sith his slumber is deaf to speech. What!"

He threw back the covers—the boy was gone!

He stared about him in speechless astonishment for a moment; noticed for the first time that his ward's ragged raiment was also missing, then he began to rage and storm, and shout for the innkeeper. At that moment a servant entered with the breakfast.

"Explain, thou limb of Satan, or thy time is come!" roared the man of war, and made so savage a spring toward the waiter that this latter could not find his tongue, for the instant, for fright and surprise. "Where is the boy?"

In disjointed and trembling syllables the man gave the information desired.

"You were hardly gone from the place, your worship, when a youth came running and said it was your worship's will that the boy come to you straight, at the bridge-end on the Southwark side. I brought him hither; and when he woke the lad and gave his message, the lad did grumble some little for being disturbed 'so early,' as he called it, but straightway trussed on his rags and went with the youth, only saying it had been better manners that your worship came yourself not sent a stranger—and so—"

"EXPLAIN, THOU LIMB OF SATAN!"

"And so thou'rt a fool!—a fool, and easily cozened—hang all thy breed! Yet mayhap no hurt is done. Possibly no harm is meant the boy. I will go fetch him. Make the table ready. Stay! the coverings of the bed were disposed as if one lay beneath them—happened that by accident?"

"I know not, good your worship. I saw the youth meddle with them—he that came for the boy."

"Thousand deaths! 'twas done to deceive me—'tis plain 'twas done to gain time. Hark ye! Was that youth alone?"

"All alone, your worship."

"Art sure?"

"Sure, your worship."

"Collect thy scattered wits—bethink thee—take time, man."

After a moment's thought, the servant said—

"When he came, none came with him; but now I remember me that as the two stepped into the throng of the Bridge a ruffian-looking man plunged out from some near place, and just as he was joining them—"

"What *then?*—out with it!" thundered the impatient Hendon, interrupting.

"Just then the crowd lapped them up and closed them in, and I saw no more, being called by my master, who was in a rage because a joint that the scrivener had ordered was forgot, though I take all the saints to witness that to blame *me* for that miscarriage were like holding the unborn babe to judgment for sins com—"

"Out of my sight, idiot! Thy prating drives me mad! Hold! whither art flying? Canst not bide still an instant? Went they toward Southwark?"

"HENDON FOLLOWED AFTER HIM."

"Even so, your worship—for, as I said before, as to that detestable joint, the babe unborn is no whit more blameless than—"

"Art here *yet*! And prating still? Vanish, lest I throttle thee!" The servitor vanished. Hendon followed after him, passed him, and plunged down the stairs two steps at a stride, muttering, "'Tis that scurvy villain that claimed he was his son. I have lost thee, my poor little mad master—it is a bitter thought—and I had come to love thee so! No! by book and bell, *not* lost! Not lost, for I will ransack the land till I find thee again. Poor child, yonder is his breakfast—and mine, but I have no hunger now—so, let the rats have it—speed, speed! that is the word!" As he wormed his swift way through the noisy multitudes upon the Bridge, he several times said to himself—clinging to the thought as if it were a particularly pleasing one—"He grumbled, but he *went*—he went, yes, because he thought Miles Hendon asked it, sweet lad—he would ne'er have done it for another, I know it well."

CHAPTER 14

Toward daylight of the same morning, Tom Canty stirred out of a heavy sleep and opened his eyes in the dark. He lay silent a few moments, trying to analyze his confused thoughts and impressions, and get some sort of meaning out of them, then suddenly he burst out in a rapturous but guarded voice—

"I see it all, I see it all! Now God be thanked, I am indeed awake at last. Come, joy! vanish, sorrow! Ho, Nan! Bet! kick off your straw and hie ye hither to my side, till I do pour into your unbelieving ears the wildest madcap dream that ever the spirits of night did conjure up to astonish the soul of man withal! . . . . Ho, Nan, I say! Bet! . . . . . ."

A dim form appeared at his side, and a voice said—

"Wilt deign to deliver thy commands?"

"Commands? . . . . O, woe is me, I know thy voice! Speak, thou—who am I?"

"Thou? In sooth, yesternight wert thou the Prince of Wales, to-day art thou my most gracious liege, Edward, king of England."

Tom buried his head among his pillows, murmuring plaintively—

"Alack, it was no dream! Go to thy rest, sweet sir—leave me to my sorrows."

"WILT DEIGN TO DELIVER THY COMMANDS?"

Tom slept again, and after a time he had this pleasant dream. He thought it was summer and he was playing, all alone, in the fair meadow called Goodman's Fields, when a dwarf only a foot high, with long red whiskers and a humped back appeared to him suddenly and said, "Dig, by that stump." He did so, and found twelve bright new pennies—wonderful riches! Yet this was not the best of it; for the dwarf said—

"I know thee. Thou art a good lad and a deserving; thy distresses shall end, for the day of thy reward is come. Dig here every seventh day, and thou shalt find always the same treasure, twelve bright new pennies. Tell none—keep the secret."

Then the dwarf vanished, and Tom flew to Offal Court with his prize, saying to himself, "Every night will I give my father a penny; he will think I begged it, it will glad his heart, and I shall no more be beaten. One penny every week the good priest that teacheth me shall have; mother, Nan and Bet the other four. We be done with hunger and rags, now, done with fears and frets and savage usage."

In his dream he reached his sordid home all out of breath, but with eyes dancing with grateful enthusiasm; cast four of his pennies into his mother's lap and cried out—

"They are for thee!—all of them, every one!—for thee and Nan and Bet—and honestly come by, not begged nor stolen!"

The happy and astonished mother strained him to her breast and exclaimed—

"It waxeth late—may it please your majesty to rise?"

Ah, that was not the answer he was expecting. The dream had snapped asunder—he was awake.

He opened his eyes—the richly clad First Lord of the Bedchamber was kneeling by his couch. The gladness of the lying dream faded away—the poor boy recognized that he was still a captive and a king. The room was filled with courtiers clothed in purple mantles—the mourning color—and with noble servants of the monarch. Tom sat up in bed and gazed out from the heavy silken curtains upon this fine company.

The weighty business of dressing began, and one courtier after another knelt and paid his court and offered to the little king his condolences upon his heavy loss, whilst the dressing proceeded. In the beginning, a shirt was taken up by the Chief Equerry in Waiting, who passed it to the First Lord of the Buckhounds, who passed it to the Second Gentleman of the Bedchamber, who passed it to the Head Ranger of Windsor Forest, who passed it to the Third Groom of the Stole, who passed it to the Chancellor Royal of the Duchy of Lancaster, who passed it to the Master of the Wardrobe, who passed it to Norroy King-at-Arms, who passed it to the Constable of the Tower, who passed it to the Chief Steward of the Household, who passed it to the Hereditary Grand Diaperer, who passed it to the Lord High Admiral of England, who passed it to the Archbishop of Canterbury, who passed it to the First Lord of the Bedchamber, who took what was left of it and put it on Tom. Poor little wondering chap, it reminded him of passing buckets at a fire.

Each garment in its turn had to go through this slow and solemn process; consequently Tom grew very weary of the ceremony; so weary that he felt an almost gushing gratefulness when he at last saw his long silken hose begin the journey down the line and knew that the end of the matter was drawing near. But he exulted too soon. The First Lord of the Bedchamber received the hose and was about to encase Tom's legs in them, when a sudden flush invaded his face and he hurriedly hustled the things back into the hands of the Archbishop of Canterbury with an astounded look and a whispered, "See, my lord!"—pointing to a something connected with the hose. The Archbishop paled, then flushed, and passed the hose to the Lord High Admiral, whispering, "See, my lord!" The Admiral passed the hose to the Hereditary Grand Diaperer, and had hardly breath enough in his body to ejaculate, "See, my lord!" The hose drifted backward along the line, to the Chief Steward of the Household, the Constable of the Tower, Norroy King-at-Arms, the Master of the Wardrobe, the Chancellor Royal of the Duchy of Lancaster, the Third Groom of the Stole, the Head Ranger of Windsor Forest, the Second Gentleman of the Bedchamber, the First Lord of the Buckhounds,—accompanied always with that amazed and frightened "See! see!"—till they finally reached the hands of the Chief Equerry in Waiting, who gazed a moment, with a pallid face, upon what had caused all this dismay, then hoarsely whispered, "Body of my life, a tag gone from a truss-point!—to the Tower with the Head Keeper of the King's Hose!"—after which he leaned upon the shoulder of the First Lord of the

"THE FIRST LORD OF THE BEDCHAMBER RECEIVED THE HOSE."

Buckhounds to regather his vanished strength whilst fresh hose, without any damaged strings to them, were brought.

But all things must have an end, and so in time Tom Canty was in a condition to get out of bed. The proper official poured water, the proper official engineered the washing, the proper official stood by with a towel, and by and by Tom got safely through the purifying stage and was ready for the services of the Hairdresser-royal. When he at length emerged from this master's hands, he was a gracious figure and as pretty as a girl, in his mantle and trunks of purple satin, and purple-plumed cap. He now moved in state toward his breakfast room, through the midst of the courtly assemblage; and as he passed, these fell back, leaving his way free, and dropped upon their knees.

After breakfast he was conducted, with regal ceremony, attended by his great officers and his guard of fifty Gentlemen Pensioners bearing gilt battle-axes, to the throne-room, where he proceeded to transact business of state. His "uncle," lord Hertford, took his stand by the throne, to assist the royal mind with wise counsel.

The body of illustrious men named by the late king as his executors, appeared, to ask Tom's approval of certain acts of theirs—rather a form, and yet not wholly a form, since there was no Protector as yet. The Archbishop of Canterbury made report of the decree of the Council of Executors concerning the obsequies of his late most illustrious majesty, and finished by reading the signatures of the Executors, to wit: the Archbishop of Canterbury; the Lord Chancellor of England; William Lord St. John; John Lord Russell; Edward Earl of Hertford; John Viscount Lisle; Cuthbert Bishop of Durham—

Tom was not listening—an earlier clause of the document was puzzling him. At this point he turned and whispered to lord Hertford—

"What day did he say the burial hath been appointed for?"

"The 16th of the coming month, my liege."

" 'Tis a strange folly. Will he keep?"

Poor chap, he was still new to the customs of royalty; he was used to seeing the forlorn dead of Offal Court hustled out of the way with a very different sort of expedition. However, the lord Hertford set his mind at rest with a word or two.

A secretary of state presented an order of the Council appointing the morrow at eleven for the reception of the foreign ambassadors, and desired the king's assent.

"A SECRETARY OF STATE PRESENTED AN ORDER."

Tom turned an inquiring look toward Hertford, who whispered—
"Your majesty will signify consent. They come to testify their
royal masters' sense of the heavy calamity which hath visited your
grace and the realm of England."

Tom did as he was bidden. Another secretary began to read a pre-
amble concerning the expenses of the late king's household, which
had amounted to £28,000 during the preceding six months—a sum so
vast that it made Tom Canty gasp; he gasped again when the fact
appeared that £20,000 of this money were still owing and unpaid;*
and once more when it appeared that the king's coffers were about
empty, and his twelve hundred servants much embarrassed for lack
of the wages due them. Tom spoke out, with lively apprehension—
"We be going to the dogs, 'tis plain. 'Tis meet and necessary that
we take a smaller house and set the servants at large, sith they be of

---

*Hume.

no value but to make delay, and trouble one with offices that harass the spirit and shame the soul, they misbecoming any but a doll, that hath nor brains nor hands to help itself withal. I remember me of a small house that standeth over against the fish-market, by Billings-gate—"

A sharp pressure upon Tom's arm stopped his foolish tongue and sent a blush to his face; but no countenance there betrayed any sign that this strange speech had been remarked or given concern.

A secretary made report that forasmuch as the late king had pro-vided in his will for conferring the ducal degree upon the Earl of Hertford and raising his brother, Sir Thomas Seymour, to the peerage, and likewise Hertford's son to an Earldom, together with similar ag-grandizements to other great servants of the crown, the Council had resolved to hold a sitting on the 16th of February for the delivering and confirming of these honors; and that meantime, the late king not having granted, in writing, estates suitable to the support of these dignities, the Council, knowing his private wishes in that regard, had thought proper to grant to Seymour "£500 lands," and to Hertford's son "800 pound lands, and 300 pound of the next bishop's lands which should fall vacant,"—his present majesty being willing.*

Tom was about to blurt out something about the propriety of pay-ing the late king's debts first, before squandering all this money; but a timely touch upon his arm, from the thoughtful Hertford, saved him this indiscretion; wherefore he gave the royal assent, without spoken comment, but with much inward discomfort. While he sat reflecting, a moment, over the ease with which he was doing strange and glittering miracles, a happy thought shot into his mind: why not make his mother Duchess of Offal Court and give her an estate? But a sorrowful thought swept it instantly away: he was only a king in name, these grave veterans and great nobles were his masters; to them his mother was only the creature of a diseased mind; they would simply listen to his project with unbelieving ears, then send for the doctor.

The dull work went tediously on. Petitions were read, and proc-lamations, patents, and all manner of wordy, repetitious and weari-some papers relating to the public business; and at last Tom sighed

---

*Hume.

pathetically and murmured to himself, "In what have I offended, that the good God should take me away from the fields and the free air and the sunshine, to shut me up here and make me a king and afflict me so?" Then his poor muddled head nodded a while, and presently drooped to his shoulder; and the business of the empire came to a stand-still for want of that august factor, the ratifying power. Silence ensued, around the slumbering child, and the sages of the realm ceased from their deliberations.

During the forenoon, Tom had an enjoyable hour, by permission of his keepers, Hertford and St. John, with the lady Elizabeth and the little lady Jane Grey though the spirits of the princesses were rather subdued by the mighty stroke that had fallen upon the royal house; and at the end of the visit his "elder sister"—afterwards the "Bloody Mary" of history—chilled him with a solemn interview which had but one merit in his eyes, its brevity. He had a few moments to himself, and then a slim lad of about twelve years of age was admitted to his presence, whose clothing, except his snowy ruff and the laces about his wrists, was of black,—doublet, hose and all. He bore no badge of mourning but a knot of purple ribbon on his shoulder. He advanced hesitatingly, with head bowed and bare, and dropped upon one knee in front of Tom. Tom sat still and contemplated him soberly a moment. Then he said—

"Rise, lad. Who art thou? What wouldst have?"

The boy rose, and stood at graceful ease, but with an aspect of concern in his face. He said—

"Of a surety thou must remember me, my lord. I am thy whipping-boy."

"My *whipping*-boy?"

"The same, your grace. I am Humphrey—Humphrey Marlow."

Tom perceived that here was some one whom his keepers ought to have posted him about. The situation was delicate. What should he do?—pretend he knew this lad, and then betray by his every utterance, that he had never heard of him before? No, that would not do. An idea came to his relief: accidents like this might be likely to happen with some frequency, now that business urgencies would often call Hertford and St. John from his side, they being members of the Council of Executors; therefore perhaps it would be well to strike out a plan himself to meet the requirements of such emer-

"THE BOY ROSE, AND STOOD AT GRACEFUL EASE."

gencies. Yes, that would be a wise course—he would practice on this boy, and see what sort of success he might achieve. So he stroked his brow perplexedly, a moment or two, and presently said—

"Now I seem to remember thee somewhat—but my wit is clogged and dim with suffering—"

"Alack, my poor master!" ejaculated the whipping-boy, with feeling; adding, to himself, "In truth 'tis as they said—his mind is gone —alas, poor soul! But misfortune catch me, how am I forgetting! they said one must not seem to observe that aught is wrong with him."

"'Tis strange how my memory doth wanton with me these days," said Tom. "But mind it not—I mend apace—a little clew doth often serve to bring me back again the things and names which had escaped me. [And not they, only, forsooth, but e'en such as I ne'er heard before—as this lad shall see.] Give thy business speech."

"'Tis matter of small weight, my liege, yet will I touch upon it an' it please your grace. Two days gone by, when your majesty faulted thrice in your Greek—in the morning lessons,—dost remember it?"

"Y-e-s—methinks I do. [It is not much of a lie—an' I had meddled

with the Greek at all, I had not faulted simply thrice, but forty times.]
Yes, I do recal it, now—go on."

—"The master, being wroth with what he termed such slovenly
and doltish work, did promise that he would soundly whip me for
it—and—"

"Whip *thee!*" said Tom, astonished out of his presence of mind.
"Why should he whip *thee* for faults of mine?"

"Ah, your grace forgetteth again. He always scourgeth me, when
thou dost fail in thy lessons."

"True, true—I had forgot. Thou teachest me in private—then if
I fail, he argueth that thy office was lamely done, and—"

"O, my liege, what words are these? I, the humblest of thy servants,
presume to teach *thee?*"

"Then where is thy blame? What riddle is this? Am I in truth gone
mad, or is it thou? Explain—speak out."

"But good your majesty, there's naught that needeth simplifying.
None may visit the sacred person of the Prince of Wales with blows;
wherefore when he faulteth, 'tis I that take them; and meet it is and
right, for that it is mine office and my livelihood."*

Tom stared at the tranquil boy, observing to himself, "Lo, it is a
wonderful thing,—a most strange and curious trade; I marvel they

have not hired a boy to take my combings
and my dressings for me—would heaven
they would!—an' they will do this thing, I
will take my lashings in mine own person,
giving God thanks for the change."
Then he said aloud—

"And hast thou been beaten,
poor friend, according to the
promise?"

"No, good your majesty, my
punishment was appointed for
this day, and peradventure it
may be annulled, as unbefit-
ting the season of mourning
that is come upon us; I know

" 'TIS I THAT TAKE THEM."   *See Note 8 at end of volume.

not, and so have made bold to come hither and remind your grace
about your gracious promise to intercede in my behalf—"

"With the master? To save thee thy whipping?"

"Ah, thou dost remember!"

"My memory mendeth, thou seest. Set thy mind at ease—thy back
shall go unscathed—I will see to it."

"O, thanks, my good lord!" cried the boy, dropping upon his knee
again. "Mayhap I have ventured far enow; and yet . . . . . ."

Seeing Master Humphrey hesitate, Tom encouraged him to go on,
saying he was "in the granting mood."

"Then will I speak it out, for it lieth near my heart. Sith thou art
no more Prince of Wales, but king, thou canst order matters as thou
wilt, with none to say thee nay; wherefore it is not in reason that
thou wilt longer vex thyself with dreary studies, but wilt burn thy
books and turn thy mind to things less irksome. Then am I ruined,
and mine orphan sisters with me!"

"Ruined? Prithee how?"

"My back is my bread, O my gracious liege! if it go idle, I starve.
An' thou cease from study, mine office is gone, thou'lt need no
whipping-boy. Do not turn me away!"

Tom was touched with this pathetic distress. He said, with a right
royal burst of generosity—

"Discomfort thyself no further, lad. Thine office shall be permanent in thee and thy line, forever." Then he struck the boy a light
blow on the shoulder with the flat of his sword, exclaiming, "Rise,
Humphrey Marlow, Hereditary Grand Whipping-Boy to the royal
house of England! Banish sorrow—I will betake me to my books again,
and study so ill that they must in justice treble thy wage, so mightily
shall the business of thine office be augmented."

The grateful Humphrey responded fervidly—

"Thanks, O most noble master, this princely lavishness doth far
surpass my most distempered dreams of fortune. Now shall I be happy
all my days, and all the house of Marlow after me."

Tom had wit enough to perceive that here was a lad who could be
useful to him. He encouraged Humphrey to talk, and he was nothing
loth. He was delighted to believe that he was helping in Tom's "cure";
for always, as soon as he had finished calling back to Tom's diseased
mind the various particulars of his experiences and adventures in

the royal school-room and elsewhere about the palace, he noticed that Tom was then able to "recal" the circumstances quite clearly. At the end of an hour Tom found himself well freighted with very valuable information concerning personages and matters pertaining to the court; so he resolved to draw instruction from this source daily; and to this end he would give order to admit Humphrey to the royal closet whenever he might come, provided the majesty of England was not engaged with other people. Humphrey had hardly been dismissed when my lord Hertford arrived with more trouble for Tom.

He said that the lords of the Council, fearing that some over-wrought report of the king's damaged health might have leaked out and got abroad, they deemed it wise and best that his majesty should begin to dine in public after a day or two—his wholesome complexion and vigorous step, assisted by a carefully guarded repose of manner and ease and grace of demeanor, would more surely quiet the general pulse—in case any evil rumors *had* gone about—than any other scheme that could be devised.

"IF YOUR MAJESTY WILL BUT TAX YOUR MEMORY."

Then the earl proceeded, very delicately, to instruct Tom as to the observances proper to the stately occasion, under the rather thin disguise of "reminding" him concerning things already known to him; but to his vast gratification it turned out that Tom needed very little help in this line—he had been making use of Humphrey in that direction, for Humphrey had mentioned that within a few days he was to begin to dine in public; having gathered it from the swift-winged gossip of the court. Tom kept these facts to himself, however.

Seeing the royal memory so improved, the earl ventured to apply a few tests to it, in an apparently casual way, to find out how far its amendment had progressed. The results were happy, here and there, in spots—spots where Humphrey's tracks remained—and on the whole my lord was greatly pleased and encouraged. So encouraged was he, indeed, that he spoke up and said in a quite hopeful voice—

"Now am I persuaded that if your majesty will but tax your memory yet a little further, it will resolve the puzzle of the Great Seal—a loss which was of moment yesterday, although of none to-day, since its term of service ended with our late lord's life. May it please your grace to make the trial?"

Tom was at sea—a Great Seal was a something which he was totally unacquainted with. After a moment's hesitation he looked up innocently and asked—

"What was it like, my lord?"

The earl started, almost imperceptibly, muttering to himself, "Alack, his wits are flown again!—it was ill wisdom to lead him on to strain them"—then he deftly turned the talk to other matters, with the purpose of sweeping the unlucky Seal out of Tom's thoughts—a purpose which easily succeeded.

CHAPTER 15

THE NEXT DAY the foreign ambassadors came, with their gorgeous trains; and Tom, throned in awful state, received them. The splendors of the scene delighted his eye and fired his imagination, at first, but the audience was long and dreary, and so were most of the addresses—wherefore, what began as a pleasure, grew into weariness and homesickness by and by. Tom said the words which Hertford put into his mouth from time to time, and tried hard to acquit himself satisfactorily, but he was too new to such things, and too ill at ease to accomplish more than a tolerable success. He looked sufficiently like a king, but he was ill able to feel like one. He was cordially glad when the ceremony was ended.

The larger part of his day was "wasted"—as he termed it, in his own mind—in labors pertaining to his royal office. Even the two hours devoted to certain princely pastimes and recreations were rather a burden to him, than otherwise, they were so fettered by restrictions and ceremonious observances. However he had a private hour with his whipping-boy which he counted clear gain, since he got both entertainment and needful information out of it.

The third day of Tom Canty's kingship came and went much as the others had done, but there was a lifting of his cloud in one way—he felt less uncomfortable than at first; he was getting a little used to his circumstances and surroundings; his chains still galled, but not all the time; he found that the presence and homage of the great afflicted and embarrassed him less and less sharply with every hour that drifted over his head.

But for one single dread, he could have seen the fourth day approach without serious distress—the dining in public; it was to begin that day. There were greater matters in the program—for on that day he would have to preside at a Council which would take his views and commands concerning the policy to be pursued toward various foreign nations scattered far and near over the great globe; on that day, too, Hertford would be formally chosen to the grand office of Lord Protector; other things of note were appointed for that fourth day, also; but to Tom they were all insignificant compared with the ordeal of dining all by himself with a multitude of curious eyes fastened upon him and a multitude of mouths whispering comments

upon his performance,—and upon his mistakes, if he should be so unlucky as to make any.

Still, nothing could stop that fourth day, and so it came. It found poor Tom low-spirited and absent-minded, and this mood continued; he could not shake it off. The ordinary duties of the morning dragged upon his hands, and wearied him. Once more he felt the sense of captivity heavy upon him.

Late in the forenoon he was in a large audience chamber, conversing with the Earl of Hertford and dully awaiting the striking of the hour appointed for a visit of ceremony from a considerable number of great officials and courtiers.

After a little while, Tom, who had wandered to a window and become interested in the life and movement of the great highway beyond the

"TOM HAD WANDERED TO A WINDOW."

palace gates—and not idly interested, but longing with all his heart
to take part in person in its stir and freedom—saw the van of a hooting and shouting mob of disorderly men, women and children of the
lowest and poorest degree approaching from up the road.

"I would I knew what 'tis about!" he exclaimed, with all a boy's
curiosity in such happenings.

"Thou art the king!" solemnly responded the earl, with a reverence.
"Have I your grace's leave to act?"

"O blithely, yes! O gladly yes!" exclaimed Tom, excitedly, adding
to himself with a lively sense of satisfaction, "In truth, being a king
is not all dreariness—it hath its compensations and conveniences."

The earl called a page, and sent him to the captain of the guard
with the order—

"Let the mob be halted, and inquiry made concerning the occasion
of its movement. By the king's command!"

A few seconds later a long rank of the royal guards, cased in flashing
steel, filed out at the gates and formed across the highway in front of
the multitude. A messenger returned, to report that the crowd were
following a man, a woman, and a young girl to execution for crimes
committed against the peace and dignity of the realm.

Death—and a violent death—for these poor unfortunates! The
thought wrung Tom's heart-strings. The spirit of compassion took
control of him, to the exclusion of all other considerations; he never
thought of the offended laws, or of the grief or loss which these three
criminals had inflicted upon their victims, he could think of nothing
but the scaffold and the grisly fate hanging over the heads of the
condemned. His concern even made him forget, for the moment, that
he was but the false shadow of a king, not the substance; and before
he knew it he had blurted out the command—

"Bring them here!"

Then he blushed scarlet, and a sort of apology sprung to his lips;
but observing that his order had wrought no sort of surprise in the
earl or the waiting page, he suppressed the words he was about to
utter. The page, in the most matter-of-course way, made a profound
obeisance and retired backwards out of the room to deliver the command. Tom experienced a glow of pride and a renewed sense of the
compensating advantages of the kingly office. He said to himself,
"Truly it is like what I was used to feel when I read the old priest's

"TOM SCANNED THE PRISONERS."

tales, and did imagine mine own self a prince, giving law and command to all, saying 'do this, do that,' whilst none durst offer let or hindrance to my will."

Now the doors swung open; one high-sounding title after another was announced, the personages owning them followed, and the place was quickly half filled with noble folk and finery. But Tom was hardly conscious of the presence of these people, so wrought up was he and so intensely absorbed in that other and more interesting matter. He seated himself, absently, in his chair of state, and turned his eyes upon the door with manifestations of impatient expectancy; seeing which, the company forbore to trouble him, and fell to chatting a mixture of public business and court gossip one with another.

In a little while the measured tread of military men was heard approaching, and the culprits entered the presence in charge of an under-sheriff and escorted by a detail of the King's Guard. The civil officer knelt before Tom, then stood aside; the three doomed persons knelt, also, and remained so; the guard took position behind Tom's chair. Tom scanned the prisoners curiously. Something about the dress or appearance of the man had stirred a vague memory in him. "Methinks I have seen this man ere now . . . . . but the when or the where fail me"—such was Tom's thought. Just then the man glanced meekly up, and quickly dropped his face again, not being able to endure the awful port of sovereignty; but the one full glimpse of the face, which Tom got, was sufficient. He said to himself: "Now is the matter clear; this is the stranger that plucked Giles Witt out of the Thames, and saved his life, that windy, bitter, first day of the New Year—a brave good deed—pity he hath been doing baser ones and got himself in this sad case. . . . . . I have not forgot the day, neither the hour; by reason that an hour after, upon the stroke of eleven, I did get a hiding by the hand of Gammer Canty which was of so goodly and admired severity that all that went before or followed after it were but fondlings and caresses by comparison."

Tom now ordered that the woman and the girl be removed from the presence for a little time; then addressed himself to the undersheriff, saying—

"Good sir, what is this man's offense?"

The officer knelt, and answered—

"So please your majesty, he hath taken the life of a subject by poison."

Tom's compassion for the prisoner, and admiration of him as the daring rescuer of a drowning boy, experienced a most damaging shock.

"The thing was proven upon him?" he asked.

"Most clearly, sire."

Tom sighed, and said—

"Take him away—he hath earned his death. 'Tis a pity, for he was a brave heart—na-na, I mean he hath the *look* of it!"

The prisoner clasped his hands together with sudden energy, and wrung them despairingly, at the same time appealing imploringly to the "king" in broken and terrified phrases—

"O my lord the king, an' thou canst pity the lost, have pity upon me!—I am innocent—neither hath that wherewith I am charged been more than but lamely proved—yet I speak not of that; the judgment is gone forth against me and may not suffer alteration; yet in mine extremity I beg a boon, for my doom is more than I can bear. A grace, a grace, my lord the king! in thy royal compassion grant my prayer—give commandment that I be hanged!"

Tom was amazed. This was not the outcome he had looked for. "Odds my life, a strange *boon!* Was it not the fate intended thee?"

"O good my liege, not so! It is ordered that I be *boiled alive!*"

The hideous surprise of these words almost made Tom spring from his chair. As soon as he could recover his wits he cried out—

"Have thy wish, poor soul! an' thou had poisoned a hundred men thou shouldst not suffer so miserable a death."

The prisoner bowed his face to the ground and burst into passionate expressions of gratitude—ending with—

"If ever thou shouldst know misfortune—which God forefend!—may thy goodness to me this day be remembered and requited!"

Tom turned to the Earl of Hertford, and said—

"My lord, is it believable that there was warrant for this man's ferocious doom?"

"It is the law, your grace—for poisoners. In Germany coiners be boiled to death in *oil*—not cast in of a sudden, but by a rope let down into the oil by degrees, and slowly; first the feet, then the legs, then—"

"O prithee no more, my lord, I cannot bear it!" cried Tom, covering his eyes with his hands to shut out the picture. "I beseech your good lordship that order be taken to change this law—O, let no more poor creatures be visited with its tortures."

The earl's face showed profound gratification, for he was a man of merciful and generous impulses—a thing not very common with his class in that fierce age. He said—

"These your grace's noble words have sealed its doom. History will remember it to the honor of your royal house."

The under-sheriff was about to remove his prisoner; Tom gave him a sign to wait; then he said—

"Good sir, I would look into this matter further. The man has said his deed was but lamely proved. Tell me what thou knowest."

"If the king's grace please, it did appear upon the trial, that this man entered into a house in the hamlet of Islington where one lay sick—three witnesses say it was at ten of the clock in the morning and two say it was some minutes later—the sick man being alone at the time, and sleeping—and presently the man came forth again, and went his way. The sick man died within the hour, being torn with spasms and retchings."

"Did any see the poison given? Was poison found?"

"Marry, no, my liege."

"Then how doth one know there was poison given at all?"

"Please your majesty, the doctors testified that none die with such symptoms but by poison."

Weighty evidence, this—in that simple age. Tom recognized its formidable nature, and said—

"The doctor knoweth his trade—belike they were right. The matter hath an ill look for this poor man."

"Yet was not this all, your majesty; there is more and worse. Many testified that a witch, since gone from the village, none know whither, did foretell, and speak it privately in their ears, that the sick man *would die by poison*—and more, that a stranger would give it—a stranger with brown hair and clothed in a worn and common garb; and surely this prisoner doth answer woundily to the bill. Please your majesty to give the circumstance that solemn weight which is its due, seeing it was *foretold*."

This was an argument of tremendous force, in that superstitious day. Tom felt that the thing was settled; if evidence was worth anything, this poor fellow's guilt was proved. Still he offered the prisoner a chance, saying—

"If thou canst say aught in thy behalf, speak."

"Naught that will avail, my king. I am innocent, yet cannot I make it appear. I have no friends, else might I show that I was not in Islington that day; so also might I show that at that hour they name, I was above a league away, seeing I was at Wapping Old Stairs; yea more, my king, for I could show, that whilst they say I was *taking* life, I was *saving* it. A drowning boy—"

"Peace! Sheriff, name the day the deed was done!"

"At ten in the morning, or some minutes later, the first day of the New Year, most illustrious—"

"Let the prisoner go free—it is the king's will!"

Another blush followed this unregal outburst, and he covered his indecorum as well as he could by adding—

"It enrageth me that a man should be hanged upon such idle, hare-brained evidence!"

A low buzz of admiration swept through the assemblage. It was not admiration of the decree that had been delivered by Tom, for the propriety or expediency of pardoning a convicted poisoner was a thing which few there would have felt justified in either admitting or admiring—no, the admiration was for the intelligence and spirit which Tom had displayed. Some of the low-voiced remarks were to this effect—

"This is no mad king—he hath his wits sound."

"How sanely he put his questions—how like his former natural self was this abrupt, imperious disposal of the matter!"

"God be thanked, his infirmity is spent! This is no weakling, but a king. He hath borne himself like to his own father."

The air being filled with applause, Tom's ear necessarily caught a little of it. The effect which

"LET THE PRISONER GO FREE!"

this had upon him was to put him greatly at his ease, and also to charge his system with very gratifying sensations.

However, his juvenile curiosity soon rose superior to these pleasant thoughts and feelings; he was eager to know what sort of deadly mischief the woman and the little girl could have been about; so, by his command the two terrified and sobbing creatures were brought before him.

"What is it that these have done?" he inquired of the sheriff.

"Please your majesty, a black crime is charged upon them, and clearly proven; wherefore the judges have decreed, according to the law, that they be hanged. They sold themselves to the devil—such is their crime."

Tom shuddered. He had been taught to abhor people who did this wicked thing. Still, he was not going to deny himself the pleasure of feeding his curiosity, for all that; so he asked—

"Where was this done?—and when?"

"On a midnight, in December—in a ruined church, your majesty."

Tom shuddered again.

"Who was there present?"

"Only these two, your grace —and *that other.*"

"Have these confessed?"

"WHAT IS IT THAT THESE HAVE DONE?"

"Nay, not so, sire—they do deny it."

"Then prithee, how was it known?"

"Certain witnesses did see them wending thither, good your majesty; this bred the suspicion, and dire effects have since confirmed and justified it. In particular, it is in evidence that through the wicked power so obtained, they did invoke and bring about a storm that wasted all the region round about. Above forty witnesses have proved the storm; and sooth one might have had a thousand, for all had reason to remember it, sith all had suffered by it."

"Certes this is serious matter." Tom turned this dark piece of scoundrelism over in his mind a while, then asked—

"Suffered the woman, also, by the storm?"

Several old heads among the assemblage nodded their recognition of the wisdom of this question. The sheriff, however, saw nothing consequential in the inquiry; he answered, with simple directness—

"Indeed, did she, your majesty, and most righteously, as all aver. Her habitation was swept away, and herself and child left shelterless."

"Methinks the power to do herself so ill a turn was dearly bought. She had been cheated, had she paid but a farthing for it; that she paid her soul, and her child's, argueth that she is mad; if she is mad she knoweth not what she doth, therefore sinneth not."

The elderly heads nodded recognition of Tom's wisdom once more, and one individual murmured, "An' the king be mad himself, according to report, then it is a madness of a sort that would improve the sanity of some I wot of, if by the gentle providence of God they could but catch it."

"What age hath the child?" asked Tom.

"Nine years, please your majesty."

"By the law of England may a child enter into covenant and sell itself, my lord?" asked Tom, turning to a learned judge.

"SEVERAL OLD HEADS NODDED THEIR RECOGNITION."

"The law doth not permit a child to make or meddle in any weighty matter, good my liege, holding that its callow wit unfitteth it to cope with the riper wit and evil schemings of them that are its elders. The *devil* may buy a child, if he so choose, and the child agree thereto, but not an Englishman—in this latter case the contract would be null and void."

"It seemeth a rude unchristian thing, and ill contrived, that English law denieth privileges to Englishmen, to waste them on the devil!" cried Tom, with honest heat.

This novel view of the matter excited many smiles, and was stored away in many heads to be repeated about the court as evidence of Tom's originality as well as progress toward mental health.

The elder culprit had ceased from sobbing, and was hanging upon Tom's words with an excited interest and a growing hope. Tom noticed this, and it strongly inclined his sympathies toward her in her perilous and unfriended situation. Presently he asked—

"How wrought they, to bring the storm?"

"*By pulling off their stockings,* sire."

This astonished Tom, and also fired his curiosity to fever heat. He said, eagerly—

"It is wonderful! Hath it always this dread effect?"

"Always, my liege—at least if the woman doth desire it, and utter the needful words, either in her mind or with her tongue."

Tom turned to the woman, and said with impetuous zeal—

"Exert thy power—I would see a storm!"

There was a sudden paling of cheeks in the superstitious assemblage, and a general, though unexpressed, desire to get out of the place —all of which was lost upon Tom, who was dead to everything but the proposed cataclysm. Seeing a puzzled and astonished look in the woman's face, he added, excitedly—

"Never fear—thou shalt be blameless. More—thou shalt go free —none shall touch thee. Exert thy power."

"O, my lord the king, I have it not—I have been falsely accused."

"Thy fears stay thee. Be of good heart, thou shalt suffer no harm. Make a storm—it mattereth not how small a one—I require naught great or harmful, but indeed prefer the opposite—do this and thy life is spared—thou shalt go out free, with thy child, bearing the king's pardon, and safe from hurt or malice from any in the realm."

The woman prostrated herself, and protested, with tears, that she had no power to do the miracle, else she would gladly win her child's life, alone, and be content to lose her own, if by obedience to the king's command so precious a grace might be acquired.

Tom urged—the woman still adhered to her declarations. Finally he said—

"I think the woman hath said true. An' *my* mother were in her place and gifted with the devil's functions, she had not stayed a moment to call her storms and lay the whole land in ruins, if the saving of my forfeit life were the price she got! It is argument that other mothers are made in like mould. Thou art free, goodwife— thou and thy child—for I do think thee innocent. *Now* thou'st naught to fear, being pardoned—pull off thy stockings!—an' thou canst make me a storm, thou shalt be rich!"

The redeemed creature was loud in her gratitude, and proceeded to obey, whilst Tom looked on with eager expectancy, a little marred by apprehension; the courtiers at the same time manifesting decided discomfort and uneasiness. The woman stripped her own feet and her little girl's also, and plainly did her best to reward the king's gener- osity with an earthquake, but it was all a failure and a disappoint- ment. Tom sighed, and said—

"There, good soul, trouble thyself no further, thy power is departed out of thee. Go thy way in peace; and if it return to thee at any time, forget me not, but fetch me a storm."*

---

*See Notes to Chapter 15 at end of the volume.

CHAPTER 16

THE DINNER HOUR drew near—yet strangely enough, the thought brought but slight discomfort to Tom, and hardly any terror. The morning's experiences had wonderfully built up his confidence; the poor little ash-cat was already more wonted to his strange garret, after four days' habit, than a mature person could have become in a full month. A child's facility in accommodating itself to circumstances was never more strikingly illustrated.

Let us privileged ones hurry to the great banqueting room and have a glance at matters there whilst Tom is being made ready for the imposing occasion. It is a spacious apartment, with gilded pillars and pilasters, and pictured walls and ceilings. At the door stand tall guards, as rigid as statues, dressed in rich and picturesque costumes, and bearing halberds. In a high gallery which runs all around the place is a band of musicians and a packed company of citizens of both sexes, in brilliant attire. In the centre of the room, upon a raised platform, is Tom's table. Now let the ancient chronicler speak:

"A gentleman enters the room bearing a rod, and along with him another bearing a table-cloth, which, after they have both kneeled three times with the utmost veneration, he spreads upon the table, and after kneeling again they both retire; then come two others, one with the rod again, the other with a salt-cellar, a plate, and bread;

when they have kneeled as the others had done, and placed what was brought upon the table, they too retire with the same ceremonies performed by the first; at last come two nobles, richly clothed, one bearing a tasting-knife, who, after prostrating themselves three times

"A GENTLEMAN BEARING A ROD."

in the most graceful manner, approach and rub the table with bread and salt, with as much awe as if the king had been present."*

So end the solemn preliminaries. Now, far down the echoing corridors we hear a bugle-blast, and the indistinct cry, "Place for the king! way for the king's most excellent majesty!" These sounds are momently repeated—they grow nearer and nearer—and presently, almost in our faces, the martial note peals and the cry rings out, "Way for the king!" At this instant the shining pageant appears, and files in at the door, with a measured march. Let the chronicler speak again:

"First come Gentlemen, Barons, Earls, Knights of the Garter, all

*Leigh Hunt's "The Town," p. 408, quotation from an early tourist.

richly dressed and bare-headed; next comes the Chancellor, between two, one of which carries the royal sceptre, the other the Sword of State in a red scabbard, studded with golden fleurs-de-lis, the point upwards; next comes the king himself—whom, upon his appearing, twelve trumpets and many drums salute with a great burst of welcome, whilst all in the galleries rise in their places, crying 'God save the king!' After him come nobles attached to his person, and on his right and left march his guard of honor, his fifty Gentlemen Pensioners, with gilt battle-axes.''

This was all fine and pleasant. Tom's pulse beat high and a glad light was in his eye. He bore himself right gracefully, and all the more so because he was not thinking of how he was doing it, his mind being charmed and occupied with the blithe sights and sounds about him—and besides, nobody can be very ungraceful in nicely-fitting beautiful clothes after he has grown a little used to them—especially if he is for the moment unconscious of them. Tom remembered his instructions,

"THE CHANCELLOR, BETWEEN TWO."

and acknowledged his greeting with a slight inclination of his plumed head, and a courteous "I thank ye, my good people."

He seated himself at table, without removing his cap; and did it without the least embarrassment; for to eat with one's cap on was the one solitary royal custom upon which the kings and the Cantys met as upon common ground, neither party having any advantage over the other in the matter of old familiarity with it. The pageant broke up and grouped itself picturesquely, and remained bareheaded.

"I THANK YE, MY GOOD PEOPLE."

Now, to the sound of gay music, the Yeomen of the Guard entered,—"the tallest and mightiest men in England, they being carefully selected in this regard"—but we will let the chronicler tell about it:

"The Yeomen of the Guard entered, bare-headed, clothed in scarlet, with golden roses upon their backs; and these went and came, bringing in each turn a course of dishes, served in plate. These dishes were received by a gentleman in the same order they were brought, and placed upon the table, while the taster gave to each guard a mouthful to eat of the particular dish he had brought, for fear of any poison."

Tom made a good dinner, notwithstanding he was conscious that hundreds of eyes followed each morsel to his mouth and watched him eat it with an interest which could not have been more intense if it had been a deadly explosive and was expected to blow him up and scatter him all about the place. He was careful not to hurry, and equally careful not to do anything whatever for himself, but wait till the proper official knelt down and did it for him. He got through without a mistake—a flawless and precious triumph.

"HE MARCHED AWAY IN THE MIDST OF HIS PAGEANT."

When the meal was over at last and he marched away in the midst of his bright pageant, with the happy noises in his ears of blaring bugles, rolling drums and thundering acclamations, he felt that if he had seen the worst of dining in public, it was an ordeal which he would be glad to endure several times a day if by that means he could but buy himself free from some of the more formidable requirements of his royal office.

CHAPTER 17

FOO-FOO THE FIRST

MILES HENDON hurried along toward the Southwark end of the Bridge, keeping a sharp lookout for the persons he sought, and hoping and expecting to overtake them presently. He was disappointed in this, however. By asking questions, he was enabled to track them part of the way through Southwark; then all traces ceased, and he was perplexed as to how to proceed. Still, he continued his efforts as best he could during the rest of the day. Nightfall found him leg-weary, half famished, and his desire as far from accomplishment as ever; so he supped at the Tabard inn and went to bed, resolved to make an early start in the morning, and give the town an exhaustive search. As he lay thinking and planning, he presently began to reason thus: The boy would escape from the ruffian, his reputed father, if possible; would he go back to London and seek his former haunts? no, would not do that, he would avoid recapture. What, then, would he do? Never having had a friend in the world, or a protector, until he met Miles Hendon, he would naturally try to find that friend again, provided the effort did not require him to go toward London and danger. He would strike for Hendon Hall, that is what he would do, for he knew Hendon was homeward bound and there he might expect to find him. Yes, the case was plain to Hendon—he must lose no more time in Southwark, but move at once through Kent, toward Monk's Holm, searching the wood and inquiring as he went. Let us return to the vanished little king, now.

The ruffian whom the waiter at the inn on the Bridge saw "about to join" the youth and the king, did not exactly join them, but fell in close behind them and followed their steps. He said nothing. His left arm was in a sling, and he wore a large green patch over his left eye; he limped slightly, and used an oaken staff as a support. The youth led the king a crooked course through Southwark, and by and by struck into the high road beyond. The king was irritated, now, and said he would stop here—it was Hendon's place to come to him, not his to go to Hendon. He would not endure such insolence; he would stop where he was. The youth said—

"Thou'lt tarry here, and thy friend lying wounded in the wood yonder? So be it, then."

The king's manner changed at once. He cried out—

"Wounded? And who hath dared to do it? But that is apart; lead on, lead on! Faster, sirrah! art shod with lead? Wounded, is he? Now though the doer of it be a duke's son, he shall rue it!"

It was some distance to the wood, but the space was speedily traversed. The youth looked about him, discovered a bough sticking in the ground, with a

"THE RUFFIAN FOLLOWED THEIR STEPS."

small bit of rag tied to it, then led the way into the forest, watching
for similar boughs and finding them at intervals; they were evidently
guides to the point he was aiming at. By and by an open place was
reached, where were the charred remains of a farm house, and near
them a barn which was falling to ruin and decay. There was no sign
of life anywhere, and utter silence prevailed. The youth entered the
barn, the king following eagerly upon his heels. No one there! The
king shot a surprised and suspicious glance at the youth, and asked—

"Where is he?"

A mocking laugh was his answer. The king was in a rage in a
moment; he seized a billet of wood and was in the act of charging
upon the youth when another mocking laugh fell upon his ear. It was
from the lame ruffian, who had been following at a distance. The
king turned and said angrily—

"HE SEIZED A BILLET OF WOOD."

"Who art thou? What is thy business here?"

"Leave thy foolery," said the man, "and quiet thyself. My disguise is none so good that thou canst pretend thou knowest not thy father through it."

"Thou art not my father. I know thee not. I am the king. If thou hast hid my servant, find him for me, or thou shalt sup sorrow for what thou hast done."

John Canty replied, in a stern and measured voice—

"It is plain thou art mad, and I am loth to punish thee; but if thou provoke me, I must. Thy prating doth no harm here, where there are no ears that need to mind thy follies, yet is it well to practice thy tongue to wary speech, that it may do no hurt when our quarters change. I have done a murder, and may not tarry at home—neither shalt thou, seeing I need thy service. My name is changed, for wise reasons; it is Hobbs—John Hobbs; thine is Jack—charge thy memory accordingly. Now, then, speak. Where is thy mother? where are thy sisters? They came not to the place appointed—knowest thou whither they went?"

The king answered, sullenly—

"Trouble me not with these riddles. My mother is dead; my sisters are in the palace."

The youth near by burst into a derisive laugh, and the king would have assaulted him, but Canty—or Hobbs, as he now called himself—prevented him, and said—

"Peace, Hugo, vex him not; his mind is astray, and thy ways fret him. Sit thee down, Jack, and quiet thyself; thou shalt have a morsel to eat, anon."

Hobbs and Hugo fell to talking together, in low voices, and the king removed himself as far as he could from their disagreeable company. He withdrew into the twilight of the farther end of the barn, where he found the earthen floor bedded a foot deep with straw. He lay down here, drew straw over himself in lieu of blankets, and was soon absorbed in thinkings. He had many griefs, but the minor ones were swept almost into forgetfulness by the supreme one, the loss of his father. To the rest of the world the name of Henry VIII brought a shiver, and suggested an ogre whose nostrils breathed destruction and whose hand dealt scourgings and death; but to this boy the name brought only sensations of pleasure, the figure it invoked wore a countenance that was all gentleness and affection. He called to mind a long succession of loving passages between his father and himself, and dwelt fondly upon them, his unstinted tears attesting how deep and real was the grief that possessed his heart. As the afternoon wasted

"HE WAS SOON ABSORBED IN THINKINGS."

away, the lad, wearied with his troubles, sank gradually into a tranquil and healing slumber.

After a considerable time—he could not tell how long—his senses struggled to a half-consciousness, and as he lay with closed eyes vaguely wondering where he was and what had been happening, he noted a murmurous sound, the sullen beating of rain upon the roof. A snug sense of comfort stole over him, which was rudely broken, the next moment, by a chorus of piping cackles and coarse laughter. It startled him disagreeably, and he unmuffled his head to see whence this interruption proceeded. A grim and unsightly picture met his eye. A bright fire was burning in the middle of the floor, at the other end of the barn, and around it, and lit weirdly up by the red glare, lolled and sprawled the motliest company of tattered gutter-scum and ruffians, of both sexes, he had ever read or dreamed of. There were huge, stalwart men, brown with exposure, long-haired, and clothed in fantastic rags; there were middle-sized youths, of truculent countenance, and similarly clad; there were blind mendicants, with patched or bandaged eyes; crippled ones, with wooden legs and crutches; there was a villain-looking pedlar with his pack; a knife-grinder, a

tinker, and a barber-surgeon, with the implements of their trades;
some of the females were hardly-grown girls, some were at prime,
some were old and wrinkled hags, and all were loud, brazen, foul-
mouthed; and all soiled and slatternly; there were three sore-faced

"A GRIM AND UNSIGHTLY PICTURE."

babies; there were a couple of starve-
ling curs, with strings about their
necks, whose office was to lead
the blind.

The night was come, the gang
had just finished
feasting, an orgie
was beginning;
the can of liquor
was passing from
mouth to mouth. A general cry broke forth—

"A song! a song from the Bat and Dick Dot-and-go-One!"

One of the blind men got up, and made ready by casting aside the
patches that sheltered his excellent eyes, and the pathetic placard
which recited the cause of his calamity. Dot-and-go-One disencum-
bered himself of his timber leg and took his place, upon sound and
healthy limbs, beside his fellow-rascal; then they roared out a rollicking ditty, and were re-inforced by the whole crew, at the end of each
stanza, in a rousing chorus. By the time the last stanza was reached,
the half-drunken enthusiasm had risen to such a pitch, that everybody

joined in and sang it clear through from the beginning, producing a volume of villainous sound that made the rafters quake. These were the inspiring words:

> "Bien Darkmans then, Bouse Mort and Ken,
> The bien Coves bings awast,
> On Chates to trine by Rome Coves dine,
> For his long lib at last.
> Bing'd out bien Morts and toure, and toure,
> Bing out of the Rome vile bine,
> And toure the Cove that cloy'd your duds,
> Upon the Chates to trine."*

Conversation followed; not in the thieves' dialect of the song, for that was only used, in talk, when unfriendly ears might be listening. In the course of it it appeared that "John Hobbs" was not altogether a new recruit, but had trained in the gang at some former time. His later history was called for, and when he said he had "accidentally" killed a man, considerable satisfaction was expressed; when he added that the man was a priest, he was roundly applauded, and had to take a drink with everybody. Old acquaintances welcomed him joyously, and new ones were proud to shake him by the hand. He was asked why he had "tarried away so many months." He answered—

"THEY ROARED OUT A ROLLICKING DITTY."

"London is better than the country, and safer, these late years, the laws be so bitter and so diligently enforced. An' I had not had that

*From "The English Rogue;" London, 1665.

accident, I had staid there. I had resolved to stay, and never more venture countrywards—but the accident has ended that."

He inquired how many persons the gang numbered now. The "Ruffler," or chief, answered—

"Five and twenty sturdy budges, bulks, files, clapper-dogeons and maunders, counting the dells and doxies and other morts.* Most are here, the rest are wandering eastward, along the winter lay. We follow at dawn."

"I do not see the Wen among the honest folk about me. Where may he be?"

"Poor lad, his diet is brimstone, now, and over hot for a delicate taste. He was killed in a brawl, somewhere about midsummer."

"I sorrow to hear that; the Wen was a capable man, and brave."

"That was he, truly. Black Bess, his dell, is of us yet, but absent on the eastward tramp; a fine lass, of nice ways and orderly conduct, none ever seeing her drunk above four days in the seven."

"She was ever strict—I remember it well—a goodly wench and worthy all commendation. Her mother was more free and less particular; a troublesome and ugly tempered beldame, but furnished with a wit above the common."

"WHILST THE FLAMES LICKED UPWARD."

nished with a wit above the common."

"We lost her through it. Her gift of palmistry and other sorts of fortune-telling begot for her at last a witch's name and fame. The law roasted her to death at a slow fire. It did touch me to a sort of tenderness to see the gallant way she met her lot—cursing and reviling all

---

*Canting terms for various kinds of thieves, beggars and vagabonds, and their female companions.

the crowd that gaped and gazed around her, whilst the flames licked upward toward her face and catched her thin locks and crackled about her old gray head—cursing them, said I?—cursing them! why an' thou shouldst live a thousand years thou'dst never hear so masterful a cursing. Alack, her art died with her. There be base and weakling imitations left, but no true blasphemy."

The Ruffler sighed; the listeners sighed in sympathy; a general depression fell upon the company for a moment, for even hardened outcasts like these are not wholly dead to sentiment, but are able to feel a fleeting sense of loss and affliction at wide intervals and under peculiarly favoring circumstances—as in cases like to this, for instance, when genius and culture depart and leave no heir. However, a deep drink all round soon restored the spirits of the mourners.

"Have any others of our friends fared hardly?" asked Hobbs.

"Some—yes. Particularly new-comers—such as small husbandmen turned shiftless and hungry upon the world because their farms were taken from them to be changed to sheep ranges. They begged, and were whipped at the cart's tail, naked from the girdle up, till the blood ran, then set in the stocks to be pelted; they begged again, were whipped again, and deprived of an ear; they begged a third time— poor devils, what else could they do?—and were branded on the cheek with a red hot iron, then sold for slaves; they ran away, were hunted down, and hanged. 'Tis a brief tale, and quickly told. Others of us have fared less hardly. Stand forth, Yokel, Burns, and Hodge— show your adornments!"

These stood up and stripped away some of their rags, exposing their backs, criss-crossed with ropy old welts left by the lash; one turned up his hair and showed the place where a left ear had once been; another showed a brand upon his shoulder—the letter V—and a mutilated ear; the third said—

"I am Yokel, once a farmer and prosperous, with loving wife and kids—now am I somewhat different in estate and calling; and the wife and kids are gone; mayhap they are in heaven, mayhap in—in the other place—but the kindly God be thanked, they bide no more in *England!* My good old blameless mother strove to earn bread by nursing the sick; one of these died, the doctors knew not how, so my mother was burnt for a witch, whilst my babes looked on and wailed.

English law!—up, all, with your cups!—now altogether and with a
cheer!—drink to the merciful English law that delivered *her* from the
English hell! Thank you, mates, one and all. I begged, from house to
house—I and the wife—bearing with us the hungry kids—but it

"THEY WERE WHIPPED AT THE CART'S TAIL."

was crime to be hungry in England—so they stripped us and lashed
us through three towns. Drink ye all again to the merciful English
law!—for its lash drank deep of my Mary's blood and its blessed
deliverance came quick. She lies there, in the potter's field, safe from
all harms. And the kids—well, whilst the law lashed me from town
to town, they starved. Drink lads—only a drop—a drop to the poor
kids, that never did any creature harm. I begged again—begged for
a crust, and got the stocks and lost an ear—see, here bides the stump;
I begged again, and here is the stump of the other to keep me minded

of it. And still I begged again, and was sold for a slave—here on my
cheek under this stain, if I washed it off, ye might see the red S the
branding-iron left there! A SLAVE! Do ye understand that word! An
English SLAVE!—that is he that stands before ye. I have run from my
master, and when I am found—the heavy curse of heaven fall on the
law and the land that hath commanded it!—I shall hang!"*

A ringing voice came through the murky air—

"Thou shalt *not!*—and this day the end of that law is come!"

"THOU SHALT *NOT!*"

All turned, and saw the fantastic figure of the little king approaching hurriedly; as it emerged into the light and was clearly revealed,
a general explosion of inquiries broke out:

"Who is it? *What* is it? Who art thou, mannikin?"

The boy stood unconfused in the midst of all those surprised and
questioning eyes, and answered with princely dignity—

*See Note 10 at end of volume.

"I am Edward, king of England."

A wild burst of laughter followed, partly of derision and partly of delight in the excellence of the joke. The king was stung. He said sharply—

"Ye mannerless vagrants, is this your recognition of the royal boon I have promised?"

He said more, with angry voice and excited gesture, but it was lost in a whirlwind of laughter and mocking exclamations. "John Hobbs" made several attempts to make himself heard above the din, and at last succeeded—saying—

"Mates, he is my son, a dreamer, a fool, and stark mad—mind him not—he thinketh he *is* the king."

"I *am* the king," said Edward, turning toward him, "as thou shalt know to thy cost, in good time. Thou hast confessed a murder—thou shalt swing for it."

"*Thou'lt* betray me?—*thou?* An' I get my hands upon thee—"

"Tut-tut!" said the burly Ruffler, interposing in time to save the king, and emphasizing this service by knocking Hobbs down with his fist, "hast respect for neither kings *nor* Rufflers? An' thou insult my presence so again, I'll hang thee up myself." Then he said to his majesty, "Thou must make no threats against thy mates, lad; and thou must guard thy tongue from saying evil of them elsewhere. *Be* king, if it please thy mad humor, but be not harmful in it. Sink the title thou hast uttered,—'tis treason; we be bad men, in some few trifling ways, but none among us is so base as to be traitor to his king; we be loving and loyal hearts, in that regard. Note if I speak truth. Now—all together: 'Long live Edward, king of England!' "

"LONG LIVE EDWARD, KING OF ENGLAND!"

The response came with such a thundergust from the motley crew that the crazy building vibrated to the sound. The little king's face lighted with pleasure for an instant, and he slightly inclined his head and said with grave simplicity—

"I thank you, my good people."

This unexpected result threw the company into convulsions of merriment. When something like quiet was presently come again, the Ruffler said, firmly, but with an accent of good nature—

"Drop it, boy, 'tis not wise, nor well. Humor thy fancy, if thou must, but choose some other title."

A tinker shrieked out a suggestion—

"Foo-foo the First, King of the Mooncalves!"

The title "took," at once, every throat responded, and a roaring shout went up, of—

"Long live Foo-foo the First, King of the Mooncalves!" followed by hootings, cat-calls, and peals of laughter.

"Hale him forth, and crown him!"

"Robe him!"

"Sceptre him!"

"Throne him!"

These and twenty other cries broke out at once; and almost before the poor little victim could draw a breath he was crowned with a tin basin, robed in a tattered blanket, throned upon a barrel, and sceptred

"KNOCKING HOBBS DOWN."

with the tinker's soldering-iron. Then all flung themselves upon their knees about him and sent up a chorus of ironical wailings and mocking supplications, whilst they swabbed their eyes with their soiled and ragged sleeves and aprons—

"Be gracious to us, O, sweet king!"

"THRONE HIM!"

"Trample not upon thy beseeching worms, O noble majesty!"

"Pity thy slaves, and comfort them with a royal kick!"

"Cheer us and warm us with thy gracious rays, O flaming sun of sovereignty!"

"Sanctify the ground with the touch of thy foot, that we may eat the dirt and be ennobled!"

"Deign to spit upon us, O sire, that our children's children may tell of thy princely condescension, and be proud and happy forever!"

But the humorous tinker made the "hit" of the evening and carried off the honors. Kneeling, he pretended to kiss the king's foot, and was indignantly spurned; whereupon he went about begging for a rag to paste over the place upon his face which had been touched by the foot, saying it must be preserved from contact with the vulgar air, and that he should make his fortune by going on the highway and exposing it to view at the rate of a hundred shillings a sight. He made himself so killingly funny that he was the envy and admiration of the whole mangy rabble.

Tears of shame and indignation stood in the little monarch's eyes; and the thought in his heart was, "Had I offered them a deep wrong they could not be more cruel—yet have I proffered naught but to do them a kindness—and it is thus they use me for it!"

CHAPTER 18

THE TROOP of vagabonds turned out at early dawn, and set forward on their march. There was a lowering sky overhead, sloppy ground under foot, and a winter chill in the air. All gaiety was gone from the company; some were sullen and silent, some were irritable and petulant, none were gentle-humored, all were thirsty.

The Ruffler put "Jack" in Hugo's charge, with some brief instructions, and commanded John Canty to keep away from him and let him alone; he also warned Hugo not to be too rough with the lad.

After a while the weather grew milder, and the clouds lifted somewhat. The troop ceased to shiver, and their spirits began to improve. They grew more and more cheerful, and finally began to chaff each other and insult passengers along the highway. This showed that they were awaking to an appreciation of life and its joys once more. The dread in which their sort was held was apparent in the fact that everybody gave them the road, and took their ribald insolences meekly, without venturing to talk back. They snatched linen from the hedges, occasionally, in full view of the owners, who made no protest, but only seemed grateful that they did not take the hedges, too.

By and by they invaded a small farm house and made themselves at home while the trembling farmer and his people swept the larder clean to furnish a breakfast for them. They chucked the housewife and her daughters under the chin whilst receiving the food from their hands, and made coarse jests about them, accompanied with insulting epithets and bursts of horse-laughter. They threw bones and vegetables at the farmer and his sons, kept them dodging all the time, and applauded uproariously when a good hit was made. They ended by buttering the head of one of the daughters who resented some of their familiarities. When they took their leave they threatened to come back and burn the house over the heads of the family if any report of their doings got to the ears of the authorities.

"THE TROOP OF VAGABONDS SET
FORWARD."

About noon, after a long and weary tramp, the gang came to a halt behind a hedge on the outskirts of a considerable village. An hour was allowed for rest, then the crew scattered themselves abroad to enter the village at different points to ply their various trades. "Jack" was sent with Hugo. They wandered hither and thither for some time, Hugo watching for opportunities to do a stroke of business but finding none—so he finally said—

"I see naught to steal; it is a paltry place. Wherefore we will beg."

"*We*, forsooth! Follow thy trade—it befits thee. But *I* will not beg."

"Thou'lt not beg!" exclaimed Hugo, eying the king with surprise. "Prithee, since when hast thou reformed?"

"What dost thou mean?"

"Mean? Hast thou not begged the streets of London all thy life?"

"I? Thou idiot!"

"THEY THREW BONES AND VEGETABLES."

"Spare thy compliments—thy stock will last the longer. Thy father says thou hast begged all thy days. Mayhap he lied. Peradventure you will even make so bold as to *say* he lied," scoffed Hugo.

"Him *you* call my father? Yes, he lied."

"Come, play not thy merry game of madman so far, mate; use it for thy amusement, not thy hurt. An' I tell him this, he will scorch thee finely for it."

"Save thyself the trouble. I will tell him."

"I like thy spirit, I do in truth; but I do not admire thy judgment. Bone-rackings and bastings be plenty enow in this life, without going out of one's way to invite them. But a truce to these matters; I believe your father. I doubt not he can lie; I doubt not he *doth* lie, upon occasion, for the best of us do that; but there is no occasion here. A wise man does not waste so good a commodity as lying for naught. But come; sith it is thy humor to give over begging, wherewithal shall we busy ourselves? With robbing kitchens?"

The king said, impatiently—

"Have done with this folly—you weary me!"

Hugo replied, with temper—

"Now harkee, mate; you will not beg, you will not rob; so be it. But I will tell you what you *will* do. You will play decoy whilst I beg. Refuse, an' you think you may venture!"

The king was about to reply contemptuously, when Hugo said, interrupting—

"Peace! Here comes one with a kindly face. Now will I fall down in a fit. When the stranger runs to me, set you up a wail, and fall upon your knees, seeming to weep; then cry out as all the devils of misery were in your belly, and say, 'O, sir, it is my poor afflicted brother, and we be friendless; o' God's name cast through your merciful eyes one pitiful look upon a sick, forsaken and most miserable wretch; bestow one little penny out of thy riches upon one smitten of God and ready to perish!'—and mind you, keep you *on* wailing, and abate not till we bilk him of his penny, else shall you rue it."

Then immediately Hugo began to moan, and groan, and roll his eyes, and reel and totter about; and when the stranger was close at hand, down he sprawled before him, with a shriek, and began to writhe and wallow in the dirt, in seeming agony.

"O dear, O dear!" cried the benevolent stranger, "O poor soul, poor soul, how he doth suffer! There—let me help thee up."

"O, noble sir, forbear, and God love you for a princely gentleman— but it giveth me cruel pain to touch me when I am taken so. My brother there will tell your worship how I am racked with anguish when these fits be upon me. A penny, dear sir, a penny, to buy a little food; then leave me to my sorrows."

"A penny! thou shalt have three, thou hapless creature"—and he fumbled in his pocket with nervous haste and got them out. "There, poor lad, take them, and most welcome. Now come hither, my boy, and help me carry thy stricken brother to yon house, where—"

"I am not his brother," said the king, interrupting.

"What! not his brother?"

"O hear him!" groaned Hugo, then privately ground his teeth. "He denies his own brother—and he with one foot in the grave!"

"Boy, thou art indeed hard of heart, if this is thy brother. For shame!—and he scarce able to move hand or foot. If he is not thy brother, who is he, then?"

"A beggar and a thief! He has got your money and has picked your pocket, like-

"BEGAN TO WRITHE AND WALLOW IN THE DIRT."

wise. An' thou wouldst do a healing miracle, lay thy staff over his shoulders and trust Providence for the rest."

But Hugo did not tarry for the miracle. In a moment he was up and off like the wind, the gentleman following after and raising the hue and cry lustily as he went. The king, breathing deep gratitude to heaven for his own release, fled in the opposite direction and did not slacken his pace until he was out of harm's reach. He took the first road that offered, and soon put the village behind him. He hurried along, as briskly as he could, during several hours, keeping a nervous watch over his shoulder for pursuit; but his fears left him at last, and a grateful sense of security took their place. He recognized, now, that he was hungry; and also very tired. So he halted at a farm house; but when he was about to speak, he was cut short and driven rudely away. His clothes were against him.

"THE KING FLED IN THE
OPPOSITE DIRECTION."

He wandered on, wounded and indignant, and was resolved to put himself in the way of like treatment no more. But hunger is pride's master; so as the evening drew near, he made an attempt at another farm house; but here he fared worse than before; for he was called hard names and was promised arrest as a vagrant except he moved on promptly.

The night came on, chilly and overcast; and still the footsore monarch labored slowly on. He was obliged to keep moving, for every time he sat down to rest he was soon penetrated to the bone with the cold. All his sensations and experiences, as he moved through the solemn gloom and the empty vastness of the night, were new and strange to him. At intervals he heard voices approach, pass by, and fade into silence; and as he saw nothing more of the bodies they belonged to than a sort of formless drifting blur, there was something spectral and uncanny about it all that made him shudder. Occasionally he caught the twinkle of a light—always far away, apparently—almost in another world; if he heard the tinkle of a sheep's bell, it was vague, distant, indistinct; the muffled lowing of the herds floated to him on the night wind in vanishing cadences, a mournful sound; now and then came the complaining howl of a dog over viewless expanses of field and forest; all sounds were remote; they made the little king feel that all life and activity were far removed from him, and that he stood solitary, companionless, in the centre of a measureless solitude.

He stumbled along, through the grewsome fascinations of this new experience, startled occasionally by the soft rustling of the dry leaves overhead, so like human whispers they seemed to sound; and by and by he came suddenly upon the freckled light of a tin lantern near at hand. He stepped back into the shadows and waited. The lantern stood by the open door of a barn. The king waited some time—there was no sound, and nobody stirring. He got so cold, standing still, and the hospitable barn looked so enticing, that at last he resolved to risk everything and enter. He started swiftly and stealthily, and just as he was crossing the threshold he heard voices behind him. He darted behind a cask, within the barn, and stooped down. Two farm laborers came in, bringing the lantern with them, and fell to work, talking meanwhile. Whilst they moved about with the light, the king made good use of his eyes and took the bearings of what seemed to be a good sized stall at the further end of the place, purposing to grope his way to it when he should be left to himself. He also noted the position of a pile of horse blankets, midway of the route, with the intent to levy upon them for the service of the crown of England for one night.

By and by the men finished and went away, fastening the door behind them and taking the lantern with them. The shivering king made for the blankets, with as good speed as the darkness would allow; gathered them up and then groped his way safely to the stall.

Of two of the blankets he made a bed, then covered himself with the
remaining two. He was a glad monarch, now, though the blankets
were old and thin, and not quite warm enough; and besides gave out
a pungent horsy odor that was almost suffocatingly powerful.

Although the king was hungry and chilly, he was also so tired and

"HE STUMBLED ALONG."

so drowsy that these latter influences soon began to get the advantage of the former, and he presently dozed off into a state of semi-
consciousness. Then, just as he was on the point of losing himself
wholly, he distinctly felt something touch him! He was broad awake
in a moment, and gasping for breath. The cold horror of that mysterious touch in the dark almost made his heart stand still. He lay
motionless, and listened, scarcely breathing. But nothing stirred, and

there was no sound. He continued to listen, and wait, during what seemed a long time, but still nothing stirred, and there was no sound. So he began to drop into a drowse once more, at last; and all at once he felt that mysterious touch again! It was a grisly thing, this light touch from this noiseless and invisible presence; it made the boy sick with ghostly fears. What should he do? That was the question; but he did not know how to answer it. Should he leave these reasonably comfortable quarters and fly from this inscrutable horror? But fly whither? He could not get out of the barn; and the idea of skurrying blindly hither and thither in the dark, within the captivity of the four walls, with this phantom gliding after him, and visiting him with that soft hideous touch upon cheek or shoulder at every turn, was intolerable. But to stay where he was, and endure this living death all night? —was that better? No. What, then, was there left to do? Ah, there was but one course; he knew it well—he must put out his hand and find that thing!

It was easy to think this; but it was hard to brace himself up to try it. Three times he stretched his hand a little way out into the dark, gingerly; and snatched it suddenly back, with a gasp—not because it had encountered anything, but because he had felt so sure it was just *going* to. But the fourth time, he groped a little further, and his hand lightly swept against something soft and warm. This petrified him, nearly, with fright—his mind was in such a state that he could imagine the thing to be nothing else than a corpse, newly dead and still warm. He thought he would rather die than touch it again. But he thought this false thought because he did not know the immortal strength of human curiosity. In no long time his hand was tremblingly groping again—against his judgment, and without his consent—but groping persistently on, just the same. It encountered a bunch of long hair; he shuddered, but followed up the hair and found what seemed to be a warm rope; followed up the rope and found an innocent calf!— for the rope was not a rope at all, but the calf's tail.

The king was cordially ashamed of himself for having gotten all that fright and misery out of so paltry a matter as a slumbering calf; but he need not have felt so about it, for it was not the calf that frightened him but a dreadful non-existent something which the calf stood for; and any other boy, in those old superstitious times, would have acted and suffered just as he had done.

The king was not only delighted to find that the creature was only a calf, but delighted to have the calf's company; for he had been feeling so lonesome and friendless that the company and comradeship of even this humble animal was welcome. And he had been so buffeted, so rudely entreated by his own kind, that it was a real comfort to him

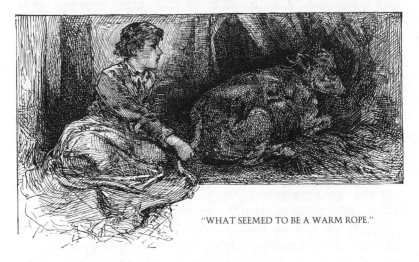

"WHAT SEEMED TO BE A WARM ROPE."

to feel that he was at last in the society of a fellow creature that had at least a soft heart and a gentle spirit, whatever loftier attributes might be lacking. So he resolved to waive rank and make friends with the calf.

While stroking its sleek warm back—for it lay near him and within easy reach—it occurred to him that this calf might be utilized in more ways than one. Whereupon he re-arranged his bed, spreading it down close to the calf; then he cuddled himself up to the calf's back, drew the covers up over himself and his friend, and in a minute or two was as warm and comfortable as he had ever been in the downy couches of the regal palace of Westminster.

Pleasant thoughts came, at once; life took on a cheerfuller seeming. He was free of the bonds of servitude and crime, free of the companionship of base and brutal outlaws; he was warm, he was sheltered; in a word, he was happy. The night wind was rising; it swept by in fitful gusts that made the old barn quake and rattle, then its forces died down at intervals, and went moaning and wailing around corners

and projections—but it was all music to the king, now that he was
snug and comfortable; let it blow and rage, let it batter and bang,
let it moan and wail, he minded it not, he only enjoyed it. He
merely snuggled the closer
to his friend, in a luxury
of warm contentment,
and drifted
blissfully
out of con-
sciousness
into a deep
and dream-
less sleep
that was full
of serenity
and peace.
The distant

"CUDDLED UP TO THE CALF."

dogs howled, the melancholy kine complained, and the winds went on raging,
whilst furious sheets of rain drove along the roof; but the majesty of
England slept on, undisturbed, and the calf did the same, it being a
simple creature and not easily troubled by storms or embarrassed by
sleeping with a king.

CHAPTER 19

THE PRINCE WITH THE PEASANTS

W HEN THE KING awoke in the early morning, he found that a wet but thoughtful rat had crept into the place during the night and made a cosy bed for itself in his bosom. Being disturbed, now, it scampered away. The boy smiled, and said, "Poor fool, why so fearful? I am as forlorn as thou. 'Twould be shame in me to hurt the helpless, who am myself so helpless. Moreover, I owe you thanks for a good omen; for when a king has fallen so low that the very rats do make a bed of him, it surely meaneth that his fortunes be upon the turn, since it is plain he can no lower go."

He got up and stepped out of the stall, and just then he heard the sound of children's voices. The barn door opened and a couple of little girls came in. As soon as they saw him their talking and laughing ceased, and they stopped and stood still, gazing at him with strong curiosity; they presently began to whisper together, then they approached nearer, and stopped again to gaze and whisper. By and by they gathered courage and began to discuss him aloud. One said—

"He hath a comely face."

The other added—

"And pretty hair."

"But is ill clothed, enow."

"And how starved he looketh."

They came still nearer, sidling shyly around and about him, examining him minutely from all points, as if he were some strange new kind of animal; but warily and watchfully, the while, as if they half feared he might be a sort of animal that would bite, upon occasion. Finally they halted before him, holding each other's hands, for protection, and took a good satisfying stare with their innocent eyes; then one of them plucked up all her courage and inquired with honest directness—

"Who art thou, boy?"

"I am the king," was the grave answer.

The children gave a little start, and their eyes spread themselves wide open and remained so during a speechless half minute. Then curiosity broke the silence—

"The *king*? What king?"

"The king of England."

The children looked at each other—then at him—then at each other again—wonderingly, perplexedly—then one said—

"Didst hear him, Margery?—he saith he is the king. Can that be true?"

"How can it be else but true, Prissy? Would he say a lie? For look you, Prissy, an' it were not true, it *would* be a lie. It surely would be. Now think on't. For all things that be not true, be lies—thou canst make naught else out of it."

It was a good tight argument, without a leak in it anywhere; and it left Prissy's half-doubts not a leg to stand on. She considered a moment, then put the king upon his honor with the simple remark—

"If thou art truly the king, then I believe thee."

"I am truly the king."

This settled the matter. His majesty's royalty was accepted without further question or discussion, and the two little girls began at once to inquire into how he came to be where he was, and how he came to be so unroyally clad, and whither he was bound, and all about his affairs. It was a mighty relief to him to pour out his troubles where they would not be scoffed at or doubted; so he told his tale with feeling, forgetting even his hunger for the time; and it was received with the deepest and tenderest sympathy by the gentle little maids. But when he got down to his latest experiences and they learned how long he had been without food, they cut him short and hurried him away to the farm house to find a breakfast for him.

"TOOK A GOOD SATISFYING STARE."

The king was cheerful and happy, now, and said to himself, "When I am come to mine own again, I will always honor little children, remembering how that these trusted me and believed in me in my time of trouble, whilst they that were older, and thought themselves wiser, mocked at me and held me for a liar."

The children's mother received the king kindly, and was full of pity; for his forlorn condition and apparently crazed intellect touched her womanly heart. She was a widow, and rather poor; consequently she had seen trouble enough to enable her to feel for the unfortunate. She imagined that the demented boy had wandered away from his friends or keepers; so she tried to find out whence he had come, in order that she might take measures to return him; but all her references to

"THE CHILDREN'S MOTHER RECEIVED THE KING KINDLY."

neighboring towns and villages, and all her inquiries in the same line, went for nothing—the boy's face, and his answers, too, showed that the things she was talking of were not familiar to him. He spoke earnestly and simply about court matters; and broke down, more than once, when speaking of the late king "his father;" but whenever the conversation changed to baser topics, he lost interest and became silent.

The woman was mightily puzzled; but she did not give up. As she proceeded with her cooking, she set herself to contriving devices to surprise the boy into betraying his real secret. She talked about cattle—he showed no concern; then about sheep—the same result—so her guess that he had been a shepherd boy was an error; she talked about mills; and about weavers, tinkers, smiths, trades and tradesmen of all sorts; and about Bedlam, and jails, and charitable retreats; but no matter, she was baffled at all points. Not altogether, either; for she argued that she had narrowed the thing down to domestic service. Yes, she was sure she was on the right track, now—he must have been a house servant. So she led up to that. But the result was discouraging.

The subject of sweeping appeared to weary him; fire-building failed to stir him; scrubbing and scouring awoke no enthusiasm. Then the goodwife touched, with a perishing hope, and rather as a matter of form, upon the subject of cooking. To her surprise, and her vast delight, the king's face lighted at once! Ah, she had hunted him down at last, she thought; and she was right proud, too, of the devious shrewdness and tact which had accomplished it.

Her tired tongue got a chance to rest, now; for the king's, inspired by gnawing hunger and the fragrant smells that came from the sputtering pots and pans, turned itself loose, and delivered itself up to such an eloquent dissertation upon certain toothsome dishes, that within three minutes the woman said to herself, "Of a truth I was right—he hath holpen in a kitchen!" Then he broadened his bill of fare, and discussed it with such appreciation and animation, that the goodwife said to herself, "Good lack! how can he know so many dishes, and so fine ones withal? For these belong only upon the tables of the rich and great. Ah, now I see! ragged outcast as he is, he must have served in the palace before his reason went astray; yes, he must have helped in the very kitchen of the king himself! I will test him."

Full of eagerness to prove her sagacity, she told the king to mind the cooking a moment—hinting that he might manufacture and add a dish or two, if he chose—then she went out of the room and gave her children a sign to follow after. The king muttered—

"Another English king had a commission like to this, in a bygone time—it is nothing against my dignity to undertake an office which the great Alfred stooped to assume. But I will try to better serve my trust than he; for he let the cakes burn."

The intent was good, but the performance was not answerable to it; for this king, like the other one, soon fell into deep thinkings concerning his vast affairs, and the same calamity resulted—the cookery got burned. The woman returned in time to save the breakfast from entire destruction; and she promptly brought the king out of his dreams with a brisk and cordial tongue-lashing. Then, seeing how troubled he was, over his violated trust, she softened at once and was all goodness and gentleness toward him.

The boy made a hearty and satisfying meal, and was greatly refreshed and gladdened by it. It was a meal which was distinguished by this curious feature, that rank was waived on both sides; yet neither recipient of the favor was aware that it had been extended. The goodwife had intended to feed this young tramp with broken victuals in a corner, like any other tramp, or like a dog; but she was so remorseful for the scolding she had given him, that she did what

"BROUGHT THE KING OUT OF HIS DREAMS."

she could to atone for it by allowing him to sit at the family table and eat with his betters, on ostensible terms of equality with them; and the king, on his side, was so remorseful for having broken his trust, after the family had been so kind to him, that he forced himself to atone for it by humbling himself to the family level, instead of requiring the woman and her children to stand and wait upon him while he occupied their table in the solitary state due to his birth and dignity. It does us all good to unbend sometimes. This good woman was made happy all the day long by the applauses which she got out of herself for her magnanimous condescension to a tramp; and the king was just as self-complacent over his gracious humility toward a humble peasant woman.

When breakfast was over, the housewife told the king to wash up the dishes. This command was a staggerer, for a moment, and the king came near rebelling; but then he said to himself, "Alfred the Great watched the cakes; doubtless he would have washed the dishes, too—therefore will I essay it."

He made a sufficiently poor job of it; and to his surprise, too, for the cleaning of wooden spoons and trenchers had seemed an easy thing to do. It was a tedious and troublesome piece of work, but he finished it at last. He was becoming impatient to get away on his journey now; however, he was not to lose this thrifty dame's society so easily. She furnished him some little odds and ends of employment, which he got through with after a fair fashion and with some credit. Then she set him and the little girls to paring some winter apples; but he was so awkward at this service, that she retired him from it and gave him a butcher knife to grind. Afterward she kept him carding

"GAVE HIM A BUTCHER KNIFE TO GRIND."

wool until he began to think he had laid the good King Alfred about far enough in the shade for the present, in the matter of showy menial heroisms that would read picturesquely in story-books and histories, and so he was half minded to resign. And when, just after the noonday dinner, the goodwife gave him a basket of kittens to drown, he did resign. At least he was just going to resign—for he felt that he must draw the line somewhere, and it seemed to him that to draw it at kitten-drowning was about the right thing—when there was an interruption. The interruption was John Canty—with a pedlar's pack on his back—and Hugo!

The king discovered these rascals approaching the front gate before they had had a chance to see him; so he said nothing about drawing the line, but took up his basket of kittens and stepped quietly out the back way, without a word. He left the creatures in an outhouse, and hurried on, into a narrow lane at the rear.

CHAPTER 20

THE HIGH HEDGE hid him from the house, now; and so, under the impulse of a deadly fright, he let out all his forces and sped toward a wood in the distance. He never looked back until he had almost gained the shelter of the forest; then he turned and descried two figures in the distance. That was sufficient; he did not wait to scan them critically, but hurried on, and never abated his pace till he was far within the twilight depths of the wood. Then he stopped; being persuaded that he was now tolerably safe. He listened intently, but the stillness was profound and solemn—awful, even, and depressing to the spirits. At wide intervals his straining ear did detect sounds, but they were so remote, and hollow, and mysterious, that they seemed not to be real sounds, but only the moaning and complaining ghosts of departed ones. So the sounds were yet more dreary than the silence which they interrupted.

It was his purpose, in the beginning, to stay where he was, the rest of the day; but a chill soon invaded his perspiring body, and he was at last obliged to resume movement in order to get warm. He struck straight through the forest, hoping to pierce to a road presently, but he was disappointed in this. He traveled on and on; but the further he went, the denser the wood became, apparently. The gloom began to thicken, by and by, and the king realized that the night was coming on. It made him shudder to think of spending it in such an uncanny place; so he tried to hurry faster, but he only made the less speed, for he could not now see well enough to choose his steps judiciously; consequently he kept tripping over roots and tangling himself in vines and briers.

And how glad he was when at last he caught the glimmer of a light! He approached it warily, stopping often to look about him and listen. It came from an unglazed window-opening in a shabby little hut. He heard a voice, now, and

felt a disposition to run and hide; but he changed his mind at once, for this voice was praying, evidently. He glided to the one window of the hut, raised himself on tiptoe, and stole a glance within. The room was small; its floor was the natural "HE TURNED AND DESCRIED TWO FIGURES." earth, beaten hard by use; in a corner was a bed of rushes and a ragged blanket or two; near it was a pail, a cup, a basin, and two or three pots and pans; there was a short bench and a three-legged stool; on the hearth the remains of a faggot fire were smouldering; before a shrine, which was lighted by a single candle, knelt an aged man, and on an old wooden box at his side, lay an open book and a human skull. The man was of large, bony frame; his hair and whiskers were very long and snowy white; he was clothed in a robe of sheepskins which reached from his neck to his heels.

"A holy hermit!" said the king to himself; "now am I indeed fortunate."

The hermit rose from his knees; the king knocked. A deep voice responded—

"Enter!—but leave sin behind, for the ground whereon thou shalt stand is holy!"

The king entered, and paused. The hermit turned a pair of gleaming, unrestful eyes upon him, and said—

"Who art thou?"

"THE KING ENTERED, AND PAUSED."

"I am the king," came the answer, with placid simplicity.

"Welcome, king!" cried the hermit, with enthusiasm. Then, bustling about with feverish activity, and constantly saying "welcome, welcome," he arranged his bench, seated the king on it, by the hearth, threw some faggots on the fire, and finally fell to pacing the floor, with a nervous stride.

"Welcome! Many have sought sanctuary here, but they were not worthy, and were turned away. But a king who casts his crown away, and despises the vain splendors of his office, and clothes his body in rags, to devote his life to holiness and the mortification of the flesh—he is worthy, he is welcome!—Here shall he abide all his days till death come." The king hastened to interrupt and explain, but the hermit paid no attention to him—did not even hear him, apparently, but went right on with his talk, with a raised voice and a growing energy. "And thou shalt be at peace here. None shall find out thy refuge to disquiet thee with supplications to return to that empty and foolish life which God hath moved thee to abandon. Thou shalt pray, here; thou shalt study the Book; thou shalt meditate upon the follies and delusions of this world, and upon the sublimities of the world to come; thou shalt feed upon crusts and herbs, and scourge thy body with whips, daily, to the purifying of thy soul. Thou shalt wear a hair shirt next thy skin; thou shalt drink water, only; and thou shalt be at peace; yes, wholly at peace; for whoso comes to seek thee shall go his way again, baffled; he shall not find thee, he shall not molest thee."

The old man, still pacing back and forth, ceased to speak aloud, and began to mutter. The king seized this opportunity to state his case; and he did it with an eloquence inspired by uneasiness and apprehension. But the hermit went on muttering, and gave no heed. And still muttering, he approached the king and said, impressively—

"'Sh! I will tell you a secret!" He bent down to impart it, but checked himself, and assumed a listening attitude. After a moment or two he went on tiptoe to the window-opening, put his head out and peered around in the gloaming, then came tiptoeing back again, put his face close down to the king's, and whispered—

"I am an archangel!"

The king started violently, and said to himself, "Would God I were with the outlaws again; for lo, now am I the prisoner of a madman!" His apprehensions were heightened, and they showed plainly in his face. In a low, excited voice, the hermit continued—

"I see you feel my atmosphere! There's awe in your face! None may be in this atmosphere and not be thus affected; for it is the very atmosphere of heaven. I go thither and return, in the twinkling of an eye. I was made an archangel on this very spot, it is five years ago, by angels sent from heaven to confer that awful dignity. Their presence filled this place with an intolerable brightness. And they knelt to me,

king! yes, they knelt to me! for I was greater than they. I have walked
in the courts of heaven, and held speech with the patriarchs. Touch
my hand—be not afraid—touch it. There—now thou hast touched a
hand which has been clasped by Abraham, and Isaac and Jacob! For I
have walked in the golden courts, I have seen the Deity face to face!''

"I WILL TELL YOU A SECRET!"

He paused, to give this speech effect; then his face suddenly changed,
and he started to his feet again, saying, with angry energy, "Yes, I am
an archangel; *a mere archangel!*—I that might have been Pope! It is
verily true. I was told it from heaven in a dream, twenty years ago; ah,
yes, I was to be Pope!—and I *should* have been Pope, for heaven had
said it—but the king dissolved my religious house, and I, poor obscure
unfriended monk, was cast homeless upon the world, robbed of my
mighty destiny!" Here he began to mumble again, and beat his fore-

head in futile rage, with his fist; now and then articulating a venomous curse, and now and then a pathetic "Wherefore I am naught but an archangel—I that should have been Pope!"

So he went on, for an hour, whilst the poor little king sat and suffered. Then all at once the old man's frenzy departed, and he became all gentleness. His voice softened, he came down out of his clouds, and fell to prattling along so simply and so humanly, that he soon won the king's heart completely. The old devotee moved the boy nearer to the fire and made him comfortable; doctored his small bruises and abrasions with a deft and tender hand; and then set about preparing and cooking a supper—chatting pleasantly all the time, and occasionally stroking the lad's cheek or patting his head, in such a gently caressing way that in a little while all the fear and repulsion inspired by the archangel were changed to reverence and affection for the man.

"CHATTING PLEASANTLY ALL THE TIME."

This happy state of things continued while the two ate the supper; then, after a prayer before the shrine, the hermit put the boy to bed, in a small adjoining room, tucking him in as snugly and lovingly as a mother might; and so, with a parting caress, left him and sat down by the fire, and began to poke the brands about in an absent and aimless way. Presently he paused; then tapped his forehead several times with his fingers, as if trying to recal some thought which had escaped from his mind. Apparently he was unsuccessful. Now he started quickly up, and entered his guest's room, and said—

"Thou art king?"

"Yes," was the response, drowsily uttered.

"What king?"

"Of England."

"Of England! Then Henry is gone!"

"Alack, it is so. I am his son."

A black frown settled down upon the hermit's face, and he clenched his bony hands with a vindictive energy. He stood a few moments, breathing fast and swallowing repeatedly, then said in a husky voice—

"Dost know it was he that turned us out into the world houseless and homeless?"

There was no response. The old man bent down and scanned the boy's reposeful face and listened to his placid breathing. "He sleeps—sleeps soundly;" and the frown vanished away and gave place to an expression of evil satisfaction. A smile flitted across the dreaming boy's features. The hermit muttered, "So—his heart is happy;" and he turned away. He went stealthily about the place, seeking here and there for something; now and then halting to listen, now and then jerking his head around and casting a quick glance toward the bed; and always muttering, always mumbling to himself. At last he found what he seemed to want—a rusty old butcher knife and a whetstone. Then he crept to his place by the fire, sat himself down, and began to whet the knife softly on the stone, still muttering, mumbling, ejaculating. The winds sighed around the lonely place, the mysterious voices of the night floated by out of the distances, the shining eyes of venturesome mice and rats peered out at the old man from cracks and coverts, but he went on with his work, rapt, absorbed, and noted none of these things.

At long intervals he drew his thumb along the edge of his knife, and nodded his head with satisfaction. "It grows sharper," he said; "yes, it grows sharper."

He took no note of the flight of time, but worked tranquilly on, entertaining himself with his thoughts, which broke out occasionally in articulate speech:

"His father wrought us evil, he destroyed us—and is gone down into the eternal fires! Yes, down into the eternal fires! He escaped us—but it was God's will, yes it was God's will, we must not repine. But he hath not escaped the fires! no, he hath not escaped the fires, the consuming, un-pitying, remorseless fires

"DREW HIS THUMB ALONG THE EDGE."

—and *they* are everlasting!"

And so he wrought; and still wrought; mumbling—chuckling a low rasping chuckle, at times—and at times breaking again into words:

"It was his father that did it all. I am but an archangel—but for him, I should be Pope!"

The king stirred. The hermit sprang noiselessly to the bedside, and went down upon his knees, bending over the prostrate form with his knife uplifted. The boy stirred again; his eyes came open for an instant, but there was no speculation in them, they saw nothing; the next moment his tranquil breathing showed that his sleep was sound once more.

The hermit watched and listened, for a time, keeping his position and scarcely breathing; then he slowly lowered his arm, and presently crept away, saying,—

"It is long past midnight—it is not best that he should cry out, lest by accident some one be passing."

He glided about his hovel, gathering a rag here, a thong there, and another one yonder; then he returned, and by careful and gentle handling, he managed to tie the king's ankles together without waking him. Next he essayed to tie the wrists; he made several attempts to cross them, but the boy always drew one hand or the other away, just as the cord was ready to be applied; but at last, when the archangel was almost ready to despair, the boy crossed his hands himself, and the next moment they were bound. Now a bandage was passed under the sleeper's chin and brought up over his head and tied fast—and so softly, so gradually, and so deftly were the knots drawn together and compacted, that the boy slept peacefully through it all without stirring.

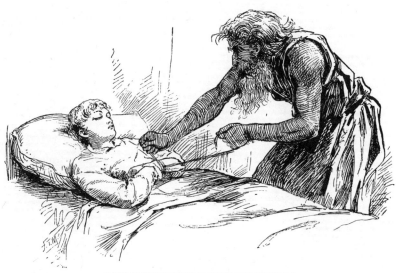

"THE NEXT MOMENT THEY WERE BOUND."

CHAPTER 21

HENDON TO THE RESCUE

THE OLD MAN glided away, stooping, stealthy, cat-like, and brought the low bench. He seated himself upon it, half his body in the dim and flickering light, and the other half in shadow; and so, with his craving eyes bent upon the slumbering boy, he kept his patient vigil there, heedless of the drift of time, and softly whetted his knife, and mumbled and chuckled; and in aspect and attitude he resembled nothing so much as a grisly, monstrous spider, gloating over some hapless insect that lay bound and helpless in his web.

After a long while, the old man, who was still gazing,—yet not seeing, his mind having settled into a dreamy abstraction,—observed on a sudden, that the boy's eyes were open—wide open and staring! —staring up in frozen horror at the knife. The smile of a gratified devil crept over the old man's face, and he said, without changing his attitude or his occupation—

"Son of Henry the Eighth, hast thou prayed?"

The boy struggled helplessly in his bonds; and at the same time forced a smothered sound through his closed jaws, which the hermit chose to interpret as an affirmative answer to his question.

"Then pray again. Pray the prayer for the dying!"

A shudder shook the boy's frame, and his face blenched. Then he struggled again to free himself—turning and twisting himself this way and that; tugging frantically, fiercely, desperately—but uselessly—to burst his fetters: and all the while the old ogre smiled down upon him, and nodded his head, and placidly whetted his knife; mumbling, from

time to time, "The moments are precious, they are few and precious—
pray the prayer for the dying!"

The boy uttered a despairing groan, and ceased from his struggles,
panting. The tears came, then, and trickled, one after the other, down
his face; but this piteous sight wrought no softening effect upon the
savage old man.

The dawn was coming, now; the hermit observed it, and spoke up
sharply, with a touch of nervous apprehension in his voice—

"I may not indulge this ecstasy longer! The night is already gone. It
seems but a moment—only a moment; would it had endured a year!
Seed of the Church's spoiler, close thy perishing eyes, an' thou fearest
to look upon . . . . ."

The rest was lost in inarticulate mutterings. The old man sunk upon
his knees, his knife in his hand, and bent himself over the moaning
boy—

"HE SUNK UPON HIS KNEES, HIS KNIFE IN HAND."

Hark! There was a sound of voices near the cabin—the knife
dropped from the hermit's hand; he cast a sheepskin over the boy and
started up, trembling. The sounds increased, and presently the voices
became rough and angry; then came blows, and cries for help; then a

clatter of swift footsteps, retreating. Immediately came a succession of thundering knocks upon the cabin door, followed by—

"Hullo-o-o! Open! And despatch, in the name of all the devils!"

O, this was the blessedest sound that had ever made music in the king's ears; for it was Miles Hendon's voice!

The hermit, grinding his teeth in impotent rage, moved swiftly out of the bedchamber, closing the door behind him; and straightway the king heard a talk, to this effect, proceeding from the "chapel:"

"Homage and greeting, reverend sir! Where is the boy—*my* boy?"

"What boy, friend?"

"What boy! Lie me no lies, sir priest, play me no deceptions!—I am not in the humor for it. Near to this place I caught the scoundrels who I judged did steal him from me, and I made them confess; they said he was at large again, and they had tracked him to your door. They showed me his very footprints. Now palter no more; for look you, holy sir, an' thou produce him not— Where is the boy?"

"O, good sir, peradventure you mean the ragged regal vagrant that tarried here the night. If such as you take interest in such as he, know, then, that I have sent him of an errand. He will be back anon."

"How soon? How soon? Come, waste not the time—can not I over-take him? How soon will he be back?"

"Thou needst not stir; he will return quickly."

"So be it, then. I will try to wait. But stop!—*you* sent him of an errand?—you! Verily this is a lie—he would not go. He would pull thy old beard, an' thou didst offer him such an insolence. Thou hast lied, friend; thou hast surely lied! He would not go for thee nor for any man."

"For any *man*—no; haply not. But I am not a man."

"*What!* Now o' God's name what art thou, then?"

"It is a secret—mark thou reveal it not. I am an archangel!"

There was a tremendous ejaculation from Miles Hendon—not altogether unprofane—followed by—

"This doth well and truly account for his complaisance! Right well I knew he would budge nor hand nor foot in the menial service of any mortal; but lord, even a king must obey when an archangel gives the word o' command! Let me—'sh! What noise was that?"

All this while the little king had been yonder, alternately quaking with terror and trembling with hope; and all the while, too, he had thrown all the strength he could into his anguished moanings, constantly expecting them to reach Hendon's ear, but always realizing, with bitterness, that they failed, or at least made no impression. So this last remark of his servant came as comes a reviving breath from fresh fields to the dying; and he exerted himself once more, and with all his energy, just as the hermit was saying—

"Noise? I heard only the wind."

"Mayhap it was. Yes, doubtless that was it. I have been hearing it faintly all the—there it is again! It is not the wind! What an odd sound! Come, we will hunt it out!"

"THEN FOLLOWED A CONFUSION OF KICKS AND PLUNGINGS."

Now the king's joy was nearly insupportable. His tired lungs did their utmost—and hopefully, too—but the sealed jaws and the muffling sheepskin sadly crippled the effort. Then the poor fellow's heart sank, to hear the hermit say—

"Ah, it came from without—I think from the copse yonder. Come, I will lead the way."

The king heard the two pass out, talking; heard their footsteps die quickly away—then he was alone with a boding, brooding, awful silence.

"THE FETTERED LITTLE KING."

It seemed an age till he heard the steps and voices approaching again—and this time he heard an added sound,—the trampling of hoofs, apparently. Then he heard Hendon say—

"I will not wait longer. I *cannot* wait longer. He has lost his way in this thick wood. Which direction took he? Quick—point it out to me."

"He—but wait; I will go with thee."

"Good—good! Why, truly thou art better than thy looks. Marry I do think there's not another archangel with so right a heart as thine. Wilt ride? Wilt take the wee donkey that's for my boy, or wilt thou fork thy holy legs over this ill-conditioned slave of a mule that I have provided for myself?—and had been cheated in, too, had he cost but the indifferent sum of a month's usury on a brass farthing let to a tinker out of work."

"No—ride thy mule, and lead thine ass; I am surer on mine own feet, and will walk."

"Then prithee mind the little beast for me while I take my life in my hands and make what success I may toward mounting the big one."

Then followed a confusion of kicks, cuffs, tramplings and plungings, accompanied by a thunderous intermingling of volleyed curses, and finally a bitter apostrophe to the mule, which must have broken its spirit, for hostilities seemed to cease from that moment.

With unutterable misery the fettered little king heard the voices and footsteps fade away and die out. All hope forsook him, now, for the moment, and a dull despair settled down upon his heart. "My only friend is deceived and got rid of," he said; "the hermit will return and—" He finished with a gasp; and at once fell to struggling so frantically with his bonds again, that he shook off the smothering sheepskin.

And now he heard the door open! The sound chilled him to the marrow—already he seemed to feel the knife at his throat. Horror made him close his eyes; horror made him open them again—and before him stood John Canty and Hugo!

He would have said "Thank God!" if his jaws had been free.

A moment or two later his limbs were at liberty, and his captors, each gripping him by an arm, were hurrying him with all speed through the forest.

CHAPTER 22

ONCE MORE "King Foo-foo the First" was roving with the tramps and outlaws, a butt for their coarse jests and dull-witted railleries, and sometimes the victim of small spitefulnesses at the hands of Canty and Hugo when the Ruffler's back was turned. None but Canty and Hugo really disliked him. Some of the others liked him, and all admired his pluck and spirit. During two or three days, Hugo, in whose ward and charge the king was, did what he covertly could to make the boy uncomfortable; and at night, during the customary orgies, he amused the company by putting small indignities upon him—always as if by accident. Twice he stepped upon the king's toes—accidentally—and the king, as became his royalty, was contemptuously unconscious of it and indifferent to it; but the third time Hugo entertained himself in that way, the king felled him to the ground with a cudgel, to the prodigious delight of the tribe. Hugo, consumed with anger and shame, sprang up, seized a cudgel, and came at his small adversary in a fury. Instantly a ring was formed around the gladiators, and the betting and cheering began. But poor Hugo stood no chance whatever. His frantic and lubberly 'prentice-work found but a poor market for itself when pitted against an arm which had been trained by the first masters of Europe in single-stick, quarter-staff, and every art and trick of swordsmanship. The little king stood, alert but at graceful ease, and caught and turned aside the thick rain of blows with a facility and precision which set the motley on-lookers

wild with admiration; and every now and then, when his practiced
eye detected an opening, and a lightning-swift rap upon Hugo's head
followed as a result, the storm of cheers and laughter that swept the
place was something wonderful to hear. At the end of fifteen minutes,
Hugo, all battered, bruised, and the target for a pitiless bombardment
of ridicule, slunk from the field; and the unscathed hero of the fight
was seized and borne aloft upon the shoulders of the joyous rabble to
the place of honor beside the Ruffler, where with vast ceremony he
was crowned King of the Game-Cocks; his meaner title being at the
same time solemnly canceled and annulled, and a decree of banishment from the gang pronounced against any who should thenceforth
utter it.

"HUGO STOOD NO CHANCE."

All attempts to make the king serviceable to the troop had failed.
He had stubbornly refused to act; moreover he was always trying to
escape. He had been thrust into an unwatched kitchen, the first day
of his return; he not only came forth empty handed, but tried to rouse

the housemates. He was sent out with a tinker to help him at his work; he would not work; moreover he threatened the tinker with his own soldering-iron; and finally both Hugo and the tinker found their hands full with the mere matter of keeping him from getting away. He delivered the thunders of his royalty upon the heads of all who hampered his liberties or tried to force him to service. He was sent out, in Hugo's charge, in company with a slatternly woman and a diseased baby, to beg; but the result was not encouraging—he declined to plead for the mendicants, or be a party to their cause in any way.

Thus several days went by; and the miseries of this tramping life, and the weariness and sordidness and meanness and vulgarity of it, became gradually and steadily so intolerable to the captive that he began at last to feel that his release from the hermit's knife must prove only a temporary respite from death, at best.

But at night, in his dreams, these things were forgotten, and he was on his throne, and master again. This, of course, intensified the sufferings of the awakening—so the mortifications of each succeeding morning of the few that passed between his return to bondage and the combat with Hugo, grew bitterer and bitterer, and harder and harder to bear.

The morning after that combat, Hugo got up with a heart filled with vengeful purposes against the king. He had two plans, in particular. One was to inflict upon the lad what would be, to his proud spirit and "imagined" royalty, a peculiar humiliation; and if he failed to accomplish this, his other plan was to put a crime of some kind upon the king and then betray him into the implacable clutches of the law.

In pursuance of the first plan, he purposed to put a "clime" upon the king's leg; rightly judging that that would mortify him to the last and perfect degree; and as soon as the clime should operate, he meant to get Canty's help, and *force* the king to expose his leg in the highway and beg for alms. "Clime" was the cant term for a sore, artificially created. To make a clime, the operator made a paste or poultice of unslaked lime, soap, and the rust of old iron, and spread it upon a piece of leather, which was then bound tightly upon the leg. This would presently fret off the skin, and make the flesh raw and angry-looking; blood was then rubbed upon the limb, which, being fully dried, took on a dark and repulsive color. Then a bandage of soiled rags was put on in a cleverly careless way which would allow the hideous ulcer to be seen and move the compassion of the passer-by.*

Hugo got the help of the tinker whom the king had cowed with the soldering-iron; they took the boy out on a tinkering tramp, and as soon as they were out of sight of the camp they threw him down and the tinker held him while Hugo bound the poultice tight and fast upon his leg.

The king raged and stormed, and promised to hang the two the moment the sceptre was in his hand again; but they kept a firm grip

"HUGO BOUND THE POULTICE TIGHT AND FAST."

upon him and enjoyed his impotent strugglings and jeered at his threats. This continued until the poultice began to bite; and in no long time its work would have been perfected, if there had been no interruption. But there was; for about this time the "slave" who had made the speech denouncing England's laws, appeared on the scene and put an end to the enterprise, and stripped off the poultice and bandage.

*From "The English Rogue;" London, 1665.

The king wanted to borrow his deliverer's cudgel and warm the jackets of the two rascals on the spot; but the man said no, it would bring trouble—leave the matter till night; the whole tribe being together, then, the outside world would not venture to interfere or interrupt. He marched the party back to camp and reported the affair to the Ruffler, who listened, pondered, and then decided that the king should not be again detailed to beg, since it was plain he was worthy of something higher and better—wherefore, on the spot he promoted him from the mendicant rank and appointed him to steal!

Hugo was overjoyed. He had already tried to make the king steal, and failed; but there would be no more trouble of that sort, now, for of course the king would not dream of defying a distinct command delivered directly from headquarters. So he planned a raid for that very afternoon, purposing to get the king in the law's grip in the course of it; and to do it, too, with such ingenious strategy, that it should seem to be accidental and unintentional; for the King of the Game-Cocks was popular, now, and the gang might not deal over-gently with an unpopular member who played so serious a treachery upon him as the delivering him over to the common enemy, the law.

Very well. All in good time Hugo strolled off to a neighboring village with his prey; and the two drifted slowly up and down one street after another, the one watching sharply for a sure chance to achieve his evil purpose, and the other watching as sharply for a chance to dart away and get free of his infamous captivity forever.

Both threw away some tolerably fair-looking opportunities; for both, in their secret hearts, were resolved to make absolutely sure work this time, and neither meant to allow his fevered desires to seduce him into any venture that had much uncertainty about it.

Hugo's chance came first. For at last a woman approached who carried a fat package of some sort in a basket. Hugo's eyes sparkled with sinful pleasure as he said to himself, "Breath o' my life, an' I can but put *that* upon him, 'tis good-den and God keep thee, King of the Game-Cocks!" He waited and watched—outwardly patient, but inwardly consuming with excitement—till the woman had passed by, and the time was ripe; then said, in a low voice—

"Tarry here till I come again," and darted stealthily after the prey.

The king's heart was filled with joy—he could make his escape, now, if Hugo's quest only carried him far enough away.

"TARRY HERE TILL I
COME AGAIN."

But he was to have no such luck. Hugo crept behind the woman, snatched the package, and came running back, wrapping it in an old piece of blanket which he carried on his arm. The hue and cry was raised in a moment, by the woman, who knew her loss by the lightening of her burden, although she had not seen the pilfering done. Hugo thrust the bundle into the king's hands without halting, saying,—

"Now speed ye after me with the rest, and cry 'Stop thief!' but mind ye lead them astray!"

The next moment Hugo turned a corner and darted down a crooked alley,—and in another moment or two he lounged into view again, looking innocent and indifferent, and took up a position behind a post to watch results.

The insulted king threw the bundle on the ground; and the blanket fell away from it just as the woman arrived, with an augmenting crowd at her heels; she seized the king's wrist with one hand,

snatched up her bundle with the other, and began to pour out a
tirade of abuse upon the boy while he struggled, without success,
to free himself from her grip.

Hugo had seen enough—his enemy was captured and the law
would get him, now—so he slipped away, jubilant and chuckling,
and wended campwards, framing a judicious version of the matter to
give to the Ruffler's crew as he strode along.

"THE KING SPRANG TO HIS DELIVERER'S SIDE."

The king continued to struggle in the woman's strong grasp, and
now and then cried out, in vexation—

"Unhand me, thou foolish creature; it was not I that bereaved
thee of thy paltry goods."

The crowd closed around, threatening the king and calling him
names; a brawny blacksmith, in leather apron, and sleeves rolled to
his elbows, made a reach for him, saying he would trounce him well,

for a lesson; but just then a long sword flashed in the air and fell
with convincing force upon the man's arm, flat-side down, the fantastic owner of it remarking pleasantly at the same time—

"Marry, good souls, let us proceed gently, not with ill blood and
uncharitable words. This is matter for the law's consideration, not
private and unofficial handling. Loose thy hold from the boy,
goodwife."

The blacksmith averaged the stalwart soldier with a glance, then
went muttering away, rubbing his arm; the woman released the boy's
wrist reluctantly; the crowd eyed the stranger unlovingly, but pru-
dently closed their mouths. The king sprang to his deliverer's side,
with flushed cheeks and sparkling eyes, exclaiming—

"Thou hast lagged sorely, but thou comest in good season, now,
Sir Miles; carve me this rabble to rags!"

CHAPTER 23

H ENDON FORCED back a smile, and bent down and whispered in the king's ear—

"Softly, softly, my prince, wag thy tongue warily—nay, suffer it not to wag at all. Trust in me—all shall go well in the end." Then he added, to himself: "*Sir* Miles! Bless me, I had totally forgot I was a knight! Lord, how marvelous a thing it is, the grip his memory doth take upon his quaint and crazy fancies! . . . . . . An empty and foolish title is mine, and yet it is something to have deserved it; for I think it is more honor to be held worthy to be a spectre-knight in his Kingdom of Dreams and Shadows, than to be held base enough to be an earl in some of the *real* kingdoms of this world."

The crowd fell apart to admit a constable, who approached and was about to lay his hand upon the king's shoulder, when Hendon said—

"Gently, good friend, withhold your hand—he shall go peaceably; I am responsible for that. Lead on, we will follow."

The officer led, with the woman and her bundle; Miles and the king followed after, with the crowd at their heels. The king was inclined to rebel; but Hendon said to him in a low voice—

"Reflect, sire—your laws are the wholesome breath of your own royalty; shall their source resist them, yet require the branches to respect them? Apparently one of these laws has been broken; when the king is on his throne again, can it ever grieve him to remember that when he was seemingly a private person he loyally sunk the king in the citizen and submitted to its authority?"

"Thou art right; say no more; thou shalt see that whatsoever the king of England requires a subject to suffer under the law, he will himself suffer while he holdeth the station of a subject."

When the woman was called upon to testify before the justice of

"GENTLY, GOOD FRIEND."

the peace, she swore that the small prisoner at the bar was the person who had committed the theft; there was none able to show the contrary, so the king stood convicted. The bundle was now unrolled, and when the contents proved to be a plump little dressed pig, the judge looked troubled, whilst Hendon turned pale, and his body was thrilled with an electric shiver of dismay; but the king remained unmoved, protected by his ignorance. The judge meditated, during an ominous pause, then turned to the woman, with the question—

"What dost thou hold this property to be worth?"

The woman curtsied and replied—

"Three shillings and eightpence, your worship—I could not abate a penny and set forth the value honestly."

The justice glanced around uncomfortably upon the crowd, then nodded to the constable and said—

"Clear the court and close the doors."

It was done. None remained but the two officials, the accused, the accuser, and Miles Hendon. This latter was rigid and colorless, and on his forehead big drops of cold sweat gathered, broke and blended together, and trickled down his face. The judge turned to the woman again, and said, in a compassionate voice—

" 'Tis a poor ignorant lad, and mayhap was driven hard by hunger, for these be grievous times for the unfortunate; mark you, he hath not an evil face—but when hunger driveth—Good woman! dost know that when one steals a thing above the value of thirteen pence ha'penny the law saith he shall *hang* for it!"

The little king started, wide-eyed with consternation, but controlled himself and held his peace; but not so the woman. She sprang to her feet, shaking with fright, and cried out—

"O, good lack, what have I done! God-a-mercy, I would not hang the poor thing for the whole world! Ah, save me from this, your worship—what shall I do, what *can* I do?"

The justice maintained his judicial composure, and simply said—

"Doubtless it is allowable to revise the value, since it is not yet writ upon the record."

"Then in God's name call the pig eightpence, and heaven bless the day that freed my conscience of this awesome thing!"

Miles Hendon forgot all decorum in his delight; and surprised the king and wounded his dignity, by throwing his arms around him and hugging him. The woman made her grateful adieux and started away with her pig; and when the constable opened the door for her, he followed her out into the narrow hall. The justice proceeded to write in his record book. Hendon, always alert, thought he would like to know why the officer followed the woman out; so he slipped softly into the dusky hall and listened. He heard a conversation to this effect—

"It is a fat pig, and promises good eating; I will buy it of thee; here is the eightpence."

"Eightpence, indeed! Thou'lt do no such thing. It cost me three shillings and eightpence, good honest coin of the last reign, that old Harry that's just dead ne'er touched nor tampered with. A fig for thy eightpence!"

"SHE SPRANG TO HER FEET."

"Stands the wind in that quarter? Thou wast under oath, and so swore falsely when thou saidst the value was but eightpence. Come straightway back with me before his worship, and answer for the crime!—and then the lad will hang."

"There, there, dear heart, say no more, I am content. Give me the eightpence, and hold thy peace about the matter."

The woman went off, crying; Hendon slipped back into the court room, and the constable presently followed, after hiding his prize in some convenient place. The justice wrote a while longer, then read the king a wise and kindly lecture, and sentenced him to a short imprisonment in the common jail, to be followed by a public flogging. The astounded king opened his mouth and was probably going to order the good judge to be beheaded on the spot; but he caught a warning sign from Hendon, and succeeded in closing his mouth again before he lost anything out of it. Hendon took him by the hand, now, made reverence to the justice, and the two departed in the wake of the constable toward the jail. The moment the street was reached, the inflamed monarch halted, snatched away his hand, and exclaimed—

"Idiot, dost imagine I will enter a common jail *alive?*"

Hendon bent down and said, somewhat sharply—

"*Will* you trust in me? Peace! and forbear to worsen our chances with dangerous speech. What God wills, will happen; thou canst not hurry it, thou canst not alter it; therefore wait, and be patient—'twill be time enow to rail or rejoice when what is to happen has happened."*

---

*See Notes to Chapter 23 at end of volume.

CHAPTER 24

THE ESCAPE

THE SHORT winter day was nearly ended. The streets were deserted, save for a few random stragglers, and these hurried straight along, with the intent look of people who were only anxious to accomplish their errands as quickly as possible and then snugly house themselves from the rising wind and the gathering twilight. They looked neither to the right nor the left; they paid no attention to our party, they did not even seem to see them. Edward the Sixth wondered if the spectacle of a king on his way to jail had ever encountered such marvelous indifference before. By and by the constable arrived at a deserted market-square and proceeded to cross it. When he had reached the middle of it, Hendon laid his hand upon his arm, and said in a low voice—

"Bide a moment, good sir, there is none in hearing, and I would say a word to thee."

"My duty forbids it, sir; prithee hinder me not, the night comes on."

"Stay, nevertheless, for the matter concerns thee nearly. Turn thy back a moment and seem not to see: *let this poor lad escape.*"

"This to me, sir! I arrest thee in—"

"Nay, be not too hasty. See thou be careful and commit no foolish error"—then he shut his voice down to a whisper, and said in the man's ear—"the pig thou hast purchased for eightpence may cost thee thy neck, man!"

The poor constable, taken by surprise, was speechless, at first, then found his tongue and fell to blustering and threatening; but Hendon was tranquil, and waited with patience till his breath was spent; then said—

"I have a liking to thee, friend, and would not willingly see thee

"THE PIG MAY COST THY NECK, MAN!"

come to harm. Observe, I heard it all—every word. I will prove it to thee." Then he repeated the conversation which the officer and the woman had had together in the hall, word for word, and ended with—

"There—have I set it forth correctly?—should not I be able to set it forth correctly before the judge, if occasion required?"

The man was dumb with fear and distress, for a moment; then he rallied and said with forced lightness—

" 'Tis making a mighty matter indeed, out of a jest; I but plagued the woman for mine amusement."

"Kept you the woman's pig for amusement?"

The man answered sharply—

"Naught else, good sir—I tell thee 'twas but a jest."

"I do begin to believe thee," said Hendon, with a perplexing mixture of mockery and half-conviction in his tone; "but tarry thou here a moment whilst I run and ask his worship—for nathless, he being a man experienced in law, in jests, in—"

He was moving away, still talking; the constable hesitated, fidgeted, spat out an oath or two, then cried out—

"Hold, hold, good sir—prithee wait a little—the judge! why, man, he hath no more sympathy with a jest than hath a dead corpse!— come, and we will speak further. Ods body! I seem to be in evil case— and all for an innocent and thoughtless pleasantry. I am a man of family; and my wife and little ones—List to reason, good your worship: what wouldst thou of me?"

"Only that thou be blind and dumb and paralytic whilst one may count a hundred thousand—counting slowly," said Hendon, with the expression of a man who asks but a reasonable favor, and that a very little one.

"BEAR ME UP, BEAR ME UP, SWEET SIR!"

"It is my destruction!" said the constable despairingly. "Ah, be reasonable, good sir; only look at this matter, on all its sides, and see how mere a jest it is—how manifestly and how plainly it is so. And even if one granted it were not a jest, it is a fault so small that e'en the grimmest penalty it could call forth would be but a rebuke and warning from the judge's lips."

Hendon replied with a solemnity which chilled the air about him—

"This jest of thine hath a name, in law—wot you what it is?"

"I knew it not! Peradventure I have been unwise. I never dreamed it had a name—ah, sweet heaven, I thought it was original."

"Yes, it hath a name. In the law this crime is called *Non compos mentis lex talionis sic transit gloria Mundi.*"

"Ah, my God!"

"And the penalty is death!"

"God be merciful to me, a sinner!"

"By advantage taken of one in fault, in dire peril, and at thy mercy, thou hast seized goods worth above thirteen pence ha'penny, paying but a trifle for the same; and this, in the eye of the law, is constructive barratry, misprision of treason, malfeasance in office, *ad hominem expurgatis in statu quo*—and the penalty is death by the halter, without ransom, commutation, or benefit of clergy."

"Bear me up, bear me up, sweet sir, my legs do fail me! Be thou merciful—spare me this doom, and I will turn my back and see naught that shall happen."

"Good! now thou'rt wise and reasonable. And thou'lt restore the pig?"

"I will, I will indeed—nor ever touch another, though heaven send it and an archangel fetch it. Go—I am blind for thy sake—I see nothing. I will say thou didst break in and wrest the prisoner from my hands by force. It is but a crazy, ancient door—I will batter it down myself betwixt midnight and the morning."

"Do it, good soul, no harm will come of it; the judge hath a loving charity for this poor lad, and will shed no tears and break no jailer's bones for his escape."

CHAPTER 25

As soon as Hendon and the king were out of sight of the constable, his majesty was instructed to hurry to a certain place outside the town, and wait there, whilst Hendon should go to the inn and settle his account. Half an hour later the two friends were blithely jogging eastward on Hendon's sorry steeds. The king was warm and comfortable, now, for he had cast his rags and clothed himself in the second-hand suit which Hendon had bought on London Bridge.

Hendon wished to guard against over-fatiguing the boy; he judged that hard journeys, irregular meals, and illiberal measures of sleep would be bad for his crazed mind; whilst rest, regularity, and moderate exercise would be pretty sure to hasten its cure; he longed to see the stricken intellect made well again and its diseased visions driven out of the tormented little head; therefore he resolved to move by easy stages toward the home whence he had so long been banished, instead of obeying the impulse of his impatience and hurrying along night and day.

When he and the king had journeyed about ten miles, they reached a considerable village, and halted there for the night, at a good inn. The former relations were resumed; Hendon stood behind the king's chair, while he dined, and waited upon him; undressed him when he was ready for bed; then took the floor for his own quarters, and slept athwart the door, rolled up in a blanket.

"JOGGING EASTWARD ON SORRY STEEDS."

The next day, and the day after, they jogged lazily along, talking over the adventures they had met since their separation, and mightily enjoying each other's narratives. Hendon detailed all his wide wanderings in search of the king, and described how the archangel had led him a fool's journey all over the forest, and taken him back to the hut, finally, when he found he could not get rid of him. Then—he said —the old man went into the bedchamber and came staggering back looking broken-hearted, and saying he had expected to find that the boy had returned and lain down in there to rest, but it was not so. Hendon had waited at the hut all day; hope of the king's return died out, then, and he departed upon the quest again.

"And old Sanctum Sanctorum *was* truly sorry your highness came not back," said Hendon; "I saw it in his face."

"Marry I will never doubt *that!*" said the king—and then told his own story; after which, Hendon was sorry he had not destroyed the archangel.

During the last day of the trip, Hendon's spirits were soaring. His tongue ran constantly. He talked about his old father, and his brother Arthur, and told of many things which illustrated their high and generous characters; he went into loving frenzies over his Edith, and was so gladhearted that he was even able to say some gentle and brotherly things about Hugh. He dwelt a deal on the coming meeting at Hendon Hall; what a surprise it would be to everybody, and what an outburst of thanksgiving and delight there would be.

It was a fair region, dotted with cottages and orchards, and the road led through broad pasture lands whose receding expanses, marked with gentle elevations and depressions, suggested the swelling and subsiding undulations of the sea. In the afternoon the returning prodigal made constant deflections from his course to see if by ascending some hillock he might not pierce the distance and catch a glimpse of his home. At last he was successful, and cried out excitedly—

"There is the village, my prince, and there is the Hall close by!

"THERE IS THE VILLAGE, MY PRINCE!"

You may see the towers from here; and that wood there—that is my father's park. Ah, *now* thou'lt know what state and grandeur be! A house with seventy rooms—think of that!—and seven and twenty servants! A brave lodging for such as we, is it not so?—Come, let us speed—my impatience will not brook further delay."

All possible hurry was made; still, it was after three o'clock before the village was reached. The travelers scampered through it, Hendon's tongue going all the time. "Here is the church—covered with the same ivy—none gone, none added." "Yonder is the inn, the old Red Lion,—and yonder is the marketplace." "Here is the May-pole, and here the pump—nothing is altered; nothing but the people, at any rate; ten years make a change in people; some of these I seem to know, but none know me." So his chat ran on. The end of the village was soon reached; then the travelers struck into a crooked, narrow road, walled in with tall hedges, and hurried briskly along it for a half mile, then passed into a vast flower garden through an imposing gateway whose huge stone pillars bore sculptured armorial devices. A noble mansion was before them.

"Welcome to Hendon Hall, my king!" exclaimed Miles. "Ah, 'tis a great day! My father and my brother, and the lady Edith will be so mad with joy that they will have eyes and tongues for none but me in the first transports of the meeting, and so thou'lt seem but coldly welcomed—but mind it not, 'twill soon seem otherwise; for when I say thou art my ward, and tell them how costly is my love for thee, thou'lt see them take thee to their breasts for Miles Hendon's sake, and make their house and hearts thy home forever after!"

The next moment Hendon sprang to the ground before the great door, helped the king down, then took him by the hand and rushed within. A few steps brought him to a spacious apartment; he entered, seated the king with more hurry than ceremony, then ran toward a young man who sat at a writing table in front of a generous fire of logs.

"Embrace me, Hugh," he cried, "and say thou'rt glad I am come again! and call our father, for home is not home till I shall touch his hand, and see his face, and hear his voice once more!"

But Hugh only drew back, after betraying a momentary surprise, and bent a grave stare upon the intruder—a stare which indicated somewhat of offended dignity, at first, then changed, in response to some inward thought or purpose, to an expression of marveling curiosity, mixed with a real or assumed compassion. Presently he said, in a mild voice—

"Thy wits seem touched, poor stranger; doubtless thou hast suffered privations and rude buffetings at the world's hands; thy looks and dress betoken it. Whom dost thou take me to be?"

"Take thee? Prithee for whom else than whom thou art? I take thee to be Hugh Hendon," said Miles, sharply.

" 'EMBRACE ME, HUGH,' HE CRIED."

The other continued, in the same soft tone—

"And whom dost thou imagine thyself to be?"

"Imagination hath naught to do with it! Dost thou pretend thou knowest me not for thy brother Miles Hendon?"

An expression of pleased surprise flitted across Hugh's face, and he exclaimed—

"What! thou art not jesting? Can the dead come to life? God be praised if it be so! Our poor lost boy restored to our arms after all these cruel years! Ah, it seems too good to be true, it *is* too good to be true—I charge thee, have pity, do not trifle with me! Quick— come to the light—let me scan thee well!"

He seized Miles by the arm, dragged him to the window, and began to devour him from head to foot with his eyes, turning him this way and that, and stepping briskly around him and about him to prove him from all points of view; whilst the returned prodigal, all aglow with gladness, smiled, laughed, and kept nodding his head and saying—

"Go on, brother, go on, and fear not; thou'lt find nor limb nor feature that cannot bide the test. Scour and scan me to thy content, my good old Hugh—I am indeed thy old Miles, thy same old Miles, thy lost brother, is't not so? Ah, 'tis a great day—I *said* 'twas a great day! Give me thy hand, give me thy cheek—lord, I am like to die of very joy!"

He was about to throw himself upon his brother; but Hugh put up his hand in dissent, then dropped his chin mournfully upon his breast, saying with emotion—

"Ah, God of his mercy give me strength to bear this grievous disappointment!"

"HUGH PUT UP HIS HAND IN DISSENT."

Miles, amazed, could not speak, for a moment; then he found his tongue, and cried out—

"*What* disappointment? Am I not thy brother?"

Hugh shook his head sadly, and said—

"I pray heaven it may prove so, and that other eyes may find the resemblances that are hid from mine. Alack, I fear me the letter spoke but too truly."

"What letter?"

"One that came from over sea, some six or seven years ago. It said my brother died in battle."

"It was a lie! Call thy father—he will know me."

"One may not call the dead."

"Dead?" Miles's voice was subdued, and his lips trembled. "My father dead!—O, this is heavy news. Half my new joy is withered now. Prithee let me see my brother Arthur—he will know me; he will know me and console me."

"He, also, is dead."

"God be merciful to me, a stricken man! Gone,—both gone—the worthy taken and the worthless spared, in me! Ah! I crave your mercy!—do not say the lady Edith—"

"Is dead? No, she lives."

"Then, God be praised, my joy is whole again! Speed thee, brother —let her come to me! An' *she* say I am not myself,—but she will not; no, no, *she* will know me, I were a fool to doubt it. Bring her—bring the old servants; they, too, will know me."

"All are gone but five—Peter, Halsey, David, Bernard and Margaret."

So saying, Hugh left the room. Miles stood musing, a while, then began to walk the floor, muttering—

"The five arch villains have survived the two-and-twenty leal and honest—'tis an odd thing."

He continued walking back and forth, muttering to himself; he had forgotten the king entirely. By and by his majesty said gravely, and with a touch of genuine compassion, though the words themselves were capable of being interpreted ironically—

"Mind not thy mischance, good man; there be others in the world whose identity is denied, and whose claims are derided. Thou hast company."

"Ah, my king," cried Hendon, coloring slightly, "do not thou condemn me—wait, and thou shalt see. I am no impostor—she will say it; you shall hear it from the sweetest lips in England. I an impostor? Why I know this old hall, these pictures of my ancestors, and all these things that are about us, as a child knoweth its own nursery. Here was I born and bred, my lord; I speak the truth; I would not deceive thee; and should none else believe, I pray thee do not *thou* doubt me—I could not bear it."

"I do not doubt thee," said the king, with a childlike simplicity and faith.

"I thank thee out of my heart!" exclaimed Hendon, with a fervency which showed that he was touched. The king added, with the same gentle simplicity—

"Dost thou doubt *me?*"

"A BEAUTIFUL LADY, RICHLY CLOTHED, FOLLOWED HUGH."

A guilty confusion seized upon Hendon, and he was grateful that the door opened to admit Hugh, at that moment, and saved him the necessity of replying.

A beautiful lady, richly clothed, followed Hugh, and after her came several liveried servants. The lady walked slowly, with her head bowed and her eyes fixed upon the floor. The face was unspeakably sad. Miles Hendon sprang forward, crying out—

"O, my Edith, my darling—"

But Hugh waved him back, gravely, and said to the lady—

"Look upon him. Do you know him?"

At the sound of Miles's voice the woman had started, slightly, and her cheeks had flushed; she was trembling, now. She stood still, during an impressive pause of several moments; then slowly lifted up her head and looked into Hendon's eyes with a stony and frightened gaze; the blood sank out of her face, drop by drop, till nothing remained but the gray pallor of death; then she said, in a voice as dead as the face, "I know him not!" and turned, with a moan and a stifled sob, and tottered out of the room.

Miles Hendon sank into a chair and covered his face with his hands. After a pause, his brother said to the servants—

"You have observed him. Do you know him?"

They shook their heads; then the master said—

"The servants know you not, sir. I fear there is some mistake. You have seen that my wife knew you not."

"Thy *wife!*" In an instant Hugh was pinned to the wall, with an

"HUGH WAS PINNED TO THE WALL."

iron grip about his throat. "O, thou fox-hearted slave, I see it all! Thou'st writ the lying letter thyself, and my stolen bride and goods are its fruit. There—now get thee gone, lest I shame mine honorable soldiership with the slaying of so pitiful a mannikin!"

Hugh, red-faced, and almost suffocated, reeled to the nearest chair, and commanded the servants to seize and bind the murderous stranger. They hesitated, and one of them said—

"He is armed, Sir Hugh, and we are weaponless."

"Armed? What of it, and ye so many? Upon him, I say!"

But Miles warned them to be careful what they did, and added—

"Ye know me of old—I have not changed; come on, an' it like you."

This reminder did not hearten the servants much; they still held back.

"Then go, ye paltry cowards, and arm yourselves and guard the doors, whilst I send one to fetch the watch," said Hugh. He turned, at the threshold, and said to Miles, "You'll find it to your advantage to offend not with useless endeavors at escape."

"Escape? Spare thyself discomfort, an' that is all that troubles thee. For Miles Hendon is master of Hendon Hall and all its belongings. He will remain—doubt it not."

CHAPTER 26

DISOWNED

THE KING SAT musing a few moments, then looked up and said—

"'Tis strange—most strange. I cannot account for it."

"No, it is not strange, my liege. I know him, and this conduct is but natural. He was a rascal from his birth."

"O, I spake not of *him*, Sir Miles."

"Not of him? Then of what? What is it that is strange?"

"That the king is not missed."

"How? Which? I doubt I do not understand."

"Indeed? Doth it not strike you as being passing strange that the land is not filled with couriers and proclamations describing my person and making search for me? Is it no matter for commotion and distress that the head of the state is gone?—that I am vanished away and lost?"

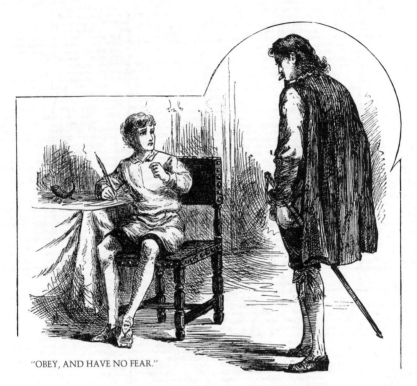

"OBEY, AND HAVE NO FEAR."

"Most true, my king, I had forgot." Then Hendon sighed, and muttered to himself, "Poor ruined mind—still busy with its pathetic dream."

"But I have a plan that shall right us both. I will write a paper, in three tongues—Latin, Greek, and English—and thou shalt haste away with it to London in the morning. Give it to none but my uncle, the lord Hertford; when he shall see it, he will know and say I wrote it. Then he will send for me."

"Might it not be best, my prince, that we wait, here, until I prove myself and make my rights secure to my domains? I should be so much the better able then, to—"

The king interrupted him imperiously—

"Peace! What are thy paltry domains, thy trivial interests, contrasted with matters which concern the weal of a nation and the integrity of a throne!" Then he added, in a gentle voice, as if he were sorry for his severity, "Obey, and have no fear; I will right thee, I will make thee whole—yes, more than whole. I shall remember, and requite."

So saying, he took the pen, and set himself to work. Hendon contemplated him lovingly, a while, then said to himself—

"An' it were dark, I should think it *was* a king that spoke; there's no denying it, when the humor's upon him he doth thunder and lighten like your true king—now where got he that trick? See him scribble and scratch away contentedly at his meaningless pot-hooks, fancying them to be Latin and Greek—and except my wit shall serve me with a lucky device for diverting him from his purpose, I shall be forced to pretend to post away to-morrow on this wild errand he hath invented for me."

The next moment Sir Miles's thoughts had gone back to the recent episode. So absorbed was he in his musings, that when the king presently handed him the paper which he had been writing, he received it and pocketed it without being conscious of the act. "How marvelous strange she acted," he muttered. "I think she knew me—and I think she did *not* know me. These opinions do conflict, I perceive it plainly; I cannot reconcile them, neither can I, by argument, dismiss either of the two, or even persuade one to outweigh the other. The matter standeth simply thus: she *must* have known my face, my figure, my voice, for how could it be otherwise? yet she *said* she knew me not, and that is proof perfect, for she cannot lie. But stop—I think I begin to see. Peradventure he hath influenced her—commanded her—compelled her, to lie. That is the solution! the riddle is unriddled. She seemed dead with fear—yes, she was under his compulsion. I will seek her; I will find her; now that he is away, she will speak her true mind. She will remember the old times when we were little playfellows together, and this will soften her heart, and she will no more betray me, but will confess me. There is no treacherous blood in her—no, she was always honest and true. She has loved me, in those old days—this is my security; for whom one has loved, one cannot betray."

He stepped eagerly toward the door; at that moment it opened, and the lady Edith entered. She was very pale, but she walked with a firm step, and her carriage was full of grace and gentle dignity. Her face was as sad as before.

Miles sprang forward, with a happy confidence, to meet her, but she checked him with a hardly perceptible gesture, and he stopped where he was. She seated herself, and asked him to do likewise. Thus simply did she take the sense of old-comradeship out of him, and transform him into a stranger and a guest. The surprise of it, the bewildering unexpectedness of it, made him begin to question, for a moment, if he *was* the person he was pretending to be, after all. The lady Edith said—

"Sir, I have come to warn you. The mad cannot be persuaded out of their delusions, perchance; but doubtless they may be persuaded to avoid perils. I think this dream of yours hath the seeming of honest truth to you, and therefore is not criminal—but do not tarry here with it; for here it is dangerous." She looked steadily into Miles's face, a moment, then added, impressively, "It is the more dangerous for that you *are* much like what our lost lad must have grown to be, if he had lived."

"Heavens, madam, but I *am* he!"

"I truly think you think it, sir. I question not your honesty in that—I but warn you, that is all. My husband is master in this region; his power hath hardly any limit; the people prosper or starve, as he wills. If you resembled not the man whom you profess to be, my husband might bid you pleasure yourself with your dream in peace; but trust me, I know him well, I know what he will do; he will say to all, that you are but a mad impostor, and straightway all will echo him." She bent upon Miles that same steady look once more, and added: "If you *were* Miles Hendon, and he knew it and all the region knew it—consider what I am saying, weigh it well—you would stand in the same peril, your punishment would be no less sure; he would deny you and denounce you, and none would be bold enough to give you countenance."

"Most truly I believe it," said Miles, bitterly. "The power that can command one life-long friend to betray and disown another, and be obeyed, may well look to be obeyed in quarters where bread and life are on the stake and no cobweb ties of loyalty and honor are concerned."

A faint tinge appeared for a moment in the lady's cheek, and she dropped her eyes to the floor; but her voice betrayed no emotion when she proceeded—

"I have warned you, I must still warn you, to go hence. This man will destroy you, else. He is a tyrant who knows no pity. I, who am his fettered slave, know this. Poor Miles, and Arthur, and my dear guardian, Sir Richard, are free of him, and at rest—better that you were with them than that you bide here in the clutches of this miscreant. Your pretensions are a menace to his title and possessions; you have assaulted him in his own house—you are ruined if you stay. Go—do not hesitate. If you lack money, take this purse, I beg of you, and bribe the servants to let you pass. O be warned, poor soul, and escape while you may."

Miles declined the purse with a gesture, and rose up and stood before her.

"Grant me one thing," he said. "Let your eyes rest upon mine, so that I may see if they be steady. There—now answer me. Am I Miles Hendon?"

"No. I know you not."

"Swear it!"

"AM I MILES HENDON?"

The answer was low, but distinct—

"I swear."

"O, this passes belief!"

"Fly! Why will you waste the precious time? Fly, and save yourself."

At that moment the officers burst into the room and a violent struggle began; but Hendon was soon overpowered and dragged away. The king was taken, also, and both were bound, and led to prison.

CHAPTER 27

IN PRISON

THE CELLS were all crowded; so the two friends were chained in a large room where persons charged with trifling offenses were commonly kept. They had company, for there were some twenty manacled and fettered prisoners here, of both sexes and of varying ages, —an obscene and noisy gang. The king chafed bitterly over the stupendous indignity thus put upon his royalty, but Hendon was moody and taciturn. He was pretty thoroughly bewildered. He had come home, a jubilant prodigal, expecting to find everybody wild with joy over his return; and instead had got the cold shoulder and a jail. The promise and the fulfilment differed so widely, that the effect was stunning; he could not decide whether it was most tragic or most grotesque. He felt much as a man might who had danced blithely out to enjoy a rainbow, and got struck by lightning.

But gradually his confused and tormenting thoughts settled down into some sort of order, and then his mind centred itself upon Edith. He turned her conduct over, and examined it in all lights, but he could not make anything satisfactory out of it. Did she know him?—or didn't she know him? It was a perplexing puzzle, and occupied him a long time; but he ended, finally, with the conviction that she did know him, and had repudiated him for interested reasons. He wanted to load her name with curses, now; but this name had so long been sacred to him that he found he could not bring his tongue to profane it.

Wrapped in prison blankets of a soiled and tattered condition, Hendon and the king passed a troubled night. For a bribe the jailer

"CHAINED IN A LARGE ROOM."

had furnished liquor to some of the prisoners; singing of ribald songs, fighting, shouting, and carousing, was the natural consequence. At last, a while after midnight, a man attacked a woman and nearly killed her by beating her over the head with his manacles before the jailer could come to the rescue. The jailer restored peace by giving the man a sound clubbing about the head and shoulders—then the carousing ceased; and after that, all had an opportunity to sleep who did not mind the annoyance of the moanings and groanings of the two wounded people.

During the ensuing week, the days and nights were of a monotonous sameness, as to events; men whose faces Hendon remembered more or less distinctly, came, by day, to gaze at the "impostor" and repudiate and insult him; and by night the carousing and brawling went on, with symmetrical regularity. However, there was a change of incident at last. The jailer brought in an old man, and said to him—

"The villain is in this room—cast thy old eyes about and see if thou canst say which is he."

Hendon glanced up, and experienced a pleasant sensation for the first time since he had been in the jail. He said to himself, "This is Blake Andrews, a servant all his life in my father's family—a good honest soul, with a right heart in his breast. That is, formerly. But none are true, now; all are liars. This man will know me—and will deny me, too, like the rest."

The old man gazed around the room, glanced at each face in turn, and finally said—

"I see none here but paltry knaves, scum o' the streets. Which is he?"

The jailer laughed.

"Here," he said; "scan this big animal, and grant me an opinion."

The old man approached, and looked Hendon over, long and earnestly, then shook his head and said—

"Marry, *this* is no Hendon—nor ever was!"

"Right! Thy old eyes are sound yet. An' I were Sir Hugh, I would take the shabby carle and—"

The jailer finished by lifting himself a-tip-toe with an imaginary halter, at the same time making a gurgling noise in his throat suggestive of suffocation. The old man said, vindictively—

"Let him bless God an' he fare no worse. An' *I* had the handling o' the villain he should roast, or I am no true man!"

The jailer laughed a pleasant hyena laugh, and said—

"Give him a piece of thy mind, old man—they all do it. Thou'lt find it good diversion."

Then he sauntered toward his ante-room and disappeared. The old man dropped upon his knees and whispered—

"God be thanked, thou'rt come again, my master! I believed thou wert dead these seven years, and lo, here thou art alive! I knew thee the moment I saw thee; and main hard work it was to keep a stony countenance and seem to see none here but tuppenny knaves and rubbish o' the streets. I am old and poor, Sir Miles; but say the word and I will go forth and proclaim the truth though I be strangled for it."

"No," said Hendon; "thou shalt not. It would ruin thee, and yet help but little in my cause. But I thank thee; for thou hast given me back somewhat of my lost faith in my kind."

The old servant became very valuable to Hendon and the king; for he dropped in several times a day to "abuse" the former, and always smuggled in a few delicacies to help out the prison bill of fare; he also furnished the current news. Hendon reserved the dainties for the king; without them his majesty might not have survived, for he was not able to eat the coarse and wretched food provided by the jailer. Andrews was obliged to confine himself to brief visits, in order to avoid suspicion; but he managed to impart a fair degree of information each time—information delivered in a low voice, for Hendon's benefit, and interlarded with insulting epithets delivered in a louder voice, for the benefit of other hearers.

"THE OLD MAN LOOKED HENDON OVER."

So, little by little, the story of the family came out. Arthur had been dead six years. This loss, with the absence of news from Hendon, impaired the father's health; he believed he was going to die, and he wished to see Hugh and Edith settled in life before he passed away; but Edith begged hard for delay, hoping for Miles's return; then the letter came which brought the news of Miles's death; the shock prostrated Sir Richard; he believed his end was very near, and he and Hugh insisted upon the marriage; Edith begged for and obtained a month's respite; then another, and finally a third; the marriage then took place, by the death-bed of Sir Richard. It had not proved a happy

"INFORMATION DELIVERED IN A LOW VOICE."

one. It was whispered about the country that shortly after the nuptials the bride found among her husband's papers several rough and incomplete drafts of the fatal letter, and had accused him of precipitating the marriage—and Sir Richard's death, too—by a wicked forgery. Tales of cruelty to the lady Edith and the servants were to be heard on all hands; and since the father's death Sir Hugh had thrown off all soft disguises and become a pitiless master toward all who in any way depended upon him and his domains for bread.

There was a bit of Andrews's gossip which the king listened to with a lively interest—

"There is rumor that the king is mad. But in charity forbear to say I mentioned it, for 'tis death to speak of it, they say."

His majesty glared at the old man and said—

"The king is *not* mad, goodman—and thou'lt find it to thy advantage to busy thyself with matters that nearer concern thee than this seditious prattle."

"What doth the lad mean?" said Andrews, surprised at this brisk assault from such an unexpected quarter. Hendon gave him a sign, and he did not pursue his question, but went on with his budget—

"The late king is to be buried at Windsor in a day or two—the 16th of the month,—and the new king will be crowned at Westminster the 20th."

"Methinks they must needs find him first," muttered his majesty; then added, confidently, "but they will look to that—and so also shall I."

"In the name of—"

But the old man got no further—a warning sign from Hendon checked his remark. He resumed the thread of his gossip—

"Sir Hugh goeth to the coronation—and with grand hopes. He confidently looketh to come back a peer, for he is high in favor with the Lord Protector."

"What Lord Protector?" asked his majesty.

"His grace the Duke of Somerset."

"What Duke of Somerset?"

"Marry, there is but one—Seymour, Earl of Hertford."

The king asked, sharply—

"Since when is *he* a duke, and Lord Protector?"

"Since the last day of January."

"And prithee who made him so?"

"Himself and the Great Council—with help of the king."

His majesty started violently. "The *king!*" he cried. "*What* king, good sir?"

"What king, indeed! (God-a-mercy, what aileth the boy?) Sith we have but one, 'tis not difficult to answer—his most sacred majesty King Edward the Sixth—whom God preserve! Yea, and a dear and gracious little urchin is he, too; and whether he be mad or no—and they say he mendeth daily—his praises are on all men's lips; and all bless him, likewise, and offer prayers that he may be spared to reign

long in England; for he began humanely, with saving the old Duke
of Norfolk's life, and now is he bent on destroying the cruelest of the
laws that harry and oppress the people."

This news struck his majesty dumb with amazement, and plunged
him into so deep and dismal a reverie that he heard no more of the old
man's gossip. He wondered if the "little urchin" was the beggar-boy
whom he left dressed in his own garments in the palace. It did not

"THE *KING!*" HE CRIED. "*WHAT* KING?"

seem possible that this could be, for surely his manners and speech
would betray him if he pretended to be the Prince of Wales—then he
would be driven out, and search made for the true prince. Could it
be that the court had set up some sprig of the nobility in his place?
No, for his uncle would not allow that—he was all-powerful and could
and would crush such a movement, of course. The boy's musings
profited him nothing; the more he tried to unriddle the mystery the
more perplexed he became, the more his head ached, and the worse
he slept. His impatience to get to London grew hourly, and his captivity became almost unendurable.

Hendon's arts all failed with the king—he could not be comforted;
but a couple of women who were chained near him, succeeded better.

Under their gentle ministrations he found peace and learned a degree of patience. He was very grateful, and came to love them dearly and to delight in the sweet and soothing influence of their presence. He asked them why they were in prison, and when they said they were Baptists, he smiled, and inquired—

"Is that a crime to be shut up for, in a prison? Now I grieve, for I shall lose ye—they will not keep ye long for such a little thing."

They did not answer; and something in their faces made him uneasy. He said, eagerly—

"You do not speak—be good to me, and tell me—there will be no other punishment? Prithee tell me there is no fear of that."

They tried to change the topic, but his fears were aroused, and he pursued it—

"Will they scourge thee? No, no, they would not be so cruel! Say they would not. Come, they *will* not, will they?"

The women betrayed confusion and distress, but there was no avoiding an answer, so one of them said, in a voice choked with emotion—

"O, thou'lt break our hearts, thou gentle spirit!—God will help us to bear our—"

"It is a confession!" the king broke in. "Then they *will* scourge thee, the stonyhearted wretches! But O, thou must not weep, I cannot bear it. Keep up thy courage—I shall come to my own in time to save thee from this bitter thing, and I will do it!"

When the king awoke in the morning, the women were gone.

"They are saved!" he said, joyfully; then added, despondently, "but woe is me!—for they were my comforters."

Each of them had left a shred of ribbon pinned to his clothing, in token of remembrance. He said he would keep these things always; and that soon he would seek out these dear good friends of his and take them under his protection.

Just then the jailer came in with some subordinates and commanded that the prisoners be conducted to the jail-yard. The king was overjoyed—it would be a blessed thing to see the blue sky and breathe the fresh air once more. He fretted and chafed at the slowness of the officers, but his turn came at last and he was released from his staple and ordered to follow the other prisoners, with Hendon.

The court or quadrangle, was stone-paved, and open to the sky.

The prisoners entered it through a massive archway of masonry, and were placed in file, standing, with their backs against the wall. A rope was stretched in front of them, and they were also guarded by their officers. It was a chill and lowering morning, and a light snow which had fallen during the night whitened the great empty space and added to the general dismalness of its aspect. Now and then a wintry wind shivered through the place and sent the snow eddying hither and thither.

"TWO WOMEN, CHAINED TO POSTS."

In the centre of the court stood two women, chained to posts. A glance showed the king that these were his good friends. He shuddered, and said to himself, "Alack, they are not gone free, as I had thought. To think that such as these should know the lash!—in England! Aye there's the shame of it—not in Heathenesse, but Christian England! They will be scourged; and I, whom they have comforted and kindly entreated, must look on and see the great wrong done; it is strange, so strange! that I, the very source of power in this broad realm, am helpless to protect them. But let these miscreants look well to themselves, for there is a day coming when I will require of them a heavy reckoning for this work. For every blow they strike now, they shall feel a hundred, then."

A great gate swung open and a crowd of citizens poured in. They flocked around the two women, and hid them from the king's view. A clergyman entered and passed through the crowd, and he also was hidden. The king now heard talking, back and forth, as if questions were being asked and answered, but he could not make out what was said. Next there was a deal of bustle and preparation, and much passing and repassing of officials through that part of the crowd that stood on the further side of the women; and whilst this proceeded a deep hush gradually fell upon the people.

Now, by command, the masses parted and fell aside, and the king saw a spectacle that froze the marrow in his bones. Faggots had been piled about the two women, and a kneeling man was lighting them!

The women bowed their heads, and covered their faces with their hands; the yellow flames began to climb upward among the snapping and crackling faggots, and wreaths of blue smoke to stream away on the wind; the clergyman lifted his hands and began a prayer—just then two young girls came flying through the great gate, uttering piercing screams, and threw themselves upon the women at the stake.

"TORN AWAY BY THE OFFICERS."

Instantly they were torn away by the officers, and one of them was kept in a tight grip, but the other broke loose, saying she would die with her mother; and before she could be stopped she had flung her arms about her mother's neck again. She was torn away once more, and with her gown on fire. Two or three men held her, and the burning portion of her gown was snatched off and thrown flaming aside, she struggling all the while to free herself, and saying she would be alone in the world, now, and begging to be allowed to die with her mother. Both the girls screamed continually, and fought for freedom; but suddenly this tumult was drowned under a volley of heart-piercing shrieks of mortal agony,—the king glanced from the frantic girls to the stake, then turned away and leaned his ashen face against the wall, and looked no more. He said, "That which I have seen, in that one little moment, will never go out from my memory, but will abide there; and I shall see it all the days, and dream of it all the nights, till I die. Would God I had been blind!"

Hendon was watching the king. He said to himself, with satisfaction, "His disorder mendeth; he hath changed, and groweth gentler. If he had followed his wont, he would have stormed at these varlets, and said he was king, and commanded that the women be turned loose unscathed. Soon his delusion will pass away and be forgotten, and his poor mind will be whole again. God speed the day!"

That same day several prisoners were brought in to remain over night, who were being conveyed, under guard, to various places in the kingdom, to undergo punishment for crimes committed. The king conversed with these,—he had made it a point, from the beginning, to instruct himself for the kingly office by questioning prisoners whenever the opportunity offered—and the tale of their woes wrung his heart. One of them was a poor half-witted woman who had stolen a yard or two of cloth from a weaver—she was to be hanged for it. Another was a man who had been accused of stealing a horse; he said the proof had failed, and he had imagined that he was safe from the halter; but no—he was hardly free before he was arraigned for killing a deer in the king's park; this was proved against him, and now he was on his way to the gallows. There was a tradesman's apprentice whose case particularly distressed the king; this youth said he found a hawk, one evening, that had escaped from its owner, and he took it home with him, imagining himself entitled to it; but the court convicted him of stealing it, and sentenced him to death.

The king was furious over these inhumanities, and wanted Hendon to break jail and fly with him to Westminster, so that he could mount his throne and hold out his sceptre in mercy over these unfortunate people and save their lives. "Poor child," sighed Hendon, "these woful tales have brought his malady upon him again—alack, but for this evil hap, he would have been well in a little time."

"THE KING WAS FURIOUS."

Among these prisoners was an old lawyer—a man with a strong face and a dauntless mien. Three years past, he had written a pamphlet against the Lord Chancellor, accusing him of injustice, and had been punished for it by the loss of his ears in the pillory, and degradation from the bar, and in addition had been fined £3000 and sentenced to imprisonment for life. Lately he had repeated his offense; and in consequence was now under sentence to lose *what remained of his ears*, pay a fine of £5000, be branded on both cheeks, and remain in prison for life. "These be honorable scars," he said, and turned back his gray hair and showed the mutilated stubs of what had once been his ears.

The king's eye burned with passion. He said—

"None believe in me—neither wilt thou. But no matter—within the compass of a month thou shalt be free; and more, the laws that have dishonored thee, and shamed the English name, shall be swept from the statute books. The world is made wrong; kings should go to school to their own laws, at times, and so learn mercy."*

---

*See Notes to Chapter 27, at end of volume.

CHAPTER 28

THE SACRIFICE

M EANTIME Miles was growing sufficiently tired of confinement
and inaction. But now his trial came on, to his great gratification,
and he thought he could welcome any sentence provided a further
imprisonment should not be a part of it. But he was mistaken about
that. He was in a fine fury when he found himself described as a
"sturdy vagabond" and sentenced to sit two hours in the pillory for
bearing that character and for assaulting the master of Hendon Hall.
His pretensions as to brothership with his prosecutor, and rightful
heirship to the Hendon honors and estates, were left contemptuously
unnoticed, as being not even worth examination.

He raged and threatened, on his way to punishment, but it did no
good; he was snatched roughly along, by the officers, and got an
occasional cuff, besides, for his unreverent conduct.

The king could not pierce through the rabble that swarmed behind;
so he was obliged to follow in the rear, remote from his good friend
and servant. The king had been nearly condemned to the stocks,
himself, for being in such bad company, but had been let off with a
lecture and a warning, in consideration of his youth. When the crowd
at last halted, he flitted feverishly from point to point around its

outer rim, hunting a place to get through; and at last, after a deal of
difficulty and delay, succeeded. There sat his poor henchman in the
degrading stocks, the sport and butt of a dirty mob—he, the body
servant of the king of England! Edward had heard the sentence
pronounced, but he had not realized the half that it meant. His anger
began to rise as the sense of this new indignity which had been put
upon him sank home; it jumped to summer heat, the next moment,
when he saw an egg sail through the air and crush itself against

"HE CONFRONTED THE OFFICER
IN CHARGE."

Hendon's cheek, and heard the crowd roar its enjoyment of the
episode. He sprang across the open circle and confronted the officer
in charge, crying—

"For shame! This is my servant—set him free! I am the—"

"O, peace!" exclaimed Hendon, in a panic, "thou'lt destroy thyself.
Mind him not, officer, he is mad."

"Give thyself no trouble as to the matter of minding him, good
man, I have small mind to mind him; but as to teaching him somewhat, to that I am well inclined." He turned to a subordinate and
said, "Give the little fool a taste or two of the lash, to mend his
manners."

"Half a dozen will better serve his turn," suggested Sir Hugh, who had ridden up, a moment before, to take a passing glance at the proceedings.

The king was seized. He did not even struggle, so paralyzed was he with the mere thought of the monstrous outrage that was proposed to be inflicted upon his sacred person. History was already defiled with the record of the scourging of an English king with whips—it was an intolerable reflection that he must furnish a duplicate of that shameful page. He was in the toils, there was no help for him: he must either take this punishment or beg for its remission. Hard conditions; he would take the stripes—a king might do that, but a king could not beg.

But meantime, Miles Hendon was resolving the difficulty. "Let the child go," said he; "ye heartless dogs, do ye not see how young and frail he is? Let him go—I will take his lashes."

"Marry, a good thought,—and thanks for it," said Sir Hugh, his face lighting with a sardonic satisfaction. "Let the little beggar go, and give this fellow a dozen in his place—an honest dozen, well laid on." The king was in the act of entering a fierce protest, but Sir Hugh silenced him with the potent remark, "Yes, speak up, do, and free thy mind—only, mark ye, that for each word you utter he shall get six strokes the more."

Hendon was removed from the stocks, and his back laid bare; and whilst the lash was applied the poor little king turned away his face and allowed unroyal tears to channel his cheeks unchecked. "Ah, brave good heart," he said to himself, "this loyal deed shall never perish out of my memory. I will not forget it—and neither shall *they!*" he added, with passion. Whilst he mused, his appreciation of Hendon's magnanimous conduct grew to greater and still greater dimensions in his mind, and so also did his gratefulness for it. Presently he said to himself, "Who saves his prince from wounds and possible death—and this he did for me—performs high service; but it is little—it is nothing!—O, less than nothing!—when 'tis weighed against the act of him who saves his prince from SHAME!"

Hendon made no outcry, under the scourge, but bore the heavy blows with soldierly fortitude. This, together with his redeeming the boy by taking his stripes for him, compelled the respect of even that forlorn and degraded mob that was gathered there; and its jibes and

"WHILST THE LASH WAS APPLIED THE POOR KING
TURNED AWAY HIS FACE."

hootings died away, and no sound remained but the sound of the
falling blows. The stillness that pervaded the place, when Hendon
found himself once more in the stocks, was in strong contrast with
the insulting clamor which had prevailed there so little a while before.
The king came softly to Hendon's side, and whispered in his ear—

"Kings cannot ennoble thee, thou good, great soul, for One who
is higher than kings hath done that for thee; but a king can confirm
thy nobility to men." He picked up the scourge from the ground,
touched Hendon's bleeding shoulders lightly with it, and whispered,
"Edward of England dubs thee earl!"

Hendon was touched. The water welled to his eyes, yet at the same
time the grisly humor of the situation and circumstances so under-
mined his gravity that it was all he could do to keep some sign of his

inward mirth from showing outside. To be suddenly hoisted, naked and gory, from the common stocks to the Alpine altitude and splendor of an Earldom, seemed to him the last possibility in the line of the grotesque. He said to himself, "Now am I finely tinseled, indeed! The spectre-knight of the Kingdom of Dreams and Shadows is become a spectre-earl!—a dizzy flight for a callow wing! An' this go on, I shall presently be hung like a very May-pole with fantastic gauds and make-

"SIR HUGH SPURRED AWAY."

believe honors. But I shall value them, all valueless as they are, for the love that doth bestow them. Better these poor mock dignities of mine, that come unasked, from a clean hand and a right spirit, than real ones bought by servility from grudging and interested power."

The dreaded Sir Hugh wheeled his horse about, and as he spurred away, the living wall divided silently to let him pass, and as silently closed together again. And so remained; nobody went so far as to venture a remark in favor of the prisoner, or in compliment to him;

but no matter, the absence of abuse was a sufficient homage in itself. A late comer who was not posted, as to the present circumstances, and who delivered a sneer at the "impostor" and was in the act of following it with a dead cat, was promptly knocked down and kicked out, without any words, and then the deep quiet resumed sway once more.

CHAPTER 29

To London

WHEN HENDON'S term of service in the stocks was finished, he was released and ordered to quit the region and come back no more. His sword was restored to him, and also his mule and his donkey. He mounted and rode off, followed by the king, the crowd opening with quiet respectfulness to let them pass, and then dispersing when they were gone.

Hendon was soon absorbed in thought. There were questions of high import to be answered. What should he do? Whither should he go? Powerful help must be found, somewhere, or he must relinquish his inheritance and remain under the imputation of being an impostor besides. Where could he hope to find this powerful help? Where, indeed! It was a knotty question. By and by a thought occurred to him which pointed to a possibility—the slenderest of slender possibilities, certainly, but still worth considering, for lack of any other that promised anything at all. He remembered what old Andrews had said about the young king's goodness and his generous

"HENDON MOUNTED AND RODE OFF WITH THE KING."

championship of the wronged and unfortunate. Why not go and try to get speech of him and beg for justice? Ah, yes, but could so fantastic a pauper get admission to the august presence of a monarch? Never mind—let that matter take care of itself; it was a bridge that would not need to be crossed till he should come to it. He was an old campaigner, and used to inventing shifts and expedients; no doubt he would be able to find a way. Yes, he would strike for the capital. Maybe his father's old friend Sir Humphrey Marlow would help him—"good old Sir Humphrey, Head Lieutenant of the late king's kitchen, or stables, or something"—Miles could not remember just what or which. Now that he had something to turn his energies to, a distinctly defined object to accomplish, the fog of humiliation and depression which had settled down upon his spirits lifted and blew away, and he raised his head and looked about him. He was surprised to see how far he had come; the village was away behind him. The king was jogging along in his wake, with his head bowed; for he, too, was deep in plans and thinkings. A sorrowful misgiving clouded Hendon's new-born cheerfulness: would the boy be willing to go again to a city where, during all his brief life, he had never known anything but ill usage and pinching want? But the question must be asked; it could not be avoided; so Hendon reined up, and called out—

"I had forgotten to inquire whither we are bound. Thy commands, my liege!"

"To London!"

"IN THE MIDST OF A JAM OF HOWLING PEOPLE."

Hendon moved on again, mightily contented with the answer—but astounded at it, too.

The whole journey was made without an adventure of importance. But it ended with one. About ten o'clock on the night of the 19th of February, they stepped upon London Bridge, in the midst of a writhing, struggling jam of howling and hurrahing people, whose beer-jolly faces stood out strongly in the glare from manifold torches—and at that instant the decaying head of some former duke or other grandee tumbled down between them, striking Hendon on the elbow and then bounding off among the hurrying confusion of feet. So evanescent and unstable are men's works, in this world!—the late good king is but three weeks dead and three days in his grave, and already the adornments which he took such pains to select from prominent people for his noble bridge are falling. A citizen stumbled over that head, and drove his own head into the back of somebody in front of him, who turned and knocked down the first person that came handy, and was promptly laid out himself by that person's friend. It was the right ripe time for a free fight, for the festivities of the morrow—Coronation Day—were already beginning; everybody was full of strong drink and patriotism; within five minutes the free fight was occupying a good deal of ground; within ten or twelve it covered an acre or so, and was become a riot. By this time Hendon and the king were hopelessly separated from each other and lost in the rush and turmoil of the roaring masses of humanity. And so we leave them.

CHAPTER 30

WHILST THE TRUE KING wandered about the land; poorly clad, poorly fed; cuffed and derided by tramps, one while; herding with thieves and murderers in a jail, another; and called idiot and impostor by all, impartially, the mock king, Tom Canty, enjoyed a quite different experience.

When we saw him last, royalty was just beginning to have a bright side for him. This bright side went on brightening more and more, every day; in a very little while it was become almost all sunshine and delightfulness. He lost his fears; his misgivings faded out and died; his embarrassments departed and gave place to an easy and confident bearing. He worked the whipping-boy mine to ever-increasing profit.

He ordered my lady Elizabeth and my lady Jane Grey into his presence when he wanted to play or talk; and dismissed them, when he was done with them, with the air of one familiarly accustomed to such performances. It no longer confused him to have these lofty personages kiss his hand, at parting.

He came to enjoy being conducted to bed in state, at night, and dressed with intricate and solemn ceremony in the morning. It came to be a proud pleasure to march to dinner attended by a glittering procession of officers of state and Gentlemen-at-Arms—insomuch, indeed, that he doubled his guard of Gentlemen-at-Arms, and made them a hundred. He like to hear the bugles sounding, down the long corridors, and the distant voices responding, "Way for the king!"

He even learned to enjoy sitting in throned state in council and seeming to be something more than the Lord Protector's mouthpiece. He liked to receive great ambassadors and their gorgeous trains, and listen to the affectionate messages they brought from illustrious monarchs who called him "brother"—O, happy Tom Canty, late of Offal Court!

"TO KISS HIS HAND, AT PARTING."

He enjoyed his splendid clothes, and ordered more; he found his four hundred servants too few for his proper grandeur, and trebled them. The adulation of salaaming courtiers came to be sweet music to his ears. He remained kind and gentle, and a sturdy and determined champion of all that were oppressed, and he made tireless war upon unjust laws. Yet upon occasion, being offended, he could turn upon an earl, or even a duke, and give him a look that would make him tremble. Once when his royal "sister," the grimly holy lady Mary, set herself to reason with him against the wisdom of his course in pardoning so many people who would otherwise be jailed or hanged or burned, and reminded him that their august late father's prisons had sometimes contained as high as sixty thousand convicts at one time, and that during his admirable reign he had delivered seventy-two thousand thieves and robbers over to death by the executioner,* the boy was filled with generous indignation, and commanded her to go to her closet and beseech God to take away the stone that was in her breast and give her a human heart.

"COMMANDED HER TO GO TO HER CLOSET."

Did Tom Canty never feel troubled about the poor little rightful prince who had treated him so kindly and flown out with such hot zeal to avenge him upon the insolent sentinel at the palace gate? Yes; his first royal days and nights were pretty well sprinkled with painful thoughts about the lost prince, and with sincere longings for his return and happy restoration to his native rights and splendors; but as time wore on and the prince did not come, Tom's mind became more and more occupied with his new and enchanting experiences, and by

*Hume's England.

little and little the vanished monarch faded almost out of his thoughts;
and finally when he did intrude upon them at intervals he was become an unwelcome spectre, for he made Tom feel guilty and
ashamed.

Tom's poor mother and sisters traveled the same road out of his
mind. At first he pined for them, sorrowed for them, longed to see
them; but later, the thought of their coming some day in their rags
and dirt, and betraying him with their kisses and pulling him down
from his lofty place and dragging him back to penury and degradation
and the slums, made him shudder. At last they ceased to trouble his
thoughts, almost wholly. And he was content, even glad; for whenever their mournful and accusing faces did rise before him now, they
made him feel more despicable than the worms that crawl.

At midnight of the 19th of February, Tom Canty was sinking to
sleep in his rich bed in the palace, guarded by his loyal vassals and
surrounded by the pomps of royalty—a happy boy; for to-morrow
was the day appointed for his solemn crowning as king of England.
At that same hour Edward the true king, hungry and thirsty, soiled
and draggled, worn with travel, and clothed in rags and shreds—his
share of the results of the riot—was wedged in among a crowd of
people who were watching, with deep interest, certain hurrying gangs
of workmen who streamed in and out of Westminster Abbey, busy as
ants; they were making the last preparations for the royal Coronation.

CHAPTER 31

RECOGNITION • PROCESSION

When Tom Canty awoke, the next morning, the air was heavy with a thunderous murmur—all the distances were charged with it. It was music to him, for it meant that the English world was out in its strength to give loyal welcome to the great day.

Presently Tom found himself once more the chief figure in a wonderful floating pageant on the Thames—for, by ancient custom, the "recognition-procession" through London must start from the Tower, and he was bound thither.

When he arrived there, the sides of the venerable fortress seemed suddenly rent in a thousand places; and from every rent leapt a red tongue of flame and a white gush of smoke; a deafening explosion followed, which drowned the shoutings of the multitude and made the ground tremble; the flame-jets, the smoke, and the explosions were repeated, over and over again, with marvelous celerity; so that in a few moments the old Tower disappeared in the vast fog of its own smoke, all but the very top of the tall pile called the White Tower; this, with its banners, stood out above the dense bank of vapor as a mountain-peak projects above a cloud-rack.

THE START FOR THE TOWER.

Tom Canty, splendidly arrayed, mounted a prancing war steed whose rich trappings almost reached to the ground; his "uncle," the Lord Protector Somerset, similarly mounted, took place in his rear; the King's Guard formed in single ranks on either side, clad in burnished armor; after the Protector followed a seemingly interminable procession of resplendent nobles attended by their vassals; after these came the Lord Mayor and the Aldermanic body, in crimson velvet robes and with their gold chains across their breasts; and after these the officers and members of all the Guilds of London, in rich raiment and bearing the showy banners of the several corporations. Also, in the procession, as a special guard of honor through the city, was the Ancient and Honorable Artillery Company, an organization already three hundred years old, at that time, and the only military body in England possessing the privilege (which it still possesses in our day,) of holding itself independent of the commands of parliament. It was a brilliant spectacle, and was hailed with acclamations all along the line, as it took its stately way through the packed multitudes of citizens. The chronicler says: "The king, as he entered the city, was received by the people with prayers, welcomings, cries, and tender words, and all signs which argue an earnest love of subjects toward their sovereign; and the king, by holding up his glad countenance to such as stood afar off, and most tender language to those that stood nigh his grace, showed himself no less thankful to receive the people's good will than they to offer it. To all that wished him well, he gave thanks. To such as bade 'God save his grace,' he said in return, 'God save you all!' and added that 'he thanked them with all his heart.' Wonderfully transported were the people with the loving answers and gestures of their king."

In Fenchurch street a "fair child, in costly apparel," stood on a stage to welcome his majesty to the city. The last verse of his greeting was in these words:

> "Welcome, O king, as much as hearts can think!
> Welcome again, as much as tongue can tell!
> Welcome to joyous tongues and hearts that will not shrink!
> God thee preserve, we pray, and wish thee ever well!"

The people burst forth in a glad shout, repeating with one voice what the child had said. Tom Canty gazed abroad over the surging sea of eager faces, and his heart swelled with exultation; and he felt that the one thing worth living for in this world was to be a king, and a nation's idol. Presently, he caught sight, at a distance, of a couple of his ragged Offal Court comrades—one of them the Lord High Admiral in his late mimic court, the other the First Lord of the Bedchamber in the same pretentious fiction—and his pride swelled higher than ever. O, if they could only recognize him, now! what unspeakable glory it would be, if they could recognize him, and realize that the derided mock king of the slums and back alleys was become a real king, with illustrious dukes and princes for his humble menials, and the English world at his feet! But he had to deny himself, and choke down his desire, for such a recognition might cost more than it would come to; so he turned away his head and left the two soiled lads to go on with their shoutings and glad adulations unsuspicious of whom it was they were lavishing them upon.

Every now and then rose the cry, "A largess! a largess!" and Tom responded by scattering a handful of bright new coins abroad for the multitude to scramble for.

The chronicler says: "At the upper end of Gracechurch street, before the sign of the Eagle, the city had erected a gorgeous arch, beneath which was a stage, which stretched from one side of the street to the other. This was a historical pageant, representing the king's immediate progenitors. There sat Elizabeth of York, in the midst of an immense white rose, whose petals formed elaborate furbelows around her; by her side was Henry VII issuing out of a vast red rose, disposed in the same manner; the hands of the royal pair were locked together, and the wedding ring ostentatiously displayed.

"WELCOME, O KING!"

From the red and white roses proceeded a stem, which reached up to a second stage occupied by Henry VIII, issuing from a red and white rose, with the effigy of the new king's mother, Jane Seymour, represented by his side. One branch sprang from this pair, which mounted to a third stage, where sat the effigy of Edward VI himself, enthroned in royal majesty; and the whole pageant was framed with wreaths of roses, red and white."

This quaint and gaudy spectacle so wrought upon the rejoicing people that their acclamations utterly smothered the small voice of the child whose business it was to explain the thing in eulogistic rhymes; but Tom Canty was not sorry, for this loyal uproar was sweeter music to him than any poetry, no matter what its quality might be. Whithersoever Tom turned his happy young face, the people recognized the exactness of his effigy's likeness to himself, the flesh and blood counterpart, and new whirlwinds of applause burst forth.

The great pageant moved on, and still on, under one triumphal arch after another, and past a bewildering succession of spectacular

"A LARGESS! A LARGESS!"

and symbolical tableaux, each of which typified and exalted some virtue or talent or merit of the little king's. "Throughout the whole of Cheapside, from every penthouse and window, hung banners and streamers; and the richest carpets, stuffs, and cloth of gold tapestried the streets, specimens of the great wealth of the stores within; and the splendor of this thoroughfare was equaled in the other streets, and in some even surpassed."

"And all these wonders and these marvels are to welcome me—me!" murmured Tom Canty.

The mock king's cheeks were flushed with excitement; his eyes were flashing; his senses swam in a delirium of pleasure. At this

point, just as he was raising his hand to fling another rich largess, he
caught sight of a pale, astounded face which was strained forward out
of the second rank of the crowd, its intense eyes riveted upon him; a
sickening consternation struck through him—he recognized his
mother! and up flew his hand, palm outward, before his eyes; that
old involuntary gesture born of a forgotten episode and perpetuated
by habit! In an instant more she had torn her way out of the press and
past the guards, and was at his side. She embraced his leg, she covered
it with kisses; she cried "O, my child, my darling!" lifting toward him
a face that was transfigured with joy and love. The same instant an
officer of the King's Guard snatched her away, with a curse, and sent

"SHE WAS AT HIS SIDE."

her reeling back whence she came, with a vigorous impulse from his strong arm. The words "I do not know you, woman!" were falling from Tom Canty's lips when this piteous thing occurred; but it smote him to the heart to see her treated so; and as she turned for a last glimpse of him, whilst the crowd was swallowing her from his sight, she seemed so wounded, so broken-hearted, that a shame fell upon him which consumed his pride to ashes and withered his stolen royalty. His grandeurs were stricken valueless, they seemed to fall away from him like rotten rags.

The procession moved on, and still on, through ever augmenting splendors, and ever augmenting tempests of welcome; but to Tom Canty they were as if they had not been. He neither saw nor heard. Royalty had lost its grace and sweetness, its pomps were become a reproach; remorse was eating his heart out. He said, "Would God I were free of my captivity!"

He had unconsciously dropped back into the phraseology of the first days of his compulsory greatness.

The shining pageant still went winding like a radiant and interminable serpent down the crooked lanes of the quaint old city, and through the huzzahing hosts; but still the king rode with bowed head and vacant eyes, seeing only his mother's face and that wounded look in it.

"Largess! largess!" The cry fell upon an unheeding ear.

"Long live Edward of England!" It seemed as if the earth shook with the explosion; but there was no response from the king. He heard it only as one hears the thunder of the surf when it is blown to the ear out of a great distance; for it was smothered under another sound which was still nearer—in his own breast, in his accusing conscience —a voice which kept repeating those shameful words, "I do not know you, woman!"

The words smote upon the king's soul as the strokes of a funeral bell smite upon the soul of a surviving friend when they remind him of secret treacheries suffered at his hands by him that is gone.

New glories were unfolded at every turning; new wonders, new marvels sprung into view; the pent clamors of waiting batteries were released; new raptures poured from the throats of the waiting multitudes; but the king gave no sign, and the accusing voice that went moaning through his comfortless breast was all the sound he heard.

By and by the gladness in the faces of the populace changed a little, and became touched with a something like solicitude, or anxiety; an abatement in the volume of applause was observable, too. The Lord Protector was quick to notice these things; he was as quick to detect the cause. He spurred to the king's side, bent low in his saddle, uncovered, and said—

"My liege! It is an ill time for dreaming! The people observe thy downcast head, thy clouded mien, and they take it for an omen! Be advised; unveil the sun of royalty and let it shine upon these boding vapors and disperse them. Lift up thy face and smile upon the people!"

"MY LIEGE! IT IS AN ILL TIME FOR DREAMING!"

So saying, the duke scattered a handful of coins to right and left, then retired to his place. The mock king did mechanically as he had been bidden. His smile had no heart in it, but few eyes were near enough or sharp enough to detect that; the noddings of his plumed head, as he saluted his subjects, were full of grace and graciousness; the largess which he delivered from his hand was royally liberal; so the people's anxiety vanished, and the acclamations burst forth again, in as mighty a volume as before.

Still, once more—a little before the progress was ended—the duke was obliged to ride forward and make remonstrance. He whispered—

"SHE WAS MY MOTHER!"

"O, dread sovereign, shake off these fatal humors—the eyes of the world are upon thee!" Then he added, with sharp annoyance, "Perdition catch that crazy pauper!—'twas she that hath disturbed your highness."

The gorgeous figure turned a lustreless eye upon the duke, and said in a dead voice—

"She was my mother!"

"My God!" groaned the Protector, as he reined his horse backward to his post, "the omen was pregnant with prophecy. He is gone mad again!"

CHAPTER 32

LET US GO BACKWARD a few hours, and place ourselves in Westminster Abbey, at four o'clock in the morning of this memorable Coronation Day. We are not without company; for although it is still night, we find the torch-lighted galleries already filling up with people who are well content to sit still and wait seven or eight hours till the time shall come for them to see what they may not hope to see twice in their lives—the coronation of a king. Yes, London and Westminster have been astir ever since the warning guns boomed at three o'clock, and already crowds of untitled rich folk who have bought the privilege of trying to find sitting-room in the galleries are flocking in at the entrances reserved for their sort.

The hours drag along, tediously enough. All stir has ceased for some time, for every gallery has long ago been packed. We may sit, now, and look and think at our leisure. We have glimpses, here and there and yonder, through the dim cathedral twilight, of portions of many galleries and balconies, wedged full with people, the other portions of these galleries and balconies being cut off from sight by intervening pillars and architectural projections. We have in view the whole of the great north transept—empty, and waiting for England's

privileged ones. We see also the ample area or platform, carpeted
with rich stuffs, whereon the throne stands. The throne occupies the
centre of the platform, and is raised above it upon an elevation of
four steps. Within the seat of the throne is enclosed a rough flat rock
—the stone of Scone—which many generations of Scottish kings sat
on to be crowned, and so it in time became holy enough to answer a
like purpose for English monarchs. Both the throne and its footstool
are covered with cloth of gold.

Stillness reigns, the torches blink dully, the time drags heavily.
But at last the lagging daylight asserts itself, the torches are extin-

"GATHERS UP THE LADY'S LONG TRAIN."

guished, and a mellow radiance suffuses the great spaces. All features
of the noble building are distinct, now, but soft and dreamy, for the
sun is lightly veiled with clouds.

At seven o'clock the first break in the drowsy monotony occurs;
for on the stroke of this hour the first peeress enters the transept,
clothed like Solomon for splendor, and is conducted to her appointed
place by an official clad in satins and velvets, whilst a duplicate of
him gathers up the lady's long train, follows after, and, when the lady
is seated, arranges the train across her lap for her. He then places her
footstool according to her desire, after which he puts her coronet
where it will be convenient to her hand when the time for the simul-
taneous coroneting of the nobles shall arrive.

By this time the peeresses are flowing in in a glittering stream, and
the satin-clad officials are flitting and glinting everywhere, seating

them and making them comfortable. The scene is animated enough, now. There is stir and life, and shifting color everywhere. After a time, quiet reigns again; for the peeresses are all come, and are all in their places—a solid acre, or such a matter, of human flowers, resplendent in variegated colors, and frosted like a Milky Way with diamonds. There are all ages, here: brown, wrinkled, white-haired dowagers who are able to go back, and still back, down the stream of time, and recal the crowning of Richard III and the troublous days of that old forgotten age; and there are handsome middle-aged dames; and lovely and gracious young matrons; and gentle and beautiful young girls, with beaming eyes and fresh complexions, who may possibly put on their jeweled coronets awkwardly when the great time comes; for the matter will be new to them, and their excitement will be a sore hindrance. Still, this may not happen, for the hair of all these ladies has been arranged with a special view to the swift and success-ful lodging of the crown in its place when the signal comes.

We have seen that this massed array of peeresses is sown thick with diamonds, and we also see that it is a marvelous spectacle—but now we are about to be astonished in earnest. About nine, the clouds suddenly break away and a shaft of sunshine cleaves the mellow atmosphere, and drifts slowly along the ranks of ladies; and every rank it touches flames into a dazzling splendor of many-colored fires, and we tingle to our finger-tips with the electric thrill that is shot through us by the surprise and the beauty of the spectacle! Presently a special envoy from some distant corner of the Orient, marching with the general body of foreign ambassadors, crosses this bar of sunshine, and we catch our breath, the glory that streams and flashes and palpitates about him is so overpowering; for he is crusted from head to heel with gems, and his slightest movement showers a dancing radiance all around him.

Let us change the tense, for convenience. The time drifted along, —one hour—two hours—two hours and a half; then the deep boom-ing of artillery told that the king and his grand procession had arrived at last; so the waiting multitude rejoiced. All knew that a further delay must follow, for the king must be prepared and robed for the solemn ceremony; but this delay would be pleasantly occupied by the assembling of the peers of the realm in their stately robes. These were conducted ceremoniously to their seats, and their coronets placed conveniently at hand; and meanwhile the multitude in the galleries were alive with interest, for most of them were beholding for the first time, dukes, earls and barons, whose names had been histori-cal for five hundred years. When all were finally seated, the spectacle from the galleries and all coigns of vantage was complete; a gor-geous one to look upon and to remember.

Now the robed and mitred great heads of the church, and their attendants, filed in up-on the platform and took their appointed places; these were fol-lowed by the Lord Pro-tector and other great officials, and these again by a steel-clad de-tachment of the Guard.

There was a waiting pause; then, at a signal, a triumphant peal of music burst forth, and Tom Canty, clothed in a long robe of cloth of gold, appeared at a door, and stepped upon the platform. The entire multitude rose, and the ceremony of the Recog-nition ensued.

"TOM CANTY APPEARED."

Then a noble anthem swept the Abbey with its rich waves of sound; and thus heralded and welcomed, Tom Canty was conducted to the throne. The ancient ceremonies went on, with impressive solemnity, whilst the audience gazed; and as they drew nearer and nearer to completion, Tom Canty grew pale, and still paler, and a deep and steadily deepening woe and despondency settled down upon his spirits and upon his remorseful heart.

At last the final act was at hand. The Archbishop of Canterbury lifted up the crown of England from its cushion and held it out over the trembling mock king's head. In the same instant a rainbow-radiance flashed along the spacious transept; for with one impulse every individual in the great concourse of nobles lifted a coronet and poised it over his or her head,—and paused in that attitude.

A deep hush pervaded the Abbey. At this impressive moment, a startling apparition intruded upon the scene—an apparition observed by none in the absorbed multitude, until it suddenly appeared, moving up the great central aisle. It was a boy, bareheaded, ill shod, and clothed in coarse plebeian garments that were falling to rags. He raised his hand with a solemnity which ill comported with his soiled and sorry aspect, and delivered this note of warning—

"I forbid you to set the crown of England upon that forfeited head. *I* am the king!"

In an instant several indignant hands were laid upon the boy; but in the same instant Tom Canty, in his regal vestments, made a swift step forward and cried out in a ringing voice—

"Loose him and forbear! He *is* the king!"

A sort of panic of astonishment swept the assemblage, and they partly rose in their places and stared in a bewildered way at one another and at the chief figures in this scene, like persons who wondered whether they were awake and in their senses, or asleep and dreaming. The Lord Protector was as amazed as the rest, but quickly recovered himself and exclaimed in a voice of authority—

"Mind not his majesty, his malady is upon him again—seize the vagabond!"

He would have been obeyed, but the mock king stamped his foot and cried out—

"On your peril! Touch him not, he is the king!"

The hands were withheld; a paralysis fell upon the house; no one moved, no one spoke; indeed no one knew how to act or what to say, in so strange and surprising an emergency. While all minds were struggling to right themselves, the boy still moved steadily forward, with high port and confident mien; he had never halted, from the beginning; and while the tangled minds still floundered helplessly, he stepped upon the platform, and the mock king ran with a glad face to meet him; and fell on his knees before him and said—

"O, my lord the king, let poor Tom Canty be first to swear fealty to thee, and say 'Put on thy crown and enter into thine own again!'"

"AND FELL ON HIS KNEES BEFORE HIM."

The Lord Protector's eye fell sternly upon the new-comer's face; but straightway the sternness vanished away and gave place to an expression of wondering surprise. This thing happened also to the other great officers. They glanced at each other, and retreated a step by a common and unconscious impulse. The thought in each mind was the same: "What a strange resemblance!"

The Lord Protector reflected a moment or two, in perplexity, then he said, with grave respectfulness—

"By your favor, sir, I desire to ask certain questions which—"

"I will answer them, my lord."

The duke asked him many questions about the court, the late king, the prince, the princesses,—the boy answered them correctly and without hesitating. He described the rooms of state in the palace, the late king's apartments, and those of the Prince of Wales.

It was strange; it was wonderful; yes, it was unaccountable—so all said that heard it. The tide was beginning to turn, and Tom Canty's hopes to run high, when the Lord Protector shook his head and said—

"It is true it is most wonderful—but it is no more than our lord the king likewise can do." This remark, and this reference to himself as still the king, saddened Tom Canty, and he felt his hopes crumbling from under him. "These are not *proofs*," added the Protector.

The tide was turning very fast, now, very fast indeed—but in the wrong direction; it was leaving poor Tom Canty stranded on the throne, and sweeping the other out to sea. The Lord Protector communed with himself—shook his head—the thought forced itself upon him, "It is perilous to the state and to us all, to entertain so fateful a riddle as this; it could divide the nation and undermine the throne." He turned and said—

"Sir Thomas, arrest this—No, hold!" His face lighted, and he confronted the ragged candidate with this question—

"Where lieth the Great Seal? Answer me this truly, and the riddle is unriddled; for only he that was Prince of Wales *can* so answer! On so trivial a thing hang a throne and a dynasty!"

It was a lucky thought, a happy thought. That it was so considered by the great officials was manifested by the silent applause that shot from eye to eye around their circle in the form of bright approving glances. Yes, none but the true prince could dissolve the stubborn mystery of the vanished Great Seal—this forlorn little impostor had been taught his lesson well, but here his teachings must fail, for his teacher himself could not answer *that* question—ah, very good, very good indeed; now we shall be rid of this troublesome and perilous business in short order! And so they nodded invisibly and smiled inwardly with satisfaction, and looked to see this foolish lad stricken with a palsy of guilty confusion. How surprised they were, then, to see nothing of the sort happen—how they marveled to hear him answer up promptly, in a confident and untroubled voice, and say—

"There is naught in this riddle that is difficult." Then, without so much as a by-your-leave to anybody, he turned and gave this command, with the easy manner of one accustomed to doing such things: "My lord St. John, go you to my private cabinet in the palace—for none knoweth the place better than you—and, close down to the floor, in the left corner remotest from the door that opens from the

"THE GREAT SEAL—FETCH IT HITHER."

ante-chamber, you shall find in the wall a brazen nail-head; press upon it and a little jewel-closet will fly open which not even you do know of—no, nor any soul else, in all the world but me and the trusty artisan that did contrive it for me. The first thing that falleth under your eye will be the Great Seal—fetch it hither."

All the company wondered at this speech, and wondered still more to see the little mendicant pick out this peer without hesitancy or apparent fear of mistake, and call him by name with such a placidly convincing air of having known him all his life. The peer was almost surprised into obeying. He even made a movement as if to go, but quickly recovered his tranquil attitude and confessed his blunder with a blush. Tom Canty turned upon him and said, sharply—

"Why dost thou hesitate? Hast not heard the king's command? Go!"

The lord St. John made a deep obeisance—and it was observed that it was a significantly cautious and non-committal one, it not being delivered at either of the kings, but at the neutral ground about half way between the two—and took his leave.

Now began a movement of the gorgeous particles of that official group which was slow, scarcely perceptible, and yet steady and persistent—a movement such as is observed in a kaleidoscope that is turned slowly, whereby the components of one splendid cluster fall away and join themselves to another—a movement which little by little, in the present case, dissolved the glittering crowd that stood about Tom Canty and clustered it together again in the neighborhood of the new-comer. Tom Canty stood almost alone. Now ensued a brief season of deep suspense and waiting—during which even the few faint-hearts still remaining near Tom Canty gradually scraped together courage enough to glide, one by one, over to the majority. So at last Tom Canty, in his royal robes and jewels, stood wholly alone and isolated from the world, a conspicuous figure, occupying an eloquent vacancy.

Now the lord St. John was seen returning. As he advanced up the mid-aisle the interest was so intense that the low murmur of conversation in the great assemblage died out and was succeeded by a profound hush, a breathless stillness, through which his footfalls pulsed with a dull and distant sound. Every eye was fastened upon him as he moved along. He reached the platform, paused a moment, then turned toward Tom Canty with a deep obeisance, and said—

"Sire, the Seal is not there!"

A mob does not melt away from the presence of a plague-patient with more haste than the band of pallid and terrified courtiers melted away from the presence of the shabby little claimant of the crown. In a moment he stood all alone, without friend or supporter, a target upon which was concentrated a bitter fire of scornful and angry looks. The Lord Protector called out fiercely—

"Cast the beggar into the street, and scourge him through the town —the paltry knave is worth no more consideration!"

Officers of the guard sprang forward to obey, but Tom Canty waved them off and said—

"Back! Whoso touches him perils his life!"

The Lord Protector was perplexed, in the last degree. He said to the lord St. John—

"Searched you well?—but it boots not to ask that. It doth seem passing strange. Little things, trifles, slip out of one's ken, and one does not think it matter for surprise; but how a so bulky thing as the Seal of England can vanish away and no man be able to get track of it again—a massy golden disk—"

Tom Canty, with beaming eyes, sprang forward and shouted—

"Hold, that is enough! Was it round?—and thick?—and had it letters and devices graved upon it?—Yes? O, *now* I know what this

"SIRE, THE SEAL IS NOT THERE!"

Great Seal is that there's been such worry and pother about! An' ye had described it to me, ye could have had it three weeks ago. Right well I know where it lies; but it was not I that put it there—first."

"Who, then, my liege?" asked the Lord Protector.

"He that stands there—the rightful king of England. And he shall tell you himself where it lies—then you will believe he knew it of his own knowledge. Bethink thee, my king—spur thy memory—it was the last, the very *last* thing thou didst that day before thou didst rush forth from the palace, clothed in my rags, to punish the soldier that insulted me."

A silence ensued, undisturbed by a movement or a whisper, and all eyes were fixed upon the new-comer, who stood, with bent head and corrugated brow, groping in his memory among a thronging multitude of valueless recollections for one single little elusive fact, which, found, would seat him upon a throne—unfound, would leave him as he was, for good and all—a pauper and an outcast. Moment after moment passed—the moments built themselves into minutes—still the boy struggled silently on, and gave no sign. But at last he heaved a sigh, shook his head slowly, and said, with a trembling lip and in a despondent voice—

"I call the scene back—all of it—but the Seal hath no place in it." He paused, then looked up, and said with gentle dignity, "My lords and gentlemen, if ye will rob your rightful sovereign of his own for lack of this evidence which he is not able to furnish, I may not stay ye, being powerless. But—"

"O, folly, O, madness, my king!" cried Tom Canty, in a panic, "wait!—think! Do not give up!—the cause is not lost! Nor *shall* be, neither! List to what I say—follow every word—I am going to bring that morning back again, every hap just as it happened. We talked— I told you of my sisters, Nan and Bet—ah, yes, you remember that; and about mine old grandam—and the rough games of the lads of Offal Court—yes, you remember these things also; very well, follow me still, you shall recal everything. You gave me food and drink, and did with princely courtesy send away the servants, so that my low breeding might not shame me before them—ah, yes, this also you remember."

"BETHINK THEE, MY KING."

As Tom checked off his details, and the other boy nodded his head in recognition of them, the great audience and the officials stared in puzzled wonderment; the tale sounded like true history, yet how could this impossible conjunction between a prince and a beggar-boy have come about? Never was a company of people so perplexed, so interested, and so stupefied, before.

"For a jest, my prince, we did exchange garments. Then we stood before a mirror; and so alike were we that both said it seemed as if there had been no change made—yes, you remember that. Then you noticed that the soldier had hurt my hand—look! here it is, I cannot yet even write with it, the fingers are so stiff. At this your highness sprang up, vowing vengeance upon that soldier, and ran toward the door—you passed a table—that thing you call the Seal lay on that table—you snatched it up and looked eagerly about, as if for a place to hide it—your eye caught sight of—"

"There, 'tis sufficient!—and the dear God be thanked!" exclaimed the ragged claimant, in a mighty excitement. "Go, my good St. John, —in an armpiece of the Milanese armor that hangs on the wall, thou'lt find the Seal!"

"Right, my king! right!" cried Tom Canty; "now the sceptre of England is thine own; and it were better for him that would dispute it that he had been born dumb! Go, my lord St. John, give thy feet wings!"

The whole assemblage was on its feet, now, and well nigh out of its mind with uneasiness, apprehension, and consuming excitement. On the floor and on the platform a deafening buzz of frantic conversation burst forth, and for some time nobody knew anything or heard anything or was interested in anything but what his neighbor was shouting into his ear, or he was shouting into his neighbor's ear. Time —nobody knew how much of it—swept by unheeded and unnoted. At last a sudden hush fell upon the house, and in the same moment St. John appeared upon the platform and held the Great Seal aloft in his hand. Then such a shout went up!

"Long live the true king!"

For five minutes the air quaked with shouts and the crash of musical instruments, and was white with a storm of waving handkerchiefs; and through it all a ragged lad, the most conspicuous figure in England, stood, flushed and happy and proud, in the centre of the

"LONG LIVE THE TRUE KING!"

spacious platform, with the great vassals of the kingdom kneeling around him.

Then all rose, and Tom Canty cried out—

"Now, O, my king, take these regal garments back, and give poor Tom, thy servant, his shreds and remnants again."

The Lord Protector spoke up—

"Let the small varlet be stripped and flung into the Tower."

But the new king, the true king, said—

"I will not have it so. But for him I had not got my crown again—none shall lay a hand upon him to harm him. And as for thee, my good uncle, my Lord Protector, this conduct of thine is not grateful toward this poor lad, for I hear he hath made thee a duke"—the Protector blushed—"yet he was not a king; wherefore, what is thy fine title worth, now? To-morrow you shall sue to me, *through him*, for its confirmation, else no duke, but a simple earl, shalt thou remain."

Under this rebuke, his grace the Duke of Somerset retired a little from the front for the moment. The king turned to Tom, and said, kindly—

"My poor boy, how was it that you could remember where I hid the Seal when I could not remember it myself?"

"Ah, my king, that was easy, since I used it divers days."

"Used it,—yet could not explain where it was?"

"I did not know it was *that* they wanted. They did not describe it, your majesty."

"Then how used you it?"

The red blood began to steal up into Tom's cheeks, and he dropped his eyes and was silent.

"Speak up, good lad, and fear nothing," said the king. "How used you the Great Seal of England?"

Tom stammered a moment, in a pathetic confusion, then got it out—

"To crack nuts with!"

Poor child, the avalanche of laughter that greeted this, nearly swept him off his feet. But if a doubt remained in any mind that Tom Canty

"TO CRACK NUTS WITH!"

was not the king of England and familiar with the august appurtenances of royalty, this reply disposed of it utterly.

Meantime the sumptuous robe of state had been removed from Tom's shoulders to the king's, whose rags were effectually hidden from sight under it.

Then the coronation ceremonies were resumed; the true king was anointed and the crown set upon his head, whilst cannon thundered the news to the city, and all London seemed to rock with applause.

CHAPTER 33

EDUARD AS KING

MILES HENDON was picturesque enough before he got into the riot on London Bridge—he was more so when he got out of it. He had but little money when he got in, none at all when he got out. The pickpockets had stripped him of his last farthing.

But no matter, so he found his boy. Being a soldier, he did not go at his task in a random way, but set to work, first of all, to arrange his campaign.

What would the boy naturally do? Where would he naturally go? Well—argued Miles—he would naturally go to his former haunts, for that is the instinct of unsound minds, when homeless and forsaken, as well as of sound ones. Whereabouts were his former haunts?

His rags, taken together with the low villain who seemed to know him and who even claimed to be his father, indicated that his home was in one or another of the poorest and meanest districts of London. Would the search for him be difficult, or long? No, it was likely to be easy and brief. He would not hunt for the boy, he would hunt for a crowd; in the centre of a big crowd or a little one, sooner or later, he should find his poor little friend, sure; and the mangy mob would be entertaining itself with pestering and aggravating the boy, who would be proclaiming himself king, as usual. Then Miles Hendon would cripple some of those people, and carry off his little ward, and comfort and cheer him with loving words, and the two would never be separated any more.

So Miles started on his quest. Hour after hour he tramped through back alleys and squalid streets, seeking groups and crowds, and finding no end of them, but never any sign of the boy. This greatly surprised him, but did not discourage him. To his notion, there was nothing the matter with his plan of campaign; the only miscalculation about it was that the campaign was becoming a lengthy one, whereas he had expected it to be short.

When daylight arrived, at last, he had made many a mile, and canvassed many a crowd, but the only result was that he was tolerably tired, rather hungry, and very sleepy. He wanted some breakfast, but there was no way to get it. To beg for it did not occur to him; as to pawning his sword, he would as soon have thought of parting with his honor; he could spare some of his clothes—yes, but one could as easily find a customer for a disease as for such clothes.

At noon he was still tramping—among the rabble which followed after the royal procession, now; for he argued that this regal display would attract his little lunatic powerfully. He followed the pageant through all its devious windings about London, and all the way to Westminster and the Abbey. He drifted here and there amongst the multitudes that were massed in the vicinity for a weary long time, baffled and perplexed, and finally wandered off, thinking, and trying to contrive some way to better his plan of campaign. By and by, when he came to himself out of his musings, he discovered that the town was far behind him and that the day was growing old. He was near the river, and in the country; it was a region of fine rural seats—not the sort of district to welcome clothes like his.

It was not at all cold; so he stretched himself on the ground in the lee of a hedge to rest and think. Drowsiness presently began to settle upon his senses; the faint and far-off boom of cannon was wafted to his ear, and he said to himself "The new king is crowned," and straightway fell asleep. He had not slept or rested, before, for more than thirty hours. He did not wake again until near the middle of the next morning.

"HE STRETCHED HIMSELF ON
THE GROUND."

He got up, lame, stiff, and half famished, washed himself in the river, stayed his stomach with a pint or two of water, and trudged off toward Westminster grumbling at himself for having wasted so much time. Hunger helped him to a new plan, now; he would try to get speech with old Sir Humphrey Marlow and borrow a few marks, and—but that was enough of a plan for the present; it would be time enough to enlarge it when this first stage should be accomplished.

Toward eleven o'clock he approached the palace; and although a host of showy people were about him, moving in the same direction, he was not inconspicuous—his costume took care of that. He watched these people's faces narrowly, hoping to find a charitable one whose possessor might be willing to carry his name to the old lieutenant—as to trying to get into the palace himself, that was simply out of the question.

Presently our whipping-boy passed him, then wheeled about and scanned his figure well, saying to himself, "An' that is not the very vagabond his majesty is in such a worry about, then am I an ass— though belike I was that before. He answereth the description to a rag—that God should make two such, would be to cheapen miracles, by wasteful repetition. I would I could contrive an excuse to speak with him."

Miles Hendon saved him the trouble; for he turned about, then, as a man generally will when somebody mesmerizes him by gazing hard at him from behind; and observing a strong interest in the boy's eyes, he stepped toward him and said—

"You have just come out from the palace; do you belong there?"

"Yes, your worship."

"Know you Sir Humphrey Marlow?"

The boy started, and said to himself, "Lord! mine old departed father!" Then he answered, aloud, "Right well, your worship."

"Good—is he within?"

"Yes," said the boy; and added, to himself, "within his grave."

"Might I crave your favor to carry my name to him, and say I beg to say a word in his ear?"

"I will despatch the business right willingly, fair sir."

"Then say Miles Hendon, son of Sir Richard, is here without—I shall be greatly bounden to you, my good lad."

The boy looked disappointed—"the king did not name him so," he said to himself—"but it mattereth not, this is his twin brother, and can give his majesty news of t'other Sir-Odds-and-Ends, I warrant." So he said to Miles, "Step in there a moment, good sir, and wait till I bring you word."

Hendon retired to the place indicated—it was a recess sunk in the palace wall, with a stone bench in it—a shelter for sentinels in bad weather. He had hardly seated himself when some halberdiers, in charge of an officer, passed by. The officer saw him, halted his men, and commanded Hendon to come forth. He obeyed, and was promptly arrested as a suspicious character prowling within the precincts of the palace. Things began to look ugly. Poor Miles was going to explain, but the officer roughly silenced him, and ordered his men to disarm him and search him.

"God of his mercy grant that they find somewhat," said poor Miles;

"I have searched enow, and failed, yet is my need greater than theirs."

Nothing was found but a document. The officer tore it open, and Hendon smiled when he recognized the "pot-hooks" made by his lost little friend that black day at Hendon Hall. The officer's face grew dark as he read the English paragraph, and Miles's blenched to the opposite color as he listened.

"ARRESTED AS A SUSPICIOUS CHARACTER."

"Another new claimant of the crown!" cried the officer. "Verily they breed like rabbits, to-day. Seize the rascal, men, and see ye keep him fast whilst I convey this precious paper within and send it to the king."

He hurried away, leaving the prisoner in the grip of the halberdiers.

"Now is my evil luck ended at last," muttered Hendon, "for I shall dangle at a rope's end for a certainty, by reason of that bit of writing.

And what will become of my poor lad!—ah, only the good God knoweth."

By and by he saw the officer coming again, in a great hurry; so he plucked his courage together, purposing to meet his trouble as became a man. The officer ordered the men to loose the prisoner and return his sword to him; then bowed respectfully, and said—

"Please you sir, to follow me."

Hendon followed, saying to himself, "An' I were not traveling to death and judgment, and so must needs economize in sin, I would throttle this knave for his mock courtesy."

The two traversed a populous court, and arrived at the grand entrance of the palace, where the officer, with another bow, delivered Hendon into the hands of a gorgeous official, who received him with profound respect and led him forward through a great hall, lined on both sides with rows of splendid flunkeys (who made reverential obeisance as the two passed along, but fell into death-throes of silent laughter at our stately scarecrow the moment his back was turned,) and up a broad staircase, among flocks of fine folk, and finally conducted him into a vast room, clove a passage for him through the assembled nobility of England, then made a bow, reminded him to take his hat off, and left him standing in the middle of the room, a mark for all eyes, for plenty of indignant frowns, and for a sufficiency of amused and derisive smiles.

Miles Hendon was entirely bewildered. There sat the young king, under a canopy of state, five steps away, with his head bent down and aside, speaking with a sort of human bird of paradise—a duke, maybe; Hendon observed to himself that it was hard enough to be sentenced to death in the full vigor of life, without having this peculiarly public humiliation added. He wished the king would hurry about it—some of the gaudy people near by were becoming pretty offensive. At this moment the king raised his head slightly and Hendon caught a good view of his face. The sight nearly took his breath away! He stood gazing at the fair young face like one transfixed; then presently ejaculated—

"Lo, the lord of the Kingdom of Dreams and Shadows on his throne!"

He muttered some broken sentences, still gazing and marveling; then turned his eyes around and about, scanning the gorgeous throng

"IT IS HIS RIGHT!"

and the splendid saloon, murmuring "But these are *real*—verily these are *real* —surely it is not a dream."

He stared at the king again—and thought, *"Is* it a dream? . . . . or *is* he the veritable sovereign of England, and not the friendless poor Tom o' Bedlam I took him for—who shall solve me this riddle?" A sudden idea flashed in his eye, and he strode to the wall, gathered up a chair, brought it back, planted it on the floor, and sat down in it!

A buzz of indignation broke out, a rough hand was laid upon him, and a voice exclaimed,—

"Up, thou mannerless clown!—wouldst sit in the presence of the king?"

The disturbance attracted his majesty's attention, who stretched forth his hand and cried out—

"Touch him not, it is his right!"

The throng fell back, stupefied. The king went on—

"Learn ye all, ladies, lords and gentlemen, that this is my trusty and well beloved servant, Miles Hendon, who interposed his good sword

"STRIP THIS ROBBER."

and saved his prince from bodily harm and possible death—and for this he is a knight, by the king's voice. Also learn, that for a higher service, in that he saved his sovereign stripes and shame, taking these upon himself, he is a peer of England, Earl of Kent, and shall have gold and lands meet for the dignity. More—the privilege which he hath just exercised is his by royal grant; for we have ordained that the chiefs of his line shall have and hold the right to sit in the presence of the majesty of England henceforth, age after age, so long as the crown shall endure. Molest him not."

Two persons, who, through delay, had only arrived from the country during this morning, and had now been in this room only five minutes, stood listening to these words and looking at the king, then at the scarecrow, then at the king again, in a sort of torpid bewilderment. These were Sir Hugh and the lady Edith. But the new earl did not see them. He was still staring at the monarch, in a dazed way, and muttering—

"O, body o' me! *This* my pauper! this my lunatic! This is he whom *I* would show what grandeur was, in my house of seventy rooms and seven and twenty servants! This is he who had never known aught but rags for raiment, kicks for comfort, and offal for diet! This is he whom *I* adopted and would make respectable! Would God I had a bag to hide my head in!''

Then his manners suddenly came back to him, and he dropped upon his knees, with his hands between the king's, and swore allegiance and did homage for his lands and titles. Then he rose and stood respectfully aside, a mark still for all eyes—and much envy, too.

Now the king discovered Sir High, and spoke out, with wrathful voice and kindling eye—

''Strip this robber of his false show and stolen estates, and put him under lock and key till I have need of him.''

The late Sir Hugh was led away.

There was a stir at the other end of the room, now; the assemblage fell apart, and Tom Canty, quaintly but richly clothed, marched down, between these liv-

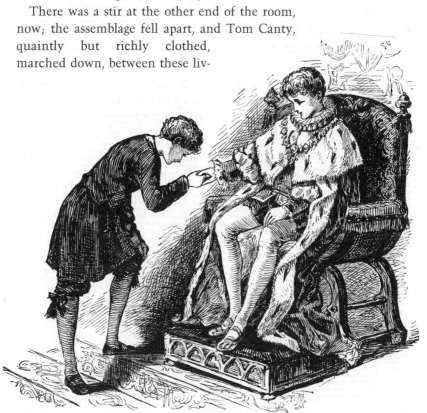

''TOM ROSE AND KISSED THE KING'S HAND.''

ing walls, preceded by an usher. He knelt before the king, who said—

"I have learned the story of these past few weeks, and am well pleased with thee. Thou hast governed the realm with right royal gentleness and mercy. Thou hast found thy mother and thy sisters again? Good; they shall be cared for—and thy father shall hang, if thou desire it and the law consent. Know, all ye that hear my voice, that from this day, they that abide in the shelter of Christ's Hospital and share the king's bounty, shall have their minds and hearts fed, as well as their baser parts; and this boy shall dwell there, and hold the chief place in its honorable body of governors, during life. And for that he hath been a king, it is meet that other than common observance shall be his due; wherefore, note this his dress of state, for by it he shall be known, and none shall copy it; and wheresoever he shall come, it shall remind the people that he hath been royal, in his time, and none shall deny him his due of reverence or fail to give him salutation. He hath the throne's protection, he hath the crown's support, he shall be known and called by the honorable title of the King's Ward."

The proud and happy Tom Canty rose and kissed the king's hand, and was conducted from the presence. He did not waste any time, but flew to his mother, to tell her and Nan and Bet all about it and get them to help him enjoy the great news.*

---

*See Notes to Chapter 33 at end of the volume.

CONCLUSION

Justice and Retribution

WHEN THE MYSTERIES were all cleared up, it came out, by confession of Hugh Hendon, that his wife had repudiated Miles by his command, that day at Hendon Hall—a command assisted and supported by the perfectly trustworthy promise that if she did not deny that he was Miles Hendon, and stand firmly to it, he would have her life; whereupon she said take it, she did not value it—and she would not repudiate Miles; then the husband said he would spare her life but have Miles assassinated! This was a different matter; so she gave her word and kept it.

Hugh was not prosecuted for his threats or for stealing his brother's estates and title, because the wife and brother would not testify against him—and the former would not have been allowed to do it, even if she had wanted to. Hugh deserted his wife and went over to the continent, where he presently died; and by and by the Earl of Kent married his relict. There were grand times and rejoicings at Hendon village when the couple paid their first visit to the Hall.

Tom Canty's father was never heard of again.

The king sought out the farmer who had been branded and sold as a slave, and reclaimed him from his evil life with the Ruffler's gang, and put him in the way of a comfortable livelihood.

He also took that old lawyer out of prison and remitted his fine. He provided good homes for the daughters of the two Baptist women whom he saw burned at the stake, and roundly punished the official who laid the undeserved stripes upon Miles Hendon's back.

He saved from the gallows the boy who had captured the stray falcon, and also the woman who had stolen a remnant of cloth from a weaver; but he was too late to save the man who had been convicted of killing a deer in the royal forest.

He showed favor to the justice who had pitied him when he was supposed to have stolen a pig, and he had the gratification of seeing him grow in the public esteem and become a great and honored man.

As long as the king lived he was fond of telling the story of his adventures, all through, from the hour that the sentinel cuffed him away from the palace gate till the final midnight when he deftly mixed himself into a gang of hurrying workmen and so slipped into the Abbey and climbed up and hid himself in the Confessor's tomb, and then slept so long, next day, that he came within one of missing the Coronation altogether. He said that the frequent rehearsing of the precious lesson kept him strong in his purpose to make its teachings yield benefits to his people; and so, whilst his life was spared he should continue to tell the story, and thus keep its sorrowful spectacles fresh in his memory and the springs of pity replenished in his heart.

Miles Hendon and Tom Canty were favorites of the king, all through his brief reign, and his sincere mourners when he died. The good Earl of Kent had too much sense to abuse his peculiar privilege; but he exercised it twice after the instance we have seen of it before he was called from the world; once at the accession of Queen Mary, and once at the accession of Queen Elizabeth. A descendant of his exercised it at the accession of James I. Before this one's son chose to use the privilege, near a quarter of a century had elapsed, and the "privilege of the Kents" had faded out of most people's memories; so, when the Kent of that day appeared before Charles I and his court and sat down in the sovereign's presence to assert and perpetuate the right of his house, there was a fine stir, indeed! But the matter was soon explained, and the right confirmed. The last earl of the line fell in the wars of the Commonwealth fighting for the king, and the odd privilege ended with him.

Tom Canty lived to be a very old man, a handsome, white-haired old fellow, of grave and benignant aspect. As long as he lasted he was honored; and he was also reverenced, for his striking and peculiar costume kept the people reminded that "in his time he had been royal;" so, wherever he appeared the crowd fell apart, making way for him, and whispering, one to another, "Doff thy hat, it is the King's Ward!"—and so they saluted, and got his kindly smile in return—and they valued it, too, for his was an honorable history.

Yes, King Edward VI lived only a few years, poor boy, but he lived them worthily. More than once, when some great dignitary, some gilded vassal of the crown, made argument against his leniency, and urged that some law which he was bent upon amending was gentle enough for its purpose, and wrought no suffering or oppression which any one need mightily mind, the young king turned the mournful eloquence of his great compassionate eyes upon him and answered—

"What dost *thou* know of suffering and oppression? I and my people know, but not thou."

The reign of Edward VI was a singularly merciful one for those harsh times. Now that we are taking leave of him, let us try to keep this in our minds, to his credit.

Note 1.—Page 68.

Christ's Hospital Costume.

It is most reasonable to regard the dress as copied from the costume of the citizens of London of that period, when long blue coats were the common habit of apprentices and serving-men, and yellow stockings were generally worn; the coat fits closely to the body, but has loose sleeves, and beneath is worn a sleeveless yellow under-coat; around the waist is a red leathern girdle; a clerical band round the neck, and a small flat black cap, about the size of a saucer, completes the costume.—Timbs' *Curiosities of London.*

Note 2.—Page 70.

It appears that Christ's Hospital was not originally founded as a *school*; its object was to rescue children from the streets, to shelter, feed, clothe them, etc.—Timbs' *Curiosities of London.*

Note 3.—Page 83.

The Duke of Norfolk's Condemnation Commanded.

The king was now approaching fast towards his end; and fearing lest Norfolk should escape him, he sent a message to the Commons, by which he desired them to hasten the bill, on pretence that Norfolk enjoyed the dignity of earl marshal, and it was necessary to appoint another, who might officiate at the ensuing ceremony of installing his son Prince of Wales.—Hume's *History of England*, vol. iii. p. 307.

Note 4.—Page 99.

It was not till the end of this reign [Henry VIII] that any salads, carrots, turnips, or other edible roots were produced in England. The little of these vegetables that was used, was formerly imported from Holland and Flanders. Queen Catherine, when she wanted a salad, was obliged to despatch a messenger thither on purpose.—Hume's *History of England*, vol. iii. p. 314.

Note 5.—Page 105.

Attainder of Norfolk.

The house of peers, without examining the prisoner, without trial or evidence, passed a bill of attainder against him and sent it down to the commons. . . . The obsequious commons obeyed his [the king's] directions; and the king, having affixed the royal assent to the bill by commissioners, issued orders for the execution of Norfolk on the morning of the twenty-ninth of January, [the next day.]—Hume's *History of England*, vol. iii. p. 307.

Note 6.—Page 120.

The Loving-Cup.

The loving-cup, and the peculiar ceremonies observed in drinking from it, are older than English history. It is thought that both are Danish importations. As far back as knowledge goes, the loving-cup has always been drunk at English banquets. Tradition explains the ceremonies in this way: in the rude ancient times it was deemed a wise precaution to have both hands of both drinkers employed, lest while the pledger pledged his love and fidelity to the pledgee, the pledgee take that opportunity to slip a dirk into him!

Note 7.—Page 129.

The Duke of Norfolk's Narrow Escape.

Had Henry VIII survived a few hours longer, his order for the duke's execution would have been carried into effect. "But news being carried to the Tower that the king himself had expired that night, the lieutenant deferred obeying the warrant; and it was not thought advisable by the Council to begin a new reign by the death of the greatest nobleman in the kingdom, who had been condemned by a sentence so unjust and tyrannical."—Hume's *History of England*, vol. iii. p. 307.

Note 8.—Page 164.

The Whipping-Boy.

James I and Charles II had whipping-boys, when they were little fellows, to take their punishment for them when they fell short in their lessons; so I have ventured to furnish my small prince with one, for my own purposes.

Notes to Chapter 15.—Page 180.

Character of Hertford.

The young king discovered an extreme attachment to his uncle, who was, in the main, a man of moderation and probity.—Hume's *History of England*, vol. iii. p. 324.

But if he [the Protector,] gave offence by assuming too much state, he deserves great praise on account of the laws passed this session, by which the rigor of former statutes was much mitigated, and some security given to the freedom of the constitution. All laws were repealed which extended the crime of treason beyond the statute of the twenty-fifth of Edward III; all laws enacted during the late reign extending the crime of felony; all the former laws against Lollardy or heresy, together with the statute of the Six Articles. None were to be accused for words, but within a month after they were spoken. By these repeals several of the most rigorous laws that ever had passed in England were annulled; and some dawn, both of civil and religious liberty, began to appear to the people. A repeal also passed of that law, the destruction of all laws, by which the king's proclamation was made of equal force with a statute.—*Ibid.*, vol. iii. p. 339.

Boiling to Death.

In the reign of Henry VIII, poisoners were, by act of parliament, condemned to be *boiled to death*. This act was repealed in the following reign.

In Germany, even in the 17th century, this horrible punishment was inflicted on coiners and counterfeiters. Taylor, the Water Poet, describes an execution he witnessed in Hamburg, in 1616. The judgment pronounced against a coiner of false money was that he should "be *boiled to death in oil*; not thrown into the vessel at once, but with a pulley or rope to be hanged under the armpits, and then let down into the oil *by degrees*; first the feet, and next the legs, and so to boil his flesh from his bones alive."—Dr. J. Hammond Trumbull's *Blue Laws, True and False*, p. 13.

The Famous Stocking Case.

A woman and her daughter, *nine years old*, were hanged in Huntingdon for selling their souls to the devil, and raising a storm by pulling off their stockings!—*Ibid.*, p. 20.

Note 10.—Page 197.

Enslaving.

So young a king, and so ignorant a peasant were likely to make mistakes—and this is an instance in point. This peasant was suffering from this law *by anticipation*; the king was venting his indignation against a law which was not yet in existence: for this hideous statute was to have birth in this little king's own reign. However, we know, from the humanity of his character, that it could never have been suggested by him.

Notes to Chapter 23.—Page 251.

Death for Trifling Larcenies.

When Connecticut and New Haven were framing their first codes, larceny above the value of twelve pence was a capital crime in England—as it had been since the time of Henry I.—Dr. J. Hammond Trumbull's *Blue Laws, True and False*, p. 13.

The curious old book called "The English Rogue" makes the limit thirteen pence ha'penny; death being the portion of any who steal a thing "above the value of thirteen pence ha'penny."

Notes to Chapter 27.—Page 284.

From many descriptions of larceny, the law expressly took away the benefit of clergy; to steal a horse, or a *hawk*, or woolen cloth from the weaver, was a hanging matter. So it was, to kill a deer from the king's forest, or to export sheep from the kingdom.—Dr. J. Hammond Trumbull's *Blue Laws, True and False*, p. 13.

William Prynne, a learned barrister, was sentenced—[long after Edward the Sixth's time]—to lose both his ears in the pillory; to degradation from the bar; a fine of £3,000, and imprisonment for life. Three years afterwards, he gave new offence to Laud, by publishing a pamphlet against the hierarchy. He was again prosecuted, and was sentenced to lose *what remained of his ears;* to pay a fine of £5,000; to be *branded on both his cheeks* with the letters S. L. (for Seditious Libeler,) and to remain in prison for life. The severity of this sentence was equaled by the savage rigor of its execution.—*Ibid.*, pp. 11–12.

Notes to Chapter 33.—Page 332.

CHRIST'S HOSPITAL, OR BLUE COAT SCHOOL, "the Noblest Institution in the World."

The ground on which the Priory of the Grey Friars stood was conferred by Henry the Eighth on the Corporation of London, [who caused the institution there of a home for poor boys and girls.] Subsequently, Edward the Sixth caused the old Priory to be properly repaired, and founded within it that noble establishment called the Blue Coat School, or Christ's Hospital, for the *education* and maintenance of orphans and the children of indigent persons. . . . . Edward would not let him [Bishop Ridley] depart till the letter was written, [to the Lord Mayor,] and then charged him to deliver it himself, and signify his special request and commandment, that no time might be lost in proposing what was convenient, and apprising him of the proceedings. The work was zealously undertaken, Ridley himself engaging in it; and the result was, the founding of Christ's Hospital for the education of poor children. [The king endowed several other charities at the same time.] "Lord God," said he, "I yield thee most hearty thanks that thou hast given me life thus long, to finish this work to the glory of thy name!" That innocent and most exemplary life was drawing rapidly to its close, and in a few days he rendered up his spirit to his Creator, praying God to defend the realm from Papistry.—J. Heneage Jesse's *London: its Celebrated Characters and Places.*

In the Great Hall hangs a large picture of King Edward VI seated on his throne, in a scarlet and ermined robe, holding the sceptre in his left hand,

and presenting with the other the Charter to the kneeling Lord Mayor. By his side stands the Chancellor, holding the seals, and next to him are other officers of state. Bishop Ridley kneels before him with uplifted hands, as if supplicating a blessing on the event; whilst the Aldermen, etc., with the Lord Mayor, kneel on both sides, occupying the middle ground of the picture; and lastly, in front, are a double row of boys on one side, and girls on the other, from the master and matron down to the boy and girl who have stepped forward from their respective rows, and kneel with raised hands before the king.—Timbs' *Curiosities of London*, p. 98.

Christ's Hospital, by ancient custom, possesses the privilege of addressing the Sovereign on the occasion of his or her coming into the City to partake of the hospitality of the Corporation of London.—*Ibid.*

The Dining-Hall, with its lobby and organ-gallery, occupies the entire story, which is 187 feet long, 51 feet wide, and 47 feet high; it is lit by nine large windows, filled with stained glass on the south side; and is, next to Westminster Hall, the noblest room in the metropolis. Here the boys, now about 800 in number, dine; and here are held the "Suppings in Public," to which visitors are admitted by tickets, issued by the Treasurer and by the Governors of Christ's Hospital. The tables are laid with cheese in wooden bowls; beer in wooden piggins, poured from leathern jacks; and bread brought in large baskets. The official company enter; the Lord Mayor, or President, takes his seat in a state chair, made of oak from St. Catherine's Church by the Tower; a hymn is sung, accompanied by the organ; a "Grecian," or head boy, reads the prayers from the pulpit, silence being enforced by three drops of a wooden hammer. After prayer the supper commences, and the visitors walk between the tables. At its close, the "trade-boys" take up the baskets, bowls, jacks, piggins, and candlesticks, and pass in procession, the bowing to the Governors being curiously formal. This spectacle was witnessed by Queen Victoria and Prince Albert in 1845.

Among the more eminent Blue Coat Boys are Joshua Barnes, editor of Anacreon and Euripides; Jeremiah Markland, the eminent critic, particularly in Greek literature; Camden, the antiquary; Bishop Stillingfleet; Samuel Richardson the novelist; Thomas Mitchell, the translator of Aristophanes; Thomas Barnes, many years editor of the London *Times*; Coleridge, Charles Lamb, and Leigh Hunt.

No boy is admitted before he is seven years old, or after he is nine; and no boy can remain in the school after he is fifteen, King's boys and "Grecians" alone excepted. There are about 500 Governors, at the head of whom are the Sovereign and the Prince of Wales. The qualification for a Governor is payment of £500.—*Ibid.*

GENERAL NOTE.

One hears much about the "hideous Blue-Laws of Connecticut," and is accustomed to shudder piously when they are mentioned. There are people in America—and even in England!—who imagine that they were a very monument of malignity, pitilessness, and inhumanity. Whereas, in reality they were about the first SWEEPING DEPARTURE FROM JUDICIAL ATROCITY which the "civilized" world had seen. This humane and kindly Blue-Law code, of two hundred and forty years ago, stands all by itself, with ages of bloody law on the further side of it, and a century and three-quarters of bloody English law on THIS side of it.

There has never been a time—under the Blue-Laws or any other—when above FOURTEEN crimes were punishable by death in Connecticut. But in England, within the memory of men who are still hale in body and mind, TWO HUNDRED AND TWENTY-THREE crimes were punishable by death!* These facts are worth knowing—and worth thinking about, too.

FINIS.

---

*See Dr. J. Hammond Trumbull's *Blue Laws, True and False*, p. 11.

APPENDIXES

APPENDIX A

MARK TWAIN'S WORKING NOTES

MARK TWAIN'S NOTES for *The Prince and the Pauper* provide a remarkably varied record of the author at work. They comprise extensive notes on English history and long lists of words and idioms which Mark Twain copied from his reading, interspersed with some of his earliest ideas for the book. Later notes, obviously made during the course of composition, show the author jotting down new ideas and refining what he had already written. All of these notes, along with a discarded page from an early version of the book, have been presented here as faithfully as the rendering of handwriting into type permits.

The notes have been grouped on the basis of physical characteristics, comparison with the manuscript, the subject matter treated within each set, internal cohesion, and topical references. When Mark Twain numbered his pages, his numbers have been printed. In addition, a number has been given to each manuscript leaf within a sequence.

No emendations have been made in Mark Twain's holograph notes. His ampersands have been retained. Words with single underlinings are rendered in italics, those with double underlinings in small capital letters. Cancellations are included and marked by angle brackets: <Hugo>. Added words or phrases are preceded and followed by carets: ∧butter-mouth∧. Additions in pencil or ink different from the original are rendered in boldface type: **Tothill fields.** Editorial explanations are in italics and enclosed in square brackets: [*circled in pencil*]. Mark Twain's alternative readings are separated by virgules: beguile/cheat.

The terms *ink 1, ink 2,* and *ink 3* are used to designate Mark Twain's writing materials. Ink 1 is the violet ink Mark Twain used for the earliest pages of his manuscript, written before the summer of 1877; ink 2 is the purple ink he used for the portions of the manuscript written between late 1877 and the spring of 1880; ink 3 is the blue ink he used for the final portion of his manuscript, written between the late spring of 1880 and 1 February 1881.

All the notes are in the Mark Twain Papers.[1] See the introduction (pp. 19–25) for full information on the works cited below by short title.

---

[1]Another manuscript page, discovered too late for inclusion here, is in the Berg collection. It contains notes drawn from the first chapter of J. A. Froude's *History of England,* volume 1.

Group A

These notes were written on a torn half-sheet of Crystal-Lake Mills station-ery measuring 20.5 by 12.5 centimeters ($8\frac{1}{16}$ by $4\frac{15}{16}$ inches), the paper used most often in the first sixteen chapters of the manuscript. The notes in A-1 were written in ink 1, whereas the notes in A-2 were written in pencil upside down on the verso of the sheet. The ink inscription is obviously a discarded page of the original Victorian manuscript featuring Jim Hubbard. The pencil notes, which refer to medieval arms, were clearly written after Mark Twain had decided to use an earlier historical setting.

A-1

3

that bowed down to the ground before the princes, made his heart ache with envy; so there was no more happiness for him. Jim's father was a steve-dore, or a coal-heaver, or something of that sort; a coarse, ignorant, passion-ate man, who often came home drunk, ∧&∧ brought a bottle of gin with him; & presently, <w> <as soon as> ∧when∧ his wife had caught up to his condition, the two would curse & fight. Jim & his brothers & sisters always came in for their share of cuffs & kicks, during the evening's performances, & then were likely to be sent to bed without any supper. ∧Jim being the eldest of the children, usually got a share of the kicks & cuffs based on the English law of primogeniture.∧ [added on the verso of the manuscript page]
    The family had but one

A-2

Bombards & culverin's
Hawberk & helmet
The King's highness
Children had to have from 7 to 15, a bow & 2 arrows.[1]

---

[1] A provision of a statute enacted by Henry VIII: "Fathers and governors of those of tender age were to teach them to shoot, having for every male child of seven years old in their houses, till he was seventeen, a bow and two shafts to induce him to learn" (Craik, *Pictorial History*, 2:759).

Group B

Mark Twain wrote these pages of notes on Crystal-Lake Mills stationery in ink 2. On some of the pages, he later made additions in pencil; on B-8, in pencil and ink 3. Most of the references are to the third volume of Hume's *History of England*. The content of these notes suggests Mark Twain had not yet begun his book and was engaged in establishing the basic historical background for it.

B-1

1

Son of Jane Seymour ∧who died in ch-bed.∧
Born Oct 12, '37. ∧in child-bed.∧
Succeeds Jan 28 '47.
∧assent to∧ Duke of Norfolk's attaint given by royal com'n the night of 27ᵗʰ **&** <2>**n of 28ᵗʰ**—king dies & he is <(I believe)> saved<.> ∧,
but lies in the Tower till accessⁿ of Mary.∧

Henry buried at Windsor Feb. 16—big funeral.

Anne Askew & 3 others burnt as Sacramentarians July 16, '46.

Edward (the real one) is crowned Feb. 20.

B-2

2

His uncle <the Lord High Admiral> ∧Protector∧ Somerset was the real king at first—<quite a warrior.>

Time, Jan. <20> **28** to Feb. 20.[1]

---

[1]More precisely, the book "begins at 9 a.m., Jan. 27, 1547," as Clemens explained to Howells on 11 March 1880, and "goes on for three weeks—till the midst of the coronation grandeurs in Westminster Abbey Feb. 20" (*MTHL*, 1:291).

B-3

3

∧*Put this in.*∧

<Cath. Parr (good sense & good talker) disputed with Henry, (she leaned to the religious reformers)<,>. Henry provoked because she disagreed. He complains to Gardiner (Arch" Cant?) who suggests her destruction. Chancellor (who?) seconds; Henry orders impeach articles; Wriothely draws them up—This paper Tom gets hold of & shows to the queen. See p. 303 Hume.>

Henry's natural son, Duke of Richmond, married a daughter of Duke of Norfolk (p. 305. Norfolk's son, the earl

B-4

4

∧Page 307∧

of Surrey. Both towered at once—Surrey beheaded Jan. 19.—let that begin this tale.

<H>Surrey had refused to marry Hertford's daughter. Henry believed he wanted to marry Mary.

Let Tom plead for Surrey.

Also for Norfolk.

Cranmer refused to help House of Lords & Commons destroy Norfolk.

Nobody with pluck enough to tell the terrible King he is going to die. Poor Tom does & gets a fine blowing up. "By the Splendor of God!" &c.

B-5

5

After Tom, Sir Anthony Denny does it, too.

He will know Lady Jane Grey, his cousin—very learned.—his own age.

Also Mary, _∧of Kath of Arragon._∧ born 1516.
Eliz, born 1533. of Anne Boleyn.

M. P.'s had 4ˢ a day, knights of shires, burgesses 2ˢ.

Katherine Howard lies in the Tower 3 mos & beheaded.

Kath Parr 4 yrs queen.

All monasteries dissolved & granted to Henry 1539.

B-6

6

E
65 [*written perpendicularly above* "burnings"]
Religious burnings.

_____

Shaxton, ∧ex-∧ Bish of Salisbury, <who preached> ex-Sacramentarian, reformed, & preached at Askew's burning, begging *her* to <re> conform. He was still alive in 1556.

_____

Anabaptists burnt.

People burnt for denying the royal authority in religious matters.

_____

Henry's marriages, page 284 Annual.

_____

No natural brothers or sisters surviving to Ed's time.

B-7

7

∧P. 314 Hume∧
Every man had to have a bow—but hand guns & X bows prohibited—no gatlings.

London could muster 15000 fighting men—that means a pop^n of 75,000.

_____

Tom sees carrots, lettuce & turnips for the first time.

_____

15000 foreign artificers in London. **& 30,000 natives, (?)—that suggests a pop of <225 to 250,000.> say 200,000.**

Plenty tramps.

_____

60,000 in prison for debt & crime at one time.
72,000 executed in Henry's reign, for *theft* & *robbery*.

B-8

8

$_\wedge$P. 317 Hume.$_\wedge$

Wages, prices of food, rent of farms.

4

{Whipping, degradation & expulsion for pronouncing Greek in the Protestant fashion! 319

{Tom's great servants—320 H. Put these around him in the beginning.

Coronation 424 Froude, 1 v.[1]

Tothill fields[2]

---

[1]A description of Anne Boleyn's spectacular coronation procession appears in the first volume of Froude's *History of England*.

[2]Mark Twain wrote this entry in pencil. The braces and the boldface numeral 4 were written in ink 3.

B-9

Mary comes like the rest to do $_\wedge$him$_\wedge$ homage as King.
<Tom's handwriting & his thoughtless signing of "Tom Canty" to a State document, betrays him>

No, he hurts his right hand & after always scrawls Edward Rex with his left.

58,000	
187,000	
40,000	485,000
200,000	50
485,000	535,

[*on verso of* B-9]

<1000>		
142,000		
90,000		
232,000	232	
58	58	
——	40	58 000
174	33,333	33,<000>333
	363,333	25 –

Group C

These notes were written in pencil on a large sheet of lined tablet paper measuring 31.7 by 20.5 centimeters ($12\frac{7}{16}$ by $8\frac{1}{16}$ inches), which has a three-part, red/blue/red, ledger-style rule 3.5 centimeters ($1\frac{3}{8}$ inches) from the left margin. The references are to Sir Walter Scott's *Fortunes of Nigel* and the fifth volume of Froude's *History of England*. In these notes Mark Twain's "v" is a roman numeral, not an abbreviation for "volume."

C-1

Alsatia (or Whitefriars) was legal refuge (See *Nigel*, introduction.

Hertford ambitious to be good to poor & have a reign of more liberty & without blood—this accounts for his allowing Tom to be kind—Froude v 17

Made in Council Feb. 16, Hertford Duke of Somerset, his brother Sir Thomas Seymour lord Seymour of Sudleye, Lord Parr Marquis of Northampton, <Lisle &> ∧Thos Lord∧ Wriothesley (<Arch[b] of Cant &> Lord Chancellor) & <Lisle> Viscount Lisle Earls of Warwick & Southampton.

Jan. 31st Hertfrd made ∧Lord∧ Protector.

The Executors (Council) F v 18.

Young Kingsale[1]

Cranmer Arch[b] of Cant

---

[1]See the explanatory note at 143.3–144.13.

Group D

Mark Twain wrote these language notes in pencil on eighteen sheets of Crystal-Lake Mills stationery and enclosed them in a folded sheet of Old Berkshire Mills stationery, which he labeled "Middle-Age phrases for a historical story." D-3 bears the number "42" written and canceled in ink 2. The top third of D-5 has been torn off.

The notes in D-1 and D-2 are primarily drawn from the scenes involving Falstaff in Shakespeare's *Henry IV, Part 1* (act 1, scene 2; act 2, scenes 1-4; act 3, scene 3; act 4, scene 2). The remainder of the notes in Group D are based on two Scott romances, *Ivanhoe* (D-3 and D-4 from chapters 1-9) and *Kenilworth* (D-5 through D-18 from chapters 1-4). Page references to Scott's works correspond to the pagination of the "Abbotsford" edition (Edinburgh and London: Robert Cadell, 1844), a handsome illustrated twelve-volume set that Clemens acquired in Edinburgh in August 1873 (Clemens' postscript on Olivia L. Clemens to Mrs. Jervis Langdon, 2–6 August 1873, Mark Twain Memorial, Hartford, Conn.).

D-1

Your highness (to the King) *Shak.*
"Room for the King!" "place for the King!" (Shak.) Enter King, attended
by 2 dukes.
  Please you, sir (to King.) Shak. Peace!
  Old sack
  Dials—
  God save thy grace
  Buff jerkin
  it jumps with my humor
S'blood—ᴧˢ'ᴧ death.
melancholy as a gib cat
'tis like, that they will know us.
Anon, anon (presently)
'Odsbody!
Nay, soft, I pray ye
Lend me thy lantern quoth 'a
foot land-rakers (footpads)
thou purple-hued malt-worm!
You muddy knave
Peace, yet fat-kidneyed rascal
Happy man be his dole (lucky be he)

D-2

Dish of skimmed milk (spiritless fellow)
Goodman—goodwife
<S>Then am I a shotten herring (rotten)
Seven, by these hilts, or I am a villain else.
3 misbegotten knaves
thou clay-brained fool
thou slave! (Shak)
hearts of gold!
What manner of man, an it like yr majesty<.>?
My noble lord (to King) Shak
Hide thee behind the arras.
He shall be answerable
Known as well as Pauls (K. Henry <IV> ᴧ4ᴧ <)>
& now you pick a quarrel to beguile/cheat me of it
Come from eating draff & husks
I cry you mercy my good lord

D-3

<**42**>

The curse of—
I am no true man
A murrain take thee
The curse of Cain upon thee
The father of mischief confound him
fain
touching these matters
son of Mahound! (Mahomet)
<Hugo>
What in the <name of> witch's name is ˄thee matter˄
Haply it is so
Haste thee, knave! (servant)
Begone!
Churl
thou ˄clown! thou˄ clod! thou <basket> ˄tub˄ of entrails
thou <sh>whey-faced, lily-livered varlet!
—hath neither the fear of earth nor awe of heaven
mighty ale—a flagon—a cup—
broach the cask
dance a measure
<Sh> Sirrah—villain
that were still somewhat on the bow-hand of fair justice

D-4

enow
Go to
Way for the King!
———————
Tilt—in Ivanhoe.
I crave pardon
drink wassail to the fair
That will I do, blithely
By the soul of my father
a bonny monk
gnaw the bowels of our nobles with usury.
I trow
Lord High Steward of England (obsolete?)
By the light of Heaven

Gramercy
in the fiend's name
Gramercy for thy courtesy (derision)
Wot ye who he is?
By my faith
Good morrow & well met
As I belong to worship (am too respectable to venture to lie)
Misfortune speed him!

D-5

　　　∧Marry come up—∧
Kingsale—Tush, man!
Pepys
Kenilworth
Giles
Tabard Inn in Southwark
Harry, Hal
Bear & Rugged Staff
Will
Loose jacket, linen breeches, ∧linen cap for cook∧ ∧landlord∧ green apron
　　∧napkin over arm, velvet cap∧
Beshrew my heart else
pewter flagon of Rhenish
best canaries—& ∧mulled∧ sack
jerkin & cloak
pike & caliver   ∧Gramercy∧

D-6

blithest news—∧how∧ durst thou
think so basely
gallants
Robin
the caliver that fired the ball
cannon
that I would give a peeled codling for
By the mass
kinsman
Michael—Mike
cavalier
warehouse—shop

Put in a printer
tapster's boy
gallows branded on left shoulder for *stealing* a caudle-cup
Slipping aside his ruff & <turning> ∧pushing∧ down the sleeve of his
  doublet from his ∧neck &∧ shoulder

D-7

Goodman—
dame
goodwife
swine
wend
indifferently
thriftless—
godless
infidel
wench
Laurence
mercer
haberdasher
lawns, cypresses & ribands
Spital
a cup of clary
Benedict
clerk of the parish
the hangman—brands people.
broad slouched hat & plume
laced wristbands
nonage
broils

D-8

prince royal—the heir
hang-dog that I am
I have suffered him to sit
guerdon
largesse! largesse!
bonny
spitchcock'd eels
I pray you of your courtesy

tankard
beaker
treason—everything is
legs swathed with a hay-wisp, a <thatched> ∧felt∧ bonnet.
their jerkin as thin as a cobweb
a pouch without ever a cross to keep the fiend from dancing it.
jovial
mar-feast
stand & deliver
crowns s. & d.
<guineas!> ∧nobles∧—<he>lo he talks in like a very lord!

D-9

wears his cloak o' one side & affects a ruffianly vaporing humor—
    his hat awry
Hounslow heath
ruffler
you wot not
'twas gospel
pluck his plumes <for>from him
worshipful
trowl the cup right merrily
jolly good ale & olde.
this savors of
swashing Will of Wallingford
swashbuckler
pursuivant's warrant
crossbow shaft
clothyard "   Dick
Tony Foster
roasted heretic for breakfast
Reeve to the abbot
purse of nobles & angels
quotha!

D-10

Anthony
poor wight
belted knight
rest her soul!
men keep such a coil about

the postern door was upon the latch
peach-colored doublet pinked out with cloth of gold
a silken jerkin & hose
what-d'ye-lack sort o' countenance
velvet bonnet, ostrich or Turkey feather—
gold brooch
shew
come, gentles,
Marry confound thine impudence
pudding face
sarsenet   ∧butter-mouth∧
hearken to him   ∧slate-face∧[1]
maugre all the gibes & quips of ∧his∧
peradventure
ambling palfrey
lattice

---

[1]Mark Twain also noted these two unusual compound words in his notebook in July 1877 (*N&J2*, p. 39).

D-11

gentlewoman
lady's dress—20, Kenilworth
lily-livered slave
quartern of sack
this bout
a piece of Hollands
lay you up in lavender (jail
the town-stocks—put him in (the wooden pinfold)
value no more'n shelled peascod
By St George
valor
Nay if it pleasure you
Nay
emprise
Wilt thou chop logic with me?
galloon lace
doughty
By St Julian
swilled
swill
smut
blasphemy

D-12

publican
salver
Three Cranes in the Vintry, the most topping tavern in London.
The Mitre in Fleet?

   Fleet Prison & marriages.
bide his wager
purlieu
new-laid eggs & muscadine <for> breakfast
<L>Giles
paid scot & lot
swasher
six-hooped pot
a carder, a dicer
mine host
Troth I know/wot not
bedizened
sold himself to the devil
Manor-house—
another clay than we are
Cicely

D-13

a wet night—drinking a cup of <fr> bastard
                                  clary
                                  canaries
                                  sack

e'en let her go her way o' God's name
how brave thou be'st, lad (dress
sad-colored suit
country-breeding
carves to me last
Coming, *friend* (makes prince mad
When the stake is made the game must be played
gamester
sack-butt
do me the grace
forfeit
Harry-nobles—gold
cold steel
wooded park

linsey-wo<o>lsey fellow
White-friars

D-14

such an unthrift
no saint & no saver
toper
his humor jumps with mine
La you there now!
swallow chaff for grain
a scant-of-grace
forsooth!
groat
a wealthy chuff
rose-nobles
make the best on't

A building—28 Ken
doublet of russet leather girt with buff belt—_∧(dudgeon dagger)_∧ long knife
    & cutlass
ingle-side
capon
friend, gossip & playfellow
gallows-bird
jail-rat

D-15

split thy wizen—weazand
as low as to thy midriff
caitiff
churl
clown
Tyburn tippet—so they did the hanging there?
Uds daggers!
fald-stool
puritanical

Prince dress—p. 31 Ken

books with great clasps & heavy bindings—Caxton & Wynk<y>in

Yeoman's service
Pshaw

Popish
papist
kennel
Gad-a-mercy

D-16

gall of bitterness & bond of iniquity (before conversion)
prithee peace
peace, dog!
mire
slop-pouch
thou canst not dance in a net & not be seen
Look you
lyme-hound to track wounded buck
gaze-hound to kill him at view
a currish proposal
ill-nurtured whelp
Milan visor—armor

Dress Tom in armor[1]
debauch
your falling band—linen falling down in front?
trunk-hose
carnal weapon—sword

---

[1]In chapter 7 of *The Prince and the Pauper* Tom amuses himself by donning a costly suit of armor he finds in the prince's apartments. For details of the costume Mark Twain referred to an illustration in chapter 5 of the "Abbotsford" edition of Scott's *Quentin Durward* and a description in chapter 8 of the same book (see E-2 and E-5).

D-17

gentleman-usher
puritan
priest with book at girdle
poniard
squire a dame
squire
esquire
hawk & hound
flat-cap'd thread-maker
mercer
give the wall to her
swaggerer   —ing word

putting a jape upon you (deceit
thou sodden-brained gull
filthy horn of stable lantern
By the holy cross of Abingdon
by the rood
sweet friend
masquer
mask
who shall gainsay me?
maiden

D-18

$_\wedge$van$_\wedge$ [*written off the page above "Harbottle"*]
Sir Harbottle Grimstone[1]
thy base unmannered tongue
Uds precious!
Knave $_\wedge$Varlet$_\wedge$
$_\wedge$Parliament bill brought to Tom in French   couldn't read it.$_\wedge$
costard—breast?
$_\wedge$away,$_\wedge$ base groom!
Avaunt
tarry not
by blood & nails
meddling coxcomb
withal
slouched hat & drooping feather
What make you here?
carrion-crow—batten
kite—maw[2]
Draw & defend
rapier (Elizabeth shortened them—let her say she will[3]
put up yr fox (sword)

---

[1]Mark Twain also made note of the "queer" name of this seventeenth-century English baronet in his notebook in March 1878 (*N&J2*, p. 59).

[2]A speech in chapter 4 of *Kenilworth*—" 'Are you come to triumph over the innocence you have destroyed, as the vulture or carrion-crow comes to batten on the lamb, whose eyes it has first plucked out?' "—evidently recalled to Mark Twain's mind these lines from act 3, scene 4, of *Macbeth:* "If charnel houses and our graves must send/Those that we bury back, our monuments/Shall be the maws of kites."

[3]As the art of fencing grew more prominent during Elizabeth's reign, the use of the rapier became more common, its "superior length" giving it a decided advantage over other dueling weapons. Elizabeth "put down this unfair practice" by stationing "grave citizens at every gate, who broke the points of the rapiers that exceeded a yard in length, and reduced them to the common standard" (Craik, *Pictorial History*, 2:869).

Group E

Mark Twain wrote these notes in pencil on torn half-sheets of unlined wove paper measuring 17.8 by 11.5 centimeters (7 by 4½ inches), the same paper he used exclusively for the second half of the book beginning with chapter 17. Nearly all the phrases were drawn from chapters 2 through 8 of *Quentin Durward*.

E-1

fine young springald
prithee, gossip, come
By St Anne but he is a <pe>proper youth
By my halidome
fair son,
my gossip (my comrade)
he hath little in his head but honesty & the fear of God
bill of charges
Rest you merry, fair master
a cup of burnt sack
hawking
paladin
pulled his bonnet over his eye
Hold, hold, most doughty man
Hark ye
mockery
ducat (not used)
Nay

E-2

Now by my father's hand (beard)
By Heaven
a flight-shot (arrow-shot) distant
hostelry
bestow
baldric
wine-pot
the brethren of the joyous science (war
the festival of St Jude last by-past.
I bethink me (I remember)
I doubt not your warranty
grand feudatories

He will give me good advice for my governance.
in guerdon of his service
gird at him
soothsayers & magicians, jugglers
a button of his jerkin
(Dress of arms about p. 54 Q. Durward)
You shall abye it (answer for it)

E-3

fair sir
with my humble duty
cavalier of honor
<c>soldier of fortune
damsel
<s>damosel
keep their state
shew
comfits—comfiture
bid yonder lady
bring hither
hark
hark in your ear
look you
the foul fiend
∧makes both serve him, for as∧ <for as> great princes as they be
good master
sirrah
old cozening quean[1]

---

[1]While most of the notes in E-3 are from chapter 4 of *Quentin Durward*, the probable source for this entry is Shakespeare's *Merry Wives of Windsor* (act 4, scene 2, line 180). The two preceding expressions also occur frequently in the same play.

E-4

squalid—squalor
halberd

Have a council concerning matters relating to foreign countries.

---

have a rouse (spree). carouse.
By my hilts!
thou shalt be dearly welcome

ay—aye
the weal or woe
fair cousin—said to a prince
By St Hubert
St Dunstan
<" Willibald>
" Swithin
Body o' me.
this brawling ruffler of the camps
his retinue of pursuivants & trumpets
coxcomb
I will nail my gauntlet to these gates
masterful
Marry & amen!
malapert ambassador
kindled with shame—kindling eye

E-5

[*on verso of* E-4]

Description of Tom in a fresh suit of armor sent to him—88 Q. Durward.
inflamed
Tom is to the King's Ward in X^s Hospital
He & Hendon are to live out the century & he longer.
A stately proclamation to Tom—90 Ib.

Group F

Mark Twain wrote most of these notes in ink 2 on the versos of sheets
from the printed playscript of *Ah Sin,* making some additions in pencil and
ink 3. He made the notes early in the composition of *The Prince and the
Pauper;* their content suggests that they were set down before he had completed chapter 7 of the manuscript.

F-1

Tom begins by abolishing all sorts of harsh laws by his simple command.
Her<bert>tfd & council object by T is firm—Am I not King? Hertford
persuades him to withhold execution a month hoping he forget. [*sidelined
in ink* 3]

Meantime, Prince is suffering these punishments & resolving to abolish them.

Sees a woman burned—going to stop that, too. Siezes axe, "I am King!" & rushes to cut her loose.

Tom & Mary talk—she urges for Pope & papacy & wants burnings. [*sidelined in ink 3*]

Tom says "No! let me but hear of a burning, & I—[*sidelined in ink 3*]

F-2

Speech-dog.

Visit queen Parr

Insert inquiry about Seal. ∧The K says, I told you do so & so with it.∧

Lords intriguing over will between 1 & daylight.

Ordering Norfolk's death by Commission.

140 servants for Tom.

Canty kills somebody & all fly.

Reflections of the 2 boys when they wake. Sir W^m. Herbert sleeps in room or closet with Tom—other servants & guards in ante-r. Tom asks, "Did I so & so yesterday, or dream it?"

Crowds of people in ante rooms—the K! the K!

F-3

∧*Champion rides in.*∧

True prince appears in rags from concealment in <Ed> Ed Confesrs tomb—hidden there & watched by his rough friend.

He offers plenty proofs—languages, &c—courtiers afraid to speak—Hertford alone says he is willing to risk his head by <calling him> fully believing in him if he can correctly answer one? Where is the great Seal? In right hand steel & gold gauntlet, <present> in cabinet. Describe this through Tom's eyes. Tom used it (to crack nuts with?)

Messenger inquires about the Cantys.

F-4

<2>

~Messire~ [*written in pencil above* "St John"]
Seems to me St John ought to manoever about the prince, too, but desire
to keep him out, since he can the better manage a mild <mad> & ignorant mad man.

He is the reason why the prince is never discovered, though always on the
point of being. His spy hunts in couples with Hertford's & so is always on
hand to prevent, by doing prince pretended favors & warnings & getting
him away.

Tom's friend suspects, & gets him away to Abbey privately, in time for cor.

Hertford says, No human creature would deny being

F-5

the prince, but would gladly lie the reverse, with so fine an opportunity—of
course the boy is mad!

<At that first luncheon the prince, out of his princely good breeding, sends
servants away lest their presence embarrass Tom.> [*written in pencil and
canceled in ink* 2]

<May I pick my teeth myself>

Wants to discharge his servants.

George ~(collar)~ & garter **where he dines in public** [*circled in ink* 3]

Mary Queen of Scots <5> ~4~ yrs ~& 1 month~ old in '47 [*sidelined in
ink* 3]

P Hertford, Mary & Bishops pester the soul of Tom with intrigues &
17 pleadings for this thing & that. [*sidelined in ink* 3]
57
6

F-6

The ball & mask after banquet—see Hunt for costumes.

Tom's first ceremonial dinner, with cup-bearers, & napkin-holders, & light-
snuffers—not allowed to do anything for himself. Eats with his fingers—is
surprised at the vegetables—asks their names.

H.—"Tis the prince's humor of his madness—humor it in all ways. Privately instructs Tom how to eat & put out his hand to be kissed."

F-7

Kings death announced in midst of Mask—confusion & hurry & excitement—mask breaks up—obsequious homage to Tom—"Live the King!" Barge it home in solemn state & slow oars, with the tide—deep tolling bells.

Purple for Mourning.

Court goes into mourning, <& pulls sad faces>

Henry's funeral—perpetual masses.

Passages between Guilford Dudley & lady Jane.

Tom—"He *is* King, & I am not"—(*at Coronation.*)

Group G

These notes were written in pencil on the front of a folded sheet of Crystal-Lake Mills stationery. The page citations refer to Lucy Aikin's *Memoirs of the Court of Queen Elizabeth,* which was first published in 1818 and several times reissued. Mark Twain apparently had originally planned to develop the role of the young Elizabeth more fully.

G-1

Elizabeth dressed with exceeding simplicity in Edward's time—60 Court of Q E.

Letter from Elizabeth to Tom about his health—62 & about H's place.

Let Tom's judgments & dining in public be put off a week. ∧but meet Council first day, as now.∧[1]

Strike out his talk with <Hum.> Eliz & Lady Jane till after his talk with Humphrey.

---

[1]Tom's judgment of the condemned prisoners (chapter 15) and the state dinner (chapter 16) originally took place the first day of Tom's kingship. Mark Twain accomplished the delay indicated in this note by revising a few lines in chapter 14 and inserting five pages (originally numbered 307A through 307E) at the beginning of chapter 15 which summarized Tom's activities on his second, third, and fourth days as king. Mark Twain did not act upon the following two recommendations for delaying episodes in the book.

Put off the talk with Humphrey several days. ∧if pos-∧

The letter accommodates matters, so Eliz returns from Hatfield— —62.

Tom teaches Eliz & Lady Jane to make mud pies.

Group H

These notes were written in pencil on the outer pages of a folded sheet of lined laid paper measuring 20.2 by 12.4 centimeters ($7^{15}/_{16}$ by $4^{7}/_{8}$ inches), embossed with a female head in profile. The page references are to Trumbull's *True-Blue Laws*. Mark Twain evidently made the notes before writing chapter 15, where the poisoner condemned to be boiled to death appears, as well as the woman and child accused of having "raised a storm by pulling off their stockings."

H-1

1

Crimes & Penalties.

Introduction to Blue Laws.

Petitioning the King against a judge for injustice, ears cut off &c.—11.
Man who wrote imprudent tract against maypoles, festivals, &c, <fined
£5000, ears cut>—he is proceeding to have the *remains* of his ears cut
off—12
     Pressing to death—12
Women's punishments for counterfeiting, irreligion &c, to be burnt alive
—12
(At Tyburn Prince may be, & see these.
Poisoners boiled to death—a law ∧of H. VIII∧ *repealed by Edward VI*. 13
2^d larceny of 13 pence, *death*—13
     The prince, in the kindness of

H-2

2

his heart, finding a crippled falcon, takes it up & succors it—it is found on him—he is accused by the real thief of stealing it, & is thrown into prison to await trial—penalty is death without benefit of clergy—13.

<The prince is badly treated by gypsies>

The prince sees 2 Dutch Baptists burnt—16

To speak in derogation of Book of Common Prayer, 100 marks; 17

Baptists could not make wills or receive legacies 17

He sees a *witch* ∧& daughter 9 yrs∧ burnt & approves. They had sold their souls to the devil—so enemies said—& raised a storm by pulling off their stockings—if Nan or Bet & Mother, they hadn't any.

Group I

Mark Twain wrote these notes in pencil on torn half-sheets of Crystal-Lake Mills stationery, making additions in ink 3 in I-6.

I-1

1

Edw. mourns for his father (weeps).

Tom dines in greater state, as King (see Lee Hunt).[1]

<Touches> ∧Tom∧ touches (his mother or sisters or father) & others for King's evil.[2]

   A bear-leader captures Ed. & makes him <put> pass the hat for pennies—This bearleader is <Canty.> of a gang of tramps who rove like gypsies (evicted to make sheep farms) In the tramp camp find Canty. Describe orgies. Miracle-playing troup for kitchens. Short card & dicing sharps (a man <pl>may play with his own servant)—see Blue Laws.

   Let them talk familiarly of this one & that one hanged, branded, burned for a witch &c, to Ed's horror. He finally blazes

---

[1]See the explanatory note at 182 *note.*

[2]See also I-4 and I-5. The ceremony of the King's Evil, dating from the reign of Edward the Confessor, grew out of a belief in the curative powers of the king's touch. Mark Twain abandoned his plans to use the ceremony in *The Prince and the Pauper,* but later introduced an anachronism into chapter 26 of *A Connecticut Yankee* by having King Arthur exercise the power over his subjects.

I-2

2

out in his royal character about what he will do, &c, to the immense amusement of the guffawing gang, who crown him, sceptre him & do him mock homage as Foo-foo the First King of the <Shadows> Mooncalves. With this gang he in time sees all the punishments inflicted. Sometimes he exercises the pardoning power & is laughed at. Gets cuffs.

He has furnished ∧a∧ letter<s> in Greek, <&> Latin & French to Hendon who is to send them to Court in evidence that he is prince. Hendon values them not, but carries them about him & forgets them. Being in a close place, later, after Ed is stolen he exhibits them as says they are certificate that he has been flogged.[1] Canty, covetous of this free pass, steals it from Hendon. Only a fragment is left, which reads: "That I am the rightful King of England I can prove; likewise that <Mar> the lady Mary & the lady E are my sisters. And I do hereby warn all,

---

[1] A statute enacted by Henry VIII in 1530 provided that a person found guilty of vagrancy should be publicly whipped and then "sent back to the place of his birth, or where he had last resided for three years, with a certificate of his whipping, 'there to put himself to labour, like as a true man oweth to do'" (Craik, *Pictorial History*, 2:905).

I-3

3

on pain of death . . . . ."
Gets to hand of officer who can read it—asks Canty if he claims all therein stated—he does—thrown in prison for high treason. Ed as King, sends pardon, but too late.

The tramps have taken away Hendon's clothes & reclothed him & sent him to beg. <—they admire him for getting>—finds favor with the gang because he has been flogged & is an old tramp & no gentleman—watches every opportunity to steal Ed away, but is watched too closely.

Night before Coronation—both boys striking for liberty, with deep-laid plans & bribed help—Tom∧'s∧ <comes> conscience will not let him be crowned. He comes within a hair of escaping—just the act of a mad King.

I-4

4

Show how Tom, finding discovery is not likely, loses his fears; then begins to take an interest in seeing how well he can play King; consequently soon begins to enjoy his pomps—requires 50 more Gents at Arms—but from that moment the struggle begins between his conscience & his <new> enjoyment of his pomps—a struggle in which conscience will finally win, & at last his only desire will be to get rid of the poisoned sceptre—he will be melancholy, hours together, & the ingenuity of the court will be taxed to amuse him.

Part of this is remorse for having touched his mother for King's evil & refused to receive her embrace or acknowledge her. ∧though he slips a handful of gold to her.∧ From that moment his pleasure is gone & he sets spies abroad to find her & the King.

His first joy is born of that state dinner.

I-5

5

One of his fears, when he is to drive in state to the city is that he may meet some member of his family & be betrayed. It is on this trip that he touches for the evil in (St Paul's?)

The progress to Paul's is for thanksgiving for his entire restoration to health & occurs between the funeral (16th) & the coronation (20th).

He ratifies <He> Somerset's dukedom Jan. 31, & Som[erset]¹ then becomes Protector.

Not *wholly* happy at the state dinner, but the dawn of happiness glimmers then.

Miss Martineau describes a coronation. See "Little Duke."²

If necessary have a tournament on the Bridge, from Scott.

Shall Edward see funeral at Windsor?

---

¹Mark Twain placed ditto marks beneath the first occurrence of Somerset's name to indicate these bracketed letters.

²Charlotte Yonge describes the ducal coronation of young Richard of Normandy in chapter 3 of *The Little Duke*. Howard G. Baetzhold has suggested that Clemens' mistaken reference to Harriet Martineau may have been caused by a confused recollection of Martineau's *The Peasant and the Prince* and Yonge's *The Prince and the Page* (Baetzhold, "Mark Twain's 'The Prince and the Pauper,'" *Notes and Queries*, n.s. 1 [September 1954]: 402). It seems clear, however, that the author was reminding himself to consult Martineau's description of Queen Victoria's coronation in the last volume of Craik's *Pictorial History* (7:584–586). Mark Twain, like Martineau, would describe the long and tedious hours of waiting, the splendid jewels and costumes of the noble onlookers illuminated by the rays of sun filtering into Westminster Abbey, and the dramatic burst of music heralding the monarch's arrival.

I-6

6

Edward must show grief for his father's death—Tom none.

Proposition of marriage with little Mary Queen of Scots, 4 yrs old.**—no, 5.**

King out in a bitter snow storm. [*written diagonally below other entries*]

Group J

Mark Twain wrote these notes in pencil on the outer pages of two folded sheets of the same paper he used for Group H.

J-1

Tom (as King) gives Father Andrew a large pension—Edward afterward confirms it. [*sidelined in ink 3*]
Tom had near <2>400 servants (page 119 MS).[1]

Hendon shall vagabondize on a bought certificate that he has been whipped & imprisoned for begging

---

[1]Page 119 of the manuscript (original pagination) corresponds to chapter 7, 98.17–28, of the present edition. The manuscript page shows that Mark Twain increased the number of royal servants from "a hundred & eighty-four" to "three hundred & eighty-four."

J-2

The prince hears of the death of the King that night & proclamation of Tom.
Prince is called Lambert Simnel & Perkin Warbeck.[1]

---

[1]Simnel and Warbeck were imposters involved in separate but equally unsuccessful intrigues to supplant Henry VII on the English throne in the late fifteenth century.

Group K

This note was written in pencil on a torn half-sheet of lined laid paper, measuring 20.2 by 12.5 centimeters ($7^{15}/_{16}$ by $4^{15}/_{16}$ inches), embossed with an ornate crest picturing a half moon and star. Although the reference to Timbs and Hunt, authors cited in *The Prince and the Pauper*, suggests that this note dates from the summer of 1879, it is possible that Clemens wrote it on one of his three earlier trips to London between 1872 and 1874. Stow's *Survey of London* was first published in 1598; "Walks" may refer to any of several pedestrian guides to London.

K-1

Page 1.

Nobody in town.—Bought Timbs—Walks—Stow<e>—Leigh Hunt, & a lot of other authorities & read about a thing, then went leisurely to see it.

Group L

Mark Twain wrote these notes in pencil on three sheets of the same paper he used for the note in K-1. The work from which the references to the Tower of London and Sir Walter Raleigh were culled has not been identified. The connection between these notes and the plot of *the Prince and the Pauper* is tenuous at best. Like K-1, these notes may date from an earlier visit to London and perhaps reflect Mark Twain's early interest in writing a travel book about England.

L-1

1

Drunken habits of James I & his court—Hunt—413

"The Tower"

∧The fascination of spots which have seen history—grass grows not where Boleyn was beheaded—nor elsewhere.∧ [*added on the verso of the manuscript page*]

⎧ Crown <je>—second-hand.
⎪ Romantic 26
⎨ <Give Wren a blast> 27
⎪ Bully graveyard—a second Westminster—30}
⎪ See & print Blood's attempt on the jewels. Old Talbot
⎩ Edward's tablet—   31

Londoner's don't visit Tower.

<It is ancient slaughter house of <nobles> Kings—>

   <Kne>Killing of Jack Straw—34

L-2

2

---

[1]The first English translation of Jean Froissart's fourteenth-century *Chronicles*, undertaken by John Bourchier at the order of King Henry VIII, appeared in 1523–1525.

[2]Charlotte Yonge's *Cameos from English History from Rollo to Edward II* (1868). Clemens owned an 1871 edition of the book in which he made two marginal notes comparing certain harsh English statutes to southern slavery (*IE*, pp. 115–116).

L-3

3

Raleigh's company in Tower while writing his history—among them his wife—had a son born there Discourses & talks on chemistry—real comfortable times—best circumstances possible in which to write.   165

Been there 8 yrs then.

Imprisoned on a trivial trumped up charge. James robbed the son of his estate because he "maun have it for Carr."—a creature.

R. couldn't even "walk up the hill within the Tower." Afterwards allowed.

Wife kept head till death, 30 yrs—like daughter of More—was it a custom? —must have been a collection of heads in most noble houses.

Group M

This note was written in ink 2 on the torn upper half of a folded sheet of lined wove paper.

M-1

Inscribe to J.

Make portraits from the same photograph, & let artist dress one in rags, 'tother *en prince*—Call one Tom, aged 6 & tother The Prince of Wales, aged 6.

APPENDIX B

A Boy's Adventure

THE ORIGINAL MANUSCRIPT of the whipping boy's story is lost; this edition reproduces the episode as it appeared in the Hartford *Bazar Budget*, 4 June 1880, pp. [1]–2. It has also been published in Kenneth R. Andrews' *Nook Farm* (pp. 243–246) and was privately printed by Merle Johnson in 1928. Mark Twain included a similar story, sometimes called "The Bull and the Bees," in Book II, chapter 36, of *Joan of Arc*.

Since there is no sequence of pages missing from the original pagination scheme of *The Prince and the Pauper*, Clemens' claim, in the introductory paragraph for the *Bazar Budget*, that this episode was extracted from "the twenty-second chapter" of the book is apocryphal. Although he wrote the whipping boy's story in May or June 1880 when he was at the mid-point of his manuscript, he made no attempt to use it until after he had completed his first draft of the entire book in mid-September 1880. He then apparently made another draft of the whipping boy episode and inserted it as part of chapter 15 in the course of renumbering the whole manuscript. After Howells' condemnation of the story as "poor fun" in December 1880, Mark Twain withdrew it, leaving a hiatus (manuscript pages 314 through 342) in the second pagination scheme. The only surviving page (314) of the story is reproduced below. It is written in blue ink (ink 3) on a torn half-sheet of the wove paper used in the second half of the manuscript. On the verso of the page the number "6A" is written and canceled in ink 3.

314

∧This chapter withdrawn & canceled.∧

The "entertainment" which _∧he_∧ got out of it consisted mainly of an absurd bit of Master Humphrey's private history. This sable-clad & solemn boy had dropped a maxim, the evening before, in answer to something the lady Elizabeth had said; & <imme> straightway had colored so violently, that Tom's curiosity was piqued, & he told Humphrey to repeat the <odd m> quaint maxim, & then asked why he had blushed.

"There's naught to blush at in the maxim," said Humphrey, "but it doth remind me of a so stupid folly of mine, that the recollection of it always scorches my cheeks with shame."

Here the principals in the scene are Tom Canty and the whipping boy, Humphrey Marlow. For the *Bazar Budget* version, however, Clemens apparently judged it expedient to substitute Prince Edward for Tom Canty. For further discussion of the story, see *MTHL*, 2:873–874.

A Boy's Adventure

[As I haven't a miscellaneous article at hand, nor a subject to make one of, nor time to write the article if I had a subject, I beg to offer the following as a substitute. I take it from the twenty-second chapter of a tale for boys which I have been engaged upon, at intervals during the past three years, and which I hope to finish, yet, before all the boys grow up. I will explain, for the reader's benefit, as follows: The lad who is talking is a slim, gentle, smileless creature, void of all sense of humor, and given over to melancholy from his birth. He is speaking to little Edward VI., King of England, in a room in the palace; the two are by themselves; the speaker was "whipping-boy" to the king when the latter was Prince of Wales. James I. and Charles II. had whipping-boys when they were little fellows, to take their punishment for them when they fell short in their lessons, so I have ventured to furnish my small prince with one, for my own purposes. The time of this scene is early in the year 1548, consequently Edward VI. is about ten years of age; the other lad is fourteen or fifteen.]

I will tell it, my liege, seeing thou hast so commanded (said the whipping-boy, with a sigh which was manifestly well freighted with painful recollections), though it will open the sore afresh, and I shall suffer again the miseries of that misbegotten day.

It was last midsummer—Sunday, in the afternoon—and drowsy, hot and breathless; all the green country-side gasped and panted with the heat. I was at home, alone; alone, and burdened with the solitude. But first it is best that I say somewhat of the old knight my father—Sir Humphrey. He was just turned of forty, in the time of the Field of the Cloth of Gold, and was a brave and gallant subject. He was rich, too, albeit he grew poor enough before he died. At the Field he was in the great cardinal's suite, and shone with the best. In a famous Masque, there, he clothed himself in a marvelous dress of most outlandish sort, imaginary raiment of some fabled prince of goblins, or spirits, or I know not what; but this I know, that it was a nine-days' wonder, even there, where the art of the broad world had been taxed in the invention of things gorgeous, strange and memorable. Even the king thy father said it was a triumph, and swore it with his great oath, "By the Splendor of God!" What a king hath praised is precious, though it were dirt before; so my father brought home this dress to England, and kept it always laid up in herbs to guard it from injurious insects and decay. When his wealth vanished, he clung to it still.

Age crept upon him, trouble wrought strangenesses in him, delusions ate into his mind. He was of so uncomfortable a piety, and so hot-spirited withal, that when he prayed, one wished he might give over, he so filled the heart with glooms of hell and the nose with the stink of brimstone; yet when he was done, his weather straightway changed, and he so raged and swore and laid about him, right and left, that one's thought was, "Would God he would pray again."

In time was he affected with a fancy that he could cast out devils—wo worth the day! This very Sunday, whereof I have spoken to your grace, he was gone, with the household, on this sort of godly mission, to Hengist's Wood, a mile and more away, where all the gaping fools in Bilton parish were gathered to hear him pray a most notorious and pestilent devil out of the carcase of Gammer Hooker, an evil-minded beldame that had been long and grievously oppressed with that devil's presence, and in truth a legion more, God pardon me if I wrong the poor old ash-cat in so charging her.

As I did advertise your grace in the beginning, the afternoon was come, and I was sore wearied with the loneliness. Being scarce out of my thirteenth year, I was ill stocked with love for solitude, or patience to endure it. I cast about me for a pastime, and in an evil hour my thought fell upon that old gala-suit my father had brought from the Field of the Cloth of Gold near thirty years bygone. It was sacred; one might not touch it and live, an my father found him in the act. But I said within myself, 'tis a stubborn devil that bides in Gammer Hooker, my father cannot harry him forth with one prayer, nor yet a hundred—there is time enow—I will have a look, though I perish for the trespass.

I dragged the marvel out from its hiding, and fed my soul with the sight. O, thou shouldst have seen it flame and flash in the sun, my liege! It had all colors, and none were dull. The hose of shining green,—lovely, silken things; the high buskins, red-heeled, and great golden spurs, jeweled, and armed with rowels a whole span long, and the strangest trunks, the strangest odd-fashioned doublet man ever saw, and so many-colored, so rich of fabric and so bespangled; and then the robe! it was crimson satin, banded and barred from top to hem with a webbed glory of precious gems, if haply they were not false—and mark ye, my lord, this robe was all of a piece, and covered the head, with holes to breath and spy through; and it had long, wide sleeves, of a most curious pattern; then there was a belt and a great sword, and a shining golden helmet, full three spans high, out of whose top sprung a mighty spray of plumes, dyed red as fire. A most gallant and barbaric dress—evil befall the day I saw it!

When I was sated with gazing at it, and would have hid it in its place again, the devil of misfortune prompted me to put it on. It was there that my sorrow and my shame began. I clothed myself in it, and girt on the sword, and fixed on the great spurs. Naught fitted—all was a world too large—yet was I content, and filled with windy vanity. The helmet sunk down and promised to smother me, like to a cat with its head fast in a flagon, but I stuffed it out

with rags, and so mended the defect. The robe dragged the ground, wherefore was I forced to hold it up when I desired to walk with freedom. Marching hither and yonder before the mirror, the grand plumes gladdened my
heart and the crimson splendors of the robe made my foolish soul to sing
for joy, albeit, to speak plain truth, my first glimpse of mine array did well
nigh fright the breath out of my lank body, so like a moving conflagration
did I seem.

Now, forsooth, could I not be content with private and secluded happiness, but must go forth from the house, and see the full sun flash upon my
majesty. I looked warily abroad on every side; no human creature was in
sight; I passed down the stairs and stepped upon the greensward.

I beheld a something, then, that in one little fleeting instant whisked
all thought of the finery out of my head, and brimmed it with a hot new
interest. It was our bull,—a brisk young creature that I had tried to mount
a hundred times, and failed; now was he grazing, all peacefully and quiet,
with his back to me. I crept toward him, stealthily and slow, and O, so eager
and so anxiously, scarce breathing lest I should betray myself—then with
one master bound I lit astride his back! Ah, dear my liege, it was but a woful
triumph. He ran, he bellowed, he plunged here and there and yonder, and
flung his heels aloft in so mad a fashion that I was sore put to it to stick
where I was, and fain to forget it was a jaunt of pleasure, and busy my mind
with expedients to the saving of my neck. Wherefore, to this end, I did take
a so deadly grip upon his sides with those galling spurs that the pain of it
banished the slim remnant of his reason that was left, and so forsook he all
semblance of reserve, and set himself the task of tearing the general world
to rags, if so be, in the good providence of God, his heels might last out the
evil purpose of his heart. Being thus resolved, he fell to raging in wide circles
round and round the place, bowing his head and tossing it, with bellowings
that froze my blood, lashing the air with his tail, and plunging and prancing,
and launching his accursed heels, full freighted with destruction, at each
perishable thing his fortune gave him for a prey, till in the end he erred, to
his own hurt no less than mine, delivering a random kick that did stave a
beehive to shreds and tatters, and empty its embittered host upon us.

In good sooth, my liege, all that went before was but holiday pastime to
that that followed after. In briefer time than a burdened man might take to
breath a sigh, the fierce insects did clothe us like a garment, whilst their
mates, a singing swarm, encompassed us as with a cloud, and waited for any
vacancy that might appear upon our bodies. An I had been cast naked into
a hedge of nettles, it had been a blessed compromise, forasmuch as nettle-
stings grow not so near together as did these bee-stings compact themselves.
Now, being moved by the anguish of this new impulse, the bull did surpass
himself. He raged thrice around the circuit in the time he had consumed to
do it once, before, and wrought final wreck and desolation upon such scattering matters as he had aforetime overlooked and spared; then, perceiving
that the swarm still clouded the air about us, he was minded to fly the place,

and leave the creatures behind—wherefore, uplifting his tail, and bowing his head, he went storming down the road, praising God with a loud voice, and in a shorter space than a wholesome pulse might take to beat a hundred was a mile upon his way—but alack, so also were the bees. I noted not whither he tended, I was dead to all things but the bees and the miserable torment; the first admonishment I had that my true trouble was but now at hand, was a wild, affrighted murmur that broke upon my ear, then through those satin eye-holes I shot a glance, and beheld my father's devout multitude of fools scrambling and skurrying to right and left with the terrors of perdition in their souls; and one little instant after, I, helmeted, sworded, plumed, and blazing in that strange unearthly panoply of red-hot satin, tore into the midst, on my roaring bull,—and my father and his ancient witch being in the way, we struck them, full and fair, and all the four went down together, Sir Humphrey crying out, in the joy of his heart, "See, 'tis the master devil himself, and 'twas I that haled him forth!"

I marvel your majesty should laugh; I see naught in it of a merry sort, but only bitterness. Lord, it was pitiful to see how the wrathful bees did assault the holy congregation and harry them, turning their meek and godly prayers into profane cursings and blasphemous execrations, whilst the whole multitude, even down to the aged mothers in Israel and frosty-headed patriarchs did wildly skip and prance in the buzzing air, and thrash their arms about, and tumble and sprawl over one another in mad endeavor to flee the horrid place. And there, in the grass, my good father rolled and tossed, hither and thither, and everywhere,—being sore beset with the bees—delivering a howl of rage with every prod he got,—ah, good my liege, thou shouldst have heard him curse and pray!—and yet, amidst all his woes, still found his immortal vanity room and opportunity to vent itself; and so, from time to time shouted he with a glad voice, saying, "I wrought to bring forth one devil, and lo, have I emptied the courts of hell!"

I was found out, my prince—ah, prithee spare me the telling what happened to me then; I smart with the bare hint of it. My tale is done, my lord. When thou didst ask me yesterday, what I could mean by the strange reply I made to the lady Elizabeth, I humbly begged thee to await another time, and privacy. The thing I said to her grace was this—a maxim which I did build out of mine own head: "All superfluity is not wealth; if bee-stings were farthings, there was a day when Bilton parish had been rich."

HARTFORD, June, 1880.

MARK TWAIN.

EXPLANATORY
NOTES

EXPLANATORY NOTES

[See the introduction (pp. 19–25) for a general discussion of the historical sources of *The Prince and the Pauper* and for complete publication information on the works cited below only by author and short title.]

49.6–14   The houses . . . like doors.] This description of London dwellings was probably based on William Harrison's *Description of England* (chapter 12, "Of the Manner of Building and Furniture of Our Houses"), first published in 1577 as part of the first volume of Raphael Holinshed's *Chronicles*.

49.16   Offal Court, out of Pudding Lane] Pudding Lane, infamous as the squalid street where the Great Fire of London began in 1666, lies between the Tower and London Bridge. Offal Court is probably Mark Twain's invention, but the name is appropriate since, as John Stow notes in his sixteenth-century *Survey of London*, "the butchers of East Cheap have their scalding house for hogs [in Pudding Lane], and their puddings, with other filth of beasts, are voided down that way to their dungboats on the Thames" (London: George Routledge and Sons, 1890, p. 216).

68.7–16   They were all dressed . . . ugly costume.] The quaint uniform described here was actually not adopted until soon after Edward VI founded Christ's Hospital in 1552, five years after the period of Mark Twain's story.

108.12–109.3 "They were dressed . . . attendants."] The source of this quotation and the source or sources of those following at 109.6–7 and 110.6–12 have not been identified. The nature of the revision in these passages and the fact that the opening and closing quotation marks were added later in ink 3 suggest that these descriptions may have been Mark Twain's own invention.

125.15–33   "Space being made . . . behold."] All but the last line of this passage is a close transcription (the only changes are those that blur historical references and effect some modernization of spelling) of Edward Hall's description of a banquet given by Henry VIII on Shrove Sunday, 1510, in the parliament chamber at Westminster (*Chronicle*, p. 513). The passage was also incorporated into Holinshed's *Chronicles* (3:555), a work from which the author quoted elsewhere in *The Prince and the Pauper*. Differences in spelling and punctuation, however, indicate that Hall, rather than Holinshed, was Clemens' source. The last line of the passage was taken from Hall's description of another pageant during the reign of Henry VIII (Hall, *Chronicle*, p. 519; Holinshed, *Chronicles*, 3:561).

126.17 Don Caesar de Bazan] Mark Twain alludes to the ruined count in Victor Hugo's play *Ruy Blas*.

132.2–134.6 This structure . . . gateways.] A footnote added here in the manuscript and then canceled (see the alterations list, 132.8) makes it clear that the source for this description of London Bridge was J. Heneage Jesse's *London* (2:278–279). The manuscript pages describing the bridge were originally numbered 13 through 17 and were apparently fragments of a sequence of pages drafted independently, perhaps even for some other project, and then incorporated into the manuscript.

139 *note* *He refers . . . creation.] The present-day title of baronet was created in 1611 by King James I. The evolution of the baronet footnote is discussed in the textual introduction (pp. 398–401).

143.3–144.13 Near four hundred years ago . . . may do.] During his 1873 trip to England Clemens saw the de Courcy tomb in Westminster Abbey and noted the probably apocryphal story of the privilege granted to John de Courcy of Kinsale (or Kingsale) in the early thirteenth century by King John (*Mark Twain's Notebooks & Journals, Volume I (1855–1873)*, ed. Frederick Anderson, Michael B. Frank, and Kenneth Sanderson [Berkeley, Los Angeles, London: University of California Press, 1975], p. 535). The story of the de Courcy privilege gained currency through its inclusion in Thomas Fuller's *History of the Worthies of England* (1662).

148.8 There was a woman] Clemens was decidedly partial to this ballad, singing it, rather inappropriately, during his wedding trip in 1870. The author included it in the raftsmen chapter from *Huckleberry Finn* published in chapter 3 of *Life on the Mississippi*. The ballad, originally a British folk song, survives in the United States from the Southern Appalachians to the Southwest under various titles—"There Was an Old Woman in Our Town," "She Loved Her Husband Dearly," and "The Rich Old Lady." A version of the same ballad, called "The Old Woman of Wexford," has been recorded in recent years by the Clancy Brothers. The ballad and Mark Twain's use of it are further discussed in *MTHL* (p. 874). The revision of the last line at William Dean Howells' suggestion is described in the textual introduction (pp. 395–396).

148.21–149.1   He did ... woman's way.] Mark Twain was apparently as bewildered as Hendon about the intricacies of threading a needle for he gave precisely the opposite information in chapter 11 of *Huckleberry Finn*—"hold the needle still and poke the thread at it—that's the way a woman most always does; but a man always does 'tother way."

160 *note*   *Hume.] Mark Twain cites David Hume's *History of England* as his source here and on page 161, but the list of executors as he gives them and the details of the late king's expenses and his gifts to important crown servants are probably from James Anthony Froude's *History of England* (5:18, 20–21, 22, 23).

182 *note*   *Leigh Hunt's ... tourist.] Leigh Hunt quotes the sixteenth-century German traveler Paul Hentzner's description of Queen Elizabeth and her attendants going to chapel at Greenwich and preparing to dine (*The Town*, pp. 407–408). All the quotations in this chapter are transpositions of parts of Hentzner's long and detailed description, with obviously inappropriate references to Elizabeth and her retinue deleted or emended and the verbs altered from the past to the present tense.

193.4–11   "Bien ... trine."] From the 1874 facsimile edition of *The English Rogue* (1:46). Mark Twain quotes only the final verses, which may be translated:

> Good night then, Drink Woman and Tavern,
> The good man goes away,
> On the gallows to hang near London gallants dining
> For his long sleep at last.
> Go out good women and watch, and watch,
> Go out of London town,
> And watch the man that stole your goods,
> Upon the gallows to hang.

194.4   "Ruffler," or chief] As Francis Grose's *Dictionary* explains, the begging crew, male and female, was divided into twenty-three distinct castes, with the "rufflers" being the premier order in that hierarchy.

194.5–7   budges ... morts] "Budges," persons who steal clothes; "bulks" and "files," pickpockets and their mates; "clapperdogeons," born beggars; and "maunders," the general cant term for beggar. "Dells," "doxies," and "morts" were terms for women. These cant terms can be found in both *The English Rogue* and Grose's *Dictionary*.

197.1–6   And still ... hang!] This information regarding the punishment of beggars and run-away slaves occurs in J. Hammond Trumbull's *True-Blue Laws* (pp. 13–14), which clearly states that the harsh statutes were instituted during Edward VI's reign. It is therefore questionable whether Trumbull was the original source for this anachronistic passage, which necessitated a clumsy footnote. Clemens did consult Trumbull's book at some point, however, since his copy (now in the Detroit Public Library) has marginal scorings and brief factual notations on these pages.

206.20–24   'O, sir, . . . ready to perish!'] This plea for alms echoes one recorded in *The English Rogue* (1:62).

241.33–242.4 "Clime" . . . passer-by.] Mark Twain paraphrases *The English Rogue* (1:61–62).

256.11–12   *Non compos mentis lex talionis sic transit gloria Mundi*] Nonsense Latin made up of well-known phrases—"Not of sound mind the law of retaliation so passes away the glory of the world."

256.19–20   *ad hominem expurgatis in statu quo*] More nonsense Latin: "to the man you cleanse in the existing state."

287.6–9   History was . . . shameful page.] Mark Twain is referring to Henry II's scourging at the tomb of Thomas à Becket in 1174.

297 note   *Hume's England.] Hume, *History of England*, 3:315.

301.37   The chronicler says] In this and the following descriptive passages, Mark Twain selectively paraphrases Holinshed's account of Queen Elizabeth's passage from the Tower through the City of London to Westminster in January 1559, several days before her coronation (*Chronicles*, 4:159–167).

337.1–13   notes 1 and 2] Both notes quote material in John Timbs's *Curiosities of London* (p. 96), although Mark Twain has silently omitted some information and slightly altered a few readings.

338.10–18   note 6] Mark Twain found this information about the loving-cup in Timbs's *Curiosities of London* (p. 395n).

339.35–340.3 notes to chapter 23] Mark Twain neglects to mention that the entire episode of the woman and the pig was taken with only minor changes from *The English Rogue* (1:63–65).

340.18–   notes to chapter 33] This information is quoted, with some
341.41   liberty, from Jesse's *London* (3:225–226) and Timbs's *Curiosities of London* (pp. 98, 99, 101).

TEXTUAL
APPARATUS

TEXTUAL INTRODUCTION

MARK TWAIN'S MANUSCRIPT of *The Prince and the Pauper* has survived, but the secretarial transcription that evidently served as printer's copy and the proof sheets that the author saw and revised have both been lost. The textual history of the first American edition, published in Boston by James R. Osgood and Company on 12 December 1881, therefore rests chiefly on the evidence obtained from collations of the author's manuscript, the publisher's prospectus, and the two states of that edition. Additional collations have shown that the first Canadian edition and the three states of the first English edition derive in complicated ways from the first American edition; all later editions are also derivative and embody no authorial revision. This evidence, in conjunction with other documents and letters, makes possible a more detailed account than has previously been available of how Mark Twain saw his book into print.

On 1 February 1881 Mark Twain wrote Osgood from Hartford, "Suppose you . . . run down here & sign, & lug off the MS—which I finished *once more* to-day."[1] Osgood presumably went to Hartford; in any event he signed the contract for the book on February 9. Whether he actually returned to Boston with the manuscript is uncertain: the contract specified only that the manuscript was to be in his hands "as soon as practicable after the date of this agreement, and not later than April 1st next ensuing."[2] But in less than a month he did indeed have it, for on March 3 Mark Twain wrote to A. V. S. Anthony, who was in charge of hiring illustrators for the book, "Very well then, I *do* say 'go

[1]Clemens to Osgood, 1 February 1881, collection of Theodore Koundakjian. Insignificant cancellations in letters have been dropped from quotations throughout. When cancellations are included, they appear within angle brackets.

[2]The contract, in MTP, is reprinted in Frederick Anderson and Hamlin Hill, "How Samuel Clemens Became Mark Twain's Publisher: A Study of the James R. Osgood Contracts," *Proof* 2 (1972): 121–124.

ahead' to the artist who is ready to make a couple of drawings on approbation."[3]

Mark Twain's manuscript probably became the house copy for the Osgood company, and may have been used by the illustrators as well, but it did not serve as printer's copy. In 1885, Mark Twain remembered that "Osgood had the Prince & Pauper copied, & sent the *copy* to the printer."[4] The manuscript has only a few minor notes and changes in another hand on the first pages, most of them added by someone in Osgood's office. Osgood himself added "Boston | James R. Osgood & Company" to the title page and moved "All rights reserved" from there to the copyright page.[5]

The printer's copy, now lost, was apparently a handwritten secretarial copy of the manuscript. Although it was Mark Twain's usual practice to revise printer's copy, he evidently had no opportunity to do so for *The Prince and the Pauper* before Osgood sent it to the printer: he confined his postmanuscript revisions to proof.

The typesetting of the first American edition was done by the Franklin Press: Rand, Avery, and Company, Boston, who also electroplated the illustrations and, later, the book itself.[6] Although the author told one correspondent on 22 April 1881 that his book was "in press,"[7] he doubtless meant only that the slow work of producing the illustrations had begun. The records of the Osgood company show that the first two "relief plates" were completed on April 21 and that these continued to be manufactured in batches until October 7.[8] The typesetting of the book itself may have begun in April, but it seems somewhat more likely that it was delayed until the company had prepared, and Mark Twain had approved, a sizable number of illustrations. On July 2 he asked the company to send him "proofs of the pictures that are thus far completed for my book," and reminded them

---

[3]Clemens to Anthony, 3 March 1881, photocopy in MTP.

[4]Clemens to Benjamin Ticknor, 12 November 1885, Yale.

[5]However, five pages of Mark Twain's manuscript were sent to the printer for evaluation very early in the production process. For nonauthorial notations that were made on the manuscript at that time, see the textual notes at 45.1, 49.5, and 51.7. This and all subsequent descriptions of the manuscript refer to Mark Twain's manuscript at the Henry E. Huntington Library and Art Gallery, San Marino, California.

[6]The Osgood company cost book lists all initial typesetting, plating, and repair costs under "R A & Co" (MS Am 1185.6, Houghton Library, Harvard, pp. 126–127).

[7]Clemens to F. A. Teall, 22 April 1881, CWB.

[8]Osgood company cost book, p. 126.

that "Osgood promised, but Osgood forgot."[9] On July 31 Mark Twain told another correspondent, "Proofs of a hundred & fifty of the engravings for my new book came yesterday, & I like them far better than any that have ever been made for me before."[10] The next day, August 1, he praised the pictures extravagantly to Benjamin H. Ticknor, Osgood's partner, and tried to arrange for special printings to be neatly bound in boards. At this time he had clearly not seen any proof sheets of the text, for he told Ticknor, "Put titles under the pictures yourself—I'll alter them in proof if any alteration shall seem necessary." And on August 14 he again praised the illustrations to Ticknor but said (apparently in response to an inquiry from the publisher), "I hain't got no proofs, yet—but there may be some in the post office now." The next day he had in fact received the first installment of proofs—an incomplete set which omitted several chapters and which contained, moreover, a problem with the illustration in chapter 1. Ticknor must have explained that this illustration had been made too large and would need to be redone—a step that probably required most of this short chapter to be reset. On August 15 Mark Twain wrote him, "Yes, that is the correct idea—do the cut over again; process it down to the required reduction." He added that he would "have to wait till you send Chap 1 again, & then begin fair & read consecutively—can't begin in the middle of the book."[11]

The illustration was eventually redone, but Mark Twain evidently could not resist the temptation to begin reading, even "in the middle of the book," and he must have read chapters 1, 3, 5, and probably 7 as well, sometime between August 15 and 23. His reaction to the quality of the typesetting was mixed, and he set it forth in a detailed letter to Ticknor while Osgood was in Europe:

If the printers will only follow copy strictly, in the matter of capitals and punctuation, my part of the proof-reading will be mere pastime. I never saw such beautiful proofs before. You will observe that in this first chapter I have not made a mark. In the other chapters I had no marks to make except in restoring my original punctuation and turning some 'tis's into "it is"—there being a dern sight too many of the

---

[9]Clemens to the Osgood company, 2 July 1881, Yale.

[10]Clemens to Mr. and Mrs. Karl Gerhardt, 31 July 1881, Boston Public Library.

[11]Clemens to Benjamin Ticknor, 1, 14, and 15 August 1881, *MTLP*, pp. 139–140, and Caroline Ticknor, *Glimpses of Authors* (Boston and New York: Houghton Mifflin Company, 1922), photofacsimile facing p. 132.

former. What I want to read proof for is for literary lapses and in-felicities (those I'll mark every time); so, in these chapters where I have had to turn my whole attention to restoring my punctuation, I do not consider that I have legitimately read proof at all. I did n't know what those chapters were about when I got through with them.

Let the printers follow my punctuation—it is the one thing I am inflexibly particular about. For corrections turning my "sprang" into "sprung" I am thankful; also for corrections of my grammar, for grammar is a science that was always too many for yours truly; but I like to have my punctuation respected. I learned it in a hundred printing-offices when I was a jour. printer; so it's got more real variety about it than any other accomplishment I possess, and I reverence it accordingly.

I have n't seen any chapter 2, nor chapter 4—nor the prefatory paragraph. But no matter; if my punctuation has been followed in them I will go bail that nobody else can find an error in them. Only, you want to be sure that they've been set up and not omitted.[12]

Shortly after writing Ticknor in this fashion Mark Twain wrote to Osgood, on August 23, and he was more than annoyed:

My dear Osgood, Welcome home again! Shall see you before you get this letter. I am sending Chapter VI back unread. I don't want to see any more until this godamded idiotic punctuating & capitalizing has been swept away & my own restored.

I didn't see this chapter until I had already read Chap. VII—which latter mess of God-forever-God-damned lunacy has turned my hair white with rage.[13]

This letter makes it clear that Mark Twain was not able to read

---

[12]This letter fragment is reprinted without a date in Caroline Ticknor's *Glimpses of Authors*, pp. 139–140. Although she does not say which book the letter refers to, she remarks that it was written "sometime previous" to another letter in which Mark Twain discusses *Life on the Mississippi*. As Mary Jane Jones writes, Benjamin Ticknor, as Osgood's partner, participated in the publication of only three of Mark Twain's books: *The Prince and the Pauper*, *The Stolen White Elephant*, and *Life on the Mississippi*. The description of proofs in this letter fits only *The Prince and the Pauper*. The *Stolen White Elephant* has no prefatory paragraph, and *Life on the Mississippi* has no profusion of the word " 'tis." *The Prince and the Pauper* has both. Mark Twain made ten changes from " 'tis" to "it is" in his manuscript, and three such variants also occur between the manuscript and the first American edition in chapter 3 (Mary Jane Jones, "A Critical Edition of Mark Twain's *The Prince and the Pauper*" [Ph.D. diss., University of Iowa, 1972], p. 336). The letter must therefore have been written between the arrival of proofs on August 15 and Mark Twain's angry letter to Osgood, cited next, on August 23.

[13]Clemens to Osgood, 23 August 1881, catalog of Sotheby Parke Bernet, sale no. 3694, 19–20 November 1974, item 89.

consecutive chapters, at least in the initial stages of proof: he looked at chapters 1, 3, 5, and 7, and that "latter mess of God-forever-God-damned lunacy" finally enraged him. At some point before August 23 he evidently received the even-numbered chapters, or at least chapter 6—which he returned "unread," presuming that the "godamded idiotic punctuating & capitalizing" was as bad there as in the odd-numbered chapters. Despite his tirades to Ticknor and to Osgood, chapters 1, 3, 5, 7, 8, 9, 10, 30, and 31 appeared in the book with their punctuation and word forms drastically altered from the manuscript readings. Chapters 2, 4, and 6, on the other hand, are fairly close to the manuscript. It therefore seems likely that alternate chapters were set by two compositors, only one of whom had been carefully or persuasively instructed in the author's preference for his own styling. Mark Twain's protest about the early chapters was ineffective: if the compositors did reset them or follow his corrections on the proofs, they did not succeed in restoring the practice of the manuscript. Nevertheless, he did eventually prevail, and of the thirty-four chapters in the first American edition, twenty-five conform fairly closely to the manuscript in the styling of accidentals.

Mark Twain met with Osgood on August 25 in Boston, and the problems with the printers were probably ironed out at that time. On September 12 he took a trip to Fredonia, New York, to visit his "mother & the rest of that family." He reported to Mary Mason Fairbanks on September 18 that when he had returned two days previously he had found "a stack" of proofs "waiting to be read." He had already read "$\frac{2}{3}$ of it in proof," he explained, and he now supposed that his "labors on that work [were] about ended."[14] Presumably he finished reading and returned the final third of the proofs promptly.

Although there is of course no direct evidence of the revisions Mark Twain made on the proofs during the summer, comparison of the manuscript with the first American edition reveals a number of "literary lapses and infelicities" that were corrected at this time, some of them undoubtedly by the author. For instance, the first American edition substitutes "Hugo" for the manuscript "Hugh" at 241.3 and 241.22. Mark Twain had mixed up the names of his villains intermit-

---

[14]Clemens to Mary Mason Fairbanks, 18 September 1881, *MTMF*, pp. 244–245.

tently throughout the work and had already corrected the mistake several times in his manuscript—for example, at 240.5 and 242.5.

In fact Mark Twain generally seems to have continued on the proofs the process of revision that he had begun on his manuscript. He polished his dialogue and narration, often choosing the modern form of a word instead of an archaic one. In addition to the substitution in chapter 3 of "It is" for the manuscript " 'Tis" (at 62.21, 64.13, and 64.37), which he mentioned in his letter to Ticknor, the first American edition substituted "since" for the manuscript "sith" at 105.30. Mark Twain had altered "sith" to "since" five times in his manuscript (at 93.11, 140.17, 143.1, 148.16, and 167.17) and was obviously making the same change on proof here.

Also consistent with his manuscript revision are several changes in italic and roman word forms. Mark Twain took great pains when marking for emphasis and often returned to his work to tinker with italics, especially in dialogue. There are eight such changes that probably occurred on proof (see the emendations at 69.14, 78.14 [twice], 139.5, 139.15, 164.8, 229.19, and 235.24).

By October 7 the publisher's prospectus was printed and ready for distribution to the canvassing agents.[15] It was made up of selected pages that would later appear in the first American edition, as well as four pages of descriptive material inserted by the publisher (including a price list), several ruled pages for subscribers' names, and samples of four bindings. Machine collation of the prospectus against the first American edition reveals that both were printed from plates rather than from standing type.

As Mark Twain indicated in his letter to Mrs. Fairbanks, he had considered his work on the book virtually finished when he returned the proofs to Osgood in late September. Nevertheless, a number of revisions were made in the plates sometime between the printing of the prospectus and the printing of the first American edition.[16] Many

---

[15]The Osgood company sheet stock book indicates that the company had received 1,010 copies (the only printing) of the prospectus by October 7 (MS Am 1185.10, Houghton Library, Harvard, p. 19).

[16]Some differences revealed in the machine collation of the prospectus against the first American edition did not result in new readings in the text of the latter. Seven pages of front matter were reset and restyled, the foliation of seven of the later pages was changed, and there was some type damage and repair.

of these changes were suggested by William Dean Howells and Edward H. House.

Between September 11 and October 12, Mark Twain sent a set of proof sheets to Howells, who had been commissioned to write a review of *The Prince and the Pauper*, which appeared in the New York *Tribune* of October 25.[17] Howells had already read the book in manuscript the year before, when Mark Twain gave it to him seeking his reaction and comments.[18] On October 12, Howells wrote to him about the proofs:

I send some pages with words queried. These and other things I have found in the book seem rather strong milk for babes—more like milk-punch in fact. If you give me leave I will correct them in the plates for you; but such a thing as that on p. 154, I can't cope with. I don't think such words as devil, and hick (for person) and basting (for beating,) ought to be suffered in your own narration. I have found about 20 such.[19]

And again on October 13 he wrote:

I send some passages marked, which I don't think are fit to go into a book for boys: your picture doesn't gain strength from [them] and [they] would justly tell against it. I venture to bring them to your notice in your own interest; and I hope you wont think I'm meddling.[20]

Mark Twain's response indicated that he did not think that Howells was meddling. On October 15 he wrote:

Slash away, with entire freedom; & the more you slash, the better I shall like it & the more I shall be cordially obliged to you. Alter any and everything you choose—don't hesitate.[21]

Despite Mark Twain's apparent willingness for Howells to make changes without consultation, Howells was actually sending him the proof sheets with queries or suggested alterations, and the author was making the decisions. He had often in the past asked Howells to read his works as an editor and as a friend; Howells had criticized *The Adventures of Tom Sawyer* before it was published, for example. And

---

[17]Howells to Clemens, 11 September and 12 October 1881, *MTHL*, 1:373–375.
[18]See the general introduction, pp. 7–8.
[19]Howells to Clemens, 12 October 1881, *MTHL*, 1:375.
[20]Howells to Clemens, 13 October 1881, *MTHL*, 1:376.
[21]Clemens to Howells, 15 October 1881, *MTHL*, 1:376.

just as he had done with *Tom Sawyer*, Mark Twain undoubtedly took some of Howells' suggestions, rejected some, and came up with new solutions in other instances.[22]

Of the problems that Howells specifically mentioned in his letter of October 12, "devils" was altered to "fiends" at 50.15, and "basting" was altered to "beating" at 115.6.[23] The word "hick" mysteriously does not appear in the manuscript, the prospectus, the first American edition, or either of the two editions set from American proof sheets (the first English and Canadian editions). Mark Twain may have added it during his first proofreading and then taken it out again before the book was printed.

In the instances already mentioned Howells may have suggested the alternative readings that Mark Twain adopted. But Mark Twain apparently supplied his own new reading for the "thing . . . on p. 154" (p. 150 of this edition) which Howells couldn't cope with changing—the last line of the ballad that Miles Hendon sings (beginning at 148.8). The manuscript reads:

> There was a woman in our town,
>   In our town did dwell—
> She loved her husband dearilee,
> But another man twice as well,—

In the first American edition the last line of the ballad was altered, in the plates, to read "But another man he loved she,—."[24]

In order to identify the other revisions resulting from the "20 such" queries that Howells mentioned in his first letter about the proofs, and the unspecified "passages marked" which he wrote of in his second, we must rely on the physical evidence provided by the altered plates. Alterations in the plates have been discovered by two methods. The first is machine collation of the prospectus against the first American

---

[22]A list of Howells' suggested changes in *Tom Sawyer* is printed in *The Adventures of Tom Sawyer, Tom Sawyer Abroad, Tom Sawyer, Detective*, ed. John C. Gerber, Paul Baender, and Terry Firkins (Berkeley, Los Angeles, London: University of California Press, 1980), Supplement B.

[23]Apparently Howells was making a real distinction between dialogue and narration when he wrote that those words ought not "to be suffered in your own narration," and he may well have intentionally passed over the later use of the word "bastings" in dialogue—for instance, in Hugo's speech at 206.2. In any case, Mark Twain apparently saw no need to alter it there even though he had changed the first instance.

[24]See the explanatory note at 148.8 and *MTHL*, 2:874, for a discussion of the ballad's history.

edition with a Hinman collator. At 90.3, for instance, such collation revealed that "styes" was cut into the plates of the first American edition.

78	*TOM*	78	*TOM*
in the slums may tell		in the **styes** may tell	
soever " —		soever " —	
Prospectus		*First American edition*	

The second method is careful sight inspection of the first American edition pages. The way the type was cut in made many plate changes apparent, because slight differences in type size, alignment, and height often resulted in uneven inking. For instance, an inspection of the first American edition reveals that "magnificent array of" was cut into the plates at 58.11–12.

> g bastions and turrets, the huge stone
>
> and its **magnificent array** of colossal
>
> signs and symbols of English royalty.
>
>)e satisfied at last? Here, indeed, was a

First American edition

About thirty plate alterations that were probably suggested by Howells have been identified.[25] Although in the absence of the proofs

---

[25]They are as follows. (Note that the following list indicates only the reading changed, not the entire alteration to the plates. For instance, at 58.11–12 "magnificent array of" was cut in to replace "imposing top-hamper of," but the list indicates only that "magnificent array" replaces "imposing top-hamper.")

51.18	himself (A)	his hide (MS)
58.11–12	magnificent array (A)	imposing top-hamper (MS)
64.6	glorious (A)	too divine (MS)
84.16	gilded (A)	gorgeous (MS)
88.37	dismayed (A)	cornered (MS)
90.2	wallow (A)	kennel (MS)
90.3	styes (A)	slums (MS, Pr)
93.1	robe, he laid himself (A)	robe de chambre, he lay (MS)
96.9	blood (A)	womb (MS)
126.8	ye again, you (A)	thee again, thou (MS)
136.10	elder (A)	big (MS)
152.9	detestable (A)	misbegotten (MS)
155.7–8	your straw and hie ye (A)	thy straw and hie thee (MS, Pr)
155.8	your (A)	thine (MS, Pr)

themselves it is of course impossible to determine their provenance with certainty, most of them reflect the sorts of concerns which Howells expressed in his letters of October 12 and 13. He undoubtedly considered the words "womb" at 96.9 and 267.4, and "misbegotten" at 152.9 and 175.37–38, "rather strong milk for babes," for example. Other alterations seem aimed at ridding the book of American colloquialisms, and one of the few criticisms that Howells offered in his review of October 25 was that "the effort to preserve the English of Henry VII.'s reign in the dialogue sometimes wavers between theatrical insistence and downright lapse into the American of Arthur's Presidency."[26]

Not long after the plate alterations presumably suggested by Howells had been ordered, House also saw a set of proof sheets and made suggestions that resulted in further alterations. House, like Howells, had read the book once before, in manuscript.[27] When he saw the proofs he became concerned about an anachronism that he had apparently not noticed the first time: by calling the Hendons baronets Mark Twain was giving them a title that did not exist in the time of Henry VIII. His discovery set off a flurry of activity to find ways to correct or rationalize the Hendons' status without having to tear up the plates of the book once again.

House wrote of his discovery to Mark Twain, who replied on October 21:

157.9	thee and Nan (A)	you and Nan (MS)
157.14	answer (A)	remark (MS)
162.2	good (A)	dear (MS)
169.9	tolerable (A)	middling (MS, Pr)
173.4	man had (A)	male one (MS, Pr)
175.37–38	hare-brained (A)	misbegotten (MS, Pr)
193.31	joyously (A)	gushingly (MS)
226.7	on (A)	along (MS)
235.35–36	obey when an archangel gives (A)	hoof it when an archangel tips (MS)
235.37	been (A)	lain (MS)
239.7	charge (A)	keep (MS)
241.31	operate (A)	be ripe (MS)
241.38	angry-looking (A)	appear decayed (MS)
242.3	the hideous ulcer to be seen (A)	parts of the sore to peep out (MS)
267.4	his birth (A)	the womb (MS)

[26]Unsigned review, New York *Tribune*, 25 October 1881, p. 6.

[27]House, who in 1890 instituted a lawsuit over the dramatization rights to *The Prince and the Pauper* (see Paul Fatout, "Mark Twain, Litigant," *American Literature* 31 [March 1959]: 30–45, for an account of the matter), wrote about his reading of the manuscript in a letter to the editor of the New York *Times*, 31 January 1890, p. 9. He had suggested one change, which may be Mark Twain's alteration in the manuscript from "treat" to "use" (see the textual note at 60.14).

No, my boy, we *couldn't* have spoken of the baronet matter (eh?); because I should have known in an instant that baronets in Henry VIII's time wouldn't begin to answer. I've suggested to Osgood a foot-note which is possibly a leather-headed way out of the difficulty, & asked him to advise with you & Howells about it. If there was no baronet but Miles, I could turn *him* into a knight, easily enough; but there's his derned old father & his brother besides, & they would make just no end of trouble, because there is so much about the transmission of the title; whereas I can't venture to let a knight transmit his title. It would be indecent.[28]

In a letter to Osgood written the same day, Mark Twain proposed two possible footnotes to follow the words "My father is a baronet" in Miles Hendon's speech at 139.23–24. The longer of the notes, which he canceled before he sent the letter, reads:

*After the plates of this book were ready for the press, <it> I chanced to remember that in England at that time, there were not yet any baronets. But it was too late to change the plates & make the correction. Now, therefore, wherever a baronet occurs in these pages, I ask the reader to kindly remember that I created him, & ought in simple right & justice to have the praise & credit of it.—M.T.

Realizing that there might be difficulty in fitting such a long footnote onto the page, he also wrote a shorter version: "*I created all the baronets that occur in this book. My plates were electrotyped & ready for the press before it recurred to my memory that in England there were no baronets in those days.—M.T."[29]

Adding a footnote meant that room had to be made for the new matter by deleting lines from the text. In the same letter Mark Twain indicated that he had "succeeded in providing the necessary room" for the shorter footnote, apparently by deleting "A grateful ... him;" (139.10–11) and making the paragraph at 139.21 run-in. The deletion and the altered paragraphing stood in the first American edition, but he adopted another solution to the baronet problem, and a different footnote was used.

Before Osgood acted on Mark Twain's letter, House wrote proposing the new solution. House's letter included a list of changes to be made where the text referred to the Hendons' rank, and suggestions for at least two alternative footnotes. The author replied to House:

---

[28]Clemens to House, 21 October 1881, CWB.
[29]Clemens to Osgood, 21 October 1881, Yale.

I am under unspeakable obligations to you, & you can bet that Mrs.
Clemens will be, too, . . . for she was totally unable to reconcile herself
to that proposed foot-note of mine—felt about it just as you did—&
she made me feel so, too, which was the reason I wanted you advised
with before anything should be done with it. . . .
And to go through the tedious work of searching out the resulting
changes in the book-text & applying the remedies was another heavy
job, too. For all of which I am most sincerely grateful. . . .
I prefer Form B, & have written Osgood explaining why; but I want
my preference to yield to yours & Osgood's. I have lent Osgood your
letter to make the emendations by, as they are all clearly set forth
in it. . . .
You have given me a prodigious sense of relief, my boy. I was in a
confoundedly awkward place. And I was taking a mighty awkward &
dangerous way to get out of it, too.[30]

"Form B" was almost certainly the footnote that appears in chapter
12 (p. 139):

He refers to the order of baronets, or baronettes,—the *barones
minores*, as distinct from the parliamentary barons;—not, it need
hardly be said, the baronets of later creation.

According to House's later statement, he was responsible for "nearly
a dozen" changes in the text, made to adjust it to the Hendons' new
status.[31] In addition to the footnote, the changes were the substitution
of the word "knight" for "baronet" (at 144 *caption*, 144.18, 145.5,
247.6, 247.9, 289.5, and 330.2), the substitution of "honors" or "show"
for "title" (at 285.9 and 331.11), the substitution of "For" for "Sir" (at
266.20), and the insertion of the phrase "one of the smaller lords, by
knight service—" following "baronet—" in Miles Hendon's speech at
139.24. Although most of these alterations were cut into the plates,
collation of the prospectus against the first American edition reveals
that the page with the footnote and the added phrase was entirely
reset.
Mark Twain was very pleased with this solution. In his letter to
Osgood explaining why he preferred "Form B" of House's footnote, he
said:

It effectually checkmates the criticaster, & at the same time it doesn't
furnish him detailed information to spread out on; whereas, if we

[30]Clemens to House, 24 October 1881, CWB.
[31]House to New York *Times*, 31 January 1890, p. 9.

furnished him these details in an elaborate Appendix-note, it is ammunition which he would try to find a way to use against us—just to show his learning. Damn him, he doesn't know where to look for it, now.[32]

Mark Twain made no mention of further revision in his correspondence after late October. But alteration of the plates continued even after printing had begun: a second state of the first American edition corrects three errors passed over in the preparation of the first state.[33]

The first American edition was published on 12 December 1881.[34] Four impressions, totaling just over 25,000 copies, were made between mid-November and the end of December. By 1 March 1882 over 21,000 copies had been sold, and soon another impression of 5,000 copies was made.[35] Most of the printing for these five impressions was done by Rand, Avery, and Company; the balance was done by John Wilson and Son.[36] Sales declined drastically thereafter, for almost 5,000 copies remained unsold by February 1884, when Osgood ceased to be Mark Twain's publisher and all rights, stock, and other material were transferred to Charles L. Webster and Company.[37]

After becoming Mark Twain's publisher in 1884, the Webster company continued to issue the first American edition of The Prince and

---

[32]Clemens to Osgood, 24 October 1881, catalog of Anderson Galleries, sale no 4228, 29–30 January 1936, item 123.

[33]The second state (Ab) substitutes the following three readings for those of the first state (Aa):

124.5	canopy of state (Ab)	canopy of estate (Aa)
237.9	do (Ab)	do not (Aa)
307.9	reined (Ab)	reigned (Aa)

See the textual notes and page 407 of this introduction for further discussion.

[34]BMT2, p. 40.

[35]The Osgood company sheet stock book (p. 19) indicates that, including overruns, 10,030 sets of pages were received by November 15, 5,050 by November 30, 5,064 by December 17, 5,075 by December 24, and 5,000 by March 14.

[36]Osgood company cost book, pp. 127 and 176. Of the first impression, Rand, Avery, and Company printed twenty out of twenty-six gatherings, and John Wilson and Son printed the remainder. The second and third impressions were printed entirely by the Rand, Avery company. Rand, Avery printed twelve gatherings of the fourth impression, and John Wilson printed fourteen. The fifth impression was printed entirely by John Wilson.

[37]The Osgood company sheet stock book (p. 19) indicates that 4,550 sets of unfolded sheets (not counting overruns) and 50 sets of folded sheets (with 110 overruns) of The Prince and the Pauper were transferred to Charles L. Webster and Company, along with 266 books in various bindings, 53 prospectuses, 13 boxes of electrotype plates, and 2 sets of binder's dies.

the Pauper until 1891. At first the unbound copies acquired from Osgood were simply cased in Webster bindings with no change of imprint, but later when new sheets were printed the title page bore the Webster company name and the date of issue.[38] The change of publishers produced no change in the text. All subsequent American editions derive from the second state of the first American edition and contribute nothing to the present text.

The first English edition, set from American proof sheets, was published earlier than the first American edition to ensure the English copyright. It was printed by Spottiswoode and Company, London, and published by Chatto and Windus on 1 December 1881.[39] Mark Twain did not see the printer's copy, nor did he read proof. The text exists in three states, the first set from proofs sent from the United States in late September and October, the second corrected against a copy of the first American edition, and the third further corrected and styled apparently by a Chatto and Windus or press proofreader. Machine collation indicates that all three states of the first English edition were printed from standing type, into which corrections were introduced.[40]

Because the English edition had to appear before the American edition, it was important to coordinate their production. The English copyright of Mark Twain's preceding book, *A Tramp Abroad*, also typeset from American proof sheets, had been threatened when the first English edition was published later than the first American edition. A misunderstanding delayed the dispatch of electroplates for the illustrations, and over a hundred pages of text had not reached England when the American Publishing Company brought out the book in the United States in March of 1880 with no advance notice to Chatto and Windus. When the final pages did reach England, Chatto and Windus quickly printed an unillustrated two-volume "Library Edition" and later, when the electroplates came, followed it up with a more expensive illustrated edition. But Andrew Chatto felt that the American Publishing Company had seriously threatened the English copyright by publishing "without giving us sufficient notice" and

---

[38]A copy of the first American edition with the Webster binding and the Osgood title page is in the collection of Theodore Koundakjian. Copies with the Webster binding and cancel title page have been seen with dates ranging from 1885 to 1891.

[39]*BAL* 3396.

[40]The Chatto and Windus records confirm that no plates were ordered for the first English edition (Ledger Book 3, p. 491, Chatto and Windus, London).

complained of the financial burden of having to make two distinct typesettings with no copyright guarantee.[41]

The following year, remembering all the difficulties with *A Tramp Abroad* and more concerned than ever about his copyright, Mark Twain wrote to Chatto on 7 October 1881 to assure him that the same thing would not happen with *The Prince and the Pauper:*

Osgood will get the pictures & advance sheets to you in ample time, & there will be no misunderstanding & no trouble about anything.[42]

Osgood did send everything to Chatto and Windus in "ample time." The publishers' records indicate that the first third of the proofs and duplicate electroplates for the illustrations had arrived by September 27. Chatto immediately placed an order with his printers for an impression of 5,000.[43] He wrote to Osgood on the same day that they would issue an illustrated edition of the book first, instead of an unillustrated edition as they had done with *A Tramp Abroad.*[44] He wrote to Mark Twain on November 1:

All goes smoothly for issuing the volume here by the date arranged . . . ; we found the illustrations so important a feature in the book that we concluded it would be better to start at once with the single volume illustrated edition at 7/6.[45]

Evidently by the time Chatto wrote, the rest of the proofs had arrived, and the first impression was complete or nearly so, for soon after, on November 3, Chatto and Windus ordered a second impression of 5,000. On the last day of the month, the company ordered a third impression of 5,000, after which no further copies of the first English edition were printed.[46]

---

[41]Moncure D. Conway to Clemens, 4 May 1880, MTP, partially printed in *MTLP*, p. 124 n. 2; Chatto to Clemens, 3 May 1880, MTP.

[42]William Bryan Gates, "Mark Twain to His English Publishers," *American Literature* 11 (March 1939): 78–80.

[43]Chatto and Windus Ledger Book 3, p. 491; another entry, dated October 2, referring to the same impression, may indicate that more proofs or electroplates arrived from the United States on that date.

[44]Chatto to Osgood, 27 September 1881, Chatto and Windus Letter Book 13, p. 434.

[45]Chatto to Clemens, 1 November 1881, Dennis Welland, *Mark Twain in England* (London: Chatto and Windus, 1978), p. 108.

[46]Chatto and Windus Ledger Book 3, p. 491. Since there were only three impressions, it is tempting to correlate the states with the impressions, but the evidence is not conclusive. Charges for corrections in the first English edition entered in the Chatto and Windus printing order ledger are undated, and changes in the standing type might have been introduced at some time during an impression as well as between impressions.

The earliest state of the first English edition incorporates the changes that Mark Twain made on the American proofs during the summer, but not all of the changes suggested by Howells in October, in particular those in the first part of the book. Spottiswoode and Company received the first installment of the American proofs and began setting type from them before all of the plate alterations had been made in the United States, but collation indicates that the printers must have received later proofs after they had been corrected or marked to include Howells' changes. In any case Mark Twain had nothing to do with the proofs forwarded to England, which were as a matter of course sent directly from the Osgood company.

However, during the flurry of activity over the American proofs set off by House's discovery of the baronet anachronism, Mark Twain did become concerned about the transmission of the alterations to England. On October 25, after sending House's list of changes to Osgood, he suggested that Osgood cable at least a footnote to Chatto and Windus:

> Wouldn't it answer to cable Chatto about thus: . . .
>
> If convenient, in paragraph . . . ., Chapter . . . ., after the words "Sir Richard Hendon," refer by the usual sign to either a foot-note or Appendix-note, said note to be worded thus:
>
> [here, in your cablegram, insert <one of> the foot-note<s> in form B.]—[or A foot-note, to be new devised BY HOUSE.] OSGOOD.
>
> How is that, Osgood? If *not* convenient, Chatto would leave things as they are, & no harm done.
>
> English critics are more likely to discover such a flaw than ours. . . .
>
> Or, send any other cablegram that suits you. Or none at all, if *that* seems best. Do just what seems best, & I am content.[47]

Apparently Osgood did cable the baronet footnote and all of House's related changes to England, for even the earliest state of the first English edition shares these readings with the first American edition.

On November 18 Ticknor informed Mark Twain that he had "mailed Chatto a complete book so that he can look the whole thing over."[48] This copy of the first American edition was probably used by the Chatto and Windus editors to correct the early printing of the first English edition and resulted in the second state. The second state differs from the first in ten substantive readings, nine of which are

---

[47]Clemens to Osgood, 25 October 1881, MTP.
[48]Ticknor to Clemens, 18 November 1881, *MTBus*, p. 176.

taken from the first American edition; for instance, "devils" becomes "fiends" at 50.15, and "make a" is corrected to "make" at 80.9.[49] The English editors were not thorough, however, and did not alter in the English edition all of the substantive readings that had been changed in the first American edition; for example, the description of the beggars at 191.22, "diseased ones, with running sores peeping from ineffectual wrappings," was retained throughout the first English edition, although it had been dropped from the American.

The third state of the first English edition reflects the efforts of a house editor or press proofreader who made further necessary corrections ("art" for "are" at 197.12), fussed with usage ("slowly" for "slow" at 59.1), and corrected for house style as well ("By-and-by" for "By and by" at 54.4). All three states of the first English edition contain a great many house conventions, as well as a number of sophistications and Anglicisms.

Although the first English edition has no primary authority, it is of interest because of its close relationship with various stages of the first American edition, which Mark Twain revised. No subsequent English edition in his lifetime has any bearing on the present text.

Like the first English edition, the first Canadian edition of *The Prince and the Pauper* was published earlier than the first American.[50] It was an unillustrated edition brought out by Dawson Brothers, Montreal, to establish Canadian copyright. Printer's copy was again a set of the American proof sheets. Although printed in Canda, it was set and plated in the United States. The author did not read proof for the edition.

Mark Twain was determined to obtain Canadian copyright in order to prevent a Canadian piracy of *The Prince and the Pauper*. Piracies of his earlier books had been sold not only in Canada but in the United States, severely undercutting the sales and profits of the American subscription editions for which he received royalties. In late September, Osgood, having read the Canadian copyright act and corresponded with Samuel Dawson, "a thoroughly honorable man and the

---

[49]The tenth substantive difference between the first state (Ea) and the second (Eb), probably due to type batter, is the absence from Eb of the word "I" at 148.19.

[50]An interim copyright was registered at the Department of Agriculture in Ottawa on 1 December 1881 and officially noted by the Canada *Gazette* on December 3 (Gordon Roper, "Mark Twain and His Canadian Publishers: A Second Look," *Papers of the Bibliographical Society of Canada* 5 [1966]: 65).

most intelligent publisher in Canada," suggested a plan whereby Mark Twain would put out an authorized edition in Canada, attempting to get Canadian copyright, but would meanwhile assign his imperial copyright to Chatto and Windus, who would be in a better legal position to fight infringers in case the effort failed. In addition, Osgood wrote, Clemens was to go to Canada for several days before and after publication, and they would "arrange to have an edition set up & printed in Canada *at the proper time.*"[51]

At first the author agreed: he wrote Osgood on October 2 to "go ahead and set up the types for Canada whenever you please." But by October 27 he had begun to have second thoughts, having realized that "in setting up and printing in Canada, we run one risk—that the sheets may be bought or stolen, and a pirated edition brought out ahead of us." He suggested as a solution that a signature here and there be left out of the Montreal printing until a few days before the Canadian publishing date. The next day he advanced another plan to Osgood whereby the first and last signatures would be typeset in Boston and the rest in Canada.

You see, what I'm after is a *preventive;* it is preferable to even the best of cures. Those sons of up there will steal anything they can get their hands on—possible suits for damages and felony would be no more restraint upon them, I think, than would the presence of a young lady be upon a stud-horse who had just found a mare unprotected by international copyright.[52]

Finally, on November 1, he wrote Osgood, "Derned if *I* can think of anything to suggest except taking a set of plates to Canada to print from. If that will answer in place of setting up the book there, I should recommend that.—They wouldn't need to be electrotyped, but only stereotyped." This idea was adopted; the book was set and plated in Boston by Rand, Avery, and Company, and the plates were sent to Dawson Brothers for printing on November 18.[53]

---

[51]Osgood to Clemens, 29 September 1881, MTP. Mark Twain did make such an assignment of copyright to Chatto and Windus, in two agreements dated 19 October and 28 October 1881 (*The Prince and the Pauper* contract, Chatto and Windus, London, photofacsimile in MTP).

[52]Clemens to Osgood, 2, 27, and 28 October 1881, *MTLP*, pp. 141, 143, 144.

[53]Clemens to Osgood, 1 November 1881, *MTLP*, p. 145; Ticknor to Clemens, 18 November 1881, *MTBus*, p. 176. The Osgood cost book (p. 128) indicates that the Osgood company got the plates on November 16.

Clemens left for Montreal on November 26 and two days later wrote Osgood from Canada, "Have just returned from visiting Mr. Dawson. He has printed an edition of 275, and they are ready to be put into the paper covers."[54] Although he was greatly concerned about the way the Canadian edition was to be produced, and was in Montreal when it was printed, he had nothing directly to do with its production. Thus the text of the Dawson edition is without authority and is of interest mainly because of its close relationship with the publication of the first American edition.

Collation indicates that printer's copy for the Dawson edition was a late stage of the American proof sheets. Once it was designated as copy for the Canadian edition, it undoubtedly did not leave the house of Rand, Avery, and Company, who were simultaneously working on the first American edition. The composition was quite accurate, and the Dawson text closely resembles that of the first American edition. The Canadian edition lacks the illustrations and the Latimer letter frontispiece and transcription, but otherwise differs from the first American edition in only six substantive readings, two of which ("cornered" at 88.37 and "slums" at 90.3) are manuscript readings that also appear in the earliest state of the English edition, apparently having been changed for the American edition only in a very late stage of proof. The other four variants appear to be due to compositor error— for example, the substitution of "unchartered" for "uncharted" at 100.5.

One odd circumstance of the Canadian edition is that of the three readings that differentiate the first and second states of the first American edition, the Canadian edition shares one reading with the first state and two readings with the second state. Perhaps the compositor first noticed the need for the two corrections in the text as he was setting type for the Canadian edition, and as a consequence they were later, along with the third correction, cut into the plates of the first American edition.[55]

Although Clemens went to Montreal to establish residency, he was not granted a Canadian copyright. The copyright law required that he

---

[54]Clemens to Elinor Howells, 25 November 1881, Houghton Library, Harvard; Clemens to Osgood, 28 November 1881, *MTLP*, p. 146.

[55]See the historical collation, 124.5, 237.9, and 307.9.

be "domiciled" in Canada, which was interpreted to mean permanent and not merely temporary residency.[56] Consequently, as he had feared, two pirated editions of *The Prince and the Pauper* appeared in Canada. The earliest, the Rose-Belford Publishing Company edition, appeared in early 1882.[57] Sometime later in the year the second piracy appeared, published by John Ross Robertson. Both piracies derive from the Dawson edition and are therefore without authority.

The second American edition, set from a copy of the second state of the first American edition, was published by the Webster company in 1892. Clemens was in Europe at the time and had no involvement with the production of the new edition. His only concern with it seems to have been financial.[58] Collation against the first American edition reveals only fourteen substantive variants, all of them probably due to compositor error.[59]

All subsequent American editions published in the author's lifetime derive from the Webster 1892 edition; Mark Twain had nothing to do with their production. The third American edition, called the "Library Edition," was set from a copy of the second and published by Harper and Brothers in 1896. The fourth American edition, the last published in Mark Twain's lifetime, was set from a copy of the third. Issued in numerous impressions with varied imprints, the fourth American edition was variously called the "Autograph Edition," the "Royal Edition," the "Japan Edition," the "De Luxe Edition," the "Riverdale Edition," the "Underwood Edition," the "Hillcrest Edition," the "Author's National Edition," and so on.

Sometime after the "Autograph Edition" was printed, a marked copy of the "Royal Edition" of *The Prince and the Pauper* was used to correct the plates.[60] It does not contain authorized revisions and corrects only those errors introduced into the text of the "Autograph

---

[56]For a complete discussion of this difference in interpretation and the entire question of the Canadian copyright of *The Prince and the Pauper*, see Gordon Roper, "Mark Twain and His Canadian Publishers," *American Book Collector* 10 (June 1960): 13–29, and the article cited earlier, "Mark Twain and His Canadian Publishers: A Second Look," pp. 62–73. See also the general introduction, p. 12.

[57]*BAL* 3629. According to Jacob Blanck (*BAL* 3397), after the Rose-Belford piracy came on the market, Dawson issued his authorized edition with a cancel title page that included the added words "Author's Canadian Edition."

[58]*MTLP*, pp. 272, 296, 304, 321, 333.

[59]Seven are omitted words and seven are mainly errors such as the substitution of "Meanwhile" for "Meantime" at 88.21 and "dropped" for "drooped" at 162.5.

[60]A marked set of the 1899 "Royal Edition" of the works of Mark Twain, found in the Yale University Library by Roger Salomon, "obviously served if not directly as copy

Edition." Collation indicates that the proofreader must have drawn his corrections from the 1896 "Library Edition," because errors that had first occurred in that edition were not corrected. Mark Twain seems to have been consulted only once, about whether to make corrections in the transcription of the Latimer letter frontispiece (see the textual note at 29.6–32).

The second English edition was ordered by Chatto and Windus from Spottiswoode and Company on the same day as they ordered the third impression of the first English edition.[61] It probably derives from one of the later states of the first English edition. The third English edition was a Chatto and Windus resetting from a copy of the third state of the first English edition. First printed in 1891, it was initially called the "7/6" and later the "3/6" edition by the publishers. In 1900 Chatto and Windus offered a set of Mark Twain's works for sale by subscription. This set, called the "Author's De Luxe Edition," was actually the 1899 American Publishing Company edition produced with a dual imprint. *The Prince and the Pauper* is volume 15 of this set. The last English edition published during Mark Twain's lifetime was printed in 1907 in an impression of 50,000 copies to sell for sixpence each.[62]

THE TEXT

Modern editorial theory stipulates that a critical text must place before the reader not only the text itself but the evidence and reasoning used by the editor to establish it. As a first step the editor designates a copy-text, the form of the text to be edited—usually the manuscript

---

for the corrected impressions, then certainly as the text where all problems were decided. . . . The copy also reports, for many readings, a lively debate between one 'FM,' a learned and opinionated corrector, and 'FEB,' or Frank E. Bliss, the proprietor of the American Publishing Company, here often forced to consult with the final authority, Twain." Colored crayons were used to indicate which of the marked corrections were to be made, and whether to charge them to the publishers or to the firm of Case, Lockwood, and Brainard, printers of the original "Autograph Edition" (William B. Todd, "Problems in Editing Mark Twain," in *Bibliography and Textual Criticism: English and American Literature 1700 to the Present*, ed. O M Brack, Jr., and Warner Barnes [Chicago and London: University of Chicago Press, 1969], p. 205).

[61]Chatto and Windus Ledger Book 3, p. 491.

[62]Unfortunately, no copies of the second English edition, the "Author's De Luxe Edition," or the 1907 sixpence edition could be obtained for collation. However, there is no evidence to suggest that Mark Twain played any part in their production. See the description of texts for further information about the editions collated in the preparation of this volume.

or first printing—which, because it is the least corrupt, provides the most satisfactory basis for establishing a text free from unauthorized readings.[63] The editor agrees to follow the copy-text in every particular except where he considers emendation justified or required. And he agrees to report and defend all such emendations, so that a reader may if he chooses reconstruct the base from which the editor has departed. The copy-text therefore becomes the source for nearly every substantive and accidental reading in the critical text, and it largely determines the form of the textual apparatus used to report the editor's decisions.

Unauthorized changes made by copyists, editors, and compositors are by this means excluded—usually silently—from the text of this edition, while authorized changes in the printer's copy, proofs, or plates, along with simple corrections supplied by the editor himself, appear in the text as emendations and are so recorded. The copy-text for the present edition is Mark Twain's manuscript for *The Prince and the Pauper*. This copy-text has been emended in the following ways:

Substantives (Words and Word Order)

(1) Variants in the first American edition considered to be Mark Twain's changes in proof are here adopted. Suggestions and alterations made by William Dean Howells and Edward House and introduced into the first American edition were presumably approved by the author and are likewise adopted.

Authorial changes in proof may be detected by analogous changes demonstrably made by Mark Twain in his manuscript (such as the change of "to't" to "to it," and "sith" to "since"), by documentary evidence (such as his letter to Benjamin Ticknor about changes of " 'tis" to "it is"), or by their length and content—criteria which make it unlikely that a compositor or editor had ventured to risk the author's wrath by altering his work (such as the omission of manuscript passages at 191.22 and 237.22–23 and the substitution of "bakeries" for "bookstores" at 132.7).

Letters establish that Howells and House suggested numerous changes that Mark Twain solicited and then adopted, presumably in

---

[63]See W. W. Greg, "The Rationale of Copy-Text," in *Collected Papers*, ed. J. C. Maxwell (London: Oxford University Press, 1966), pp. 374–391.

proof. Howells' substitution of "beating" for "basting" at 115.6 and House's alterations from "baronet" to "knight" at 144.18 and 145.5 are typical.

(2) Variants in the first American edition that correct simple errors in the manuscript are adopted here. These include corrections of tense and agreement (such as "ordered" for "order" at 328.5 and "houses" for "house" at 49.11), of omitted words and dittography (such as "to and fro" for "to fro" at 107.10 and "after" for "after after" at 324.13), and of misidentification (such as "Hugo" for "Hugh" at 241.3). These corrections would be adopted in any case, but their appearance in the first American edition indicates that the author himself may have supplied them.

(3) Variants in the first American edition that apparently result from errors in transcription or from editorial sophistication are rejected. When it is possible to compare the copy-text with the prospectus, the first American edition, the first English edition, and the first Canadian edition, precise discrimination about even very small variants is possible. For instance, the manuscript reading "splatter" is rejected in favor of the first American edition "spatter" (63.9), because the agreement of the manuscript with the first English edition shows that the manuscript reading was initially typeset correctly and remained unchanged at least through the stage of proof from which the English edition was set, and the change must therefore have been made at a relatively late stage of production, when only an author would think to alter his text.

(4) When Mark Twain transcribed material from a source he often adapted it to fit his text; for instance, he cut inappropriate references to Queen Elizabeth and altered verbs from the past to the present tense in his quotations from Hunt, pp. 143–145. He also made changes that did not materially alter the sense of the passage; for instance, he substituted "from" for "in" in the quotation from Trumbull at 340.7. The copy-text reading is preferred to the original source in every case.

Accidentals (Paragraphing, Punctuation, and Word Forms)

(1) A conservative policy regarding the accidentals of the copy-text has been followed. Old-fashioned spellings ("recal" and "pedlar") have been retained. Mark Twain's punctuation has been emended

here and there to correct mechanical errors (omitted quotation marks in dialogue, periods instead of question marks), but otherwise has been respected, even when it appears idiosyncratic.

(2) On succeeding stages of his work, Mark Twain often revised italic word forms and exclamation points for emphasis, and such emphasis variants in the first American edition are here adopted as authorial revisions in proof. An exception to this policy is made for nine chapters in the first American edition (1, 3, 5, 7, 8, 9, 10, 30, and 31), because they are so drastically different from the manuscript. The presumption is that in these instances the author's alterations and the compositor's unauthorized ones are inextricably tangled. Moreover, Mark Twain's changes in emphasis there were made in a corrupt text in a vain effort to restore his manuscript punctuation. For example, in chapter 3, where Mark Twain had to turn his "whole attention to restoring" his punctuation, the following emphasis variants occur:

Manuscript: O, he was a prince! a prince! a living prince,
First American edition: Oh! he was a prince—a prince, a living prince,

a real prince, without the shadow of a question, and the prayer of
a real prince—without the shadow of a question; and the prayer of

the pauper-boy's heart was answered at last!
the pauper-boy's heart was answered at last.

There is no profitable way to determine which of these alterations were Mark Twain's. In this and numerous similar instances the editor runs the risk of seriously distorting or misrepresenting the author's intentions, whether he adopts the whole set of variants or tries to extract Mark Twain's revisions from the compositor's. Thus in the nine chapters a conservative policy is followed, and the copy-text is the authority for emphasis.

(3) Mark Twain was not as careful about his spelling, capitalization, and hyphenation, as he was about his punctuation. His work contains outright errors (such as his habitual misspelling "sieze") and lapses stemming from haste or carelessness (such as the omission of a letter in "straigtway" at 90.16–17). Moreover, he was often pointlessly inconsistent in such matters. He found the chore of hunting down and changing such inconsistent forms distasteful and expected it to be performed by the editors and compositors of his published works. In the manuscript of *The Prince and the Pauper*, he did make an effort to

do some of this type of correcting; for instance, he went over his manuscript and numerous times added an apostrophe to the word "an" (meaning "if"). He nevertheless left many inconsistencies. Because he expected others to smooth the formal texture of his work, and because inconsistencies can be distracting to a reader, emendations for consistency have been adopted whenever retaining the inconsistency would serve no conceivable purpose and the author's preference is discernible. As a rule, the resolution of inconsistencies is guided by his preponderant usage throughout the work. Out of well over a hundred references to the prince, for example, Mark Twain capitalized only seven times, all in the early pages of his manuscript. The frequency of occurrence within the book is sometimes inconclusive, and in these cases reference has been made to other writings of the same period. And in a few instances, as with the spellings "beggar-boy" and "beggar boy," Mark Twain seems to have been utterly indifferent, and the editor's choice is essentially arbitrary. In every case, however, the form chosen has the warrant of the author's usage.[64]

(4) Mark Twain's manuscript contains numerous instances of a device characteristic of his manuscripts of the 1870s and 1880s: when the end of a sentence fell short of the right margin of the page, and there was not enough room on the same line for the following word, he often inscribed a dash to fill out the line. The device was probably a holdover from Clemens' days as a printer—a translation into hand-

---

[64]For a fuller discussion of the principle of emendation to attain uniformity, see the textual introduction to the Iowa-California edition of *A Connecticut Yankee in King Arthur's Court*, ed. Bernard L. Stein, with an introduction by Henry Nash Smith (Berkeley, Los Angeles, London: University of California Press, 1979). In the present text the following emendations were made to correct inconsistent usages: 61.1, 61.4, 65.19, 66.7, 66.11, 70.32, 77.6, 77.7, 84.13, 84.13, 85.6, 85.13, 86.4, 87.10, 88.4, 88.37, 90.4, 90.12, 93.8, 94.1, 96.1, 96.15, 96.15, 96.16 ("prince"), 97.11, 105.6, 105.10, 108.2, 109.5 ("Duke"), 115.17, 119.13, 119.14, 120.3, 120.3, 125.37, 128.4, 131.3, 132.2, 133.7, 134.7, 136.3, 137.7, 137.8, 137.10, 153.9, 155.14, 156.1 ("Prince"), 162.36, 162.37, 164.2, 164.17, 165.12, 166.2, 170.30, 172.15, 175.33, 187.2, 188.8, 195.15, 205.20, 206.14, 207.17, 207.22, 216.26, 227.10, 228.3, 234.11, 235.16 ("an' "), 235.25, 239.1, 243.31, 267.12, 278.25, 279.1, 279.9, 289.7, 295.4, 300.15, 301.27, 303.10, 307.5, 313.6, 313.29, 314.19, 315.18, 317.2, 320.4, 320.11, 320.22, 322.1, 328.9, 328.9, 328.17, 330.14, 330.14, 333.14, 334.25, 337.23, 338.8 ("day.]—"), 338.30, 338.30, 340.40, and 341.22.

Similarly, Mark Twain's citations to his notes at the end of the book have been emended to correct inconsistent usages, sometimes necessitating minor substantive changes in addition to changes in capitalization, punctuation, and type style (see the textual note at 337.9, and the emendations list, 337.9–342 *note*).

writing of a common newspaper technique for justifying a line following terminal punctuation (and for signaling that no paragraph break
was intended). Newspaper compositors would often fill in such spaces
with a dash rather than respace the line. The amanuensis who transcribed Mark Twain's manuscript for the printer must have copied at
least some of his end-line dashes after terminal punctuation, for a few
are preserved in the first American edition. The compositors evidently
interpreted such dashes as a justifying device, for almost none of them
were typeset. In fact, in five of the six instances where the compositors
typeset them in the main body of the text, they probably did so for
their own convenience: these five dashes occur at the ends of lines in
that edition as well (at 150.21, 164.16, 205.4, 320.30, and 328.32). The
sixth instance, at 226.4, is discussed below.

It is not always possible, however, to interpret manuscript end-line
dashes after terminal punctuation as a mere justifying device of no
further significance. For example, Mark Twain used dashes following
terminal punctuation to separate his historical notes from their source
citations (pp. 337–342). In addition, he sometimes used them within a
manuscript line to represent a pause or a continued thought, or to
link a question and response (for instance, at 318.9–10 "Was it round?
—and thick?—and had it letters and devices graved upon it?—Yes?"
and at 263.8–9 "My father dead!—O, this is heavy news"). The decision about whether to retain Mark Twain's end-line dashes must
therefore take into account their literary significance.

Three categories of end-line dashes following terminal punctuation
have been identified. The first and by far the largest category comprises all instances in which manuscript end-line dashes clearly have
no rhetorical or stylistic function. In these instances, the dashes have
been rejected in this edition as superfluous.[65]

[65]At 47.11 ("together.—"), 50.23 ("beggar.—"), 58.18 ("armor.—"), 67.7
("elsewhere.—"), 73.9 ("captivity.—"), 77.12 ("servants.—"), 79.4 ("so.'—"), 93.5
("alone.—"), 97.2 ("dinner.—"), 103.8 ("without.—"), 105.3 ("king.—"), 105.14
("point.—"), 108.19 ("edge.—"), 111.18 ("it.—"), 111.22 ("eyes.—"), 114.25
("business.—"), 120.13 ("him.—"), 120.26 ("time.—"), 121.10 ("usurper.—"), 121.12
("impostor.—"), 126.4 ("fury.—"), 126.26 ("dangerous!'—"), 133.29 ("it.—"), 147.9
("it.'—"), 150.21 ("innkeeper.—"), 158.10 ("hose.—"), 160.12 ("due them.—"), 164.16
("simplifying.—"), 169.9 ("success.—"), 179.20 ("cataclysm.—"), 181.6 ("month.—"),
189.13 ("distance.—"), 191.18 ("of.—"), 204.10 ("made.—"), 205.4 ("trades.—"),
209.29 ("meanwhile.—"), 211.12–13 ("intolerable.—"), 212.4 ("welcome.—"), 212.8
("lacking.—"), 253.5 ("twilight.—"), 253.10 ("it.—"), 287.10 ("remission.—"), 291.8

The second category comprises instances of dashes in Mark Twain's historical notes. The dashes in this section, some of which occur at the ends of manuscript lines following terminal punctuation, are retained in this edition (as they were in the first American edition) because Mark Twain used them to separate the text of each note from its source citation.

The third category comprises sixteen doubtful cases of end-line dashes following terminal punctuation whose significance is ambiguous. In these cases, the dashes occur in passages of dialogue and internal monologue, where Mark Twain's punctuation tends to be particularly idiosyncratic and rhetorical. The first American edition printed a dash in only one of these instances, at 226.4 (but changed the following word from the manuscript "Here" to "here"). The present edition retains the dashes in six cases in which they seem to serve an identifiable literary purpose,[66] but rejects them in the remaining ten as superfluous.[67]

(5) When Mark Twain interlined revisions in his manuscript, he sometimes inserted new punctuation without deleting the original punctuation. For instance, at 329.9 he wrote "for?", inserted a caret between "for" and the question mark, and interlined "—who shall solve me this riddle?" above, inadvertently leaving two question marks. Similarly, he sometimes inserted a new word at the beginning of a sentence without changing the capital letter of the word that originally began the sentence to a lowercase letter. For instance, at 326.26 he wrote "He," added "So" in front of it, and left standing the capital *H*. In order to avoid excessive listing of these mechanical emendations, such cases of double punctuation and capitalization are reported only in the list of alterations in the manuscript.

(6) In addition to the superfluous end-line dashes and instances of double punctuation and capitalization just discussed, a few mechanical changes are made without notation in the list of emendations.

("answered.—"), 292.7 ("way.—"), 304.10 ("love.—"), 314.19 ("Wales.—"), 317.30 ("crown.—"), 320.30 ("unnoted.—"), 320.33 ("up!—"), 322.2 ("moment.—"), 328.32 ("away!—"), 340.13 ("hierarchy.—"), 341.29 ("formal.—"), and 342.5 ("inhuman-ity.—").

[66]At 78.6 ("prince?—"), 96.16 ("exaltation?—"), 117.35 ("forgot!—"), 173.36 ("me!—"), 226.4 ("welcome!—"), and 260.4 ("so?—").

[67]At 62.1 ("say.—"), 81.12 ("faintness.—"), 82.3 ("permanent.—"), 115.1 ("madam.—"), 142.23 ("crown.—"), 179.25 ("thee.—"), 235.24 ("go.—"), 254.6 ("harm.—"), 256.28 ("it.—"), and 270.8 ("perils.—").

a. Mark Twain's ampersands are expanded to "and."[68]

b. Superscript letters are lowered to the line.

c. Mark Twain's chapter headings have been standardized to "CHAPTER" followed by an arabic numeral (in the manuscript Mark Twain designated chapter headings with a variety of abbreviations in upper or lower case); periods and flourishes following headings have been dropped.

d. The headings to Mark Twain's notes (for instance, "Note 1.— Page") which he varied in minor ways in the manuscript have been standardized to follow the first American edition, and the page numbers of the present edition are silently supplied.

e. The opening words of each chapter appear in small capitals with an ornamental initial letter as an editorial convention.

f. Punctuation following italic words is italicized according to the usual practice, whether or not Mark Twain underlined the mark of punctuation.

Moreover, because it was Mark Twain's intent that they be published as part of his book, the table of contents, chapter titles, list of illustrations, and illustrations and their captions are adopted from the first American edition, although they are styled to accord with this edition.[69]

V.F.

---

[68]In the manuscript, Mark Twain always wrote out the word "And" at the beginning of sentences. In addition, he wrote out the word "and" in the following instances: at 31 title, 33.3, 65.3, 76.4, 88.26, 103.3, 111.21, 134.11, 134.38 ("and curses"), 139.8, 139.18 ("and work"), 141.7 ("and other"), 150.14, 150.36, 164.5, 164.11, 167.22, 172.9, 173.38, 191.2 ("himself, and"), 194.6 ("and maunders"), 195.26, 195.28, 208.4, 209.3 ("new and"), 209.5, 227.10, 229.21, 238.5 ("return and"), 239.4 ("and Hugo"), 249.14, 249.31, 260.1, 265.8 ("and turned"), 279.10, 282.11 ("and wreaths"), 283.13, 284.29, 285.6, 295.10 ("and gave"), 301.7, 301.15, 301.34 ("and Tom"), 304.5, 311.2 ("and shifting"), 312.35 ("and thus"), 313.21, 313.24, 313.36, 314.2, 326.18, and 335.14. All other instances of "and" in this edition were ampersands in the manuscript.

[69]A number of the illustrations have been reduced or enlarged slightly in size to accommodate them to the page width of this edition, and some of the rules around the pictures have been dropped. In five captions minor substantive changes have been made to bring them into accord with the present text. In the caption on page 80, "a" replaces the first American edition reading "with"; on page 143, "upon" replaces "on"; on page 191, "thinkings" replaces "thinking"; on page 194, "upward" replaces "upwards"; and on page 288, "Whilst" replaces "While." In addition, on page 236, the caption of the first English edition replaces that of the first American edition (see the textual note).

GUIDE TO THE TEXTUAL APPARATUS

Description of Texts identifies and discusses editions published in Mark Twain's lifetime and specifies copies collated and examined in the preparation of this edition.

Textual Notes specify those features of the text discussed generally in the textual introduction, record all of Mark Twain's marginalia in the manuscript, and discuss adopted readings and aspects of Mark Twain's revision which require fuller explanation.

Emendations of the Copy-Text lists every departure from the copy-text and records the source of the reading in the present text. It includes the reading adopted when a compound word is hyphenated at the end of a line in the copy-text.

Historical Collation records all variant substantive readings among the significant texts.

Alterations in the Manuscript provides a description of the manuscript and a record of every revision that the author made in it.

Word Division in This Volume lists ambiguous compounds hyphenated at the end of a line in this volume, and gives their correct form for quotation.

DESCRIPTION OF TEXTS

The following texts have been collated, and the collation results are reported in the textual apparatus because of the light they shed on the writing and revision of *The Prince and the Pauper*. The symbols on the left are used in this volume to identify the texts. Following the description of texts is a list of the specific copies of each edition used in the preparation of this volume.

MS   Manuscript. HM 1327 in the Henry E. Huntington Library, San Marino, California. A full description of the manuscript will be found in the list of alterations in the manuscript, pages 455–458.

Pr   Prospectus. Boston: James R. Osgood and Company, 1882. The prospectus contains five leaves of front matter—including the dedication and the photographic facsimile and transcript of the Latimer letter, but not the epigraph from *The Merchant of Venice* or the introductory paragraph that immediately precedes the first chapter in the book. The text of the prospectus, which was printed in a single impression from the plates prepared for the first American edition, corresponds to the following passages in this edition:

47 *title*–9	CHAPTER . . . holiday,
50.4–38	organized . . . Latin,
53.3–54.4	splashing . . . wrought
55.7–56.9	eat . . . before
57 *title*–10	CHAPTER . . . street—but
59.8–60.13	fastened . . . out:
61.7–62.1	"Doth . . . always
62.31–63.1	neither . . . more."
64.21–66.2	then at the . . . shouting:
68.6–16	jumping . . . costume. [*including footnote*]
73 *title*–12	CHAPTER . . . be if
74.12–75.14	ante-chamber . . . lord?"
77.8–78.3	Poor . . . reverence,
78.14–79.29	"Thou . . . toward the
80.5–16	a growing . . . replied—
82.17–83.8	One . . . place. [*including footnote*]
85 *title*–86.1	CHAPTER . . . proceed, Hert[ford]
87.17–88.13	such . . . again.
90.2–30	in the styes . . . play. Where[fore]
91.8–92.4	the asking . . . came straight[way]
94.14–95.7	St. John . . . held it

97 *title*–98.5	CHAPTER . . . highness the
99.14–100.2	of importing . . . dead [*including footnote*]
101.8–102.5	By his . . . naturally
103 *title*–104.16	CHAPTER . . . what
107 *title*–108.14	CHAPTER . . . roses, and
109.7–110.15	satin . . . this!
111 *title*–22	CHAPTER . . . one—
113.1–14	"O, poor . . . wandering
114.37–115.20	to their . . . would
117.6–25	to sleep . . . William!"
118.19–119.16	thy . . . into
120.31–121.15	imaginary . . . treason. [*including footnote*]
123 *title*–125.7	CHAPTER . . . knife.
127.1–13	troop . . . assemblage
131 *title*–133.3	CHAPTER . . . before
134.31–135.3	would . . . odds
137.3–16	He . . . ill-[conditioned]
138.9–139.28	Hendon . . . rich, [*without footnote*]
142.18–33	ragamuffin . . . get
145.2–12	wrought . . . content."
147 *title*–16	CHAPTER . . . this."
155 *title*–157.2	CHAPTER . . . more be
157.34–158.13	to the . . . enough in
159.19–29	a form, and . . . for?"
162.34–163.8	to happen . . . forgetting!
164.20–165.13	Tom . . . reason
167.20–28	totally . . . succeeded.
169 *title*–22	CHAPTER . . . all
171.5–25	"I would . . . victims,
173.4–17	dress . . . comparison."
175.34–177.21	"Let . . . again.
296.4–16	He . . . make
299 *title*–10	CHAPTER . . . thousand
301.4–33	nigh . . . upon.
305.11–17	splendors . . . greatness
306.10–307.11	vapors . . . again!"

A   First American edition. Boston: James R. Osgood and Company, 1882 (*BAL* 3402), and New York: Charles L. Webster and Company, 1885–1891. This is the only edition for which Mark Twain read proof. Collation indicates that the text, printed from electrotype plates, occurs in two states, here designated Aa and Ab. Comparison of wear, damage, and repair of type in some fifteen copies shows that the three readings that identify the first state occur only in the copies printed earliest and suggests that those readings were altered after the first impression had left the press and before the second impression was begun. The bindings of the Osgood copies of this edition also occur in two states, noted by Jacob Blanck, who correctly stated that two sets of brasses must have been used to stamp them.[1] However, there is no absolute correlation between the earliest state of the text and the binding that Blanck identifies as the earliest binding—copies of both states of the text are found with both states of the binding.

E   First English edition. London: Chatto and Windus, 1881–1882 (*BAL* 3396). Collation indicates that the text of this edition, set from American proofsheets and printed from standing type, occurs in three states, here designated Ea, Eb, and Ec. Of the copies examined, only the third state bears the 1882 date on the title page.

C   First Canadian edition. Montreal: Dawson Brothers, 1881 (*BAL* 3397). This edition was set from American proofsheets and printed from stereotype plates. All copies examined are textually identical, although later copies substitute a title page with the added words "Author's Canadian Edition."

The following editions of *The Prince and the Pauper* were found to be derivative and without authority.

Continental edition. Leipzig: Bernhard Tauchnitz, 1881.

Unauthorized Canadian edition. Toronto: Rose-Belford Publishing Company, 1882 (*BAL* 3629).

Unauthorized Canadian edition. Toronto: John Ross Robertson, 1882.

Third English edition. London: Chatto and Windus, 1891.

Second American edition. New York: Charles L. Webster and Company, 1892.

Third American edition. New York: Harper and Brothers, 1896.

Fourth American edition. Hartford: American Publishing Company, 1899, and New York: Harper and Brothers, 1903.

---

[1]*BAL* 3402; Osgood company cost book, p. 126. Blanck's distinction between the binding states is based partly on what he implies are two different patterns of rosettes occurring on the spines of the two states. In fact, the rosette pattern is the same in both binding states, but it stands one way up in one binding and the other way up in the other. When the Webster company became the publishers of *The Prince and the Pauper*, the binding style remained the same except that on the spine the publisher's name was changed, and the title and author's name were moved to correspond to the position of those elements on the spine of the Webster company's *Huckleberry Finn*.

The following sight and machine collations were performed in the course of preparing this edition.[2] All emendations, manuscript revisions, and readings that were confused or obscure on the microfilm of the manuscript were exhaustively checked against the manuscript itself, and at every stage variant readings were checked in every relevant copy available in the Mark Twain Papers; the University of California Library, Berkeley; and the collection of Theodore H. Koundakjian. Printer's copy for this edition is an emended photocopy of MTP Morrison.

SIGHT COLLATIONS

Photocopy of manuscript *vs.* Ab (photocopy of MTP Morrison), three collations

Ab (MTP Morrison) *vs.* Eb (MTP Tufts) and C (photocopy of CWB copy of Dawson 1881)

Ea (Koundakjian copy) *vs.* Eb (MTP Tufts)

Eb (MTP Tufts) *vs.* Ec (Northwestern copy C62.pr.1882)

Eb (MTP Tufts) *vs.* Chatto and Windus 1892 third English edition (MTP Appert 104), a partial collation covering chapters 1–5 and 22–27

Eb (MTP Tufts) *vs.* Tauchnitz 1881 Continental edition (Harvard copy AL 1059.59), a partial collation covering chapters 1, 2, 18, 19, and 33

MACHINE COLLATIONS

Aa (Koundakjian copy 3) *vs.* Pr (MTP copy, missing one leaf, pp. 113 and 116)

Pr (MTP) *vs.* photocopy of Pr (CWB copy PS 1316.A1.1882a)

Aa (Koundakjian copy 3) *vs.* Ab (MTP Tufts); Ab (MTP Morrison); Ab, University Press imprint (MTP Hibbitt); and Ab, Webster 1885 (MTP W. Webster)

In addition, a photocopy of the manuscript and copies of the prospectus, first American, first English, and first Canadian editions were sight collated at the University of Iowa Textual Center, along with copies of the second, third, and fourth American editions, and the third English edition. Several copies of the first American edition were machine collated, as were copies of the first English edition and later American editions—in particular, several impressions of the fourth American edition.

---

[2]*Sight collation* means the collation of two or more copies that either are not typeset or are printed from different settings of type and hence cannot be collated by machine. *Machine collation* means the collation on the Hinman collator of two copies printed from the same typesetting or from plates cast from the same typesetting. The Hinman machine, by superimposing the images of the two copies on each other, enables the operator to quickly detect any typographic differences, even very small ones.

Textual Notes

These notes specify features of the text which are treated generally in the textual introduction, and discuss adopted readings and aspects of authorial revision which require fuller explanation. Mark Twain's marginalia in the manuscript are included here in full; usually they are self-explanatory or explained by their context, and are therefore merely quoted and described without comment. Other features of the manuscript included here are drafts of letters, notes or fragments from other literary works, and notations in handwriting other than Mark Twain's.

The terms *ink 1, ink 2,* and *ink 3* designate Mark Twain's writing materials (see the list of alterations in the manuscript for a full discussion of the ink colors). Cancellations are enclosed by angle brackets: <they>. A vertical rule indicates the end of a line in the manuscript.

Although a note may cite the first American edition as the source for an emendation, the emendation may be listed in the emendations list with the symbol Pr if it first occurred in the prospectus.

See the historical sources section of the introduction (pp. 19–25) for complete information on the works cited below only by author and short title.

29.6–32   Ryght . . . Lorde.] This edition follows Mark Twain's source for both the facsimile and the transcription of the Latimer letter, the second part of James's *Facsimiles of National Manuscripts* (p. 60). Although the printer's copy for the first American edition is not extant, it seems probable that the transcription was typeset directly from the printed source along with the letter itself. The author wrote to A. V. S. Anthony on 28 April 1881 that he would "hand that book to Osgood" to take to Boston, and added, "If it is too bulky, I guess we'll tear out that particular fac-simile & let him take *that.*" If he did tear out the facsimile, he probably tore out and sent the printed transcription along with it.

In 1900 an editor examined the American Publishing Company's 1899 "Royal Edition" of *The Prince and the Pauper* to determine which plates could be reused without alteration and which would need correction and repair. He must have compared the transcription in that edition with the facsimile, for he marked his corrections on the page and wrote, "I don't know whose deciphering this is, but it is *wrong* in many places. FM." Frank Bliss, president of the American Publishing Company, replied, "Clemens wrote Dec 31, 1900 to let it stand & not make corrections. 'They are not important' " (Yale).

This edition ignores Mark Twain's instruction of 1900, since it arose from a different set of circumstances. The author apparently neither made nor even copied out the transcription, and so he had no hand in introducing the errors that appeared in the first American edition and derivative versions such as the "Royal Edition." Furthermore, it is unlikely that he introduced any changes for literary purposes. He must originally have intended to print the transcription exactly as given in *Facsimiles* (which modernized some spellings, for instance turning "yt" into "that" at 29.14), and therefore that source has been made the authority here.

A list of rejected prospectus and first American edition (A) readings follows. A wavy dash (∼) on the right of the dot stands for the word on the left and signals that only a punctuation mark is changed. A caret ($_\wedge$) indicates the absence of a punctuation mark.

29.6	honorable. *(Facs)* • ∼, (A)
29.6	*Jesu.* And *(Facs)* • ∼, and (A)
29.8	was, *(Facs)* • ∼$_\wedge$ (A)
29.8	trow) *(Facs)* • ∼), (A)
29.9	berer *(Facs)* • ∼, (A)
29.9	Evance *(Facs)* • Erance, (A)
29.21	*depravetur.* Butt *(Facs)* • ∼. [¶] Butt (A)
29.26	youres *(Facs)* • Youres, (A)
29.26	Wurcestere *(Facs)* • ∼, (A)

31.1–4   *The Prince and the Pauper ... AGES]* Mark Twain took pains with the title and subtitle of his book. The manuscript includes a title page (written in ink 3 on white wove paper) which originally read "The Little Prince | AND THE | Little Pauper. | A Tale of the Sixteenth Century. | BY MARK TWAIN. | (Samuel L. Clemens.) | [*All rights reserved.*] | 1880." He revised the title, canceling both instances of "Little," changed the subtitle to read "A Tale for Young Folks of all ages," and changed the date from "1880" to "1881." Later, on a sheet of Osgood company stationery, he wrote another title page (Yale) which reads "The Prince & the Pauper. | A Tale for Young People of all Ages. | Scene laid in the Sixteenth Century. | By Mark Twain. | Boston: | J.R. Osgood & Co. | London: | Chatto & Windus. | 1881." He evidently revised again, for in the first American edition "Scene laid in the Sixteenth Century" does not appear, although the title page there does show the change from "Folks" to "People" in the subtitle and drops "(Samuel L. Clemens.)" Except for differences of typographic style, this edition adopts the title and subtitle of the first American edition.

Mark Twain's manuscript also includes a copyright page (written in ink 3 on white wove paper) on which he wrote

"Copyright by S. L. Clemens, 1880." His publisher, Osgood, made changes on both the original title page and the copyright page. On the title page, he canceled "[*All rights reserved*]" and wrote "Boston | James R. Osgood & Company" above the cancellation; on the copyright page, he altered Mark Twain's date from "1880" to "1881" and added "All rights reserved."

45.1 I WILL set] In the top left margin of the manuscript page beginning here, Mark Twain wrote and canceled in ink 3 the incomplete instruction "Put this paragra." Next to that in pencil in an unidentified hand, evidently that of an editor at the Osgood company, is the canceled inscription "10 to 14 to RA & Co"—noting that pages 10 through 14 of the manuscript had been sent to Rand, Avery, and Company, the printers of the first American edition, for word count and assessment. Following the canceled inscription is the penciled abbreviation "ntd," perhaps indicating that information concerning the five pages was noted elsewhere or that the pages had been returned. Some specifications for the book were written on the verso of manuscript page 10 (see the textual note at 49.5).

49.1 LET US SKIP] At the top of the manuscript page on which chapter 2 begins, Mark Twain wrote in pencil "View of London?"—possibly a suggestion to the illustrators.

49.5 Canty lived] At the top of the manuscript page beginning here, Mark Twain wrote in pencil the cue words "Tom Canty." Apparently an editor at the Osgood company (or the printer, when five pages of the manuscript were submitted to him) later wrote in pencil on the verso "$4\frac{1}{2} \times 6\frac{1}{2}$ | S. p. modern | 1700–1800 letters." The specifications refer to the size of the block of type on each page, the type size and face (small pica modern), and the approximate number of letters per page in the first American edition.

51.7 time of] Preceding "of" near the bottom of manuscript page 14 is a bracket, first written in pencil and then redrawn in green crayon—evidently a printer's mark made when pages 10–14 were submitted to the printer for evaluation.

52.7 Offal Court] As in the first American edition here and at 60.37, 60.38, 63.2, 70.1, and 75.18. The manuscript reads "Offal court" in these six instances. (In eleven other instances the manuscript and first American edition both read "Offal Court.") Though Mark Twain may not have been responsible for the change, the reading of the first American edition has been adopted as a necessary correction.

57.6 furthest] As in the manuscript. The reading of the first American edition, "farthest" (and the subsequent change from "further" to "farther" at 223.19), is almost certainly a sophistication.

58.12   other the] Although Mark Twain could have inadvertently dropped "of" from "other of the" or transposed "the" and "other," it appears that he intended this rather archaic locution. He revised this sentence in the manuscript (see the alterations list, 58.10, 58.11, and 58.12–13) and later made or approved another change in it, probably at the suggestion of Howells (see the emendations list, 58.11–12). In neither instance did he change this reading, nor, apparently, did the locution bother the editors of the first editions, all of whom set "other the."

60.14   use . . . use] The two alterations in the manuscript here from "treat" to "use" were apparently suggested by Edward House during his first reading of The Prince and the Pauper in 1881. Later neither he nor Mark Twain seemed to remember the change very clearly. In 1890, at the time of the lawsuit over rights to the Prince and the Pauper play, Mark Twain wrote his final words on the subject:

The truth is that he suggested only one correction—a verbal one. He thought—but did not claim to be certain—that the word "entreated," to signify "used," (kindly treated, badly treated, etc.,) had disappeared from speech before the time of Edward VI. But . . . it was an error. The expression was still in use in Elizabeth's time, as Shakspeare will testify. (DV 305, MTP)

Since there is no alteration of "entreated" in the manuscript, Mark Twain was probably remembering this change from "treat" to "use." At the time, he apparently considered the change to be of some importance, since collation indicates that he made the same correction at 201.10 on the proofs for the first American edition. Thus in spite of his inaccurate memory of the incident, his repudiation of the change seems to have come more from his anger at House in 1890 than from any wish to go back and change the reading.

60.21   Prince of Limitless Plenty] As in the first American edition. The manuscript reads "Prince of limitless Plenty." Mark Twain may well have capitalized the l on the proof sheets, and the capital has been adopted here as a likely authorial correction.

60.37   Pudding Lane] In the manuscript Mark Twain originally wrote "Mincing lane" in ink 2. Later he interlined above it in pencil "or Pudding?—see Ch 1." Still later in ink 3 he canceled "or" and "see Ch 1." and retraced the word "Pudding" in his interlineation. The name "Pudding Lane" appears only one other time, in chapter 2 at 49.16. The *l* of "lane" in the manuscript has been emended here to accord with the earlier reading at 49.16 and the reading of the first American edition.

62.28   Know'st] As in the first American edition. The manuscript reads "Knowst." Although it is possible that the amanuensis misread the manuscript or that the compositor was trying to correct Mark Twain's dialect, the change is accepted here as consistent with the way that Mark Twain sometimes revised his dialect in the manuscript or on proof. The same reasoning applies to two other emendations, "knowest" at 79.17 ("knowst" in the manuscript) and "fearest" at 83.10 ("fear'st" in the manuscript). In both cases the first American edition reading is adopted.

63.9   spatter] As in the first American edition. The manuscript and the first English edition read "splatter." Since the first English edition was set from early proofs of the first American, the change must have been made deliberately on a later set of American proofs, almost certainly by Mark Twain. The first American edition seems to bear out that theory since there is an extra space in front of "spatter" as if the change were introduced into an already set page by a typesetter who did not then evenly space out the line.

64.31   when the brute] At the top of the manuscript page beginning here, on which Tom's bruised hand is revealed, Mark Twain wrote in pencil and canceled in ink 3 "This bruise spoils his handwriting." He never made use of the plot device suggested here, although he had Tom allude to his bruised hand again at 320.10–11.

71.4   foul] As in the manuscript. Mark Twain's handwriting here is easily misread as "front," the reading of the first American edition.

82.14–15   confirm it.] The manuscript reads "confirm it.!" Mark Twain apparently squeezed in the period to replace his original exclamation point, which he then neglected to cancel. The period is adopted here as the later reading.

82.16   Hertford."] Followed by Mark Twain's uncanceled "(?)" in ink 3 in the right margin of the manuscript page. He had originally written "Herbert" in ink 2 (here and at 83.7, 84.8–9, 87.5, 87.15, and 96.4). When he substituted "Hertford" in ink 3, he apparently was still unsure of which name it was to be and followed it with another ink 3 "(?)," which he later canceled. Even after making his final decision he neglected to cancel the original "(?)" left standing in the margin.

83 *note*   of volume] As in the manuscript; the first American edition reads "of the volume," probably a sophistication. A similar sophistication occurred at 180 *note*, where the manuscript reads "at end" and the first American edition reads "at the end"; again, the manuscript reading is preserved.

90.2–3   wallow in the styes] As in the first American edition. The evolution of this phrase is as follows:
            1. kennel in the slums (MS)
            2. [*not in*] in the slums (Pr)
            3. kennel in the slums (Ea)
            4. wallow in the slums (C)
            5. wallow in the styes (A)
            6. kennel in the styes (Eb)
            The first state of the English edition (Ea) and the Canadian edition (C) were set from early stages of proof for the first American edition (A). Apparently Mark Twain made the first change (from "kennel" to "wallow") after the early proofs had been sent to England but before the Canadian edition was set. At some time after the prospectus (Pr) was printed, he then further revised the reading (from "slums" to "styes") for the first American edition. That reading is adopted here. The reading of the second state of the first English edition (Eb), which was corrected against the American edition to incorporate late changes, does not represent another Mark Twain revision, but rather an incomplete correction.

90.35   that] The reading of the first American edition, "their," is rejected as a memorial error or unconscious repetition from the two previous instances of "their" in the sentence, although it is conceivable that Mark Twain made the change when he changed "albeit" to "although" in the line below.

92.10   down upon his knees] At the top of the manuscript page beginning here, Mark Twain wrote and canceled in pencil "(Mustn't take off his buskins)."

93.4   and theirs.] Originally followed in the manuscript by a centered line, which Mark Twain wrote in ink 2 and later canceled in ink 3 when he substituted the instruction "(Double space)."

96.16   against] As in the first American edition. In the manuscript Mark Twain originally wrote "against," then canceled the "a" and substituted an apostrophe. Possibly the copyist read through his alteration, but it is more likely that he reversed himself again, as he frequently did (see, for instance, the alterations list, 205.15).

99.31   appealingly, first at one] The manuscript reads "appealingly at first to one." The reading of the first American edition has been adopted here as Mark Twain's alteration on proof. Even though this alteration occurs in one of the nine chapters of the first American edition with consistent nonauthorial changes in punctuation, the comma after "appealingly" has also been adopted here as part of Mark Twain's alteration.

100.9   nature] The manuscript reads "Nature." Originally the word began the sentence, and when Mark Twain interlined "At last" he left the capital standing. Perhaps he wanted the word to remain a proper noun, but it is more likely that he simply overlooked the correction, as he did for instance at 96.13 (see the alterations list).

102.5   naturally] The first American edition reading is adopted here as Mark Twain's change from the manuscript reading, "actually," although it is tempting to reject it as a memorial error.

102.11   present.] Mark Twain's note written in pencil and canceled in ink 3 follows in the manuscript: "Let him hide the Seal."

105.34   Commission] At the top of the manuscript page beginning here, Mark Twain wrote in ink 2 and canceled in ink 3 "Both tanned & brown with out-door sports."

111.1   WE LEFT] At the top of the manuscript page on which chapter 10 begins, Mark Twain wrote in pencil and canceled in ink 3 "Offal Court in Cole Harbor."

111.12   ground among the] At the bottom of the manuscript page ending here, Mark Twain wrote and canceled in pencil "Let this be father Andrew—."

119.10   I tell thee!"] On the manuscript page ending here, Mark Twain wrote in pencil and canceled in ink 3 "Insert here the route <they> prince took, & sort of buildings."

124.5   canopy of state] The manuscript, the first state of the first American edition, and the first English and first Canadian editions all read "canopy of estate." The reading of the second state of the first American edition, a late correction, is adopted here. It is one of three substantive changes in the second state of the first American edition (see the textual notes at 237.9 and 307.9 for the other two). The change was probably made to correct the discrepancy between the uncorrected text reading and the caption of the illustration on the same page.

127.6   Return we] Preceding these words on the manuscript page, Mark Twain wrote and canceled in pencil "Return to Tom."

128.3   Hertford.] Followed in the manuscript by Mark Twain's "(?),"
            which he wrote and later canceled in ink 3.

129.7   Hertford] Followed in the margin of the manuscript page by
            Mark Twain's "(?)," which he wrote and later canceled in ink 3.

129.9   king of England!"] At the bottom of the manuscript page ending
            here, Mark Twain wrote and canceled in ink 3 "(Barge it home
            in solemn state & slow oars, with the tide—deep tolling bells.)"

133.37–134.2 When ... London Bridge.] Mark Twain wrote in pencil and
            later canceled in ink 3 the words "cut here" in the margin of the
            manuscript page alongside this sentence. Though he may have
            been referring to an intended illustration, it is more likely that
            he wrote it as a direction to himself when he was integrating
            these pages into his narrative (see the alterations list, 132.4–
            134.6). He did not cut until near the end of the next para-
            graph ("gateways.")

136.17–137.8 boy's form ... the prince] On the verso of this manuscript page
            are some miscellaneous notes by Mark Twain in black ink and
            pencil, mainly a list of characters' names for *Ah Sin*.

137.38–   "Good sir ... stepped briskly] On the verso of this manuscript
138.10   page are four words in Bret Harte's hand, "last. I have
            [reasoned]," presumably a discarded page from *Ah Sin*.

139.10–11   a grateful ... him;] As in the manuscript and prospectus. This
            passage was apparently deleted from the first American edition
            at the behest of Mark Twain to accommodate the introduction
            of eight new words of text at 139.24 and the footnote at the
            bottom of the same page (139 *note*). Since the deletion occurred
            only because of the exigencies of the moment and not out of
            any aesthetic consideration, the passage is here restored (see the
            textual introduction, p. 399).

139.21   "I would] As in the manuscript and prospectus. These words
            originally began a new paragraph and were printed run-on in the
            first American edition presumably only to create more space for
            the additions at 139.24 and 139 *note*.

140.15   truth] As in the manuscript. The first American edition read-
            ing, "troth," seems to have resulted from the copyist's mis-
            reading of the manuscript, in which the u is written over the
            original o.

142.18–27   a homeless ... duty and] On the verso of this manuscript page
            is a draft of a letter dated 22 November [1875], from Mark
            Twain to Mr. [C. E.] Flower, about the plan to build by sub-
            scription a Shakespeare memorial theater in Stratford on Avon.

155.7   last.] The manuscript reads "last.!" Mark Twain originally fol-
            lowed "last" with an exclamation point in ink 2. He later

squeezed in a period in ink 3 without canceling the exclamation point, perhaps undecided about which of the two marks of punctuation to adopt. The first American edition prints the exclamation point, perhaps because the copyist overlooked the period. The period, however, is adopted here as the later reading.

157.29   Third Groom] In the manuscript Mark Twain wrote in pencil and canceled in ink 3 two question marks above the word "Third."

165.23   shall] The manuscript reads "shalt." Though Mark Twain's manuscript *t* could easily have been misread as an *l* here, the first American edition reading is adopted as a necessary correction.

171.27   even made him] As in the manuscript. The reading of the first American edition, "made him even," is rejected as a mechanical or memorial transcription error.

173.7   meekly] As in the manuscript. The reading of the first American edition, "quickly," is rejected as a memorial error or an eye skip to the phrase that follows immediately ("and quickly dropped his face again").

174.22–31 picture . . . said—] A receipt in an unknown hand is written on the verso of this manuscript page, probably by one of Clemens' employees. It notes a transaction with Clemens' neighbor, Marshall Jewell—"For Exchange Cows 45 dollers." It is headed "Hartford" and dated 8 July 1878.

175.7   poison."] Mark Twain interlined the word "Remark" in pencil as a reminder to interrupt his dialogue here. He later crossed it out when he added "Weighty . . . said—" (175.8–9) in ink 3 on the verso of the manuscript page.

177.35   is serious matter] As in the manuscript. The reading of the first American edition, "is a serious matter," is rejected as a sophistication.

179.13   woman doth desire] As in the manuscript. The omission of "doth" in the first American edition is rejected as a sophistication or eye skip.

185.5   mistake—a flawless] As in the manuscript. The first American edition omits the word "a," probably a transcription error.

187.1   MILES HENDON] At the top of the manuscript page on which chapter 17 begins, Mark Twain wrote in ink 2 and canceled in ink 3 "he has the k's clothes."

188.6   wood] As in the first American edition. The manuscript reads "road." Though it is possible that Mark Twain's handwriting was misread, it is more likely that the change was made intentionally. Either "road" or "wood" makes sense, as Miles does search for the king in both places, but the later reading is adopted here as authoritative.

191.5   sank] As in the manuscript. The first American edition reads "sunk," possibly a misreading of Mark Twain's manuscript *a* for *u*, or a sophistication.

195.6   imitations left,] Although Mark Twain may have intended a kind of rhetorical pause when he punctuated his manuscript "imitations, left," it is just as likely that he changed the direction of his sentence after writing "imitations," but neglected to cancel his comma. In either case, the comma seems so obtrusive that the first American edition reading is adopted here as a correction.

198.24   uttered,—] Mark Twain originally followed "uttered" with a semicolon. He canceled the top portion of the semicolon with a dash and he may have tried to wipe out the remaining comma, as it is somewhat smeared. However, since the comma appears to be uncanceled and Mark Twain commonly used the comma-dash construction, it has been retained here.

205.2   village] Presumably as a note of his intention to expand the king's adventures with Hugo, Mark Twain wrote and later canceled the words "as usual" in ink 3 at the top of the manuscript page which originally followed at this point (see the alterations list, 205.4 and 243.36). When he added the new pages, he wrote that the king was sent out in Hugo's charge, "as usual," but later apparently dropped the words from his text (see the emendations list, 241.7).

212   *illustration*] Howells' daughter, Winifred, wrote to Mark Twain on 18 January 1882, after receiving her copy of *The Prince and the Pauper*: "I think the loveliest place I have read is where the Prince finds the calf in the barn and is so glad to cuddle up to something warm and alive. After his horror at first feeling something beside him it was such a relief to find what it really was that I was almost angry with the picture for letting me know a little too soon" (*MTHL*, p. 383). The picture has been moved to follow the text in this edition.

215.5   be shame] Although the first American edition reading, "be a shame," may be due to Mark Twain's revision to less archaic diction, the manuscript reading is retained here because of the number of similar variants apparently caused by compositorial sophistication or transcription error.

218   *illustration*] When John J. Harley designed this illustration for

the first American edition, he gave it an irregular shape, apparently intending that the printer fill the notch with type. The printer, however, simply centered the illustration, making a strangely unbalanced page. The shape of the picture has been altered to accommodate it to the specifications of this edition.

First American edition

220.11   due to his] As in the manuscript. The first American edition reads "due his," probably a sophistication.

235.37   been] As in the first American edition. The manuscript reads "lain." Although the first American edition reading is quite possibly a memorial error, the large number of revisions by Mark Twain in these pages makes it more likely that he made the change.

236 *caption*   "THEN . . . PLUNGINGS."] The first American edition caption reads "GOD MADE EVERY CREATURE BUT YOU!" The caption was drawn from a passage in the manuscript where Miles Hendon curses the mule, which was omitted from the first American edition, possibly at the suggestion of Howells (see the emendations list, 237.22–23). The editors of the first English edition noticed the discrepancy and recaptioned the illustration; that reading is adopted here.

237.9   do think there's not] The corrupted reading "do not think there's not" appeared in the first state of the first American edition, possibly introduced by the compositor when the line was reset to drop "in all hell's dominions." The corruption was carried over into the first English edition, one of the two editions set from the American proofs. The reading was corrected in the first Canadian edition and the second state of the first American edition. See the textual introduction, page 407.

237.12–14   myself?— . . . work.] As in the first American edition. The manuscript reads "myself— . . . work?" The first American edition reading may well have been Mark Twain's change and appears to be a necessary correction.

242.12   strugglings] As in the manuscript. The first American edition reading, "struggling," is probably due to a misreading of Mark Twain's badly formed final *s* in his manuscript.

244.11–13   alley,— . . . results.] In the manuscript Mark Twain originally ended his sentence with "alley." He later revised the manuscript to expand the sentence, adding "—and . . . results." on the verso of the page with instructions to turn it over, but neglected to alter his old terminal punctuation. The reading was corrected in the first American edition by substituting a comma for the period after "alley," and that reading is adopted here.

244.16   king's wrist] In the top left corner of the manuscript page beginning here, Mark Twain wrote and canceled "release" in ink 3, presumably a note to himself about his intentions for the king as the episode continued.

253.6   nor the left] As in the manuscript. The first American edition reading, "nor to the left," is rejected as a probable sophistication.

260.21   tongues] As in the manuscript. The first American edition reading, "tongue," is probably a misreading or a sophistication.

267.1   THE KING] At the top of the manuscript page on which chapter 26 begins, Mark Twain wrote and canceled in ink 3 "Make H very strong."

268.4   I have a plan] In the margin of the manuscript page near these words, Mark Twain wrote and canceled in ink 3 "(or a paper)."

278.4   goodman] The first American edition reads "good man," very likely a misreading of Mark Twain's manuscript, in which the word is hyphenated at the end of a line. The manuscript reading is preferred.

283.19–21   If he . . . unscathed.] Apparently Mark Twain considered having the king demand the woman's release after all. In the margin of the manuscript page here he wrote and canceled in ink 3 "No.—let him do it."

296.17   grimly holy] As in the manuscript and first English edition. The first American edition reads "grimly, holy." Although "grimly" does have an adjectival sense (the 1870 Webster's dictionary defines it as "having a hideous or stern look"), the comma is rejected here as nonauthorial. It was probably introduced by the compositor, perhaps when he reset to accommodate Mark Twain's change in the same line from "sick; and once" to "tremble. Once" (see the emendations list, 296.17). The first English edition was set from proofs for the first American edition, but in this case agrees with the manuscript—presumably the English compositor decided the comma was in error and dropped it.

298.23   preparations] As in the manuscript. The first American edition reading, "preparation," is probably a transcription error or a sophistication.

307.9   reined] The manuscript and the first state of the first American edition read "reigned." The reading was corrected to "reined" in the second state of the first American edition as well as in the first Canadian (see the textual introduction, p. 407). The editors of the first English edition also made the necessary correction, and it is adopted here.

317.26   turned] As in the manuscript. The first American edition reading, "moved," is probably an unconscious repetition from the line above.

322.27   applause.] At the bottom of the manuscript page ending here, Mark Twain wrote and canceled in ink 3 "Champion."

325.18   the old lieutenant] In the right margin of the manuscript page on which these words appear, Mark Twain wrote and canceled in ink 3 "head lieutenant of the late kings <kitchen> household don't know exact title." In the left margin he wrote and canceled in ink 3 "—no, head ranger of the late kings cabbage orchards." It is impossible to tell in which order he wrote and canceled the two marginal notes, but in any case he finally decided to let "the old lieutenant" stand as is. He had also been vague about Sir Humphrey's title and position earlier in the text, at 292.9–11.

332 note   volume.] At the bottom of the manuscript page ending here, Mark Twain wrote and circled his signature in light pencil, then retraced the signature and the circle in heavier pencil.

337.9   Timbs' . . . London.] As in the first English edition. Mark Twain wrote his notes hastily and out of their final order, leaving his citations in a jumble for his editors to fix. For instance, in the manuscript note 3 cites *"Hume,"* note 4 *"Hume's History of England,"* and note 5 *"Hume's England."* Although the editors of the first American edition made some attempt to standardize

the citations, they left many anomalies, and the forms of citations adopted here are from the first English edition.

339.33   own reign] As in the first American edition. The manuscript
reads *"own reign,"* as does the first English edition, set from
proofs of the first American edition. Mark Twain, already in
some embarrassment at having to explain the king's pronouncing the end of a law that did not yet exist, must have decided
not to emphasize that the "hideous statute" was instituted in
Edward's own reign. He probably dropped the italics from late
proofs of the first American edition.

341.41   *Ibid.*] At the bottom of the manuscript page ending here, Mark
Twain wrote in ink 3 "(The 'General Note' follows, here,
<either> after the dash.)" He followed his note with a curved
dash, centered on the next line.

342.1   GENERAL NOTE] In the top left corner of the manuscript page
beginning here, Mark Twain wrote in ink 3 "Last." In the top
right portion of the page he wrote and canceled the direction
"Put this paragraph in large type, leaded."

EMENDATIONS OF THE COPY-TEXT

Readings adopted in this edition from a source other than the copy-text, Mark Twain's manuscript, are recorded here. The only copy-text readings changed without listing are the forms peculiar to the written page and the typographical features discussed in the textual introduction. Mechanical errors in inscription occasioned by incomplete revision in the manuscript are noted in the list of alterations in the manuscript.

In each entry, the reading of this edition is given first, its source identified by a symbol in parentheses; it is separated by a dot from the rejected copy-text reading on the right, thus: fiends (A) • devils. The following symbols refer to sources of emendation:

Pr   Publisher's prospectus for the first American edition

A   First American edition

Ab   Second state of the first American edition

I-C   This edition (Iowa-California)

This list also records the form adopted in this edition when a compound word is hyphenated at the end of a line in Mark Twain's manuscript. The form chosen has been determined by other occurrences of the word and parallels within this work, and by the appearance of the word in Mark Twain's other works of the period.

The symbol I-C follows any emendation whose source is not an authoritative text—Pr or A—even if the same correction was made in a subsequent, derivative, edition. A wavy dash (∼) on the right of the dot stands for the word on the left and signals that only a punctuation mark is emended. A caret (∧) indicates the absence of a punctuation mark, so that the entry "myself? (A) • ∼∧" shows that a question mark follows "myself" in the first American edition, while no punctuation follows "myself" in the copy-text. A vertical rule (word | word) indicates the end of a line in the manuscript. Information in square brackets, such as [not in], is editorial. Emendations marked with an asterisk are discussed in the textual notes.

35.5	thronèd (I-C) • thronéd
49.11	houses (A) • house
50.15	fiends (A) • devils
51.12	grandmother (I-C) • grand-|mother
51.18	himself (A) • his hide
*52.7	Court (A) • court
53.3	solely (Pr) • merely
53.6	May-pole (I-C) • May-|pole
55.15	barefooted (I-C) • bare-|footed

58.11–12	magnificent array (A) • imposing top-hamper
*60.21	Limitless (A) • limitless
60.37	Court (A) • court
*60.37	Lane (A) • lane
60.38	Court (A) • court
61.1	grandam (I-C) • granddam
61.4	grandam (I-C) • grand-dam
62.21	It is (A) • 'Tis
62.23	lackeys (A) • lackies
*62.28	Know'st (A) • Knowst
62.33	Court. (Pr) • ~?
63.2	Court (A) • court
*63.9	spatter (A) • splatter
64.6	glorious (A) • too divine
64.13	It is (A) • 'Tis
64.36	king (I-C) • king my father [Pr reads "King"]
64.37	It is (Pr) • 'Tis
65.8	seized (Pr) • siezed
65.19	highness (I-C) • Highness
66.7	highness (I-C) • Highness
66.11	highness (I-C) • Highness
68.8	serving-men (Pr) • serving-|men
68 note	Note (Pr) • Notes
69.14	am (A) • *am*
70.1	Court (I-C) • court
70.12	charity."* (I-C) • ~.*"
70.32	Prince (A) • prince
75.18	Court (A) • court
77.6	prince (A) • Prince
77.7	prince (A) • Prince
78.14	Thou (Pr) • *Thou*
78.14	*king* (I-C) • king [Pr reads "King"]
79.17	knowest (Pr) • knowst
80.8	so! (Pr) • ~.
81.14	Thou'lt (A) • Thoul't
81.15	thou'lt (A) • thoul't
*82.15	it. (A) • ~.!
83.6	grievously!"* (I-C) • ~!*"

83.10	fearest (A) • fear'st
84.11	death-blow (A) • death-|blow
84.13	The prince (A) • The Prince
84.13	prince (A) • Prince
84.16	gilded (A) • gorgeous
85.6	Earl (I-C) • earl
85.13	Earl (I-C) • earl
86.4	St. John (A) • St John
86.7	To wit (I-C) • To-|wit
87.3	show (A) • shew
87.9	His (A) • his
87.10	St. John (A) • St John
87.13	doth (A) • ~,
88.4	St. John's (Pr) • St John's
88.6	shown (Pr) • shewn
88.18	show (A) • shew
88.37	lady (A) • Lady
88.37	dismayed (A) • cornered
89.1	to-day (A) • to-|day
89.9	dangerous ground (A) • pretty thin ice
*90.2	wallow (A) • kennel
*90.3	styes (A) • slums
90.4	St. John's (Pr) • St John's
90.12	an' (Pr) • an
90.16–17	straightway (Pr) • straigtway
90.21	overlooking (Pr) • over-|looking
90.36	although (A) • albeit
92.4	gentleman (A) • gentlemen
92.4–5	straightway (I-C) • straight-|way
92.7	seized (A) • siezed
92.13	Beshrew (A) • Be-|shrew
93.1	robe (A) • robe de chambre
93.1	laid himself (A) • lay
93.7	head-shaking (A) • head-|shaking
93.8	St. John (A) • St John
94.1	loth (I-C) • loath
94.4	manner! (A) • ~?
96.1	St. John (A) • St John

96.9	blood (A) • womb
96.13	called himself (A) • said he were
96.15	called prince (A) • called Prince
96.15	prince by (A) • Prince by
96.16	prince (A) • Prince
*96.16	against (A) • 'gainst
96.17	mad! (A) • ~.
97.7	it (Pr) • them
97.11	Earl (Pr) • earl
*99.31	appealingly, first at one (Pr) • appealingly at first to one
*100.9	nature (A) • Nature
*102.5	naturally (Pr) • actually
105.2	that—" (I-C) • ~—∧
105.6	empty handed (I-C) • empty-handed
105.10	recal (I-C) • recall
105.30	since (A) • sith
107.10	to and fro (Pr) • to fro
108.2	cloth of gold (I-C) • cloth-of-gold
108.15	Feathers, (I-C) • ~∧ [A reads "feathers,"]
109.5	Duke (A) • duke
109.5	gateway (A) • gate-|way
111.10	Thou'lt (Pr) • Thoul't
114.8	horse-laugh (A) • horse-|laugh
114.37	grandmother (Pr) • grand-|mother
115.6	beating (A) • basting
115.17	defense (I-C) • defence
115.23	back, drowned in tears, to her bed (A) • back to her bed drowned in tears
119.4	household (Pr) • house-|hold
119.13	Bridge (I-C) • bridge
119.14	Bridge (I-C) • bridge
120.3	Bridge (I-C) • bridge
120.3	Bridge (I-C) • bridge
120.29	waterman (A) • water-|man
120.34	dived (A) • dove
121.5	To wit (Pr) • To-wit
123.14	Dowgate (Pr) • Dow-|gate
*124.5	canopy of state (Ab) • canopy of estate

125.5	leftward (Pr) • left-|ward
125.37	Prince (I-C) • prince
126.8	ye (A) • thee
126.8	you (A) • thou
126.35	mob-tide (A) • mob-|tide
127.7	bugle-note (Pr) • bugle-|note
128.4	lord (A) • Lord
131.3	Bridge (Pr) • bridge
132.2	Bridge (Pr) • bridge
132.7	bakeries (Pr) • bookstores
133.7	Bridge (A) • bridge
134.7	Bridge (A) • bridge
134.9	thou'rt (A) • thour't
134.9	Thou'lt (A) • Thoul't
134.11	thou'lt (A) • thoul't
134.19	head-piece (A) • head-|piece
136.3	Prince (I-C) • prince
136.10	elder (A) • big
136.13	it! (A) • ~.
137.7	Prince (I-C) • prince
137.8	Prince (I-C) • prince
137.10	fantasy (Pr) • phantasy
138.8	Prithee (A) • Prythee
138.13	boy's (Pr) • boys
139.5	*king* (Pr) • king
139.15	*must* (Pr) • must
139.24	one . . . service*— (A) • [*not in*]
139.36–38	*He . . . creation. (A) • [*not in*]
144.15–16	to wit (A) • to-wit
144.18	Knight (A) • Baronet
145.5	knight (A) • baronet
147.23	thou'lt (A) • thoul't
150.11	he loved she (A) • twice as well
151.1	thou'rt (A) • thour't
151.13	worship. (A) • ~?
152.9	detestable (A) • misbegotten
153.9	Bridge (A) • bridge
*155.7	last. (I-C) • ~.!

155.7	your straw (A) • thy straw
155.8	ye (A) • thee
155.8	your unbelieving (A) • thine unbelieving
155.14	woe (Pr) • wo
156.1	wert (Pr) • wast
156.1	Prince (I-C) • prince
157.9	thee and Nan (A) • you and Nan
157.14	answer (A) • remark
158.23–24	truss-point (I-C) • truss-|point
159.24	to wit (I-C) • to-wit
160.6	household (A) • house-|hold
162.2	good (A) • dear
162.36	St. John (Pr) • St John
162.37	Council of Executors (I-C) • council of executors
164.2	recal (I-C) • recall
164.8	always (A) • *always*
164.17	Prince (I-C) • prince
165.12	Prince (I-C) • prince
165.19	thou'lt (A) • thoul't
*165.23	shall (A) • shalt
166.2	recal (I-C) • recall
169.6	homesickness (Pr) • home-|sickness
169.9	tolerable (A) • middling
170.2	embarrassed (A) • embarassed
170.30	Earl (I-C) • earl
171.17	highway (Pr) • high-|way
171.22	heart-strings (Pr) • heart-|strings
172.15	King's Guard (I-C) • king's guard
173.4	man had (A) • male one
175.4	liege. (A) • ~?
175.33	New Year (I-C) • new year
175.35	outburst (Pr) • out-|burst
175.37–38	hare-brained (A) • misbegotten
177.1	superior (Pr) • suprior
180.2	goodwife (A) • good-|wife
180.11	earthquake (A) • earth-|quake
180.15	storm."* (A) • ~.*"
181.4	ash-cat (A) • ash-|cat

184.8	bareheaded (A) • bare-|headed
187.2	Bridge (I-C) • bridge
*188.6	wood (A) • road
188.8	Bridge (I-C) • bridge
188.24	Thou'lt (A) • Thoul't
189.11	seized (A) • siezed
191.16	weirdly (A) • wierdly
191.22	crutches; (A) • crutches; diseased ones, with running sores peeping from ineffectual wrappings;
192.22	re-inforced (A) • re-|inforced
193.31	joyously (A) • gushingly
194.2	countrywards (I-C) • country-|wards
194.16	midsummer (A) • mid-|summer
194.30	beldame (A) • bel-|dame
194.33	fortune-telling (A) • fortune-|telling
195.4	thou'dst (I-C) • thoud'st
*195.6	imitations (A) • ~,
195.15	new-comers (I-C) • new comers
195.27	criss-crossed (A) • criss-|crossed
195.33	mayhap in (A) • may-|hap in
198.24	hast (A) • has
198.27	England!' (A) • ~!∧
199.5	Mooncalves (A) • Moon-|calves
201.10	use (A) • treat
205.10	Thou'lt (A) • Thoul't
205.14	I (A) • *I*
205.15	Thy (A) • Your
205.16	thou hast (A) • you have
205.16	thy (A) • your
205.20	An' (A) • An
206.14	an' (A) • an
207.17	An' (A) • An
207.22	heaven (I-C) • Heaven
211.3	drowse (A) • drowze
211.36	non-existent (A) • non-|existent
216.26	an' (A) • an
218.10	surprise (A) • surprize
221.2	self-complacent (A) • self-|complacent

222.14	outhouse (I-C) • out-|house
224.24	sheepskins (A) • sheep-|skins
226.7	on (A) • along
226.19	seized (A) • siezed
227.10	heaven (I-C) • Heaven
228.3	Pope (I-C) • pope
229.19	he (A) • *he*
230.20	archangel (A) • arch-|angel
230.22	bedside (A) • bed-|side
231.8	midnight (A) • mid-|night
233.1	cat-like (A) • cat-|like
234.9	this ecstasy (A) • the ecstasy of this ravishing dalliance
234.11	an' (A) • an
235.7	straightway (I-C) • straight-|way
235.12	who (A) • whom
235.16	an' (A) • an
235.16	not— Where (A) • not, I will carve thy withered heart out o' thy body with as small compunction as I would a vicious dog's! Where
235.20–21	overtake (A) • over-|take
235.24	you (A) • *you*
235.25	an' (A) • an
235.35	obey (A) • hoof it
235.36	gives (A) • tips
*235.37	been (A) • lain
236.13	sheepskin (A) • sheep-|skin
237.9	archangel with (A) • archangel in all hell's dominions with
237.11	ill-conditioned slave (A) • misbegotten devil
*237.12	myself? (A) • ∼∧
*237.14	work. (A) • ∼?
237.22	a (A) • this
237.22–23	mule, which must have broken its spirit, (A) • mule— [¶] "Ye stubborn and rebellious limb, ye son of shame! you came into the world with disgraceful parentage, and are going out of it without hope of leaving posterity behind! And you are not belonging among the works of God, neither; God made every beast and bird and creature that's in the world but you—and you're the vile invention of man!" [¶] This cruel speech must have broken the spirit of the mule,

239.1	Foo-foo (I-C) • Foo-Foo
239.7	charge (A) • keep
239.15	seized (A) • siezed
240.3	storm of (A) • roars and
240.7	seized (A) • siezed
241.3	Hugo (A) • Hugh
241.7	charge, (A) • charge, as usual,
241.22	Hugo (A) • Hugh
241.31	operate (A) • be ripe
241.38	angry-looking (A) • appear decayed
242.3	the hideous ulcer to be seen (A) • parts of the sore to peep out
242.17	enterprise (A) • enterprize
243.13	headquarters (A) • head-|quarters
243.14	afternoon (A) • after-|noon
243.29	first. (A) • ~!
243.31	an' (A) • an
*244.11	alley,— (A) • ~.—
244.16	seized (A) • siezed
246.7	goodwife (I-C) • good-|wife
247.6	knight (A) • baronet
247.9	spectre-knight (A) • spectre-baronet
249.5	eightpence (A) • eight-|pence
250.3	Thou'lt (A) • Thoul't
250.10	eightpence (A) • eight-|pence
250.16	eightpence (A) • eight-|pence
255.2	fidgeted (I-C) • fidgetted
256.17	seized (A) • siezed
256.25	thou'rt (A) • thour't
256.25	thou'lt (A) • thoul't
259.5	gladhearted (A) • glad-|hearted
260.2	thou'lt (A) • thoul't
260.10	yonder (A) • yonnder
260.10	marketplace (A) • market-|place
260.10	May-pole (I-C) • May-|pole
260.22	thou'lt (A) • thoul't
260.25	thou'lt (A) • thoul't
260.32	thou'rt (A) • thour't
261.19	seized (A) • siezed

261.19	arm, (A) • arm, excited and agitated,
262.6	thou'lt (A) • thoul't
263.14	Ah! (A) • ~,
264.10	seized (A) • siezed
266.6	seize (A) • sieze
266.20	For (A) • Sir
267.4	his birth (A) • the womb
267.10–11	person (A) • peron
267.12	state (I-C) • State
269.27	playfellows (A) • play-|fellows
270.21	straightway (A) • straight-|way
274.7	condition (A) • character
274.11	midnight (A) • mid-|night
275.29	Thou'lt (A) • Thoul't
*278.4	goodman (I-C) • good-|man
278.25	Earl (I-C) • earl
278.31	"What (A) • ∧~
279.1	Duke (I-C) • duke
279.9	Prince (I-C) • prince
279.11	court (I-C) • Court
280.22	stonyhearted (A) • stony-|hearted
283.29	half-witted (A) • half-|witted
285.9	honors (A) • title
286.13	thou'lt (A) • thoul't
287.4	seized (A) • siezed
287.35	outcry (A) • out-|cry
288.9	whispered (A) • whipered
289.5	spectre-knight (A) • spectre-baronet
289.7	May-pole (I-C) • may-pole
295.4	mock king (I-C) • mock-king
296.17	tremble. Once (A) • sick; and once
300.15	parliament (I-C) • Parliament
301.23	Bedchamber (Pr) • Bed-|chamber
301.27	mock king (Pr) • mock-king
301.37	Gracechurch (A) • Grace-|church
302.35	counterpart (A) • counter-|part
303.3	Cheapside (A) • Cheap-|side
303.3	penthouse (A) • pent-|house

303.10	mock king's (A) • mock-king's
306.8	downcast (A) • down-|cast
307.5	highness (I-C) • Highness
*307.9	reined (Ab) • reigned
309.16	galleries (A) • galleeries
310.10	daylight (A) • day-|light
310.21–22	simultaneous (A) • simutaneous
311.6	white-haired (I-C) • white-|haired
313.6	mock king's (I-C) • mock-|king's
313.29	majesty (I-C) • Majesty
313.29	seize (A) • sieze
314.19	Prince (A) • prince
315.18	Prince (A) • prince
317.2	St. John (A) • St John
320.4	beggar-boy (I-C) • beggar boy
320.11	highness (I-C) • Highness
320.22	St. John (A) • St John
322.1	Duke (I-C) • duke
324.13	after (A) • after after
326.1	whipping-boy (A) • whipping-|boy
327.3	pot-hooks (A) • pot-|hooks
327.8	Seize (A) • Sieze
328.5	ordered (A) • order
328.9	judgment (A) • judgement
328.9	economize (A) • economise
328.17	scarecrow (I-C) • scare-crow
330.2	knight (A) • baronet
330.14	lady (I-C) • Lady
330.14	earl (I-C) • Earl
331.11	show (A) • title
333.14	Earl (I-C) • earl
334.25	Earl (I-C) • earl
335.19	credit. (A) • ~. | [centered] The end.
*337.9	Timbs' *Curiosities of London.* (I-C) • *Timbs'* "~~~.
337.13	Timbs' *Curiosities of London.* (I-C) • *Timbs'* "~~~.
337.15	*The Duke of Norfolk's Condemnation Commanded* (A) • The Duke of Norfolk's Condemnation Commanded
337.20–21	Hume's *History of England,* vol. iii. (I-C) • *Hume, vol.* III,

337.23	Henry VIII (A) • ~~.
337.27	Hume's (I-C) • *Hume's*
337.27	iii. (A) • III.,
338.8	day.]— (A) • ~.]∧
338.8	Hume's *History of England* (I-C) • *Hume's England*
338.8–9	vol. iii. p. (A) • *vol. III, p.*
338.9	307 (I-C) • *306*
338.26–27	Hume's *History of England* (I-C) • *Hume's England*
338.27	vol. iii. p. 307 (A) • *vol. III, p. 307*
338.30	James I (A) • ~~.
338.30	Charles II (A) • ~~.
338.36	Hume's *History of England* (I-C) • *Hume's England*
338.37	vol. iii. p. 324 (A) • *vol. III, p. 324*
339.10–11	*Ibid.*, vol. iii. p. 339 (A) • *Ibid, vol. III, p. 339*
339.21–22	Dr. J. Hammond Trumbull's *Blue Laws, True and False,* (I-C) • *Dr. J. Hammond Trumbull's* "~~, ~~~,"
339.26	*Ibid.* (A) • ~∧
*339.33	own reign (A) • *own reign*
339.39–40	Dr. J. Hammond Trumbull's *Blue Laws, True and False,* p. (I-C) • *Dr. J. Hammond Trumbull's* "~~, ~~~," p.
339.40	13 (I-C) • *17*
340.8–9	Dr. J. Hammond Trumbull's *Blue Laws, True and False,* p. 13 (I-C) • *Dr. J. Hammond Trumbull's* "~~, ~~~," p. 13
340.17	*Ibid.* (A) • ~∧
340.17	pp. 11–12 (I-C) • *p. 12*
340.38–39	J. Heneage Jesse's *London: its Celebrated Characters and Places.* (I-C) • *J. Heneage Jesse's* "~, ~~~~~."
340.40	Edward VI (A) • ~~.
341.9	Timbs' *Curiosities of London,* p. (I-C) • *Timbs'* "~~~," *p.*
341.22	St. Catherine's (A) • *St Catherine's*
341.36	Hunt. (A) • ~.—
342.2	*"hideous Blue-Laws of Connecticut,"* (A) • "~" ~-~~~, ∧
342.11	*never been a time* (A) • NEVER BEEN A TIME
342 note	*Blue Laws, True and False,* (I-C) • "Blue Laws, True and False,"

HISTORICAL COLLATION

This collation records all variant substantive readings among the following texts:

MS Mark Twain's manuscript

Pr Publisher's prospectus for the first American edition

A First American edition

E First English edition

C First Canadian edition

In each entry, a dot separates the adopted reading on the left from the rejected variant or variants on the right. Variant states of a single edition are designated by lowercase letters following the symbol for the edition. Thus, Aa and Ab represent the first and second states of the first American edition. Likewise, Ea, Eb, and Ec represent the first, second, and third states of the first English edition. When consecutive states agree on a reading, they are listed thus: Ea–b. When nonconsecutive states agree, they are listed thus: Ea, Ec.

Texts that agree substantively do not necessarily agree in all their accidental or stylistic features; in the entry at 285.9, for example, the first English edition reads "honours" not "honors."

When a reading occurs for the first time in the present text (among the texts included in the collation), it is reported first with the Iowa-California symbol (I-C) and then followed with the historical information (see the entry at 64.36).

If contemporary dictionaries indicate that two spellings are simply alternative, or are English and American spellings of the same word, the difference is not considered substantive, and they are not included in this list—"center" and "centre," for instance. But if the dictionary assigns separate listings or gives distinct definitions to the words—as in "farther" and "further" or "O" and "Oh"—they are included here. Likewise, forms such as "sith" and "since" or "troth" and "truth" will be found in this list.

When Mark Twain revised a passage in the manuscript and then canceled it in proof, the record of his manuscript revisions is reported in the list of alterations and keyed to this table. A superscript number within an entry (see 237.22–23) refers the reader to the list of alterations. Information in square brackets, such as [not in], is editorial. A vertical rule (word | word) indicates the end of a line in the manuscript. Entries marked with an asterisk are discussed in the textual notes.

47 *title*	CHAPTER (MS, E) • THE PRINCE AND THE PAUPER. | CHAPTER (A, C); TOM CANTY. | CHAPTER (Pr)
49.11	houses (A, E, C) • house (MS)
50.15	fiends (A, Eb–c, C) • devils (MS, Pr, Ea)
51.18	himself (A, Eb–c, C) • his hide (MS, Ea)

53.3	solely (Pr, A, E, C) • merely (MS)
*57.6	furthest (MS) • farthest (Pr, A, E, C)
58.11–12	magnificent array (A, E, C) • imposing top-hamper (MS)
59.1	slow (MS, A, Ea–b, C) • slowly (Ec)
59.10	O (MS) • Oh (Pr, A, E, C)
61.13	O (MS) • Oh (Pr, A, E, C)
62.11	O (MS) • Oh (A, E, C)
62.21	It is (A, E, C) • 'Tis (MS)
*62.28	Know'st (A, E, C) • Knowst (MS)
*63.9	spatter (A, C) • splatter (MS, E)
64.6	O (MS) • Oh (A, E, C)
64.6	glorious (A, E, C) • too divine (MS)
64.13	It is (A, E, C) • 'Tis (MS)
64.36	king (I-C) • King (Pr, A, E, C); king my father (MS)
64.37	It is (Pr, A, E, C) • 'Tis (MS)
68 note	Note (Pr, A, E, C) • Notes (MS)
*71.4	foul (MS) • front (A, E, C)
75.1	sprung (MS, A, C) • sprang (E)
75.3	O . . . O (MS) • Oh . . . Oh (A, E, C)
75.14	O (MS) • Oh (A, E, C)
75.20	O (MS) • Oh (A, E, C)
79.19	knowest (Pr, A, E, C) • knowst (MS)
79.24	O (MS) • Oh (Pr, A, E, C)
80.8	matters (MS) • matter (Pr, A, E, C)
80.9	make (MS, Pr, A, Eb–c, C) • make a (Ea)
83.10	fearest (A, E, C) • fear'st (MS)
83.12	oh (MS) • O (A, E, C)
*83 note	of (MS) • of the (Pr, A, E, C)
84.16	gilded (A, E, C) • gorgeous (MS)
87.3	show (A, E, C) • shew (MS)
88.6	shown (Pr, A, E, C) • shewn (MS)
88.18	show (A, E, C) • shew (MS)
88.37	dismayed (A, Eb–c) • cornered (MS, Ea, C)
89.9	dangerous ground (A, Eb–c, C) • pretty thin ice (MS, Ea)
*90.2	wallow (A, C) • kennel (MS, E)
*90.3	styes (A, Eb–c) • slums (MS, Pr, Ea, C)
90.35	that (MS) • their (A, E, C)
90.36	although (A, E, C) • albeit (MS)

92.4	gentleman (A, E, C) • gentlemen (MS)
93.1	robe (A, Eb–c, C) • robe de chambre (MS, Ea)
93.1	laid himself (A, Eb–c, C) • lay (MS, Ea)
95.2	ear (MS) • ears (Pr, A, E, C)
96.9	blood (A, Eb–c, C) • womb (MS, Ea)
96.13	called himself (A, E, C) • said he were (MS)
*96.16	against (A, E, C) • 'gainst (MS)
97.7	it (Pr, A, E, C) • them (MS)
*99.31	first at one (Pr, A, E, C) • at first to one (MS)
100.5	uncharted (MS, A, E) • unchartered (C)
*102.5	naturally (Pr, A, E, C) • actually (MS)
105.30	since (A, E, C) • sith (MS)
107.10	to and fro (Pr, A, E, C) • to fro (MS)
113.1	O (MS, Pr, A, C) • Oh (E)
113.5	O (MS, Pr, A, C) • Oh (E)
113.12	O (MS, Pr, A, C) • Oh (E)
115.6	beating (A, E, C) • basting (MS, Pr)
115.23	back, drowned in tears, to her bed (A, E, C) • back to her bed drowned in tears (MS)
115.29	O (MS, A, C) • Oh (E)
117.2	sprung (MS, A, C) • sprang (E)
117.10	O (MS, Pr, A, C) • Oh (E)
117.18	O (MS, Pr, A, C) • oh (E)
117.35	O (MS, A, C) • Oh (E)
118.2	sunk (MS, A, C) • sank (E)
120.34	dived (A, E, C) • dove (MS, Pr)
*124.5	canopy of state (Ab) • canopy of estate (MS, Pr, Aa, E, C)
126.5	sprung (MS, A, Ea–b, C) • sprang (Ec)
126.8	ye (A, E, C) • thee (MS)
126.8	you (A, E, C) • thou (MS)
127.15	sunk (MS, A, Ea–b, C) • sank (Ec)
131.11	sprung (MS, Pr, A, Ea–b, C) • sprang (Ec)
132.7	bakeries (Pr, A, E, C) • bookstores (MS)
136.10	elder (A, E, C) • big (MS)
137.21	sprung (MS, A, Ea–b, C) • sprang (Ec)
138.1	O (MS, A, C) • Oh (E)
138.13	boy's (Pr, A, E, C) • boys (MS)
*139.10–11	a grateful . . . him; (MS, Pr) • [not in] (A, E, C)

139.24   one ... service*— (A, E, C) • [not in] (MS, Pr)

139 note   *He ... said, the ... creation. (A, C) • *He ... said, to the ... creation. (E); [not in] (MS, Pr)

*140.15   truth (MS) • troth (A, E, C)

144.18   Knight (A, E, C) • Baronet (MS)

145.5   knight (A, E, C) • baronet (MS, Pr)

148.19   I (MS, A, Ea, Ec, C) • [not in] (Eb)

*150.11   he loved she (A, E, C) • twice as well (MS)

152.9   detestable (A, E, C) • misbegotten (MS)

155.7   your straw (A, E, C) • thy straw (MS, Pr)

155.8   ye (A, E, C) • thee (MS, Pr)

155.8   your unbelieving (A, E, C) • thine unbelieving (MS, Pr)

156.1   wert (Pr, A, E, C) • wast (MS)

157.9   thee and Nan (A, E, C) • you and Nan (MS)

157.14   answer (A, E, C) • remark (MS)

159.29   day (MS, Pr, A, E) • [not in] (C)

160.9   were (MS, A, C) • was (E)

162.2   good (A, E, C) • dear (MS)

164.12   O (MS, A, C) • Oh (E)

165.7   O (MS, A, C) • Oh (E)

*165.23   shall (A, E, C) • shalt (MS)

166.14   by a (MS, A, E) • by (C)

169.9   tolerable (A, E, C) • middling (MS, Pr)

*171.27   even made him (MS) • made him even (A, E, C)

173.4   man had (A, E, C) • male one (MS, Pr)

*173.7   meekly (MS) • quickly (Pr, A, E, C)

174.23   O (MS, A, C) • oh (E)

175.37–38   hare-brained (A, E, C) • misbegotten (MS, Pr)

*177.35   is (MS) • is a (A, E, C)

*179.13   doth (MS) • [not in] (A, E, C)

179.24   O (MS, A, C) • Oh (E)

180 note   at (MS) • at the (A, E, C)

184.6   as (MS) • [not in] (A, E, C)

184.13   Yeomen (MS, E) • Yeoman (A, C)

*185.5   mistake—a (MS) • mistake— (A, E, C)

*188.6   wood (A, E, C) • road (MS)

190.11   is it (MS, A, C) • it is (E)

*191.5   sank (MS, E) • sunk (A, C)

191.22   crutches; (A, C) • crutches; diseased ones, with running sores
              peeping from ineffectual wrappings; (MS, E)

192.16   Dick (MS, A, C) • Dick and (E)

193.4   Darkmans (MS, A, C) • Darkman's (E)

193.31   joyously (A, E, C) • gushingly (MS)

197.6   and (MS) • of (A, E, C)

197.12   art (MS, A, Ec, C) • are (Ea–b)

198.24   hast (A, E, C) • has (MS)

201.10   use (A, E, C) • treat (MS)

205.15   Thy (A, E, C) • Your (MS)

205.16   thou hast (A, E, C) • you have (MS)

205.16   thy (A, E, C) • your (MS)

206.20   O (MS, A, C) • Oh (E)

206.32   O (MS, A, C) • Oh (E)

*215.5   be (MS) • be a (A, E, C)

219.14   goodwife (MS, A, E) • good wife (C)

*220.11   due to (MS) • due (A, E, C)

221.18   Afterward (MS, A, C) • Afterwards (E)

223.19   further (MS) • farther (A, E, C)

226.7   on (A, E, C) • along (MS)

234.9   this ecstasy (A, E, C) • the ecstasy of this ravishing dalliance
              (MS)

234.13   sunk (MS, A, Ea–b, C) • sank (Ec)

235.4   O (MS, A, C) • Oh (E)

235.12   who (A, E, C) • whom (MS)

235.16   not— Where (A, E, C) • not, I will carve thy withered heart out
              o' thy body with as small compunction as I would a vicious
              dog's! Where (MS)

235.17   O (MS, A, C) • Oh (E)

235.18   take (MS, A, C) • take an (E)

235.35   obey (A, E, C) • hoof it (MS)

235.36   gives (A, E, C) • tips (MS)

*235.37   been (A, E, C) • lain (MS)

*237.9   do (MS, Ab, C) • do not (Aa, E)

237.9   archangel with (A, E, C) • archangel in all hell's dominions
              with (MS)

237.11   ill-conditioned slave (A, E, C) • misbegotten devil (MS)

237.22   a (A, E, C) • this (MS)

237.22–23   mule, which must have broken its spirit, (A, E, C) • mule—

[¶] "Ye stubborn and rebellious limb, ye son of shame! you came into the world with disgraceful parentage, and are going out of it without hope of leaving posterity behind![1] And you are not belonging among the works of God, neither; God made every beast and bird and creature that's in the world but you—and you're the vile invention of man!" [¶] This cruel speech must have broken the spirit of the mule, (MS)

239.7	charge (A, E, C) • keep (MS)
240.3	storm of (A, E, C) • roars and (MS)
241.3	Hugo (A, E, C) • Hugh (MS)
241.7	charge, (A, E, C) • charge, as usual, (MS)
241.22	Hugo (A, E, C) • Hugh (MS)
241.31	operate (A, E, C) • be ripe (MS)
241.38	angry-looking (A, E, C) • appear decayed (MS)
242.3	the hideous ulcer to be seen (A, E, C) • parts of the sore to peep out (MS)
*242.12	strugglings (MS) • struggling (A, E, C)
247.6	knight (A, E, C) • baronet (MS)
247.9	spectre-knight (A, E, C) • spectre-baronet (MS)
248.1	sunk (MS, A, Ea–b, C) • sank (Ec)
249.23	O (MS, A, C) • Oh (E)
250.5	nor (MS, A, C) • or (E)
*253.6	nor (MS) • nor to (A, E, C)
260.15	a half (MS, A, C) • half a (E)
*260.21	tongues (MS) • tongue (A, E, C)
261.19	arm, (A, E, C) • arm, excited and agitated, (MS)
263.9	O (MS, A, C) • oh (E)
264.17	O (MS, A, C) • Oh (E)
266.1	O (MS, A, C) • Oh (E)
266.20	For (A, E, C) • Sir (MS)
267.4	his birth (A, E, C) • the womb (MS)
267.5	O (MS, A, C) • Oh (E)
271.6	O (MS, A, C) • Oh (E)
272.3	O (MS, A, C) • Oh (E)
274.7	condition (A, E, C) • character (MS)
*278.4	goodman (I-C) • good man (A, E, C); good-|man (MS)
280.19	O (MS, A, C) • Oh (E)
280.22	O (MS, A, C) • Oh (E)
285.9	honors (A, E, C) • title (MS)

285.13   unreverent (MS, A, C) • irreverent (E)

286.13   O (MS, A, C) • Oh (E)

287.33   O (MS, A, C) • oh (E)

289.5   spectre-knight (A, E, C) • spectre-baronet (MS)

295.4   a quite (MS, A, C) • quite a (E)

296.17   tremble. Once (A, E, C) • sick; and once (MS)

*298.23   preparations (MS) • preparation (A, E, C)

301.35   Every (MS, A, Ea–b, C) • [not in] (Ec)

302.3   a historical (MS, A, C) • an historical (E)

305.35   sprung (MS, A, Ea–b, C) • sprang (Ec)

306.3   of (MS, A, C) • of the (E)

*307.9   reined (Ab, E, C) • reigned (MS, Pr, Aa)

314.4   O (MS, A, C) • Oh (E)

*317.26   turned (MS) • moved (A, E, C)

318.5   a so bulky (MS, A, C) • so bulky a (E)

318.10   O (MS, A, C) • Oh (E)

319.12   O . . . O (MS, A, C) • Oh . . . oh (E)

320.16   dear (MS, A, C) • good (E)

324.13   after (A, E, C) • after after (MS)

327.5   Miles's (MS) • Miles (A, E, C)

328.5   ordered (A, E, C) • order (MS)

330.2   knight (A, E, C) • baronet (MS)

330.17   O (MS, A, C) • Oh (E)

331.11   show (A, E, C) • title (MS)

335.19   credit. (A, E, C) • ~. | [centered] The end. (MS)

337.8   round (MS) • around (A, E, C)

337.20   Hume's (E) • *Hume* (MS, A, C)

337.20–21   *History of England* (E) • [not in] (MS, A, C)

338.8   *History of* (E) • [not in] (MS, A, C)

338.9   307 (I-C) • *306* (MS, A, E, C)

338.26–27   *History of* (E) • [not in] (MS, A, C)

338.36   *History of* (E) • [not in] (MS, A, C)

339.26   *Ibid.* (MS, A, C) • Dr. J. Hammond Trumbull's *Blue Laws,
              True and False* (E)

339.40   13 (I-C) • *17* (MS, A, E, C)

340.17   pp. 11–12 (I-C) • p. 12 (MS, A, E, C)

ALTERATIONS IN THE MANUSCRIPT

The list of alterations records every change made by Mark Twain in the manuscript. The only exceptions are the essential corrections that he made as he wrote or reread his work. These fall into six categories: (1) letters or words that have been mended, traced over, or canceled and rewritten for clarity; (2) false starts and slips of the pen; (3) corrected eye skips; (4) words or phrases that have been inadvertently repeated, then canceled; (5) corrected misspellings; and (6) inadvertent additions of letters or punctuation that have been subsequently canceled—for instance, an incorrect "they" or "then" altered to "the," or superfluous quotation marks canceled at the end of a narrative passage. The first words of chapters appear in this list as Mark Twain wrote them, although they are styled in the text of this edition with a full capital followed by small capital letters.

If an altered reading has been emended, the fact is noted in the entry here. In descriptions of Mark Twain's revisions, use of the word "above" signals that new writing is interlined, while use of the word "over" means that something is written in the same space as the reading it supplants, covering it. The term "wiped out" signifies that Mark Twain obliterated a word by smearing it with his finger. "Follows" and "followed by" are spatial, not necessarily temporal, descriptions. A vertical rule indicates the end of a line in the manuscript.

Description of the Manuscript

The manuscript of *The Prince and the Pauper*, in the Henry E. Huntington Library, San Marino, California, consists of 866 pages, inscribed in three distinct colors of ink with some revision in pencil. In this edition, Mark Twain's writing materials are designated as follows:

Ink 1 is violet, a bright bluish purple. The earliest pages of *The Prince and the Pauper* were written in this ink. Though it has not been possible to date the pages precisely, they were written sometime before the summer of 1877, perhaps in late 1876.

Ink 2 is dark brownish purple. This ink was used on those pages of the manuscript written from late 1877 through early 1878 and again in the winter and spring of 1880. Ink 2 was also used to revise pages written in ink 1.

Ink 3 is blue. This ink was used for the final portion of the manuscript, from May or June 1880 until its completion on 1 February 1881. It was also used to revise the earlier pages written in inks 1 and 2.

Pencil was used intermittently for revision throughout the manuscript.

The following list identifies the sections of Mark Twain's manuscript according to the color of the ink in which they were originally written. The list of alterations in the manuscript gives a full account of writing materials, including revisions.

		Ink color	MS pages
31.1–35.6	*The Prince ... Venice.*	ink 3	1–4
45.1–54.3	I will ... enough,	ink 2	5–19
54.3–55.15	on the ... bare[footed]	ink 3	20–25
55.15–56.20	[bare]footed ... tears.	ink 1	26–28
57 *title*–60.2	CHAPTER 3 ... last!	ink 2	29–34
60.3–60.30	Tom's ... before	ink 1	35–37
60.30–65.5	except ... grounds in	ink 2	38–50
65.5–66.10	his bannered ... down	ink 1	51–52
66.10–115.23	the road ... bed.	ink 2	53–176
115.24–117.23	As she ... Presently	ink 3	177–185
117.23–145.4	while ... cured."	ink 2	188–255
145.4–145.12	After ... content."	ink 3	255–256
147 *title*–169.18	CHAPTER 13 ... of it.	ink 2	257–317
169.19–169.21	The third ... little	ink 3	318
169.21–201.10	used ... for it!"	ink 2	319–414
203 *title*–342.16	CHAPTER 18 ... p. 11.	ink 3	415–866

The manuscript of *The Prince and the Pauper* is something of an exception to Walter Blair's observation that in a manuscript of any length Mark Twain "was fairly sure to use three to six kinds of paper and to change from one kind to another in a seemingly capricious fashion."[1] In this manuscript Mark Twain's use of five varieties of paper follows a pattern of sorts. Crystal-Lake Mills paper was used for the earliest pages, written in ink 1, and for many of the pages written in ink 2. Three varieties of paper—buff, white laid, and P & P—were used only for pages written in ink 2. White wove paper was used for some pages written in ink 2, but mainly for the pages written in ink 3. A description of the papers follows:

Crystal-Lake Mills (CLM) is white, unwatermarked, wove stationery, ruled horizontally in blue, and torn into half-sheets measuring 20.5 by 12.5 centimeters ($8\frac{1}{16}$ by $4\frac{15}{16}$ inches). It is embossed in the upper left corner with a picture of a building and the words "Crystal-Lake Mills."

---

[1] "When Was *Huckleberry Finn* Written?" *American Literature* 30 (March 1958): 6–7.

Buff is a buff-colored, laid stationery which is torn into half-sheets measuring 19.9 by 12.4 centimeters ($7^{13}\!/_{16}$ by $4^{7}\!/_{8}$ inches) with vertical chain-lines 2.5 centimeters ($^{15}\!/_{16}$ inch) apart.

P & P is a white, laid stationery, ruled horizontally in blue, and torn into half-sheets measuring 20.3 by 12.4 centimeters (8 by $4^{7}\!/_{8}$ inches). It has horizontal chain-lines 2.2 centimeters ($^{7}\!/_{8}$ inch) apart. A device with the initials "P & P," often quite faint, is embossed in the upper left corner of some of the pages.

White laid (WL) is a white, laid stationery, ruled horizontally in blue, and torn into half-sheets measuring 20.1 by 12.4 centimeters ($7^{7}\!/_{8}$ by $4^{7}\!/_{8}$ inches). It has vertical chain-lines 2 centimeters ($^{3}\!/_{4}$ inch) apart.

White wove (WW) is a white, unwatermarked, wove stationery, torn into half-sheets measuring 17.8 by 11.5 centimeters (7 by $4^{1}\!/_{2}$ inches).

The following list identifies Mark Twain's use of each of the five varieties of paper in his manuscript.

		Paper	MS pages
31.1–35.6	*The Prince ... Venice.*	WW	1–4
45.1–54.3	I will ... enough,	CLM	5–19
54.3–55.15	on the ... bare[footed]	WW	20–25
55.15–115.23	[bare]footed ... bed.	CLM	26–176
115.24–117.23	As she ... Presently	WW	177–185
117.23–132.4	while ... affair,	CLM	186–221
132.4–134.6	for a ... digress.	buff	222–226
134.7–145.6	Hendon's ... truly,	CLM	227–255
145.6–145.12	for one ... content."	WW	256
147 *title*–150.27	CHAPTER 13 ... trembling	P & P	257–265
150.27–156.5	syllables ... sorrows."	CLM	266–274
156.6–159.13	Tom ... cere[mony]	buff	275–285
159.13–160.3	[cere]mony ... heavy	CLM	286–288
160.3–166.3	calamity ... with	buff	289–310
166.3–169.11	very ... ended.	CLM	311–316
169.12–18	The larger ... of it.	P & P	317
169.19–21	The third ... little	WW	318
169.21–170.10	used ... Hertford	P & P	319
170.10–174.31	would ... said—	CLM	320–334
174.32–180.13	"Good ... power	buff	335–356

Alterations List

Written in ink 3 from 31 title through 35.6.
Written in ink 2 from 45.1 through 54.3 ('enough,').

47 *title*   CHAPTER 1] *in the MS* 'CHAPTER 1.' *added in ink 3.*

47.1–47.2   In . . . century,] *originally* 'In the ancient city of London, on the 12*th* of October, 1537,'; 'don, on a certain autumn day in' *interlined in ink 3 above uncanceled* 'don, [*of* 'London,'] on . . . of'; *the entire passage canceled and* 'In . . . century,' *interlined in ink 3.*

47.2   poor] *interlined.*

47.4   rich] *interlined.*

47.6   longed for him, and hoped for him, . . . God for him,] *the commas added in ink 3.*

47.7   went nearly] *originally* 'nearly went'; 'went' *canceled in ink 3; then* 'went' *interlined before* 'nearly' *in ink 3.*

47.10   very mellow] *interlined above canceled* 'fuddled'.

47.11   By] *follows canceled* 'The'.

48.4   Tom Canty,] *follows canceled* 'Edward Canty,'.

49.1   number of] *interlined in ink 3 above canceled* 'matter of near ten'.

49.2–3   —for that] *follows canceled* 'for that'.

49.3   think] *followed by a canceled comma.*

49.3–4   double as many.] *interlined in ink 3 above canceled* 'more than that.'

49.4   dirty,] *the comma possibly mended from a period.*

49.6   London Bridge.] *interlined in ink 3 above canceled* 'The Tower.'

49.9   strong] *followed by a comma canceled in ink 3.*

49.15   foul] *follows canceled* 'little'.

49.17   ricketty] *originally* 'rickety'; *the additional* 't' *squeezed in.*

49.17   wretchedly] *follows canceled* 'pauper'.

49.18   a room] *follows canceled* 'one'.

50.4   be called] *follows canceled* 'be cons'.

50.6	service.] *followed by canceled* 'There was generally a fight over the selection, too, between the grandmother and the sisters.'
50.27	Among,] *follows canceled* 'There was'; *the comma added.*
50.27	but not of,] *interlined.*
50.37–38	a little Latin, and how] *interlined.*
51.7	Yet little Tom] *in the MS* 'Little Tom' *follows canceled* 'Tom'; 'Yet' *interlined;* 'L' *not reduced to* 'l'.
51.11	first,] *the comma added in ink 3.*
51.13	starving] *interlined.*
51.16	beaten] *follows* 'kicked and' *canceled in ink 3.*
51.16	for it] *interlined.*
51.20	listening] *follows canceled* 'reading'.
51.21	fairies,] *followed by canceled* 'and about'; *the comma mended from a semicolon.*
52.1	as he] *follows canceled* 'he'.
52.3	unleashed] *follows canceled* 'gave bridle to his'.
52.8	was glad] *follows canceled* 'kept his'.
53.9	Tower, by land or boat.] *originally* 'Tower.'; *the comma added on the line and* 'by land or boat.' *interlined; two periods inadvertently left standing.*

Written in ink 3 from 54.3 ('on the') *through 55.15* ('bare[footed]').

54.8	But] *interlined.*
54.8	began to] *interlined.*
54.8	now,] *interlined.*
54.18	family—] *the dash apparently mended from a period; followed by canceled* 'only'.
54.18	only,] *interlined.*
54.19	after a while,] *interlined.*
54.20	guards,] *interlined.*
55.1	mock] *interlined.*
55.11	at last] *interlined.*

Written in ink 1 from 55.15 ('[bare]footed') *through 56.20.*

55.15	barefooted] *actually* 'bare-|footed'; 'bare-' *written in ink 3 and* 'footed' *written on the following page in ink 1;* 'footed' *follows*

a passage written in ink 1 and canceled in ink 2: 'house there were twenty-two families. In describing the Hubbards and their quarters and their odious ways, all these twenty-two wretched families have been described. [¶] One day Jim tramped all about Whitechapel, bare-|'; *'odious' interlined above canceled* 'dreadful'.

55.18   they were—] *interlined.*

55.19   good] *interlined above canceled* 'rare'.

55.19   rain;] *the semicolon added; followed by canceled* 'all day;'.

56.1   it was] *follows canceled* 'every'.

56.1   At] *interlined above canceled* 'That'.

56.1   Tom] *interlined in ink 2 above canceled* 'Jim'.

56.3   father and grandmother] *interlined in ink 2 above canceled* 'parents'.

56.4   —after their fashion; wherefore] *interlined in ink 3 above a canceled semicolon.*

56.4   a brisk] *interlined in ink 3 above canceled* 'a sound'.

56.5   long] *originally* 'longer'; *'er' canceled.*

56.6   going on in the building] *interlined in ink 2 above a canceled comma.*

56.7   far, romantic lands,] *interlined in ink 2 above canceled* 'Arabia and Persia'.

56.8   who] *interlined in ink 3 above canceled* 'that'.

56.9   or flying] *'or' interlined above canceled* 'and running'; *'or' possibly substituted for* 'and' *before* 'running' *was canceled.*

56.10   as usual,] *interlined in ink 3 following a comma added in ink 3.*

56.11   himself.] *the period added in ink 3 to replace a canceled exclamation point.*

56.12   royal estate] *follows canceled* 'rega'.

56.14   music,] *followed by canceled* 'that'; *the comma possibly added later.*

56.16   here] *interlined.*

56.16   and there] *follows canceled* 'here'.

56.18–20 him, his . . . tears.] *interlined in ink 3. Mark Twain originally wrote* 'him his dream had' *in ink 1. He canceled that in ink 1 and followed it with* 'him, it was not the same it had been before. His dream had intensified its sordidness a thousand fold. He well nigh cried his eyes out, and his heart was like to break.' *Then in ink 2 he mended the period after* 'before' *to a semicolon and following it squeezed in the word* 'for', *neglect-*

ing to lower the 'H' of 'His' to 'h'. Later in ink 2 he canceled 'for His dream had intensified' *and interlined* 'for this, which was much the finest dream he had dreamed yet, had intensified'. *Finally, in ink 3 he canceled the entire passage* 'him, it was . . . break.' *and interlined* 'him, his . . . tears.'

Written in ink 2 from 57 title through 60.2.

57.1	hungry] *followed by* 'in the morning,' *canceled in ink 3.*
57.1–2	away but with . . . dreams.] *originally* 'away, but with his thoughts busy with that wonderful dream.'; 'but with . . . wonderful dream.' *canceled and the comma after* 'away' *mended to a period;* 'but with . . . dreams.' *interlined to follow* 'away'; *two periods inadvertently left standing; all revisions in ink 3.*
57.5	musing] *interlined in ink 3 above canceled* 'dreaming'.
57.7	traveled] *followed by* 'before' *canceled in ink 3.*
57.10–11	though . . . one side] *interlined in ink 3 above canceled* 'there was only one row of houses on one side'.
57.11–12	there were] *interlined in ink 3 above canceled* 'and'.
57.12	other,] *the comma mended from a period.*
57.13	rich] *interlined in ink 3 above canceled* 'great'.
58.4	bereaved] *follows canceled* 'mourning'.
58.5	days;] *the semicolon mended in ink 3 from a comma.*
58.7	stately] *follows what appears to be canceled* 'nob'.
58.8	far more] *follows canceled* 'still'.
58.10	pile] *interlined above canceled* 'mass'.
58.11	its gilded] 'its' *interlined.*
58.11	bars] *followed by a canceled comma.*
58.12–13	of English] 'of' *interlined above canceled* 'and'.
58.14–15	a prince of . . . blood,] *interlined.*
58.16–17	an erect and stately] *originally* 'a stiff and state'; 'a' *mended to* 'an', 'stiff and state' *canceled and followed by* 'erect and stately'.
58.20–22	Splendid . . . enclosure.] 'Splendid carriages' *squeezed in and* 'with . . . enclosure.' *added on the verso of the MS page with instructions to turn over.*
58.22	other] *interlined.*
59.1	approached, and was moving] *interlined above canceled* 'moved'.

59.2–3   when all at] *follows canceled* 'and all at'.
59.3   the golden] *follows canceled* 'the gilded'.
59.4   comely] *interlined in ink 3 above canceled* 'pale'.
59.4–5   tanned . . . exercises,] *interlined in ink 3.*
59.6   jewels;] *the semicolon mended in ink 3 from a comma.*

Written in ink 1 from 60.3 through 60.30 ('encountered before').

60.3   Tom's] *interlined in ink 2 following canceled* 'in the British army Jim's'; *marked to begin a new paragraph with a paragraph sign in ink 3.*

60.4   wonder and delight.] *originally* 'wonder.'; 'and delight.' *interlined in ink 2; the two periods inadvertently left standing; followed by canceled* 'Here was a prince, here a palace—his darling book was true, then!'.

60.4   Everything] *originally began a new paragraph; marked to run in with a line in ink 2 to* 'delight.'

60.6   devouring] *interlined in ink 2 without a caret above canceled* 'satisfying'.

60.7   gate-bars] *originally* 'grate-bars'; 'r' *canceled.*

60.9   of country . . . London idlers.] *originally* 'of country . . . London scum' *added in ink 2 following* 'that is always before those palace gates. The soldier' *canceled in ink 2;* 'idlers' *added in ink 3 following canceled* 'scum'.

60.9   The soldier] *interlined in ink 2.*

60.10   thy] *interlined in ink 2 above canceled* 'your'.

60.10   thou] *interlined in ink 2 above canceled* 'you'.

60.14   dar'st thou use a poor] *originally* 'dare you treat a poor'; ' 'st' *written over* 'e' *and* 'thou' *interlined without a caret above canceled* 'you', *in ink 2;* 'use' *interlined without a caret above canceled* 'treat' *in ink 3.*

60.14   like that!] *interlined in ink 2 above canceled* 'like that!' *following an unrecovered canceled interlineation of two letters.*

60.14   dar'st thou use the] *originally* 'dare you treat the'; ' 'st' *written over* 'e' *and* 'thou' *interlined above canceled* 'you', *in ink 2;* 'use' *interlined without a caret above canceled* 'treat' *in ink 3.*

60.14–15   the king my father's meanest subject] *originally* 'the poorest British subject'; 'king my father's' *interlined in ink 2 before* 'poorest', *and* 'British' *canceled to read* 'the king my father's poorest subject'; *then* 'poorest' *canceled and* 'meanest' *interlined in ink 3.*

60.17–18   and shout . . . Wales!"] *squeezed in follo~~~~ a canceled period.*

60.19   presented] *follows* 'made the military salute,' *canceled in ink 2.*

60.19   with their halberds,] *interlined in ink 2.*

60.21   Prince] *originally* 'prince'; 'P' *written over* 'p'.

60.22   Edward] *follows* 'Albert' *canceled in ink 2; followed by* 'Tudor' *interlined in ink 2.*

60.23   Thou lookest] *originally* 'You look'; 'Thou' *interlined in ink 2 above canceled* 'You'; 'est' *interlined in ink 2 to follow* 'look'.

60.23   thou'st] *interlined in ink 2 above canceled* 'you have'.

60.26   a right royal] *interlined above canceled* 'a'.

60.27   stock still] *interlined.*

60.27–28   were, like so many statues.] *originally* 'were.'; *the comma added on the line and* 'like . . . statues.' *interlined; two periods inadvertently left standing.*

60.28   Edward] *follows* 'Albert' *canceled in ink 2.*

60.28   Tom] *interlined in ink 2 above canceled* 'Jim'.

60.28   palace] *followed by a canceled comma.*

60.29   his command] 'his' *interlined.*

60.29   a repast] *follows* 'a splendid flunkey brought' *canceled in ink 2; followed by* 'was brought' *interlined in ink 2.*

60.29   Tom] *interlined in ink 2 above canceled* 'Jim'.

Written in ink 2 from 60.30 ('except') *through 65.4–5* ('grounds in').

60.30–33   the prince . . . ate.] *added on the verso of the MS page with instructions to turn over; replaces canceled* 'and while he ate, Edward asked questions.' *on the recto.*

60.31   princely] *follows canceled* 'true'.

60.37   Pudding] *interlined in ink 3 above canceled* 'Mincing'; *traced over an earlier pencil interlineation,* 'Pudding'; *see textual note.*

61.1   grandam] *the MS reads* 'granddam' *(emended); originally* 'grandmother'; 'dam' *interlined above canceled* 'mother'.

61.3   Bet.] *mended in ink 3 from original* 'Bess.'

61.5   other] *followed by canceled* 'beside,'.

61.6   evil] *apparently originally 'evils'; the 's' canceled.*

61.10   beatings] *canceled, then restored with the instruction 'stet' in ink 3.*

61.12   Beatings?] *the question mark written over an exclamation point.*

61.15   hie her] *interlined in ink 3.*

61.16   you] *interlined in ink 3 above canceled* 'thou'.

61.16   forget,] *originally* 'forgettest,'; *'gettest,' canceled and 'get,' squeezed in in ink 3.*

62.3   neither] *interlined in ink 3.*

62.3   sorrow] *followed by a comma canceled in ink 3.*

62.6   an'] *the apostrophe added in ink 3.*

62.9   do thy] *originally* 'doth your'; *the 'th' of 'doth' canceled and 'thy' interlined above canceled* 'your'.

62.14   undress at night?] *interlined above canceled* 'to bed?'.

62.15   attireth] *follows canceled* 'tireth'.

62.21–22   had not meant] *follows canceled* 'meant not'.

62.23   and lackeys] *the MS reads* 'lackies' *(emended); follows canceled* 'and ser'.

62.23   to it.] *originally* 'to 't.'; *'it.' interlined in ink 3 above canceled* ' 't.'

62.29   I doubt."] *interlined in ink 3 above canceled* '—I fear me." '

62.30   hard only] *originally* 'only hard'; *transposed with a line in pencil.*

62.31   I think,] *interlined in ink 3 above canceled* 'methinks,'.

62.33   Hast] *follows canceled* 'What is it'.

62.36   play] *follows canceled* 'do'.

63.3   like to the] *follows canceled* 'as do the'.

63.5   "Marry,] *interlined in ink 3 above canceled* ' "Sooth to say,'.

63.11   enjoy] *follows canceled* 'taste'.

64.7   thine] *follows canceled* 'your'.

64.9   crown!"] *the exclamation point apparently written over a question mark; the quotation marks added in ink 3.*

64.12   "Oho,] *interlined in ink 3 above canceled* ' "Ho,'.

64.13   will be] *interlined in ink 3.*

64.16   A few] *follows canceled* 'In'; *'A' written over 'a'.*

64.21   then at each] *follows canceled* 'that'.

64.24   It is] *interlined in ink 3 above canceled* ' 'Tis'.

64.26   I] *the underlining added, canceled, and added again in ink 3.*

64.26   hast] *originally* 'has'; *the* 't' *squeezed in.*

64.26–27   the same voice and manner,] *interlined in ink 3.*

64.27   stature] *follows canceled* 'hei'.

64.30   thou] *interlined above canceled* 'you'.

64.33   it is] *interlined in ink 3 above canceled* ''tis'.

64.35   "Peace!] *interlined in ink 3 above canceled* ' "Silence!'.

64.35   It was] *originally* ' 'Twas'; ' 'T' *canceled and* 'It' *squeezed in in ink 3.*

64.35   a cruel] 'a' *interlined.*

64.35   little] *follows canceled* 'ragged'.

64.36   foot.] *followed by canceled* 'and darting fire from his eyes.'; *the period added.*

64.38–65.5   had snatched . . . grounds in] *added on the verso of the MS page in ink 3 with instructions to turn over; replaces* 'was out and flying through the palace grounds in' *canceled on the recto;* 'out and' *interlined.*

Written in ink 1 from 65.5 ('his bannered'*) through 66.10 (*'far down'*).*

65.5   his] *interlined in ink 2.*

65.6   glowing] *interlined in ink 3 above canceled* 'blazing'.

65.13   Tom,] *interlined in ink 2 without a caret above canceled* 'Jim,'.

65.14   promptly;] *interlined in ink 2 without a caret above canceled* 'instantly;'.

65.14–15   the prince . . . portal,] *interlined in ink 2 above canceled* 'Albert Edward came marching forth,'.

65.16   royal wrath,] *originally* 'princely indignation,'; 'indignation,' *canceled and* 'wrath,' *interlined in ink 1; then* 'princely wrath,' *canceled and* 'royal wrath,' *interlined in ink 2.*

65.17   ear] *interlined above canceled* 'side of his head'.

65.17   roadway,] *interlined in ink 2 without a caret above canceled* 'gutter,'.

65.18   thou beggar's] 'thou' *interlined in ink 2 without a caret above canceled* 'you'.

65.18   thou got'st] 'thou' *interlined in ink 2 without a caret above canceled* 'you'; ' 'st' *interlined in ink 2.*

65.18–19   his highness] *originally* ' 'is royal 'Ighness'; 'h' *written over the first apostrophe,* 'royal' *canceled, and* 'Hi' *written over* ' 'I' *(emended); all revisions in ink 2.*

66.1   The prince] *interlined in ink 2 above canceled* 'Albert Edward'.

66.2   fiercely] *interlined in ink 2 above canceled* 'furiously'.

66.3   my person is sacred;] *interlined; the semicolon mended from a comma in ink 3.*

66.3   thou shalt] 'thou' *interlined in ink 2 above canceled* 'you'; 'shalt' *mended from* 'shall' *in ink 2.*

66.4   thy] *interlined in ink 2 without a caret above canceled* 'your'.

66.5   The] *originally* 'But the'; 'But' *canceled and* 'T' *written over* 't'.

66.5   brought] *follows canceled* 'deridingly dropped'.

66.5   halberd] *interlined in ink 2 above canceled* 'musket'.

66.5–6   mockingly] *follows a comma apparently mended from a colon or what may be canceled opening quotation marks.*

66.7   highness] *follows* 'royal' *canceled in ink 2;* 'Hi' *written over* ' 'I' *in ink 2 (emended).*

66.7   thou] *interlined in ink 2 above canceled* 'you'.

66.9   jeering] *followed by a canceled comma and canceled* 'roaring'.

Written in ink 2 from 66.10 ('the road') through 115.23 ('to her bed.')

67 title   CHAPTER 4] *in the MS* 'Chapter 4.' *added in ink 3.*

67.1   persecution,] *the comma added in ink 3.*

67.2   As long] *follows canceled* 'He had become so footsore and weary, and so tired of raging'.

67.6   use] *follows canceled* 'any'.

67.13   a few] *follows canceled* 'a sca'.

67.13   prodigious] *interlined in ink 3.*

67.14   about,] *the comma added in ink 3.*

67.15   of workmen;] *follows canceled* 'of artisan'; *the semicolon mended in ink 3 from a comma.*

67.16   now] *follows canceled* 'no'.

67.17   "It is] *interlined in ink 3 above canceled* ' " 'Tis'.

68.3   that son] *follows canceled* 'h'.

68.8–9   'prentices*] *the asterisk interlined and the footnote added to the bottom of the MS page in ink 3; see entry at 68 note.*

68.9   had on] *follows canceled* 'wore'.

68.10–11   it being] 'it' *interlined.*

68.13   blue] *follows canceled* 'long'.

68.14   as low] *follows canceled* 'to'.

68.15	yellow] *follows canceled 'red'.*
68 note	*See Note 1, . . . volume.] *added to the bottom of the MS page in ink 3; originally '*See "Notes" at . . . volume.'; the quotation marks canceled and '1,' interlined; the 's' of 'Notes' inadvertently left uncanceled (emended).*
69.1	The boys] *originally run-on; marked to begin a new paragraph with a paragraph sign in ink 3.*
69.4	desireth] *follows canceled 'crav'.*
69.7	face] *follows 'pale' canceled in ink 3.*
69.24	a gibbet] *'a' interlined.*
69.34–35	city. . . . bleeding] *originally 'city again. He wan'; Mark Twain canceled 'He wan' and wrote 'His face and hands were bruised and bleeding'; later in ink 3 he canceled 'again.', added the period after 'city', canceled the words 'His face and' and 'bruised and', and interlined 'His body was bruised, his'.*
70.2	before] *interlined in ink 3 above canceled 'ere'.*
70.9	starved,] *the comma added in ink 3.*
70.11–12	thereby; for . . . charity."*] *originally 'thereby."'; the period mended to a semicolon, 'for learning' written over the quotation marks, and 'softeneth . . . charity."' added on the verso of the MS page with instructions to turn over. The asterisk was interlined in ink 3 on the verso following 'charity.' (emended) when the footnote was added; see entry at 70 note.*
70.20	an'] *the apostrophe added in ink 3.*
70.21	am I] *transposed from 'I am' with a line and instructions in pencil.*
70.21	John] *added in pencil in a space originally left blank.*
70.23	shoulder,] *the comma added in ink 3.*
70 note	*See Note . . . volume.] *written in ink 3 on the verso of the MS page.*
71.4	swarm] *interlined in ink 3 above canceled 'rabble'.*
71.5	of human vermin] *follows canceled 'of human ver'.*
73 title	CHAPTER 5] *the MS reads 'Chap. 5.'; '5.' added in ink 3 in a space originally left blank.*
73.1	left alone . . . cabinet,] *interlined in ink 3 following a comma added in ink 3.*
73.2–3	the great] *'the' interlined in ink 3 above canceled 'the'.*
73.3	away,] *the comma added; followed by canceled 'from it,'.*
73.3	imitating] *originally 'trying to imitate'; 'trying to' canceled in ink 3; the 'e' of 'imitate' mended to 'i' and 'ng' added in ink 3.*
73.5	kissing] *follows canceled 'and kissed'.*

73.7–8   when delivering] *follows canceled* 'into whose hands he was delivering'.

73.8   lords of Norfolk and] *interlined without a caret; follows the canceled interlineation* 'Duke', *above canceled* 'earl of'.

73.11   how] *follows* 'of' *canceled in pencil.*

73.12   Court] *apparently written over* 'c'.

74.7   he grew] *follows canceled* 'he began'.

74.9   explain!] *the exclamation point added in ink 3 replacing a canceled question mark.*

74.11   higher;] *the semicolon mended in ink 3 from a comma.*

74.14   gorgeous] *follows canceled* 'tall and'.

74.14   gentlemen-servants] *follows canceled* 'ser'.

74.14   degree,] *the comma added in ink 3.*

75.1   butterflies,] *the comma added in ink 3.*

75.3   tell!] *the exclamation point replaces a canceled question mark; followed by canceled* 'What'.

75.7–8   trifling sound.] 'sound' *interlined in ink 3 above* 'trifling'; *Mark Twain had neglected to finish his sentence, ending one MS line with* 'trifling' *and beginning the next with* 'Presently'.

75.12   girl,] *originally* 'girl about Tom's own age' *followed by interlined* 'and richly clad,'; *then in ink 3 the comma added after* 'girl' *and* 'about . . . and' *canceled.*

75.18   City] *originally* 'city'; *the* 'c' *underlined three times in ink 3.*

76.2   eyes] *followed by canceled* 'and' *and an unrecovered canceled word of about four letters.*

76.4   me] 'me' *underlined in ink 3.*

76.9   dreadful] *follows canceled* 'a'.

77.1   IN . . . KING!] *interlined;* 'In the name of the king!' *underlined twice in pencil and followed by a mark for extra space.*

77.2   upon] *follows canceled* 'nor'.

77.6   Soon] *follows canceled* 'Soon there was a'.

77.6–7   there was . . . comes!"] *interlined above canceled* 'a musical bugle blast rang down the echoing corridors, followed by these words: [¶] "Way for the high and mighty, the lord Edward, Prince of Wales!" '.

77.8   trying] *follows canceled* 'staring about him'.

77.11   them,] *the comma added in ink 3.*

77.15   reclined] *interlined in ink 3 above canceled* 'was'.

77.16   and a stern] 'and' *interlined.*

77.17   His] *originally* 'He ha'; 'He' *mended to* 'His' *and* 'ha' *canceled.*

77.18	—like] *the dash added in ink 3; follows canceled* 'but not on it—'.
78.1	swollen] *follows canceled* 'legs'.
78.3	silence now;] *apparently originally* 'silence.'*; the period mended to a semicolon and* 'now' *interlined.*
78.4	except] *interlined above canceled* 'but'.
78.4–5	This ... Henry VIII.] *Mark Twain drew a line alongside this sentence and wrote the word* 'strike' *in ink 2; he canceled the line and the instruction in ink 3.*
78.7	cozen] *interlined above canceled* 'entertain'.
78.7	and kindly] *follows a canceled dash.*
78.11–12	as instantly] 'as' *interlined.*
78.12	a shot] *follows canceled* 'his'.
78.12	there. Lifting] *originally* 'there, and lifted'*; the period written over the comma,* 'and' *canceled,* 'L' *mended from* 'l', *and* 'ing' *written over* 'ed'.
78.13	hands,] *follows canceled* 'beseeching' *and canceled interlineation* 'h'*; followed by a canceled dash and squeezed-in* 'he exclaimed,—'.
78.14	king?] *the MS reads* 'king?' *(emended); followed by canceled closing quotation marks and canceled* 'he exclaimed.'*; the question mark written over an exclamation point.*
78.14	Then] *follows canceled opening quotation marks.*
79.2–5	in a ... not well."] *written on the verso of the MS page with instructions to turn over; replaces* 'gently— [¶] "Come to thy father, child, thou art not well." ' *canceled on the recto.*
79.12	child?] *the question mark written over an exclamation point in ink 3.*
79.16–17	Thou art] *follows canceled* 'Thy ill dream'.
79.17	now;] *followed by a canceled dash; the semicolon possibly mended from a comma.*
79.20	grace] *follows canceled* 'great'.
79.21	being] *follows canceled* 'and'.
79.23	blameful.] *the period written over a comma; followed by canceled* 'though nathless'.
79.23	I am] *follows canceled* 'O,'.
79.27	Tom] *follows canceled opening quotation marks.*
79.27	with a glad cry,—] *interlined above canceled* 'crying out—'.
79.29	land] *follows canceled* 'people'.
79.31	save] *follows canceled* 'no'.

79.32   grave] *follows what appears to be canceled 'de'.*

79.32   a little confused,] *'a little' interlined; the comma possibly added; followed by canceled 'a little,'.*

79.33   timidly] *interlined.*

80.2   used,] *followed by canceled 'do'.*

80.5   with] *follows a canceled dash.*

80.11   delighted,] *the comma added in ink 3.*

80.15   stricken] *follows canceled 'de'.*

81.6   silent] *interlined without a caret above canceled 'abashed'.*

81.12   it is] *originally ' 'tis'; 'it' interlined and ' 't' canceled in ink 3.*

81.12   scurvy] *follows canceled 'faint'.*

81.12   me!] *the exclamation point added in ink 3.*

81.14   heart] *followed by a canceled comma.*

82.1   company;] *the semicolon mended from a comma in ink 3; followed by 'and' canceled in ink 3.*

82.1–2   manner . . . said—] *squeezed in in ink 3 to replace canceled 'manner changed to sternness. He said,—'.*

82.3   it is] *interlined in ink 3 above canceled ' 'tis'.*

82.5   to it] *originally 'to 't'; 'it' interlined in ink 3 above canceled ' 't'.*

82.8   still] *follows canceled 'y'.*

82.9   hear] *followed by canceled 'h'.*

82.14   Prince] *originally 'prince'; 'P' written over 'p'.*

82.14–15   confirm it.] *the MS reads 'confirm it.!'; Mark Twain apparently squeezed in the period to replace the exclamation point which he then neglected to cancel; emended.*

82.15   in his princely dignity,] *interlined in ink 3 above a comma written and canceled in ink 3.*

82.16   form.] *followed by canceled closing quotation marks.*

82.16   Hertford.''] *interlined in ink 3 above canceled 'Herbert.'' '; see textual note.*

82.18   Hereditary Great Marshal] *originally 'hereditary great marshal'; 'h', 'g', and 'm' underlined three times in ink 3.*

83.3   earl] *follows canceled 'm'.*

83.4   invest] *follows canceled 'speed'.*

83.5   before] *interlined in ink 3 above canceled 'ere'.*

83.6   grievously!''*] *the asterisk interlined in ink 3 following 'grievously!' (emended) and the footnote added to the bottom of the MS page in ink 3; see entry at 83 note.*

83.7   Hertford] *interlined in ink 3 above canceled 'Herbert'.*

83.8	law;] *the semicolon mended in ink 3 from a comma.*
83.9	wrath] *follows canceled* 'f'.
83.10	me,] *the comma added in ink 3.*
83.15	thee!] *the exclamation point added in ink 3.*
83.15	thy heart] *follows canceled* 'thee'.
83.16	even though] 'even' *interlined.*
83.16	wert] *originally* 'were'; 't' *written over* 'e'.
83.17	gentle] *interlined above canceled* 'merciful'.
83 note	*See . . . volume.] added to the bottom of the MS page in ink 3.*
84.4	is it] *originally* 'is't'; 'it' *interlined in ink 3 above canceled* ' 't'; *follows canceled* 'isnt'.
84.4	liege] *follows canceled* 'gracious'.
84.5	not live] 'not' *interlined.*
84.5	but for] *follows canceled* 'wer't not'.
84.6	worthy.] *at this point on the MS page, originally numbered 83, Mark Twain interlined the instruction* '(insert 83½ &c.)'; *he apparently changed his mind and canceled the instruction instead.*
84.8	rest.] *followed by canceled closing quotation marks.*
84.8–9	Hertford and] *interlined in ink 3 above canceled* 'Herbert and'.
84.12–13	buzz of low . . . comes!"] *originally* 'bu-|gle note and the herald's proclamation—* [¶] "Way for the high and mighty, the lord Edward Prince of Wales!"'; 'zz' *written over the hyphen after* 'bu', 'gle . . . Wales!"' ' *canceled, and* 'of low . . . comes!"' ' *squeezed in.*
84.16	forever] *follows canceled* 'one'.
84.17	friendless] *follows canceled* 'fettered'.
84.17	his] *interlined in ink 3 above canceled* 'His'.
84.22	but . . . dreary!] *appears to be squeezed in at the bottom of the MS page, following a semicolon mended from a period.*
85 title	CHAPTER 6] *the MS reads* 'Chap. 6.'; '6.' *added in ink 3 in a space originally left blank.*
85.2	since] *interlined without a caret above canceled* 'seeing'.
85.3	elderly men] *followed by a comma added in ink 3 and then wiped out.*
85.13	you] *interlined in ink 3 above canceled* 'thee'.
86.1	seem to] *interlined in ink 3.*
86.3	gentlemen] *follows canceled* 'lords'.
86.5	that for] *follows canceled* 'my'.
86.7	power,] *the comma apparently mended from a period.*

86.11   which] *interlined with a caret above canceled* 'that'.

86.16   semblance] *follows canceled* 'sur'.

87.5   Hertford or my] *interlined in ink 3 above canceled* 'Herbert or mine'.

87.6   till] *followed by canceled* 'that'.

87.13 ·   chafe,] *originally interlined in pencil without a caret as an alternative reading to* 'bind,'*; later in ink 3* 'bind,' *canceled,* 'chafe,' *retraced, and a caret added.*

87.15   Hertford] *interlined in ink 3 above canceled* 'Herbert'.

88.12   grieves] *originally* 'grieveth'*;* 'es' *interlined in ink 3 above canceled* 'eth'.

88.13   voice;] *the semicolon mended from a comma in ink 3.*

88.16   the young girls] *follows canceled* 'the ladies'.

88.19   it will] *originally* ''twill'*;* 'it' *interlined in ink 3 above canceled* ''t'.

88.19   to note] 'to' *originally* 'too'*; the second* 'o' *canceled;* 'note' *interlined above canceled* 'see'.

88.22   his majesty's] *follows canceled* 'the'.

88.24   art much] *follows canceled* 'at'.

88.31   precaution,] *the comma added in ink 3.*

88.32   became] *follows canceled opening parenthesis.*

88.34   part;] *the semicolon mended from a comma in ink 3.*

89.7   is it] *originally* 'is't'*;* 'it' *interlined in ink 3 above canceled* ''t'.

89.12   wert] *interlined in ink 3 above canceled* 'wast'.

89.13   Thou'lt] *originally* 'Thoul't'*; the original apostrophe canceled and a new apostrophe added between* 'u' *and* 'l'.

89.15   prince."] *followed by an asterisk written and canceled in ink 3.*

90.8   "brother's"] *the opening and closing quotation marks originally added in pencil, then retraced in ink 3.*

90.9   between] *follows canceled* 'ca'.

90.9   but caressingly] 'but' *interlined above canceled* 'and'.

90.14   princess] *originally* 'prince's'*; the apostrophe canceled and the final* 's' *added.*

90.14   saw] *follows canceled* 'noted'.

90.17   changed] *interlined above canceled* 'turned'.

90.18   wore on] *followed by a canceled comma.*

90.20   lovingly] *followed by canceled* 'bent u'.

90.23   relief] *follows canceled* 'de'.

90.29   channel] *follows two unrecovered canceled letters.*

90.33	been sufficiently] *originally* 'had a sufficient'; 'been' *interlined above canceled* 'had a'; 'ly' *added.*
90.34–35	make that] *follows canceled* 'steer her through the'.
90.38	splendid] *follows canceled* 'charming and'.
91.7	Indeed] *originally* 'In sooth'; 'deed' *interlined in ink 3 above canceled* 'sooth'.
91.7	your ladyships] *follows canceled* 'my lady's'.
91.7	can] *interlined above canceled* 'could'.
91.10	Give ye] 'ye' *interlined in pencil above canceled* 'thee'.
91.10	ye!"] *interlined in pencil above canceled* 'thee!" '.
91.11	naught] *apparently originally* 'nought'; 'a' *mended from* 'o'.
91.19	it is for you] 'it is' *interlined in ink 3 above canceled* ' 'tis'.
91.19	it is for us] 'it is for' *interlined in ink 3 to replace* ' 'tis for' *which was interlined and canceled above canceled* 'and'.
92.6	water;] *the semicolon mended in ink 3 from a comma.*
92.8	Next] *follows canceled* 'Tom'.
92.9	timidly] *follows canceled* 'humbly'.
93.1	to sleep] *follows canceled* 'too s'.
93.4	—and theirs.] *originally added in pencil, then retraced in ink 3; the preceding comma mended in ink 3 from a period.*
93.6	with much] *follows canceled* 'then'.
93.9	this.] *the period added in pencil replacing a canceled question mark.*
93.10	mad will] *follows canceled* 'and'.
93.11	since] *interlined in ink 3 above canceled* 'sith'.
93.12	have you] *interlined in ink 3 above canceled* 'hast thou'.
93.17	Speak] *written over* 'G'.
94.1	in my] 'in' *interlined in ink 3 above canceled* 'upon'.
94.4	manner!] *the MS reads* 'manner?'; *the question mark apparently squeezed in; emended.*
95.6	Baron] *follows canceled* 'Marquis'.
95.7	years,] *the comma added in ink 3.*
95.10	hand] *interlined in ink 3.*
96.4	lord Hertford] *follows canceled* 'lord Herbert'.
96.6	thought,] *the comma added in ink 3.*
96.7	mutter.] *the period added in ink 3 replacing a canceled dash.*
96.9	there] *follows canceled* 'that'.
96.11–17	folly!" [¶] Presently ... mad!"] 'folly!" ' *originally followed by* [¶] 'After further perplexing thought and further pacing,

he said— [¶] "But if it *could* be? .... if it *might* be?
.... The morrow shall resolve the doubt. I will move heed-
fully and in secret—not by public proclama-|' *and by one
MS page now missing; the dash following* 'secret' *mended from
a period; then* [¶] 'Presently ... mad.''' *(96.12–17) (emended)
added to follow* 'folly!''' *on the verso of the MS page with
instructions to turn over; later,* 'After ... proclama-|' *can-
celed in ink 3, and the MS page which followed presumably discarded.*

96.13   "Now were] *originally* '"Were'; '"Now' *added and the original quotation marks canceled;* 'W' *not reduced to* 'w'.

96.15–16   prince by the court, prince] *the MS reads* 'Prince ... Prince'
(emended); originally 'prince ... prince'; 'P' *written over*
'p' *(twice).*

96.16   against] *the MS reads* '*gainst'; *originally* 'against'; *the* 'a'
canceled and an apostrophe added; emended.

96.17   By the soul] *follows canceled* 'Who, then, *could* refuse a
princedom so forced upon him?'.

97 title   CHAPTER 7] *the MS reads* 'Chap. 7.'; '7.' *added in ink 3 in
a space originally left blank.*

97.5   table] *followed by a canceled comma and canceled* 'whose
furniture was all of'.

97.6   Its furniture was all] *interlined without a caret to replace
interlined and canceled* 'Its plates and dishes were all' *which in
turn was interlined above canceled* 'Its furniture was all'.

97.8   Benvenuto.] *follows canceled* 'old'; *followed by canceled* 'A
priest said grace'.

97.8–9   chaplain] *interlined in ink 3 above canceled* 'priest'.

97.11   who fastened] *follows canceled* 'in'.

98.10   at this time] *follows canceled* 'however'.

98.10–11   seldom] *interlined in ink 3 above canceled* 'never'.

98.12   function] *followed by a caret added and canceled in ink 3.*

98.17   was not] *follows what appears to be canceled* 'so' *and canceled*
'n' *or* 'u'.

98.19   strange;] *the semicolon replaces a canceled semicolon.*

98.21   goodness] *interlined in ink 3 to replace canceled* 'God'.

98.22   Lord] *originally* 'lord'; 'L' *written over* 'l'.

98.25–26   and the Lord Head Cook,] *interlined in ink 3 above a canceled
comma;* 'Head Cook,' *follows canceled* 'High Admiral,'.

98.26   three] *interlined in pencil above canceled* 'a'.

98.31–32	to be careful] 'be careful' *interlined above canceled* 'instructed'; 'to' *added in pencil and then retraced in ink 3.*
98.33	they] 'these' *interlined in pencil without a caret above* 'they' *and canceled in ink 3.*
98.37	curiously,] *the comma added in ink 3.*
98.39	said,] *the comma added in ink 3.*
99.16–17	Holland.*] *the asterisk interlined in ink 3 and the footnote added to the bottom of the MS page in ink 3; see entry at 99 note.*
99.24	be aware of it] *follows canceled* 'consider it'.
99.29	the muscles] *follows canceled* 'his'.
99.31	first at one] *the MS reads* 'at first to one' *(emended);* 'to' *interlined in pencil.*
99.35	cruelly!] *followed by canceled closing quotation marks.*
99 note	*See Note . . . volume.] *added to the bottom of the MS page in ink 3; originally* 'note'; 'N' *written over* 'n'.
100.1	smiled] *follows canceled* 'sp'.
100.2	in deep] *follows canceled* 'for'.
100.2	behold,] *interlined above canceled* 'alas,'.
100.5	sea,] *the comma apparently mended from a period.*
100.5	to solve] 'to' *interlined in ink 3.*
100.8	Tom's] *interlined in pencil.*
100.9	At last nature] *originally* 'Nature', *followed by* 'at last' *interlined in ink 3 and canceled; then* 'At last' *interlined in ink 3; the* 'N' *not reduced to* 'n' *(emended); see textual note.*
100.12	himself.] *followed by canceled* [¶] 'His next act was to commit a blunder without knowing it—he got up and left the table without waiting for his chaplain to ask a blessing.'
100.13	broad] *interlined.*
100.15	my lord] *follows canceled* 'the'.
100.17	draught] *originally* 'draft'; 'f' *canceled and* 'ugh' *interlined in ink 3.*
100.19	hath] *originally* 'has'; 'th' *written over* 's'.
101.1	eccentricity] *interlined above canceled* 'proof'.
101.1	mind] *followed by a comma canceled in ink 3.*
101.5	uplifted hands] *follows canceled* 'clas' *or possibly* 'clos'.
101.12	in gold] *originally* 'in gold'; 'in' *canceled and* 'with' *interlined in pencil;* 'with' *canceled and* 'in' *interlined in ink 3.*
101.12	This] *follows canceled* 'It belonged'.

102.3	Grand] *originally 'grand'; 'g' underlined three times in ink 3.*
102.4	services; so] *originally 'services. So'; the period mended to a semicolon in ink 3; 'S' not reduced to 's'.*
102.8	of the English court.] *originally 'of courts and princes.'; 'the English' interlined, the 's' of 'courts' and 'and princes.' canceled, and the period added after 'court'; all revisions in ink 3.*
102.10	Let us] *follows canceled 'Leav'.*
102.10	there] *follows canceled 'there an hour.'*
103 title	CHAPTER 8] *the MS reads 'Chap. 8.'; '8.' added in ink 3 in a space originally left blank.*
103.1	Henry VIII] *interlined in ink 3 above canceled 'the king'.*
103.2	himself,] *followed by a canceled dash.*
103.2	Troublous] *followed by a wiped-out comma.*
103.4	Presently] *follows canceled 'A wicked light'.*
103.4	flamed up] *'up' interlined in ink 3.*
103.4	eye,] *the comma added in ink 3.*
103.13	realm,] *the comma added in ink 3.*
103.17	before] *follows canceled 'for'.*
103.19	an ashen] *originally 'a deadly'; the 'n' added to 'a', 'deadly' canceled, and 'ashen' interlined; all revisions in ink 3.*
103.23	cometh] *followed by a canceled exclamation point.*
104.1	my Great Seal] *follows canceled 'the'; originally 'my great seal'; the 'G' and 'S' written over 'g' and 's'.*
104.1	that shall] *follows canceled 'thou'.*
104.2	Speed ye,] *the comma added in ink 3.*
104.7	keepeth] *originally 'keepest'; 'eth' written over 'est' in ink 3.*
104.8	since,] *interlined in ink 3 above canceled 'gone,'.*
104.11	remember it.] *followed by canceled closing quotation marks.*
104.15	into] *originally 'in|to'; altered to 'into' with a hyphen added in ink 3.*
104.16	time,] *the comma possibly mended from a period.*
105.1	you gave] *originally 'thou gavest'; 'you' interlined in ink 3 to replace canceled 'thou'; 'st' canceled in ink 3.*
105.1	Great] *originally 'great'; 'G' written over 'g'.*
105.8	grieveth] *follows 'sore' canceled in ink 3.*
105.10	Seal.] *the period mended from a comma and followed by canceled 'neither can he find it in his cabinet where he is, nor I neither, that holp him seek.'*
105.12	array] *interlined in ink 3 above canceled 'list'.*
105.17	my heart] *followed by canceled 'of hearts'.*

105.21	and gazed] 'and' *interlined in ink 3.*
105.24	By the] *follows canceled* 'Is thy'.
105.24	glory] *possibly* 'Glory'; *a large* 'g' *written over the original* 'g' *appears to be an attempt to clarify rather than to capitalize the letter.*
105.24	an'] *the apostrophe added in ink 3.*
105.35	work] *follows canceled* 'doom'.
105.37	Norfolk.*] *the asterisk added in ink 3.*
105 note	*See . . . volume.] *added in ink 3.*
107 title	CHAPTER 9] *the MS reads* 'Chap. 9.'; '9.' *added in ink 3 in a space originally left blank.*
107.1	in the evening] *follows canceled* 'that'.
107.2–3	as far . . . citywards,] *interlined.*
107.4	colored lanterns] *follows canceled* 'lan'.
107.4	and gently] *follows canceled* 'that'.
107.8	was a picture] *follows canceled* 'was empty'.
107.9	polished] *interlined in ink 3 to replace canceled* 'shining'.
107.13	steps.] *followed by canceled* 'except the guards ranked upon either hand.'; *the period added.*
107.13	heavy] *follows canceled* 'filled' *and canceled* 'thi'.
107.14	carry,] *the comma added in ink 3.*
107.16	from the glare] *follows canceled* 'with'.
107.16–17	toward the palace.] *more than a third of the MS page was torn off below these words; ink marks on the torn edge appear to be the tops of letters written on the missing part of the sheet before it was torn away; originally this page was followed by that now beginning with the interlineation* 'high aloft' *(110.1); the text that intervenes is on seven pages inserted in the MS.*
108.1	banners] *follows canceled* 'clo'.
108.3	flags] *interlined above canceled* 'pennons'.
108.4	which] *interlined above canceled* 'that'.
108.4	tiny] *interlined.*
108.5	others] *follows canceled* 'still'.
108.5	since] *followed by a canceled comma.*
108.9	glossy] *interlined in ink 3 above canceled* 'polished' *which follows canceled* 'hel'.
108.11	The advance-guard] *follows canceled* [¶] 'Out from the great gate'.
108.12–109.3	"They . . . attendants."] *the quotation marks added in ink 3.*
108.12	dressed] *follows canceled opening quotation marks.*

108.16   halberd] *originally* 'halbert'; 'd' *written in ink 3 over* 't'.

108.20   in the gold] *follows canceled* 'in the liveries'.

108.25   civic] *interlined.*

108.25–26   City's Sword] *apparently originally* 'city's Sword'; 'C' *apparently written over* 'c' *and underlined three times in ink 3.*

108.27   Garter King-at-Arms] *originally* 'garter king-at-arms'; 'g', 'k', *and* 'a' *underlined three times in ink 3.*

108.30   then the lord] 'then' *interlined above canceled* 'and finally'.

108.32   scarlet cloaks] *follows canceled* 'cloaks'.

108.32   then the heads] *follows canceled* 'fin'.

108.36   and took] *follows canceled* 'to'.

108.38   cavaliers] *follows canceled* 'Span'.

109.5–6   arrayed] *follows canceled* 'w'.

109.6–7   "doublet . . . silver."] *the quotation marks added in ink 3.*

109.8   bent] *follows canceled* 'and'.

109.9   trumpet-blast] *followed by a canceled comma.*

109.10   followed,] *the comma mended from a semicolon; followed by canceled* 'high aloft'.

110.1   high aloft] *interlined at the beginning of an MS page; the preceding dash interlined in ink 3 at the end of the preceding MS page; see entry at* 107.16–17.

110.2   the massed] *follows* 'all' *canceled in ink 3.*

110.6   He was] *follows canceled* [¶] 'He was superbly arrayed in white cloth of gold, he wore his George and Garter, and wherever the light fell upon him jewels responded with a blinding flash. He was attended by the queen's brother the earl of Hertford, and two dukes, attired in costumes'; 'He was attended . . . costumes' *apparently canceled before the rest of the paragraph.*

110.6–12   "magnificently . . . orders,"] *the quotation marks added in ink 3.*

110.9   the triple-feather crest,] *originally* 'his crest,'; 'his' *canceled and* 'the Wales' *interlined; then* 'the Wales crest,' *canceled and* 'the triple-feather crest,' *interlined; all revisions in ink 3.*

110.11   the order] 'the' *interlined in ink 3 above canceled* 'his'.

110.13   O, Tom] *follows what may be closing quotation marks and a dash canceled in ink 3.*

111 title   CHAPTER 10] *the MS reads* 'Chap. 10.'; '10.' *added in ink 3 in a space originally left blank.*

111.5   to rage] 'to' *interlined.*

111.9   and the blow] *follows canceled* 'but the blow descended'.

111.12	a dim form] *follows canceled* 'the'.
111.13	mob] *follows canceled* 'mob scudded to their several holes with one impulse'.
111.15	abode,] *interlined above canceled* 'foul den,'.
111.21	withered] *follows canceled* 'lean'.
112.3	an'] *the apostrophe added in ink 3.*
112.7	thou] *interlined above canceled* 'you'.
112.7	to speak] 'to' *interlined in ink 3.*
112.8	Wales,] *the comma added in ink 3.*
112.13	laughter] *follows canceled* 'brutal'.
112.15	woe and] *interlined above canceled* 'grief and'.
113.2	put] *follows canceled* 'took' *or possibly* 'look'.
113.13	ruin] *squeezed in; possibly added later.*
114.5	scum,] *interlined above canceled* 'sluts,'.
114.13	An'] *the apostrophe added in ink 3.*
114.14	but let] *follows canceled* 'let'.
114.24	the father's] *follows canceled* 'John'.
114.29	gathered,] *followed by a canceled exclamation point and canceled closing quotation marks; the comma added.*
114.33	shoulder] *interlined in ink 3 above canceled* 'cheek'.
114.33	from] *interlined above canceled* 'with'.
114.34	staggering] *interlined in ink 3 above canceled* 'reeling'.
114.34	Goodwife] *interlined in pencil to replace canceled* 'Mrs.'
114.35	pelting] *follows canceled* 'pl'.
114.35	cuffs] *written over canceled* 's'.
114.36	person.] *interlined in ink 3 above canceled* 'head.'
115.5	right soundly,] *interlined in ink 3 above canceled* 'until he was nearly senseless,'.
115.7	has] *interlined in ink 3 above canceled* 'hath'.
115.9	out,] *the comma apparently mended from a period.*
115.16	appetite,—] *the dash interlined.*
115.22	anew,] *interlined above canceled* 'again,'.

Written in ink 3 from 115.24 through 117.23 ('Presently').

115.24	As she lay] *follows* [¶] 'Pain, hunger' *written and canceled in ink 2, and* [¶] 'Gradually the prince's pains ceased, and utter weariness sealed his eyes in a deep sleep. Hour after hour

slipped away. Still he slept like the dead. Thus, nearly five hours passed. Then his stupor began to lighten. Presently' *written in ink 2 and canceled in ink 3.*

115.36	Ah yes] *follows canceled* 'A happy thought'.
116.2	promising test] *follows canceled* 'test'.
116.8	measured] *interlined above canceled* 'soft'.
116.11	combined.] *interlined above canceled* 'put together.'
116.11	at once] *interlined.*
116.14	startled] *followed by canceled* 'out o'.
116.15	his dreams] *originally* 'his'; 'his' *canceled and followed by* 'a dream'; *then* 'a' *canceled,* 'his' *interlined, and* 's' *added to* 'dream'.
117.1	by his ear] *follows canceled* 'a'.
117.3	special] *interlined.*
117.10	so old] *follows canceled* 'an'.
117.12	before;] *the semicolon apparently mended from a comma; followed by canceled* 'and'.
117.13–14	the test . . . so she] *Mark Twain originally wrote* 'the test until she had'; *then he added a semicolon after* 'test', *canceled* 'until she had', *and interlined* 'so she' *to read* 'test; so she'. *Then he canceled* 'so she' *and interlined* 'she must try again—the failure must have'. *Finally, he canceled the entire passage and wrote* 'the test . . . so she' *on the verso of the MS page with instructions to turn over.*
117.16	had marked] 'had' *interlined.*
117.17	to bed,] *interlined.*
117.17–18	asleep, . . . boy!"] *originally probably* 'to sleep.'; 'to' *canceled,* 'a' *interlined, and the period apparently mended to a comma;* 'saying . . . be my' *squeezed in at the bottom of the MS page, and* 'boy!"' *written on the following MS page.*

Written in ink 2 from 117.23 ('while') through 145.4 ('cured."').

117.30	What! is] *originally* 'Beshrew me are'; 'are' *canceled and followed by* 'is'; *then in ink 3* 'What!' *interlined above canceled* 'Beshrew me'.
117.30	chamber] *originally* 'bedchamber'; 'bed' *canceled in ink 3.*
117.32	whisper] *follows canceled* 'muffled'.
117.36	Thou'rt] *follows canceled* 'That'.

118.3	with a moan] *follows canceled* 'again'.
118.5	all] *interlined.*
118.10	hilarious] *interlined to replace canceled* 'dull, far off'.
118.11	apparently . . . away.] *interlined following a comma mended from a period.*
118.12–13	from snoring] 'from' *interlined in ink 3.*
118.16	it was] *originally* ' 'twas'*; 'it' interlined in ink 3 to replace canceled* ' 't'.
118.18	An'] *the apostrophe added in ink 3.*
119.1	He roused] *follows canceled* ' ''Up'.
119.2	commanded,] *followed by a canceled dash.*
119.4	street] *follows canceled* 'dark'.
119.6	way] *originally* 'ways'*; the* 's' *canceled.*
119.6	giving] *follows canceled* 'now and then'.
119.8	fool,] *the comma added in ink 3.*
119.9	a new name] *interlined above canceled* 'another'.
119.14	tarry] *follows canceled* 'not go'.
119.14–15	will we flee] 'will' *interlined in ink 3 above canceled* 'shall'.
119.17	multitude] *follows canceled* 'swarming'.
120.3–4	Southwark Bridge, likewise;] *the MS reads* 'Southwark bridge, likewise;' *(emended); interlined without a caret above canceled* '(also Southwark'.
120.6	thick] *interlined.*
120.7	dazzling] *follows canceled* 'b'.
120.7	almost] *follows canceled* 'seemed'.
120.11	and hopelessly] *follows canceled* 'in an instant'.
120.13	Canty] *interlined above canceled* 'he'.
120.15	liquor,] *the comma added in ink 3.*
120.20	thee not,''] *originally* 'not thou,'' '. *Apparently as an alternative reading, Mark Twain interlined* 'thee' *above* 'thou', *in pencil and without a caret; later in ink 3 he canceled* 'not thou,'' ' *and added* 'not,'' ' *to the interlineation.*
120.23	that,] *the comma apparently mended from a period.*
120.29	brought;] *the semicolon replaces a canceled comma.*
120.30	his other] 'his' *interlined above canceled* 'the'.
120.33	custom.*] *the asterisk interlined and the footnote added to the bottom of the MS page in ink 3; see entry at 120 note.*
120.34	hand-free] 'hand-' *interlined.*
120.34	dived] *the MS reads* 'dove' *(emended); follows canceled* 'dar'.

120 *note*   *See Note . . . volume.] *added to the bottom of the MS page in ink 3.*

121.8   Canty,] *the comma added in ink 3.*

121.10   a usurper] 'a' *originally* 'an'; *the* 'n' *canceled.*

121.11   make himself known,] *follows canceled* 'and'; *the comma added in ink 3.*

121.12   impostor] *follows canceled* 'usur'.

121.14–15   in cases . . . treason.] *written in ink 3 on the verso of the MS page with instructions to turn over; the preceding comma mended from a period in ink 3.*

123 *title*   CHAPTER 11] *the MS reads* 'Chap. 11.'; '11.' *added in ink 3 in a space originally left blank.*

123.3–4   beruffled with joy-flames;] *interlined without a caret above canceled* 'lined with bonfires; as the procession'.

123.7   along,] *follows canceled* 'do'; *the comma added in ink 3.*

123.12   side] *follows canceled* 'little friends'.

123.14   was towed] 'was' *interlined in ink 3 above canceled* 'were'.

123.19   ancient] *follows canceled* 'walled'.

123.19   gallant] *interlined without a caret above canceled* 'gorgeous'.

124.1   Cheapside and made] *originally* 'Cheap-|side and marched'; 'side and marched' *canceled and followed by* 'side and made'.

124.5   a rich] *follows canceled* 'seats under'.

124.11   city;] *the semicolon mended from a colon; followed by canceled* 'and'.

125.5   fat] *interlined in ink 3 above canceled* 'portly'.

125.6   with impressive] *follows canceled* 'a'.

125.6   solemnity] *interlined above canceled* 'gravity'.

125.7   Beef,] *the comma mended from a period.*

125.8   After grace,] *interlined.*

125.10   from her] *follows canceled* 'and she'.

125.23   pykes" . . . "turned] *the quotation marks added in ink 3.*

125.25   voyded] *originally* 'voyded'; *the underline canceled.*

125.26   cannell-bone] *originally* 'cannell-bone'; *the underline canceled.*

126.14   than] *mended from* 'that'.

126.17   Don Caesar de Bazan in] *interlined in ink 3 above canceled* 'Ruy Blas in'; 'Bazan' *possibly followed by a canceled dash.*

126.22   a long] *followed by a canceled comma and canceled* 'straight'.

126.26   "Marry,] *interlined in ink 3 above canceled* ' "Sooth,'.

126.33   who] *written over 'y'.*

126.36–37   champion] *follows canceled 'prince's'.*

126.37–38   his destruction certain,] *interlined.*

127.2   upon the] *follows canceled 'the'.*

127.3   bold] *follows canceled 'brave'.*

127.8   silence,] *the comma mended from a semicolon.*

127.14   accord; ... moments;] *the semicolons mended in ink 3 from commas.*

128.1   Poor Tom's] *follows canceled* [¶] *'We will let the curtain descend upon this picture.'*

128.4   He said,] *followed by a canceled dash.*

128.4   lord Hertford's ear—] *originally 'Hertford's ear—'; 'Hertford's' canceled and 'Lord St. John's' interlined to replace it; then in ink 3 'Lord St. John's' and 'ear—' canceled and 'Lord Hertford's ear—' interlined; emended.*

128.5   faith and honor!] *interlined in ink 3 above canceled 'head!'.*

129.1   in a strong] *follows canceled 'with'.*

129.3   from this day] *follows what appears to be canceled 'and so'.*

129.4–5   To ... decrees the Duke] *originally 'The Duke'; 'To ... decrees' interlined; 'T' of 'The Duke' not reduced to 't'.*

129.5   die!"*] *followed by canceled 'To the Tower with thy message!" '; the quotation marks following 'die!' apparently added; the asterisk added in ink 3 and the footnote added to the bottom of the MS page in ink 3; see entry at 129 note.*

129.8   prodigious] *interlined in ink 3 above canceled 'mighty' which follows canceled 'mighty'.*

129.9   is ended!] *follows canceled 'is done!'.*

129 note   *See Note ... volume.] *added in ink 3 to the bottom of the MS page; originally 'note'; 'N' written over 'n'; originally followed by three MS pages that now open chapter 14 (155 title–156.5).*

131 title   CHAPTER 12] *the MS reads 'Chap. 12'; '12' added in ink 3 in a space originally left blank.*

131.2   mob] *follows canceled 'crowd'.*

131.6   it from] *follows canceled 'it, and'.*

131.12   outcast] *follows canceled 'forgotten and'.*

131.16   KING!"] *originally 'KING OF ENGLAND!" '; 'OF ENGLAND!" ' canceled in pencil and ink 3; the exclamation point and quotation marks after 'KING' added in ink 3.*

132.4–134.6   for a closely ... gateways.] *written in ink 2 on five sheets of buff paper originally numbered 13–17; apparently inscribed earlier than surrounding MS pages, and originally part of a sequence of which only these remain, these pages were subsequently re-numbered in sequence with the larger MS (see the explanatory note at 132.2–134.6 and the textual note at 133.37–134.2); 'for a closely' follows canceled* 'more than six hundred years. For six centuries families dwelt upon this noisy and bustling highway;'; *'gateways.' is followed by canceled* 'We can imagine the Bridge school-marm (of th', *in which* '(of th' *follows canceled* '(of 1305'; *these canceled passages are also in ink 2.*

132.5   sides of it,] 'it,' *interlined above canceled* 'the bridge,'.

132.5   bank] *interlined in pencil as an alternative reading to* 'side'; *later in ink 3* 'side' *canceled and a caret added.*

132.8   church.] *followed by a canceled asterisk and the following canceled footnote written on the verso of the MS page with instructions to turn over. The superior numbers refer to Mark Twain's revisions which are listed following the passage.*

'Footnote [¶] *Of the forty-three houses burnt down in a frightful conflagration which nearly consumed the Bridge in 1633, one was inhabited by a needle-maker, eight by haber-dashers of small wares, six by hosiers, five by hatters, one by a shoemaker, three by silkmen, one by a milliner, two by glovers, two by mercers, one by a distiller of strong waters, one by a girdler, one by a linen-draper, two by woolen-drapers, one by a salter, two by grocers, one by a scrivener, one by the curate of St. Magnus Church, one by the clerk, and one by a female whose occupation is not stated, while two others were unoccupied. [¶] The rent of several of the houses (in Edward I.'s time, when the Bridge[1] was ending its first century,) amounted to no more than three half-pence, and twopence halfpenny; and a fruiterer's shop, described to have been two yards and a half and one thumb in length, and three yards and two thumbs in depth, was let on a lease from a bridgemaster at[2] a rental of twelve pence.—[Jesse's "London."' '

1. Bridge] *followed by canceled* 'was ending its first cen'; 'ending' *interlined above canceled* 'its'.
2. bridgemaster at] *followed by canceled* 'twelve pence.—'.

132.8   looked] *follows canceled* 'was probably'.

132.8   upon] *followed by canceled* 'its'.

133.2   all] *follows canceled* 'his'.

133.5   families] *followed by canceled* 'who'.

133.6   old] *interlined.*

133.6   or six] *interlined.*

133.9   level,] *interlined.*

133.10   It was] *marked to begin a new paragraph with an interlined paragraph sign; the paragraph sign then canceled.*

133.11   self-conceited.] *the period added in ink 3; followed by a dash and* 'ten to one it had a tolerably poor opinion of London.' *canceled in ink 3;* 'ten' *interlined to replace canceled* 'a hundred'.

133.13   were] *interlined above canceled* 'and'.

133.15   having] *followed by canceled* 'h'.

133.20   mighty] *followed by canceled* 'procession'.

133.29   least] *followed by canceled* 'it was'.

133.30   windows,] *followed by canceled* 'for a'.

133.32   affording] *follows* 'the' *canceled in pencil.*

133.34   Bridge] *originally* 'bridge'; 'B' *written over* 'b'.

134.2   lashing] *follows canceled* 'raging'.

134.2   London] *follows canceled* 'the'.

134.3   times of . . . writing,] *follows canceled* 'old'; 'of . . . writing,' *interlined.*

134.4   English] *follows canceled* 'his'.

134.6   But we digress.] *added in ink 3; follows canceled* 'We . . . th' *as reported in the entry at 132.4–134.6.*

134.11   us] *follows canceled* 'up'.

134.11   mayhap] *written over* 'and'.

134.20   scurvy] *interlined above canceled* 'filthy'.

134.22   threat,] *the comma mended from a period.*

134.30   sword] *interlined.*

134.31   thou] *interlined above canceled* 'you'.

134.33   fate?] *follows canceled* 'for'.

134.34   lie—] *followed by canceled* 'death'.

135.7   two or three o'clock] *follows* 'half past' *canceled in ink 3;* 'or three o'clock' *interlined in ink 3.*

135.11   immediately.] *followed by canceled* [¶] 'Hendon'.

136.10   his malady;] *interlined above canceled* 'him; he shall'.

136.12   burnt] *interlined as an alternative reading to* 'damned'; *later* 'damned' *canceled in ink 3.*

136.15   tenderly] *interlined.*

136.16   slight] *follows what appears to be canceled* 'li'.

136.18   was,] *interlined above canceled* 'is,'.

137.8   was] 'was' *underlined in ink 3.*

137.9   king,] *the comma apparently mended from a period.*

137.12   foreign] *follows 'dismal' canceled in ink 3.*

137.14   Arthur;] *follows canceled 'Hugh;'.*

137.15   *he*] 'he' *underlined in ink 3.*

137.19   departure,] *follows canceled 'leave'.*

137.20   cheap] *written over what appears to be wiped-out 'in'.*

137.21   sprung] *follows canceled 'startled' and canceled 'rose'.*

137.21–22   posture, and] *'and' interlined preceding canceled 'glanced
             sharply about him'.*

137.34–35   look, that . . . somewhat] *originally* 'look, some-|what'; 'some-'
             canceled and 'that . . . some-' *interlined in ink 3.*

138.11   bidding,] *the comma written over a period.*

138.12–13   up a towel,] *originally* 'a towel up,'; 'up,' *canceled and* 'up'
             interlined; the comma following 'towel' *added; all revisions in
             ink 3.*

138.14   his own face] *interlined in ink 3 above canceled 'himself'.*

138.17   then] *written over 'and'.*

138.18   said,] *followed by a canceled dash.*

139.6   faith,] *originally* 'i' faith,' *interlined above canceled 'beshrew
             me'; 'i' ' canceled in ink 3.*

139.6   Tower,] *the 'T' possibly mended from 't'.*

139.9   capable of.] *followed by canceled* [¶] 'When the king had
             finished, he felt greatly refreshed, in body and spirit'.

139.11   relaxed] *follows canceled 'unbent'.*

139.26   has] *interlined in ink 3 above canceled 'hath'.*

139.33   past,] *interlined in ink 3 above canceled 'gone,'.*

139.33   nineteen] *written over 's'.*

140.1   heiress] *interlined above canceled 'mistress'.*

140.2   lapsed] *originally* 'relapsed'; 're' *canceled.*

140.10   best] *follows canceled 'most'.*

140.14   be] *follows canceled 'bem'.*

140.15   in truth I] *originally* 'it troth'; 'in' *interlined above canceled
             'it'; 'u' written over 'o' of 'troth'; 'I' interlined; all revisions in
             ink 3.*

140.16   say] *follows 'e'en' canceled in ink 3.*

140.17   since] *interlined in ink 3 above canceled 'sith'; the preceding
             comma added in ink 3.*

140.17   brought] *follows canceled 'but s'.*

140.18   any taint] *interlined in ink 3 above canceled 'aught'.*

140.20	faults] *follows canceled* 'little'.
141.4	brother] *followed by a canceled comma.*
141.4	make] *originally* 'made'; 'k' *written over* 'd'.
141.6	by] *interlined above canceled* 'with'.
141.14	I was] *originally* 'was I'; 'I' *canceled and another* 'I' *interlined preceding* 'was' *in ink 3.*
141.16	won] *interlined in ink 3 above canceled* 'did win'.
142.3	its] *follows canceled* 'and'.
142.5	abused!] *the exclamation point written over a comma.*
142.6	cross] *interlined in ink 3 above canceled* 'mass'.
142.9	ears] *the* 's' *possibly added later.*
142.13	out] *followed by what appears to be canceled* 'h'.
142.13	wherewith] *interlined.*
142.13	hath] *originally* 'has'; 'th' *written over* 's'.
142.14	romaunt.] *originally* 'romaunt of'; 'of' *canceled and the period added.*
142.14	lack] *followed by* 'or' *canceled in ink 3.*
142.15	living.] *followed by canceled closing quotation marks.*
142.16	cured!] *the exclamation point added in ink 3.*
142.17	proud] *written over* 'I'.
142.24	it is] *interlined in ink 3 above canceled* ' 'tis'.
142.29	offer—] *the dash written over a period.*
142.33	it were] *originally* ' 'twere'; ' 't' *canceled and* 'it' *interlined in ink 3.*
142.34	has] *interlined in ink 3 to replace canceled* 'hath'.
142.35	it is.] *followed by canceled closing quotation marks.*
142.36	did not throw] *originally* 'threw not'; 'did' *interlined in ink 3 above canceled* 'threw'; 'throw' *interlined in ink 3.*
143.1	duty,] *originally* 'duty; wherefore'; *the semicolon and* 'wherefore' *canceled and the comma added.*
143.1	since] *interlined in ink 3 above canceled* 'sith'.
143.2	hold] *interlined in ink 3 above canceled* 'deem'.
143.3	as your grace knoweth,] 'as ... knoweth' *interlined in pencil and later retraced in ink 3; the comma added in ink 3.*
143.4	England,] *the comma added in ink 3.*
143.7	Spanish] *written over* 's'.
143.7	witness] *follows canceled* 'jud'.
143.11	monarch] *follows canceled* 'king'.

144.2   I and] 'and' *interlined.*

144.3–4   and hold] *interlined.*

144.6   kings] *originally* 'king'; *expanded to* 'kings' *in ink 3; the* 's' *canceled, then another* 's' *interlined above it, also in ink 3.*

144.9   and] *followed by canceled* 'from'.

144.14   this] *written over* 'o'.

144.18–19   "Rise, Sir . . . "rise, and] *originally* ' "Rise," *said the king, gravely,* "and'; *the closing quotation marks after* ' "Rise,' *canceled and* 'Sir Miles Hendon, Baronet," ' *(emended) interlined in ink 3;* 'gravely,' *and the opening quotation marks preceding* 'and' *canceled and* 'gravely . . . "rise,' *interlined in ink 3.*

144.21   lapse."] *the quotation marks added in ink 3; followed by* 'The king hath spoken." ' *canceled in ink 3.*

144.22   His majesty] *follows canceled* [¶] 'Hendon'.

145.2   grievously] *interlined in ink 3 above canceled* 'sorely'.

Written in ink 3 from 145.4 ('After'*) through 145.12.*

145.11   raiment!] *followed by canceled* 'Some might smile.'

Written in ink 2 from 147 title through 201.10.

147 *title*   CHAPTER 13] *the MS reads* 'Chap. 13.'; '13.' *added in ink 3 in a space originally left blank.*

147.1   comrades.] *the period mended from a semicolon.*

147.3   rags"—] *originally* 'rags." '; *the dash squeezed in, canceling the period.*

147.4   remark, tucked] *the comma mended from a semicolon;* 'tucked' *interlined above canceled* 'covered'.

147.17   rose,] *originally followed by* 'took the boy's measure with a string, and slipped softly out.'; 'took' *written at the bottom of the MS page and* 'the boy's . . . out.' *written on a new MS page; the comma after* 'string' *mended to a period and* 'and . . . out.' *canceled; then* 'took . . . string.' *canceled; the verso of the MS page upon which* 'the boy's . . . out.' *was written then used to continue the MS.*

147.18   ward— . . . time,—] *the dashes interlined.*

147.20   complained] *follows canceled* 'and'.

148.2	thirty or forty] *originally* 'twenty or thirty'; 'twenty or' *canceled and* 'or forty' *interlined.*
148.3	wear;] *the semicolon added in ink 3.*
148.10	less thunderous] *interlined in ink 3 above canceled* 'milder'.
148.14	two] *interlined in ink 3 above canceled* 'twain'.
148.16	dry—] *followed by canceled* 'w'.
148.16	since he has] *interlined in ink 3 above canceled* 'sith he hath'.
148.18	getteth] *mended from* 'gets'.
148.18	sufficiency] *follows canceled* 'supp'.
148.19	needle] *followed by canceled* 'for'.
148.20	thread it!] *the exclamation point apparently replaces a period.*
148.22	held] *follows canceled* 'en'.
149.1	way.] *followed by canceled* 'The thread missed the'.
149.6	lap,] *the comma apparently mended from a period.*
149.7	inn] *interlined above canceled* 'landlord'.
149.7	included] *follows canceled* 'likewise—'.
149.10	awaits] *interlined in ink 3 above canceled* 'awaiteth'.
150.3	likewise] *interlined.*
150.11	he loved she,—] *the MS reads* 'twice as well,—' *(emended); the comma and dash replace what was either a period or a semicolon following* 'well'.
150.19	moment;] *the semicolon mended in ink 3 from a comma.*
150.20	also] *interlined.*
150.32	hither;] *the semicolon mended in ink 3 from a comma.*
150.32	message,] *the comma added in ink 3.*
151.1	fool!] *the exclamation point added in ink 3.*
151.4	hurt] *interlined above canceled* 'harm'.
151.4	Possibly] *follows canceled* 'I will'.
151.12	Hark ye!] *originally* 'Harkye!'; 'ye!' *follows canceled* 'ye!'.
151.15	"Sure, your worship."] *squeezed in with a caret and marked with a paragraph sign.*
151.19	two . . . ruffian-] *interlined in ink 3 to replace canceled* 'two joined the throng of the bridge, a ruffian-'; 'throng' *in the cancellation follows* 'moving' *canceled earlier in ink 3.*
151.20	joining them—"] *originally* 'laying his hand upon the smaller boy—" ', *which was tentatively canceled in pencil and followed by* 'joining them—" ' *in pencil; then* 'joining them—" ' *interlined in ink 3, and* 'laying . . . boy—" ' *and the penciled* 'joining them—" ' *canceled in ink 3.*

151.21   then] 'then' *underlined in ink 3.*

152.1   I] *followed by a canceled comma.*

152.3   scrivener] *followed by canceled* 'ord'.

152.11   yet] 'yet' *underlined in ink 3.*

153.1–2   servitor vanished. Hendon . . . muttering,] 'Hendon . . . mut-
            tering,' *added on the verso of the MS page with instructions
            to turn over; another instruction to turn over canceled follow-
            ing* 'vanished.'; 'Hend' *interlined without a caret above*
            'servitor' *and then canceled.*

153.3   poor] *followed by canceled* 'poor'.

153.4   it is] *interlined in ink 3 to replace canceled* ' 'tis'.

153.5   by book and bell,] *interlined in ink 3 above canceled* 'by the
            mass,'; 'by' *in the interlineation written over what may be* 'in'.

153.5   not] 'not' *underlined in ink 3.*

153.6   yonder] *interlined above canceled* 'there'.

153.7   now—] *followed by canceled* 'neither time to spare for eating, if
            I had it.'' '

153.7   let] *originally* 'lets'; 's' *canceled.*

153.9   himself—] *followed by what appears to be canceled* 'then'.

155 title– CHAPTER . . . sorrows."] *these three MS pages originally fol-*
156.5   *lowed* 'volume.' *(129 note).*

155 title   CHAPTER 14] *the MS reads* 'Chap. 14.'; '14.' *added in ink 3 in a
            space originally left blank.*

155.1   of the same morning,] *interlined.*

155.3   impressions,] *the comma added in ink 3.*

155.5   rapturous] *followed by canceled* 'whisper'.

155.7   last.] *the MS reads* 'last.!' *(emended); the period squeezed in in
            ink 3 without canceling the exclamation point.*

155.7   Ho] *follows canceled* 'Ho'.

155.9   wildest madcap] 'madcap' *interlined;* 'wildest' *followed by a
            canceled comma.*

155.14   voice!] *follows canceled* 'voice! Thou'rt Sir William Herbert in
            my fatal dream'; 'fatal' *follows canceled* 'dis'.

156.7–8   in . . . Fields,] *Mark Twain originally left a blank space fol-
            lowing* 'in'; *following the space he wrote* 'field,' *followed
            by another, larger blank space. Then in ink 3 he wrote*
            'Goodman's' *in the first blank space, altered* 'field,' *to* 'Fields,',
            and wrote 'a fair meadow,' *in the second blank space to produce
            the reading* 'Goodman's Fields, a fair meadow,'. *Finally, in ink 3
            he canceled* 'Goodman's Fields,' *wrote* 'the' *over* 'a', *canceled*

the comma *after* 'meadow', *and added* 'called Goodman's Fields,' *following* 'meadow'.

156.8   only] *interlined.*

156.11   pennies—] *the dash written over a period.*

157.3   good] *followed by canceled* 'priest that tau'.

157.9   are for thee] 'thee' *interlined in pencil without a caret above* 'you', *apparently as an alternative reading; later in ink 3* 'you' *canceled and a caret added.*

157.11   happy] *followed by canceled* 'mo'.

157.11   mother] *followed by canceled* 'p'.

157.19–20   courtiers clothed ... color—] 'courtiers' *follows canceled* 'gorgeous'; 'clothed ... color—' *interlined.*

157.21   upon] *followed by canceled* 'this brilliant spectacle.'

157.24   offered] *followed by canceled* 'his'.

157.28   Second] *interlined above canceled* 'First'.

157.33   the Chief] 'the' *interlined.*

157.35   of England,] *interlined above a canceled comma.*

158.11   and] *interlined.*

158.11   Lord] *mended from* 'lord'.

158.23   tag] *follows canceled* 'truss-'.

159.6   Tom] *followed by canceled* 'was'.

159.11   assemblage; and] *followed by canceled* 'where'.

159.19   to ask] *originally* 'and asked'; 'to' *interlined above canceled* 'and'; 'ed' *of* 'asked' *canceled.*

159.22   Executors] *followed by* 'appointing February 16th of the coming month for' *interlined without a caret and canceled in pencil.*

159.29   day] *followed by canceled* 'have'.

159.33   hustled] *follows canceled* 'his'.

160.1   Tom turned] 'Tom' *added without a caret preceding* 'Turned'; 'T' *of* 'Turned' *not reduced to* 't'.

160.8   gasp;] *the semicolon apparently squeezed in preceding a canceled dash.*

160.9   unpaid;*] *the asterisk interlined in ink 3 and the footnote added to the bottom of the MS page in ink 3; see entry at 160 note.*

160.11   empty,] *the comma mended from a period.*

160 note   *Hume.] *added to the bottom of the MS page in ink 3.*

161.1   delay,] *the comma added in ink 3.*

161.7	there] *interlined.*
161.9	A] *interlined following canceled* 'Another'.
161.12	and likewise . . . Earldom,] *interlined.*
161.20	willing.*] *the asterisk interlined in ink 3 and the footnote added to the bottom of the MS page in ink 3; see entry at 161 note.*
161.22	first,] *follows canceled* 'before'.
161.27	mind:] *the colon added in ink 3 preceding a canceled dash.*
161.30	great] *follows canceled* 'gra'.
161 note	*Hume.] *added to the bottom of the MS page in ink 3.*
162.5	shoulder;] *the semicolon mended in ink 3 from a comma.*
162.9–10	by . . . St. John,] *interlined.*
162.11–12	though . . . house] *added on the verso of the MS page with instructions to turn over.*
162.13	the visit] *interlined above canceled* 'it'.
162.14	interview] *interlined above canceled* 'visit'.
162.17	presence,] *the comma apparently mended from a period.*
162.18	of black,—] *follows canceled* 'all'; *the dash added in ink 3.*
162.32	his] *interlined.*
162.34	An idea] *follows canceled* 'Had'.
162.36	his side] 'his' *interlined above canceled* 'his' *which appears to be written over* 'the'.
162.38	himself] *followed by canceled* 'for'.
163.1	—he] *followed by canceled* 'would begin with this boy'.
163.3	a moment or two,] *interlined.*
163.4	remember] *followed by canceled* 'me'.
163.12	bring] *follows canceled* 'ta' *or* 'la'.
163.13	forsooth,] *interlined.*
163.14	before] *followed by a canceled exclamation point.*
163.14	see.] *the period mended from an exclamation point.*
163.17	lessons,] *followed by canceled* ' 'twas'.
163.18	[It is] *interlined in ink 3 above canceled* '['Tis'.
164.3	termed] *followed by canceled* 'such ignorant and'.
164.10	True, true] *followed by a canceled exclamation point.*
164.19	livelihood."*] *the asterisk interlined in ink 3 and the footnote added to the bottom of the MS page in ink 3; see entry at 164 note.*
164.21	thing,—] *the comma and dash replace the original semicolon.*
164.24	thing,] *interlined above a canceled comma.*

164.34–35   unbefitting] *originally* 'unfitting'; 'be' *interlined.*

164 *note*   *See Note . . . volume.] added in ink 3 to the bottom of the MS page.

165.21   He] *followed by canceled* 'commanded Humphrey to rise, and'.

165.22   burst of] *interlined.*

165.29   shall the] *interlined above canceled* 'will the'.

165.29   business] *follows canceled* 'serious'.

165.29   augmented."] *interlined in ink 3 above canceled* 'increased." '

165.30   The grateful . . . fervidly—] *added on the verso of the MS page with instructions to turn over.*

165.31   O] *followed by a canceled comma.*

165.32   surpass] *interlined above canceled* 'o'erpass'.

165.37   Tom's] *interlined above canceled* 'his'.

166.6   would give order] *interlined above canceled* 'sent orders to his guards and pages'; *originally* 'would give orders'; 's' *canceled.*

166.7   whenever] *follows canceled* 'at'.

166.9   Hertford] *interlined above canceled* 'St. John'.

166.12   that] *followed by canceled* 'the'.

166.13   begin to] *interlined.*

166.13   after] *interlined above canceled* 'for'.

166.15   more surely] *follows canceled* 'quiet the g'.

167.1   instruct] *follows canceled* ' "remind" Tom'.

167.2   the rather] *follows canceled* 'the rather'.

167.6   within a few days] *interlined.*

167.7   begin to] *interlined.*

167.7   public;] *the semicolon mended in ink 3 from a comma.*

167.14   voice] *interlined without a caret above canceled* 'way'.

167.16   the puzzle] 'the' *written over what appears to be* 'a'.

167.16   of the Great Seal—a loss] *interlined.*

167.17   although] *originally* 'though'; 'al' *squeezed in.*

167.17   since] *interlined above canceled* 'sith'.

167.28   easily] *interlined in ink 3.*

167.28   succeeded.] *followed by canceled* [¶] 'Presently the mock king, who had wandered to a window and become interested in' *written at the bottom of the MS page; the passage originally continued on a new MS page with* 'the life' *(170.37) but was canceled when the material now intervening was added.*

169 *title*   CHAPTER 15] *the MS reads* 'CHAP. 15.'; *added in ink 3 to the upper left corner of the MS page.*

169.2   trains;] *the semicolon mended in ink 3 from a comma.*

169.2   in awful state,] *interlined above canceled* 'and sceptred,'.

169.3   imagination] *follows canceled* 'a'.

169.4   long] *followed by a canceled comma.*

169.4   most] *interlined without a caret above canceled* 'many'.

169.5   wherefore,] *interlined above canceled* 'so'.

169.5   grew] *follows canceled* 'turned'.

169.14   princely] *originally* 'principal'; *the same character used for* 'i'
             and 'e'; 'ly' *written over wiped-out* 'pal'.

169.18   needful] *follows canceled* 'needed'.

169.19–21   The third day . . . little] *added on a new MS page in ink 3,*
             following the heading 'Chap. 16.' *written and canceled in ink 3;*
             follows [¶] 'The third day of his kingship came and went much
             as the others had done, but there was a lifting of his cloud in one
             way—he felt less uncomfortable than at first; he was getting a
             little' *canceled in ink 3 at the bottom of the preceding MS page.*
             The new passage, essentially the same as the canceled passage,
             was written to follow the addition of about 40 MS pages, almost
             all now lost, comprising what is now called "A Boy's Adven-
             ture" (see Appendix B, pp. 376–380). When Mark Twain de-
             leted the pages of "A Boy's Adventure" he canceled the
             chapter heading as well.

170.4   But] *follows canceled* 'The'.

170.6   program] *originally* 'programme'; 'me' *canceled.*

170.9   near] *followed by canceled* 'al'.

170.10   too] *follows canceled* 'two'.

170.10   grand] *interlined above canceled* 'great'.

170.11   Lord Protector] 'Lord' *interlined; an asterisk interlined in ink 3*
             following 'Protector' *and canceled in ink 3.*

170.15–17   performance,—and upon . . . any.] *originally* 'performance.'; *a*
             comma written over the period and followed by 'and noticing';
             then the dash interlined, 'noticing' *canceled, and* 'upon . . .
             any.' *squeezed in.*

170.32   a visit] *follows canceled* 'the reception of a'.

171.2   saw] *follows canceled* 'observed'.

171.7   solemnly] *interlined.*

171.9   "O . . . yes!" exclaimed] ' "O . . . yes!" ' *interlined in pencil*
             without a caret, presumably as an alternative reading, above
             ' "Of a surety, yes!" '; 'surety, yes' *followed by a wiped-out*
             comma; later in ink 3 ' "Of a surety, yes!" ex-|' *canceled and*
             ' "O . . . yes!" ex-|' *written over the penciled interlineation.*

171.10   being] *follows canceled 'the'.*

171.15   command!] *the exclamation point mended from a period in ink 3.*

171.16   flashing] *interlined in ink 3 following canceled 'shining'.*

171.17   gates and . . . highway] *'gates', followed by a canceled comma, is at the bottom of an MS page; 'and . . . highway' begins the next page; 'and . . . highway' was originally written at the beginning of another page, then canceled; the verso of that page was subsequently used at a later point in the MS.*

171.26   grisly] *'grim' written in pencil without a caret above 'grisly' as an alternative reading and later canceled in ink 3.*

171.27   even] *follows canceled 'm'.*

171.28   but] *'only' written in pencil without a caret above 'but' as an alternative reading and later canceled in ink 3.*

171.31   lips;] *the semicolon mended from a comma in ink 3.*

171.36   glow] *follows 'happy' canceled in pencil and again in ink 3.*

171.37   advantages] *interlined in pencil without a caret above canceled 'charms'; retraced and a caret added in ink 3.*

172.4–12   Now . . . another.] *added on the verso of the MS page with instructions to turn over.*

172.4   open;] *the semicolon mended from a comma in ink 3.*

172.6   folk] *written over 'and'.*

172.9   state,] *the comma added in ink 3.*

172.10   manifestations] *follows canceled 'every'.*

172.12   public] *interlined above canceled 'state'.*

172.13   In a little] *follows canceled 'The'.*

172.14   an] *interlined in ink 3 above canceled 'the'.*

173.4   stirred] *follows canceled 'fas'.*

173.8   sovereignty;] *originally, perhaps as a reminder of a possible alternative reading, 'sover' interlined in pencil without a caret above 'royalty;'; later in ink 3 'sovereignty;' written over 'sover', 'royalty;' canceled, and a caret added.*

173.10   the stranger] *originally 'he'; 't' added to 'he' to create 'the', and 'stranger' interlined.*

173.11   Thames,] *follows 'cold' canceled in pencil and again in ink 3.*

173.11   life,] *followed by canceled 'that day . . . . . . what day was it? . . . . . . ah, yes,'.*

173.12   baser] *originally interlined in pencil without a caret as an alternative reading to 'worser'; later in ink 3 'worser' canceled, 'baser' retraced, and a caret added.*

173.13   forgot the day, neither] 'forgot' *originally followed by* 'him, nor yet the day, nor'; *then in pencil* 'him, nor yet' *canceled and* 'neither' *and* 'for' *interlined without carets as possible alternative readings to* 'nor'; *finally in ink 3* 'him, nor yet the day, nor' *and the two interlineations canceled and* 'the day, neither' *interlined without a caret.*

173.14   eleven,] *interlined in pencil without a caret above canceled* 'ten,'; *the alteration retraced and a caret added in ink 3.*

173.17   fondlings and caresses] *interlined in ink 3 above canceled* 'holiday amusements'.

173.18   Tom] *follows canceled* 'Now'.

173.19   time;] *the semicolon mended in ink 3 from a comma.*

173.27   he asked.] *added in pencil and retraced in ink 3.*

173.37   that;] *the semicolon mended in ink 3 from a comma.*

174.2   king!] *followed by a canceled dash.*

174.4   had] *interlined in pencil and retraced in ink 3.*

174.5   boon!] *originally* 'boon, meseemeth!'; 'meseemeth!' *canceled in pencil and again in ink 3; the exclamation point following* 'boon' *written in ink 3 over the comma.*

174.5   Was it] *originally* 'Was't'; ''t' *canceled and* 'it' *interlined in ink 3.*

174.6   alive!"] *followed by an asterisk written in pencil and canceled in ink 3.*

174.10   miserable a] *originally* 'horrible a'; 'miserable' *originally interlined in pencil without a caret as an alternative reading to* 'horrible'; *later in ink 3* 'miserable' *retraced,* 'a' *added to the interlineation,* 'horrible a' *canceled, and a caret added.*

174.17   ferocious] *originally* 'grewsome'; 'cruel' *interlined in pencil without a caret above* 'grewsome' *as an alternative reading; later in ink 3* 'ferocious' *written over* 'cruel', 'grewsome' *canceled, and a caret added.*

174.21   cried Tom,] *interlined.*

174.25   profound] *interlined.*

174.26   very] *interlined.*

174.26   common] *written over* 'v'.

174.28   words] *followed by a canceled comma.*

174.32   has] *interlined in ink 3 above canceled* 'hath'.

174.35   entered] *originally* 'did enter'; 'did' *canceled and* 'ed' *added in ink 3.*

174.36   at ten] *follows canceled* 'upon'.

175.1   hour,] *the comma mended from a period.*

175.8–9	Weighty . . . and said—] *added in ink 3 on the verso of the MS page with instructions to turn over.*
175.12	worse.] *originally* 'worser.'; 'r.' *canceled and the period after* 'worse' *added in ink 3.*
175.14	the sick] 'the' *written over* 'a'.
175.19	seeing] *follows canceled* 'f'.
175.21	day.] *interlined in ink 3 above canceled* 'age.'
175.21	settled;] *originally* 'settled—'; *the dash canceled and the semicolon added in ink 3.*
175.25	my king] *follows canceled* 'your gracious maj'.
175.27	name,] *followed by* 'I name' *canceled in pencil and again in ink 3.*
175.32	some minutes later,] *interlined in ink 3 above canceled* 'betwixt it and eleven,'.
176.1	admiration] *interlined above canceled* 'wonder'.
176.2	decree] *interlined above canceled* 'judgment'.
176.2	delivered] *follows canceled* 'ren'.
177.7	upon] *written over* 'o'.
177.21	Tom] *follows canceled opening quotation marks.*
177.28	witnesses] *originally* 'wo'; 'itnesses' *written over* 'o'.
177.29	bred the] 'the' *interlined.*
177.35	turned] *followed by canceled* 'the grave'.
178.5	dearly] *followed by canceled* 'earned'.
178.7	if she is mad] 'is' *interlined above canceled* 'be'.
178.10	An'] *originally* 'An' '; *the apostrophe canceled in ink 2; then another apostrophe interlined in ink 3.*
178.14	child?"] *the question mark mended from a comma.*
178.17	a learned judge.] *follows canceled* 'the earl of Hertford.'
178.21	*devil*] 'devil' *underlined in ink 3.*
178.23	void."] *followed by canceled* [¶] ' " 'Tis said the devil's wit outs'.
179.9	*By pulling off their stockings*] 'By . . . stockings' *underlined in ink 3.*
179.10	curiosity] *follows canceled* 'a'.
179.11	said,] *interlined above canceled* 'asked,'.
179.12	wonderful!] *follows canceled* 'a'.
179.13	liege—] *the dash apparently written over a period.*
179.14	either] *followed by canceled* 'to hersel'.
179.31	miracle,] *followed by canceled* 'and must be content to lose her life'.

179.32   alone,] *interlined.*

179.32   by obedience] *Mark Twain wrote* 'obedience to the king's command' *at the top of a page, canceled it, wrote* 'if' *to begin a new line below the cancellation, and then canceled* 'if'; *he then turned the sheet over end for end and wrote on its other side the page that now begins* 'by obedience'.

179.33   acquired.] *follows canceled* 'com'.

179.36   An'] *originally* 'An''; *the apostrophe canceled in ink 2; then another apostrophe interlined in ink 3.*

179.36   my] 'my' *underlined in ink 3.*

179.38   whole] *interlined in ink 3.*

179.38   if] *followed by* 'giving me back' *canceled in ink 2 and again in ink 3.*

180.1–2   got! It is . . . mould.] *originally* 'got for it.'; 'for it.' *canceled in ink 3 and the exclamation point added;* 'It is . . . mould.' *added in ink 3 on the verso of the MS page with instructions to turn over.*

180.5–13   make me a storm, . . . thy power] *the verso of this MS page is numbered* '309' *and contains the single word* 'again.', *apparently the terminal fragment of a sentence; this MS fragment, however, does not fit into any of the existing pagination schemes of the MS.*

180.7   eager] *follows canceled* 'strong'.

180.8   apprehension;] *followed by canceled* 'and' *which is followed in turn by* 'and' *interlined and canceled; the semicolon mended in ink 3 from a comma.*

180.8   at the same time] *interlined.*

180.15   storm."*] *the asterisk interlined in ink 3 following* 'storm.' *(emended).*

180 *note* *See Notes to . . . volume.] *squeezed in in ink 3;* 'Notes . . . at' *originally* 'Note 9 at'; '9 at' *canceled,* 's' *added to* 'Note', *and* 'to Chapter 15 at' *added.*

181 *title* CHAPTER 16] *the MS reads* 'CHAP. 16'; *originally* 'CHAP. 17.' *was inserted in ink 3; then* '17.' *was canceled and* '16' *was interlined in ink 3.*

181.4–5   garret, after . . . habit,] 'after . . . habit,' *interlined; the comma after* 'garret' *probably added.*

181.10   imposing] *interlined in ink 3 above canceled* 'stately'.

181.10   spacious] *interlined in ink 3 above canceled* 'gorgeous'.

181.15   raised] *follows* 'slightly' *canceled in ink 3.*

181.18   have] *interlined above canceled* 'had'.

181.19   spreads] *the terminal 's' added.*

181.20   retire] *originally 'retired'; the 'd' canceled.*

182.3   richly clothed,] *interlined.*

182.6   awe] *follows canceled 'awe'.*

182.6   present."*] *the asterisk added in ink 3 and the footnote added to the bottom of the MS page in ink 3; see entry at 182 note.*

182.8   indistinct] *interlined.*

182 note *Leigh . . . tourist.] *added in ink 3 to the bottom of the MS page.*

183.1   Chancellor,] *followed by canceled* 'bearing the seals in a silk purse,'.

183.4   himself] *interlined; followed by canceled* '—whom when'; *'whom' mended from* 'who,'.

183.16   besides] *follows canceled* 'then'.

184.3   He] *interlined above canceled* 'Tom'.

184.3   removing] *follows canceled* 'lay'.

184.3   cap;] *originally* 'cap,—a royal custom'; '—a royal custom' *canceled; the comma mended to a semicolon in ink 3.*

184.6   common] *interlined above canceled* 'equal'.

184.9–10 entered,] *followed by canceled* 'bringing the dinner'.

185.4–5   He got . . . triumph.] *squeezed in to replace canceled* 'He even overcame the strong impulse to pocket nuts for private eating; this was his finest triumph.'

185.5   flawless] *follows canceled* 'happy'.

185.9   public] *follows canceled* 'it'.

187 title CHAPTER 17] *the MS reads* 'Chap. 17.'; '17.' *added in ink 3 following canceled* '18.'

187.3   disappointed] *follows canceled* 'en'.

187.4   however.] *follows canceled* 'but'.

187.10   morning,] *the comma mended from a period.*

188.6   searching] *follows canceled* 'in'.

188.6–7   Let us . . . now.] *squeezed in in ink 3.*

188.9   king,] *follows* 'little' *canceled in ink 3.*

188.12   used] *follows canceled* 'assisted' *which follows canceled* 'supported'.

188.20   endure] *interlined in ink 3 above canceled* 'abide'.

188.34   he shall rue it!"] *interlined in ink 3 above canceled* 'it shall avail him nothing—he shall hang!" '.

189.1   way] *interlined above canceled* 'king'.

189.4   near] *written over* 'a'.

189.5   them a] *interlined in ink 3 above canceled* 'it a'.

189.7   there!] *the exclamation point mended from a period in ink 3.*

189.10   mocking] *follows* 'rude,' *canceled in ink 3.*

189.12   youth] *interlined above canceled* 'mocker'.

189.13   from] *interlined in ink 3.*

190.6   sup sorrow for] *interlined in ink 3 above canceled* 'rue'.

190.11   ears] *followed by canceled* 'to n'.

190.13   murder,] *the comma added in ink 3.*

190.13   tarry] *interlined in ink 3 above canceled* 'bide'.

190.17   sisters?] *followed by canceled closing quotation marks.*

190.19   The] *follows canceled opening quotation marks.*

190.23–24   —prevented] *follows canceled* '—interfered.'

190.28   together, in low voices,] *originally* 'together. [¶] Thou hast
             tarried many months away,'' said Hugo. [¶] ''London is better
             than'; [¶] 'Thou ... than' *canceled; the period following*
             'together' *mended to a comma and* 'in low voices,' *added.*

190.33   soon absorbed] *follows canceled* 'soon steeped in reverie.'

190.33   griefs,] *followed by canceled* 'upon his head-roll, but the minor
             ones were forgotten, almost,'; *the comma following* 'griefs'
             probably added.

190.35   the name] *interlined above canceled* 'it'.

191.20   youths,] *interlined following canceled* 'brutes,'.

191.23   was a villain-looking pedlar] *originally* 'were villain-looking
             pedlars'; 'was a' *interlined above canceled* 'were'; *the* 's' *of*
             'pedlars' *canceled.*

191.23   his pack;] *originally* 'their packs;'; 'his' *interlined above
             canceled* 'their'; *the* 's' *of* 'packs' *canceled.*

192.1   barber-surgeon,] *interlined in ink 3 above canceled* 'tooth-
             puller,'.

192.3   were old] *follows canceled* 'ol'.

192.3–4   foul-mouthed;] *the semicolon mended in ink 3 from a comma.*

192.15   broke] *interlined in ink 3 above canceled* 'burst'.

192.16   a song] *followed by a canceled exclamation point.*

192.16   Dot-and-go-One!''] 'O' *written over* 'o' *in ink 3;* 'and-go-One!'' '
             follows canceled 'and-go-One.'

192.19   Dot-and-go-One] *originally* 'Dot-and-go-one'; 'o' *underlined
             three times in ink 3.*

193.11   trine.''*] *the asterisk interlined and the footnote added to the
             bottom of the MS page in ink 3; see entry at 193 note.*

193.14–15   used, in talk,] *the comma following* 'used' *added in ink 3 and*
             'in talk,' *interlined in ink 3.*

193.26	added] *follows canceled 'h'.*
193.27	roundly] *interlined in ink 3 above canceled 'lavishly'.*
193.37	An'] *the apostrophe added in ink 3.*
193 note	*From . . . 1665.] *added to the bottom of the MS page in ink 3.*
194.6	and maunders] *'and' interlined in ink 3 above a canceled comma.*
194.7	morts.*] *followed by canceled closing quotation marks.*
194.14	over hot] *originally 'over-|hot'; the hyphen canceled.*
194.19	was he,] *the comma added in ink 3.*
194.20	of us] *'of' interlined above canceled 'with'.*
194.20	yet,] *the comma mended from a period.*
194.27	commendation.] *followed by canceled closing quotation marks.*
194.35	see] *follows canceled 'hear the'.*
194.35	all] *followed by canceled 'that'.*
195.1	around] *interlined above canceled 'about'.*
195.2	thin] *interlined in ink 3 above canceled 'white'.*
195.3	about] *written over 'and'.*
195.3	gray] *interlined in ink 3.*
195.3	them,] *the comma added; followed by a canceled exclamation point.*
195.4	an'] *the apostrophe added in ink 3.*
195.11–12	circumstances—as . . . no heir.] *originally 'circumstances.'; '—as . . . no heir.' added in ink 3 on the verso of the MS page with instructions to turn over; two periods inadvertently left standing.*
195.18	girdle] *interlined in ink 3 above canceled 'shoulders'.*
195.19	ran, then . . . pelted;] *originally 'ran;'; the comma added preceding the semicolon and 'then . . . pelted;' interlined following 'ran,'; two semicolons inadvertently left standing.*
195.20	and deprived] *follows canceled 'lost'.*
195.22	iron,] *followed by canceled 'set in the'.*
195.27	backs,] *follows canceled 'scarred'.*
195.28	been;] *interlined in ink 3 above canceled 'resided;'.*
195.35	*England*] *'England' underlined in ink 3.*
195.35	blameless] *interlined in ink 3 above canceled 'tender'.*
196.6	three] *originally 'three'; 'three' canceled and 'six' interlined in ink 3; then 'six' canceled and 'three' interlined in ink 3.*
197.2	stain,] *followed by canceled 'ye'.*
197.3	SLAVE] *'slave' underlined twice in ink 3.*

197.4	SLAVE!] 'slave' *underlined twice in ink 3; the exclamation point added in ink 3.*
197.6	hang!''*] *the asterisk interlined and the footnote added to the bottom of the MS page in ink 3; see entry at* 197 *note.*
197.7	through the murky air—] *possibly added later; follows a canceled dash.*
197.10	as] *followed by canceled* 'the'.
197.11	general] *follows canceled* 'general shout'.
197 note	*See . . . volume.] *added to the bottom of the MS page in ink 3.*
198.1	Edward,] *interlined above canceled* 'the'; *the interlineation was originally* 'Edward the Sixth,'; 'the Sixth,' *canceled and the comma following* 'Edward' *added in ink 3.*
198.5	vagrants,] *follows canceled* 'base-born'.
198.14	cost,] *followed by canceled* 'be'.
198.15	swing] *originally* 'hang'; 'hang' *canceled and* 'die' *interlined above it in ink 3; then* 'die' *canceled and* 'swing' *interlined in ink 3.*
198.16	An'] *originally* 'An''; *the apostrophe canceled in ink 3 and then restored in ink 3.*
198.19	An'] *originally* 'An''; *the apostrophe canceled in ink 2 and later restored in ink 3.*
198.24	uttered,—] *originally* 'uttered;'; *a dash written over the top portion of the semicolon; see textual note.*
198.28	"LONG . . . ENGLAND!''] 'Long . . . England' *underlined twice in ink 3.*
198.29	thundergust] *interlined in ink 3 following canceled* 'rousing heartiness'.
198.30	vibrated] *originally* 'quaked'; 'quaked' *canceled and* 'rocked' *interlined above it in ink 3; then* 'rocked' *canceled and* 'vibrated' *interlined in ink 3.*
198.35	merriment.] *interlined in ink 3 above canceled* 'laughter.'
198.35	When] *followed by canceled* 'it had'.
198.37	Humor] *follows canceled* 'Be'.
199.3	The] *follows canceled* 'At'.
199.6	hootings, cat-calls, and] *interlined in ink 3.*
199.11	twenty] *interlined in ink 3 above canceled* 'fifty'.
199.11	broke out at] *interlined in ink 3 above canceled* 'burst forth at'.
200.2–3	of ironical . . . supplications,] *interlined in ink 3 to replace canceled* 'of imploring and tearful wailings,'.
201.2	contact with] 'with' *interlined in ink 3 above canceled* 'from'.
201.7	eyes;] *the semicolon mended in ink 3 from a comma.*

The remainder of the manuscript (from 203 title) written in ink 3.

203 title   CHAPTER 18] *the MS reads* 'Chap. 18.'; *originally* 'chap. 19.'; 'C' *written over* 'c'; '18.' *follows canceled* '19.'

203.7   commanded] *follows canceled* 'told'.

203.8   lad.] *followed by canceled* [¶] 'After a'; *then* 'The troop followed the high road' *added following* 'lad.' *and canceled.*

203.14   was held] 'was' *interlined above canceled* 'were'.

203.15   took] *follows canceled* 'nobody'.

203.16   venturing] *follows canceled* 'offering'.

204.2   seemed] *follows canceled* 'looked'.

204.2   grateful] *originally* 'thank-|ful'; 'thank-' *canceled and* 'grate' *interlined.*

204.6   from] *follows canceled* 'for'.

204.7   about] *follows canceled* 'upon'.

204.14   authorities.] *following this word on the MS page originally numbered 406, Mark Twain wrote and canceled* 'O' *(perhaps intending to write* 'OVER'*); then he wrote and canceled* 'See 406½'; *next he wrote instructions to turn over and, on the verso,* 'Insert here, pages 406A [406]B [406]C etc etc' *(using ditto marks below the first* '406'*); finally he canceled the note on the verso and the instructions to turn over. No pages 406½ or 406A etc. are known to exist. Later, after renumbering the MS, Mark Twain added 128 new MS pages at 205.4 below.*

205.4   village] *at this point Mark Twain inserted 128 new MS pages (205.4–243.35);* 'village' *is written at the bottom of an MS page and was followed originally by a page beginning* 'at different points and ply their various trades. "Jack" was sent with Hugo. They wandered through the streets a good while, Hugo watching for opportunities to do a stroke of business but finding none. At last a woman passed by with a package of some sort in a basket. Hugo said—'; *this page was moved to follow the 128 new MS pages and the above passage* 'at different . . . said—' *was canceled when the intervening pages were added.*

205.15   Thy] *the MS reads* 'Your' *which follows canceled* 'Thy'; *emended.*

205.17   even] *interlined.*

206.23   smitten] *follows canceled* 'stri'.

206.26   Hugo] *originally* 'Hugh'; 'o' *written over* 'h'.

207.5   Hugo] *originally* 'Hugh'; 'o' *written over* 'h'.

207.8   foot.] *followed by canceled closing quotation marks.*

207.16–17	likewise.] *followed by canceled closing quotation marks.*
207.19	Hugo] *originally* 'Hugh'; 'o' *written over* 'h'.
208.2	grateful] *follows canceled* 'grateful'.
208.3	tired] *follows what appears to be canceled* 'tre'.
208.6	wounded] *interlined above canceled* 'chafed'.
209.10	muffled] *interlined.*
209.19	overhead,] *followed by a canceled interlined dash.*
209.19	sound;] *followed by a canceled dash.*
209.23	still,] *followed by canceled* 'that he resolved'.
209.25	swiftly] *followed by canceled* 'and softly'.
209.31	stall] *followed by canceled* 'partly filled'.
210.3	quite] *interlined.*
210.6	influences] *followed by canceled* 'were'.
210.7	into] *followed by what appears to be canceled* 'a ha' *and canceled* 's'.
210.10	moment,] *the comma possibly mended from a period.*
211.3	once more,] *interlined without a caret above canceled* 'again,'.
211.10	dark,] *followed by canceled* 'between the'.
211.11	him, and] *followed by three separate cancellations in the following order:* 'touching him', 'visiting', *and* 'and w'.
211.22	This] *follows canceled* 'He'.
211.25	would] *originally* 'could'; 'w' *written over* 'c'.
211.25	But] *followed by canceled* 'this'.
211.31	calf!] *the exclamation point apparently squeezed in.*
211.37	those] *follows canceled* 'that'.
212.13	calf;] *originally* 'calf's back;'; ' 's' *and* 'back;' *canceled and the semicolon added after* 'calf'.
212.13	himself] *followed by canceled* 'close'.
212.17	at once;] *interlined above canceled* 'right away;'.
212.20	in a word, he was happy.] *interlined to replace canceled* 'yes, and he was homeward bound and should have his own again!'; 'he was happy.' *follows canceled* 'he was contented,'.
212.20	rising;] *followed by a canceled dash.*
213.3	minded] *follows canceled* 'was'.
213.6	contentment,] *followed by canceled* 'and sank'.
213.22	simple] *followed by canceled* 'sort'.
215 *title*	CHAPTER 19] *the MS reads* 'Chap. 19.'; '19.' *follows canceled* '20.'
215.6	myself so helpless.] *originally* 'so helpless myself.'; 'myself'

	interlined preceding 'so'; 'myself.' *canceled; the period following* 'helpless' *added.*
215.7	very] *interlined.*
215.7	make] *follows canceled* 'blandly'.
215.8	fortunes] *followed by canceled* 'a'.
215.8	since] *followed by canceled* 'he can no'.
215.10	heard] *followed by canceled* 'a noise'.
215.13	still,] *originally* 'still;'; *the semicolon canceled and the comma added.*
215.15	By and by] *followed by canceled* 'one of them said, timidly—'.
216.7	all] *followed by canceled* 'points, but warily and watch'.
216.9	occasion.] *followed by canceled* 'At last one of them plucked'.
216.10	holding] *follows canceled* 'with'.
216.12	up] *followed by canceled* 'her'.
216.25	a lie?] *follows canceled* 'that'; *followed by canceled closing quotation marks.*
217.7	now,] *interlined above canceled* 'again,'; *the preceding comma apparently added.*
217.13	crazed] *follows canceled* 'dis'.
218.1	inquiries] *follows canceled* 'q'.
218.13	weavers] *follows canceled* 'ne'.
219.4	subject] *interlined above canceled* 'matter'.
219.4	surprise,] *follows canceled* 'vast'.
219.5	hunted] *follows canceled* 'tracked him'.
219.6–7	proud, too, of . . . it.] *originally* 'proud of . . . it, too.'; 'too.' *canceled and the comma following* 'it' *mended to a period;* 'too,' *interlined and the comma following* 'proud' *apparently added.*
219.9	gnawing] *interlined following canceled* 'frantic'.
219.10	such] *followed by canceled* 'another'.
219.11	dissertation upon] *follows canceled* 'dissertation upon'.
219.11	toothsome] *interlined above canceled* 'noble'.
221.4	housewife] *followed by canceled* 'suggested' *and canceled* 'told up'.
221.9	and to] 'and' *interlined.*
221.9	too,] *interlined.*
221.12–16	He was . . . Then she] *added on the verso of the MS page with instructions to turn over, replacing* 'Then she' *canceled on the recto.*

221.17   service,] *interlined.*

222.2   present,] *followed by canceled* 'as far as'.

222.6   he felt that] *interlined to replace canceled* 'it seemed to him that'.

222.9   Canty] *followed by canceled* 'and Hugo!'.

222.11   discovered] *interlined above canceled* 'saw'.

223 title   CHAPTER 20] *the MS reads* 'CHAP. 20.', *which was inserted with a caret at the top of the MS page;* '20.' *originally* '21.'; '0' *written over* '1'.

223.1   The] *originally run-on; marked to begin a new paragraph with an interlined paragraph sign.*

223.7   stopped; being persuaded] *interlined to replace canceled* 'climbed up among the great branches of an old oak, and felt'.

223.8   safe.] *followed by canceled* 'It was'.

223.9   awful,] *follows canceled* 'even'.

223.11   mysterious,] *followed by what may be canceled* 'not'.

223.11   real] *interlined above canceled* 'living'.

223.12   only] *follows canceled* 'the'.

223.12–13   departed ones.] *originally followed by an MS page inscribed with* [¶] 'It was his purpose, in the beginning,'; *the second page apparently abandoned and its verso subsequently used at a later point in the MS.*

223.15   where he was,] *interlined to replace canceled* 'in the tree'.

223.17   resume] *follows canceled* 'quit the tree and'.

223.18   a road] *follows canceled* 'the hi'.

224.3   over] *follows canceled* 'of'.

224.15   small;] *follows canceled* 'very'; *followed by canceled* 'and there was but the one;'; *the semicolon following* 'small' *possibly mended from a comma.*

226.5   come] *originally* 'cometh'; 'th' *canceled.*

226.15   and thou] *followed by a canceled dash and canceled closing quotation marks.*

226.17   molest] *follows canceled* 'no'.

226.23   'Sh!] *interlined.*

226.23   secret!"] *the exclamation point possibly mended from a period.*

226.37   confer that awful dignity.] *interlined to replace canceled* 'do that solemn office.'; 'solemn' *interlined.*

227.3   be not] *follows canceled* 'there'.

227.5   walked] *followed by canceled* 'the'.

227.7   energy,] *followed by a canceled dash.*

227.9–10 ah, yes,] *followed by canceled* 'I should'.

227.10 and I] 'and' *interlined*.

228.6 out of] 'of' *interlined*.

229.2–3 in a small adjoining room,] *interlined*.

229.4 might;] *interlined above canceled* 'would;'.

229.6 then] *interlined above canceled* 'and'.

229.7 fingers,] *followed by canceled* 'af'.

229.9 entered his guest's room,] *interlined to replace canceled* 'approached the bed,'.

229.23 frown] *followed by canceled* 'on the hermit's face'.

229.24 of evil satisfaction. A] *originally* 'of coar'; 'coar' *canceled and followed by* 'joy. A'; 'joy.' *canceled and* 'beaming satisfaction.' *interlined above it;* 'of beaming satisfaction. A' *canceled, and* 'of evil satisfaction. A' *added;* 'A' *followed by canceled* 'sm'.

229.25–26 he turned] 'he' *interlined*.

229.28 toward] *follows canceled* 'at'.

229.35 peered] *followed by canceled* 'at'.

230.18 low] *followed by a canceled comma and canceled* 'malignant'.

230.22 noiselessly] *interlined*.

230.23 form] *followed by a canceled comma and canceled* 'f'.

231.9 some one] *followed by canceled* 'might'.

231.18 sleeper's] *interlined*.

231.20 compacted,] *originally* 'com-|pleted'; 'pleted' *canceled and* 'pacted,' *interlined*.

233 title CHAPTER 21] *the MS reads* 'Chap. 21'; '21' *interlined above canceled* '22.'

233.2 half] *follows canceled* 'with'.

233.3 craving] *interlined above canceled* 'gloating'.

233.7 grisly,] *originally* 'grim,'; 'sly' *written over* 'm'.

233.9 the old] 'the' *written over what appears to be* 'a'.

233.9–10 gazing,— . . . abstraction,—] *the dashes interlined*.

233.16 at the same time] *interlined*.

233.19 dying!''] *followed by canceled* [¶] 'The boy struggled again'.

234.3 uttered] *originally* 'uttering'; 'ed' *written over* 'ing'.

234.7 The dawn] *originally run-on; marked to begin a new paragraph with a paragraph sign.*

234.7 hermit] *followed by canceled* 'of'.

234.11 spoiler,] *interlined above canceled* 'enemy,'.

234.16 voices] *follows canceled* 'angry'.

235.6   teeth] *followed by a canceled comma.*

235.17   peradventure] *interlined following canceled* 'mayhap'.

235.20   time] *followed by a canceled exclamation point.*

235.22   stir;] *followed by canceled* 'thou wouldst'.

235.23   stop!—] *interlined above canceled* 'hold—'.

235.24   —you!] *the MS reads* '—you!' *(emended); interlined; the ex-clamation point written over a question mark.*

235.25   didst] *originally* 'did'; 'st' *interlined.*

235.25–26   lied, friend;] *originally* 'lied;'; *the semicolon canceled and the comma added;* 'friend;' *interlined.*

235.26   go] *followed by a canceled comma.*

236.4   as comes a] *interlined to replace canceled* 'like a'.

236.7   only] *interlined following canceled* 'naught but'.

236.11   tired] *interlined above canceled* 'weary'.

237.2   sound,—] *the dash interlined.*

237.7   —but] *follows canceled* 'went'; *followed by canceled* 'thou wouldst never f'.

237.10   wilt] *mended from* 'will'.

237.12   myself?—] *the MS reads* 'myself—' *(emended); the dash inter-lined above a canceled semicolon.*

237.13   indifferent sum of a month's] *interlined.*

237.15   ride] *mended from* 'run'.

237.21   by a] *interlined above canceled* 'with a'.

237.22   mule,] *the MS reads* 'mule—' *(emended); followed by a passage which was revised in the MS, then canceled in a later stage. See the historical collation for the text of the deleted passage, in which the position of the following revision is indicated by a superior number.*

             1. behind!] *originally* 'behind you!'; 'you!' *canceled, and the exclamation point added following* 'behind'.

238.2   fade] *followed by canceled* 'and die'.

238.2–3   for the moment,] *interlined.*

238.5   He] *follows canceled* 'A'.

238.6   so] *interlined.*

238.6–7   again, that . . . sheepskin.] 'that . . . sheepskin.' *squeezed in; the comma mended from a period.*

238.9   knife] *interlined above canceled* 'marrow'.

239 *title*   CHAPTER 22] *the MS reads* 'Chap. 22'; '22' *follows can-celed* '23.'

239.2   their coarse jests] 'their' *mended from* 'the'; 'jests' *followed by canceled* 'of'.

239.21   trick of] 'of' *interlined above canceled* 'and'.

239.23   set] *follows canceled* 'set the crowd of'.

240.3   result, the] *followed by canceled* 'mad hurricane of'.

240.5   Hugo,] *follows* 'poor' *canceled in ink 3 and again in pencil;* 'Hugo' *originally* 'Hugh'; 'o' *interlined in pencil without a caret above canceled* 'h'.

240.8   ceremony] *follows canceled* 'honor'.

240.16   to rouse] *follows canceled* 'to al'.

241.26   this,] *followed by canceled* 'it was'.

241.29   purposed] *follows canceled* 'put'.

241.30   mortify him] 'him' *interlined.*

241.33   "Clime"] *originally* 'A "clime" '; 'A' *canceled and* 'C' *written over* 'c'; *the quotation marks possibly added.*

241.35   soap] *follows canceled* 'and'.

241.35   and spread] 'and' *interlined.*

241.38   angry-looking] *the MS reads* 'appear decayed' *(emended);* 'appear' *written over* 'seem'.

242.4   passer-by.*] *the asterisk interlined and the footnote added to the bottom of the MS page; see entry at 242 note.*

242.5   Hugo] *mended from* 'Hugh'.

242.6   soldering-iron;] *followed by canceled* 'and'; *the semicolon possibly added.*

242.6   boy] *follows canceled* 'unsuspecting'.

242.6   out on a tinkering] *interlined above canceled* 'on an early-morning'; 'out on' *may have been interlined first above canceled* 'on'.

242.12   and enjoyed] *follows canceled* 'and laughed at his'.

242.14   time] *followed by canceled* 'the'.

242 note   *From . . . 1665.] *added to the bottom of the MS page.*

243.1   warm] *follows canceled* 'settle'.

243.7   should not be] 'not' *interlined; followed by canceled* 'ad' *and* 'no more required'.

243.22   another,] *followed by canceled* 'both'.

243.26   both,] *followed by canceled* 'were'; *the comma probably added.*

243.26   sure] *interlined above canceled* 'certain'.

243.28   uncertainty] *interlined above canceled* 'risk'.

243.31   "Breath] *follows canceled* ' "Lord, an I can'.

243.36   "Tarry] *follows the canceled passage* 'at different . . . said—' *described in the entry at 205.4.*

243.36   prey.] *interlined above canceled* 'woman.'

243.38   now,] *interlined.*

244.1   But] *originally run-on; marked to begin a new paragraph with a paragraph sign.*

244.11–13   —and . . . results.] *added on the verso of the MS page with instructions to turn over.*

244.11   two he] *follows canceled* 'two crept back again'; 'he' *interlined.*

244.14   The] *originally run-on; marked to begin a new paragraph with a paragraph sign.*

244.15   from it] *followed by a canceled comma.*

245.1   snatched] *follows canceled* 'and'.

245.4–9   Hugo . . . in vexation—] *added on the verso of the MS page with instructions to turn over; replaces canceled* 'He cried out, in vexation—' *on the recto;* 'out,' *in the cancellation followed by a canceled dash.*

246.3   pleasantly] *interlined.*

246.6   handling.] *followed by canceled closing quotation marks.*

246.6   thy] *interlined above canceled* 'thine'.

246.9   away,] *followed by canceled* 'and'; *the comma apparently added.*

246.13   comest] *apparently mended from* 'camest'.

246.14   Sir Miles;] *originally* 'Miles Hendon;'; 'Hendon;' *canceled and the semicolon added following* 'Miles'; 'Sir' *interlined.*

247 title   CHAPTER 23] *originally* 'CHAP. 24' *interlined at the top of the MS page;* '23.' *interlined above canceled* '24'.

247.4–11   Then . . . this world."] *added on the verso of the MS page with instructions to turn over.*

247.6   Lord,] *interlined above canceled* 'Now'.

247.7   quaint and crazy] *originally* 'wild and crazy'; 'wild' *canceled;* 'queer' *interlined above it and canceled; then* 'quaint' *interlined.*

247.9   honor] *follows canceled* 'worthy'.

247.9   spectre-knight] *the MS reads* 'spectre-baronet' *(emended);* 'spectre-' *interlined.*

247.11   an earl] *interlined above canceled* 'a lord'.

247.12   apart to] *originally* 'apart, deferentially, to'; *the commas and* 'deferentially' *canceled.*

247.12–13   and was about] *follows canceled* 'and laid his hand'.

247.15   friend,] *the comma replaces what appears to be a canceled*
           semicolon.

247.15   your hand] *originally* 'thine hand'; 'thine' *mended to* 'thy' *and*
           then canceled; 'your' *interlined.*

247.15   peaceably;] *originally* 'peacefully;'; 'fully;' *canceled and* 'ably;'
           interlined.

247.19   said] *follows canceled* 'w'.

247.21   royalty] *follows canceled* 'loyalty'.

248.4   requires] *follows canceled* 'o'.

248.5   station] *interlined above canceled* 'position'.

248.11   troubled, whilst] *follows canceled* 'grave and'; *the comma*
           mended from a semicolon; 'whilst' *interlined above canceled*
           'and'.

248.12   thrilled . . . dismay;] *squeezed in to replace canceled* 'racked
           with a sudden convulsion of dismay;'; 'sudden' *interlined.*

249.1–2   an ominous] *interlined above canceled* 'a portentous'.

249.3   dost] *follows canceled* 'doth'.

249.12   broke and blended] *interlined above canceled* 'melted';
           'blended' *mended from* 'blent'.

249.14   in . . . voice—] *follows a canceled dash.*

249.15   was] *interlined.*

249.16   grievous] *interlined to replace canceled* 'evil'.

249.17   woman!] *the exclamation point written over a comma.*

249.18   thirteen] *originally* 'thirteen'; 'thirteen' *canceled and* 'twelve'
           interlined and canceled; then 'thirteen' *interlined.*

249.20   consternation,] *interlined above canceled* 'dismay,'.

249.22   shaking] *interlined above canceled* 'quaking'.

249.24   the whole] *follows canceled* 'all'.

249.26   and simply] *follows canceled* 'and sa'.

249.27   since] *follows a canceled dash.*

249.28   writ] *originally* 'written'; 'ten' *canceled.*

249.31   surprised] *interlined without a caret above canceled* 'aston-
           ished'.

249.32   by] *mended from* 'but'.

249.38   dusky] *follows canceled* 'murky'.

250.1   pig . . . eating;] *interlined to replace canceled* 'and comely pig,
           and'.

250.3   indeed!] *followed by canceled* 'It cost'.

250.7   in] *originally* 'i' '; *the apostrophe canceled and* 'n' *added.*

250.9   saidst] *followed by canceled* 'it cost'.

250.15   dear] *interlined above canceled* 'good'.

250.18   The . . . crying;] *interlined.*

250.21   lecture,] *the comma apparently added later.*

250.22   imprisonment] *follows canceled* 'term in the'.

250.22   a public flogging.] *interlined above canceled* 'a whipping.'

250.23   astounded] *interlined above canceled* 'astonished'.

251.6   inflamed] *follows canceled* 'street'.

251.6   snatched . . . hand,] *interlined above canceled* 'stamped his foot,'.

251.7   I] *follows canceled* 'the majesty of'; *originally* 'I'; *the underlining canceled.*

251.10   dangerous] *follows canceled* 'reckless'.

251.11   be] *follows canceled* 'pe'.

251.13   happened."*] *the asterisk and the following footnote added later.*

251 note   Notes . . . 23] *originally* 'Note 10'; '10' *canceled,* 's' *added to* 'Note' *and* 'to Chapter 23' *interlined.*

253 title   CHAPTER 24] *the MS reads* 'Chap. 24.'; '24.' *follows canceled* '20'.

253.2   straight] *interlined.*

253.3   anxious] *followed by canceled* 'to get'.

253.8   had] *interlined.*

253.21–22   error"—then . . . ear—"the] *originally* 'error—the'; 'then . . . ear—' *interlined following the dash; the closing quotation marks following* 'error' *and the opening quotation marks preceding* 'the' *added.*

254.3   tranquil,] *interlined above canceled* 'cool,'.

254.3   patience] *follows canceled* 'tranquil'.

254.3   his] *interlined above canceled* 'the man's'.

254.4   said] *follows canceled* 'he'.

254.9   should not] *interlined above canceled* 'would'.

254.10   if] *follows canceled* 'thu'.

254.20   nathless] *originally* 'natheless'; 'e' *canceled.*

255.4–5   the . . . hath] *originally* 'he hath'; 't' *added to* 'he', *and* 'judge! why, man, he' *interlined preceding* 'hath'.

256.4   e'en] *follows canceled* 'e'.

256.7   a solemnity . . . him—] *interlined above canceled* 'impressive solemnity—'.

256.8	name, in law—] *originally* 'name—'; *the comma added and* 'in law' *interlined.*
256.9	have been unwise.] *interlined above canceled* 'am lost!"'.
256.17	thirteen pence] *follows canceled* 'three and eight-|pence'.
256.19	barratry,] *interlined above canceled* 'theft,'.
256.28	archangel] *interlined above canceled* 'angel'.
256.28	Go] *follows canceled* 'Out'.
256.29	break in and] *interlined.*
256.30	force.] *followed by canceled closing quotation marks.*
256.33	this] *interlined above canceled* 'yon'.
256.33	jailer's] *follows canceled* 'kee'.
257 title	CHAPTER 25] 'CHAP. 25.' *interlined in MS;* '25' *mended from* '21'.
257.4	blithely] *interlined.*
257.5	sorry steeds.] *interlined above canceled* 'donkeys.'
257.10	mind;] *originally* 'mind and must'; 'and must' *canceled and the semicolon added.*
257.12	and its] *interlined above canceled* 'and the poor little chap's'.
257.13	move] *follows canceled* 'choke down'.
257.21	bed; then . . . slept] *originally* 'bed, and slept'; *the comma mended to a semicolon,* 'and' *canceled, and* 'then . . . quarters, and' *interlined preceding* 'slept'.
258.2–16	over the adventures . . . archangel.] *added on the verso of the MS page with instructions to turn over; replaces* 'and planning, and allowing themselves liberal noonings.' *which was canceled on the recto.*
258.4	described] *follows canceled* 'ended'.
258.12	old Sanctum Sanctorum] *interlined above canceled* 'he'.
259.1	the last] 'the' *interlined above canceled* 'this'.
259.1	of the trip,] *interlined.*
259.3	Arthur, and] *followed by canceled* 'the lovely Edith,'.
259.4	loving] *interlined to replace canceled* 'endless adoring'.
259.4	Edith] *follows canceled* 'lovely'.
259.5	he was even able] *originally* 'he even managed'; 'managed' *canceled;* 'was' *and* 'able' *interlined.*
259.5	some] *interlined.*
259.10	receding] *interlined.*
259.10	marked] *possibly squeezed in later.*
260.5	my] *interlined following canceled* 'mine'.

260.5   delay."] *the period mended from an exclamation point;*
             'CHAP. 21.' interlined following 'delay." ', then canceled.

260.6   it] *follows canceled 'the'.*

260.10   Lion,] *followed by canceled closing quotation marks.*

260.18   them.] *followed by canceled quotation marks.*

260.26   after!"] *interlined above canceled 'more!" '.*

260.28   door, helped . . . and] *originally 'door, and siezing the king*
             in his arms,'; 'and . . . arms,' canceled, and 'helped . . . and'
             interlined.

260.30   seated . . . then] *interlined to replace canceled 'put the king*
             down, and'.

260.33–34   shall touch . . . see . . . hear] *originally 'have touched . . . seen*
             . . . heard'; 'shall' interlined above canceled 'have', 'ed' of
             'touched' canceled, 'n' of 'seen' canceled, and 'd' of 'heard'
             canceled.

260.35   back, . . . surprise,] *interlined above canceled 'back, angrily'.*

260.36   grave] *interlined following a canceled unrecovered word of five*
             or six letters.

261.3   Thy] *apparently mended from 'Tho'.*

261.6   . Prithee] *apparently written over 'Fr'.*

261.6   art] *originally 'are'; 'e' mended to 't'.*

261.8   other] *follows canceled 'co'.*

261.11   brother] *followed by a canceled comma.*

261.17   do] *originally 'do'; the underlining canceled.*

261.19   dragged] *follows canceled 'and'.*

262.4   laughed] *follows canceled 'chuckled,'.*

262.7   and scan] *follows canceled 'and scan'; followed by canceled 'w'*
             and canceled 'me good,'.

262.9   is't] *follows canceled 'isn't'.*

262.10   lord,] *interlined following canceled ' 'Odsbody,'.*

262.12   throw] *follows canceled 'spring'.*

262.17   amazed,] *followed by canceled 'and stupefied,'.*

262.19   disappointment?] *followed by canceled closing quotation*
             marks.

262.21   eyes may] *'may' apparently written over 'and'.*

263.6   know me."] *followed by canceled [¶] ' "He is dead.'*

263.9   dead!] *the exclamation point squeezed in.*

263.14   crave your] *originally 'cry you'; 'crave' interlined above*
             canceled 'cry', and 'you' expanded to 'your'.

263.15   do not say] *originally* 'say not'; 'do not' *interlined before* 'say' *and* 'not' *canceled after* 'say'.

263.18   An'] *the apostrophe apparently added later.*

263.18   am] *interlined above canceled* 'be'.

263.25   leal and] *interlined.*

263.28   gravely,] *followed by a canceled dash.*

263.32   derided.] *followed by canceled closing quotation marks.*

263.34   coloring] *interlined above canceled* 'blushing,'.

264.2   should] *follows canceled* 'though'.

264.6   with] *follows canceled* 'with'.

264.10   grateful] *followed by canceled* 'enough'.

264.14   slowly,] *interlined.*

264.16   sprang] *follows canceled* 'stepped eagerly'.

264.18   said] *followed by a canceled comma and a canceled dash.*

265.1   Do you] *originally* 'Dost thou'; 'st' *of* 'Dost' *canceled and* 'you' *interlined above canceled* 'thou'.

265.2   Miles's] *follows an unrecovered cancellation of three letters.*

265.5   looked] *follows canceled* 'fixed a stony'.

265.13   heads;] *followed by canceled* 'then, at a sign, they retired.'

265.13   said] *followed by what may be canceled* 'to'.

265.14   you] *interlined above canceled* 'thee'.

265.14   fear] *followed by an unrecovered cancellation of two or three letters.*

265.15   You have] *interlined above canceled* 'Thou hast'.

265.15   you] *interlined above canceled* 'thee'.

266.3   shame] *interlined above canceled* 'smirch'.

266.4   the slaying] *follows canceled* 'the shedding of'.

266.7   of them] 'of' *written over* 's'.

266.8   weaponless."] *followed by canceled* [¶] ' "Then'.

266.9   Upon] *follows canceled* 'Y'.

266.11   an'] *the apostrophe possibly added later.*

266.16   watch," said Hugh.] *originally* 'watch." '; *the closing quotation marks canceled; the comma and a new set of closing quotation marks added and* 'said Hugh.' *interlined; two periods inadvertently left standing.*

266.17   "You'll] *interlined above canceled* ' "Thou't'.

266.17   your] *interlined to replace canceled* 'thy'.

266.18   at escape] *follows canceled* 'to'.

266.19   "Escape?] *followed by canceled closing quotation marks.*

266.19   an'] *the apostrophe possibly added later.*

266.20   all] *followed by canceled 'of'.*

267 title   CHAPTER 26] *the MS reads* 'Chap. 26.'; '26.' *follows canceled* '22.'

268.2   pathetic] *follows canceled 'mad'.*

268.4   plan] *followed by a canceled period.*

268.4   a paper,] *originally* 'a paper'; 'them' *interlined preceding* 'a'; *then apparently* 'them a' *canceled,* 'paper' *expanded to* 'papers', *and the comma added; finally the* 's' *of* 'papers' *canceled and* 'a' *interlined.*

268.6   with it] 'it' *interlined above canceled* 'them'.

268.6   Give it] 'it' *interlined above canceled* 'them'.

268.7   see it,] 'it,' *interlined above canceled* 'them,'.

268.7   wrote it.] 'it.' *interlined above canceled* 'them.'

268.10   domains] *follows canceled* 'title and'.

268.17   whole.] *followed by canceled* 'Re'.

269.4   when] *follows canceled* 'he hath a'.

269.8   diverting him] *interlined above canceled* 'turning me'.

269.9   wild] *interlined.*

269.12–14   So absorbed . . . act.] *added on the verso of the MS page with instructions to turn over.*

269.17   plainly;] *follows canceled* 'plainly; I cannot r'.

269.17   dismiss] *followed by canceled* 'one'.

269.20   otherwise?] *the question mark interlined without a caret above a canceled comma or what may have been a semicolon.*

269.36   Miles] *follows canceled* 'Sir'.

270.3   question,] *interlined above canceled* 'doubt,'.

270.4   if] *interlined above canceled* 'that'.

270.6   have] *interlined.*

270.34   but] *followed by canceled* 'there'.

271.5   purse] *follows canceled* 'm'.

271.14–272.2 "Swear . . . swear."] *added on the verso of the MS page with instructions to turn over.*

272.4   yourself."] *followed at the bottom of the MS page by a paragraph which was canceled:* [¶] ' "No! You *shall* confess me—and when that is done, others shall follow.'; *the following MS page has apparently been lost, since the succeeding page now surviving begins in mid-sentence of a passage which was revised and then canceled. The canceled passage is reproduced below. The superior numbers refer to Mark Twain's revisions, which are listed following the passage.*

'days—ah, you wince; that shot went home, then!—I[1] could empty a quiver-full of the like into thy wooden heart, an I chose, thou poor false Edith. Enjoy these acres—thou hast dearly earned them; I will come no more to trouble thee with frights about thy precious lands and dignities and shekels."[2]'

1. I] *followed by canceled* 'could follow it'.
2. shekels."] *follows canceled* 'sheckels.'

272.7	prison.] *followed by canceled* [¶] 'The first act of his majesty's captivity was'.
273 title	CHAPTER 27] *the MS reads* 'Chap. 27.'; '27.' *follows canceled* '23.'
273.2–3	commonly] *follows canceled* 'kept.'
273.4	ages,] *the comma mended from a period.*
273.6	moody] *follows canceled* 'tacitur'.
273.11	stunning] *possibly mended from* 'sh'.
273.11	he] *follows canceled* 'it s'.
273.12	danced blithely out] *originally* 'danced out hilariously'; 'hilariously' *canceled and* 'blithely' *interlined.*
273.15	centred] *follows canceled* 'se'.
273.16	He] *originally* 'Her'; *the* 'r' *canceled.*
274.4	interested] *follows canceled* 'motives'.
274.5	curses,] *interlined without a caret above canceled* 'reproaches,'.
274.5	this name] *interlined above canceled* 'it' *which follows canceled* 'he'.
274.9	singing] *written over* 'and'.
274.9	of ribald] 'of' *interlined in ink 3 above* 'of' *canceled in pencil;* 'ribald' *possibly squeezed in.*
274.10	was . . . consequence] *originally* 'were . . . consequences'; 'was' *interlined above canceled* 'were'; *the* 's' *of* 'consequences' *canceled.*
274.14	about the head and shoulders] *interlined.*
274.18	were of] *interlined following canceled* 'had'.
275.4	at last.] *followed by canceled* 'One day t'.
275.8	"This] *follows canceled* ' "Wh'.
275.14	said—] *followed by canceled* [¶] ' "These be all strangers to me'.

275.21   An'] *the apostrophe apparently added later.*

275.22   shabby] *interlined above canceled* 'scurvy'.

275.26   an'] *the apostrophe apparently added later.*

275.26   An'] *the apostrophe apparently added later.*

275.34   wert] *mended from* 'were'.

275.37   o'] *originally* 'of'; *the* 'f' *canceled and the apostrophe added.*

276.7   Hendon] *follows canceled* 'But for'.

276.10   Andrews] *originally* 'Andrews's'; ' 's' *canceled.*

277.5   return;] *followed by canceled* 'two years went by and'.

277.11   nuptials] *interlined above canceled* 'marriage'.

278.2   for] *followed by what appears to be canceled* 'it'.

278.3   glared] *originally* 'stared'; 'gl' *written over* 'st'.

278.10   in a day or two—] *interlined; originally* 'in a few days—'; *then* 'few', *the* 's' *of* 'days', *and the dash canceled, and* 'or two—' *added.*

278.18   resumed] *followed by canceled* 'his'.

278.19   grand] *follows canceled* 'great'.

278.19   hopes. He] 'hopes.' *followed by canceled* ' 'Tis thought the lapsed title in the lady Edith's family will be revived in him, and that'; 'He' *mended from* 'he'.

278.20   a peer,] *originally* 'an earl'; 'n' *of* 'an' *canceled and* 'peer,' *interlined following canceled* 'earl'.

278.23   Duke] *originally* 'duke'; 'D' *written over* 'd'.

278.24   Duke] *originally* 'duke'; 'D' *written over* 'd'.

278.25   Earl] *the MS reads* 'earl' *(emended); follows canceled* 'Hert'.

278.30   king."] *followed by canceled* [¶] 'The'.

278.35   Sixth—whom God preserve!] *originally* 'Sixth."'; *the period and the quotation marks canceled, and* '—. . . preserve!' *interlined.*

278.35   dear] *follows canceled* 'most'.

278.36   little urchin] *interlined above canceled* 'king'.

279.5   old] *follows canceled* 'talk'.

280.4   why] *follows canceled* 'what'.

280.5   Baptists,] *followed by canceled* 'he said'.

280.7   lose ye] 'ye' *interlined above canceled* 'thee'.

280.7   keep ye] 'ye' *interlined above canceled* 'thee'.

280.16   betrayed confusion] *follows canceled* 'were distressed a'; 'bet' *of* 'betrayed' *mended from* 'bre'; 'confusion' *written over* 's'.

280.27   me!—for . . . comforters."] *the exclamation point squeezed in*

	to replace a canceled exclamation point and closing quotation marks; '—for . . . comforters." ' added.
280.32	came] interlined.
281.2	standing] follows canceled 'with'.
281.7	shivered] interlined above canceled 'sighed'.
281.16–34	To think . . . hundred, then."] added on the verso of the MS page with instructions to turn over; replaces 'And I, the very source of power, am helpless to protect them in this their time of bitter need!—must even look on' canceled on the recto.
281.25	done;] followed by canceled 'I'.
281.33	they] follows canceled 'that'.
281.35	citizens] follows canceled 'cl'.
282.4	the further] follows canceled 'the side fur'.
282.5	people.] followed by canceled 'and they ceased to stir or speak.'; the period following 'people' added.
282.11	away] interlined above what appears to be canceled 'aside'.
283.5–6	the burning portion of] interlined.
283.6	snatched] interlined above canceled 'torn'.
283.10–11	a volley of . . . shrieks] 'volley of' interlined; 'shrieks' expanded from 'shriek'.
283.15	there;] followed by canceled 'till I die'; the semicolon apparently added.
283.17	Hendon] follows canceled 'Th'.
283.23	That same day] interlined to replace canceled 'Some days later,'; 'Some' interlined above canceled 'Two'.
283.26–28	—he had . . . offered—] added on the verso of the MS page with instructions to turn over.
283.28	the opportunity] 'the' interlined.
283.32	he had] 'he' interlined.
284.2	mount] originally 're-mount'; 're-' canceled.
284.9	strong] follows canceled 'brave'.
284.16	and degradation] 'and' interlined.
284.26	life.] followed by canceled quotation marks.
284.36–note	mercy."* . . . volume.] the asterisk and the following footnote added.
285 title	CHAPTER 28] the MS reads 'Chap. 28.'; '28.' follows canceled '24.'
285.2	But now] interlined above canceled 'At last'.
285.5–6	described . . . and] interlined.

285.8–9   rightful heirship] *follows canceled* 'heir'; 'ship' *of* 'heirship'
            squeezed in in pencil.

285.11   threatened,] *followed by canceled* 'but'.

285.14   rabble] *interlined above canceled* 'crowd'.

285.14   swarmed] *interlined above canceled* 'followed'.

286.1   through;] *the semicolon apparently replaces a wiped-out
            period.*

286.3   degrading] *follows canceled* 'stocks'.

286.12   free!] *followed by canceled* 'I that am the king, command it!" '.

286.17   well inclined."] *interlined above canceled* 'nothing loath." '

286.18   a taste] *interlined above canceled* 'a touch'.

286.19   manners."] *followed by canceled* [¶] ' "Half' *and* [¶] 'The king
            was siezed'.

287.2   up,] *followed by what appears to be* 'en' *or* 'eg' *interlined and
            then canceled.*

287.16   "Marry,] *followed by canceled* ' 'tis well thought of—yes,'.

287.16   thought,] *followed by canceled* 'truly'.

287.21   you utter] *interlined above a canceled comma.*

287.23   and his . . . bare;] *interlined.*

287.26–27   never . . . memory.] *interlined to replace canceled* 'not be for-
            got. He shall'; *closing quotation marks following* 'forgot.'
            canceled.

287.28–34   passion. Whilst . . . SHAME!"] 'passion.' *originally followed by*
            [¶] 'Hendon made no out-|', *which was canceled, then re-
            copied following the addition of* 'Whilst . . . SHAME!" '.

287.29   grew] *followed by canceled* 'apace in his mind,'.

287.31   wounds] *follows canceled* 'death,—and this'.

287.36   redeeming] *follows canceled* 'taking the boy's stripes'.

288.2   that pervaded] *interlined above canceled* 'of'.

288.3–289.12 contrast with . . . power." The dreaded . . . spurred] 'con-|'
            was originally followed on a new MS page by 'trast with the
            insulting clamor which had prevailed there so little a while
            before. As the dreaded Sir Hugh rode'; 'trast . . . before.' *was
            canceled when* 'trast with . . . power." ' *(288.3–289.11) was
            added on three intervening MS pages. Then* 'As the dreaded
            Sir Hugh rode' *was canceled and* 'The dreaded . . . spurred'
            squeezed in to replace it.

288.5   came . . . his] *interlined above canceled* 'came and whispered
            in Hendon's'.

288.9   lightly] *follows canceled* 'wit'.

289.4	indeed!] *follows canceled* 'indeed'.
289.6	spectre-earl!] *the exclamation point squeezed in.*
289.6	An'] *follows canceled* 'Ah, well, dear heart,'.
289.8	But] *interlined following canceled* 'Ah, well, dear heart,'.
289.9–10	of mine,] *interlined above a canceled comma.*
289.10	right] *interlined above canceled* 'pure'.
289.11	interested] *follows canceled* 'self'.
289.14	remained] *follows canceled* 'they'.
289.14	so far] *follows canceled* 'to'.
289.15	in favor] *follows what may be canceled* 'or'.
290.2–3	and who] *interlined.*
291 title	CHAPTER 29] *the MS reads* 'Chap. 29.'; '29.' *follows canceled* '25.'
291.3	mule and his donkey.] *originally* 'his donkeys.'; 'mule and his' *interlined, the* 's.' *of* 'donkeys.' *canceled and a new period added.*
291.7	thought.] *the period mended from a comma.*
291.16	Andrews] 's' *apparently added later.*
292.6	inventing] *follows canceled* 's'.
292.8–11	Maybe ... which.] *added on the verso of the MS page with instructions to turn over.*
292.12	fog] *follows canceled* 'night'.
293.2	sorrowful] *interlined.*
293.4	during] *follows canceled* 'he'.
293.10	mightily] *interlined above canceled* 'well'.
293.10	with] *written over* 'a'.
293.11	astounded] *interlined to replace canceled* 'wondering'.
293.13	one. About] *originally* 'one;—for, about'; *the semicolon and* '—for,' *canceled and* 'A' *written over* 'a' *of* 'about'.
293.14	they] *follows an unrecovered cancellation of two letters.*
293.15	people,] *interlined to replace canceled* 'human beings—and at that instant a'.
293.17	the decaying] 'the' *interlined above canceled* 'a'.
293.17–294.1	head ... grandee] *interlined above canceled* 'human head'; 'human' *may have been canceled earlier.*
294.4	grave,] *originally followed by an MS page inscribed with* 'and already his bridge-adornments are falling'; *the second page apparently abandoned and its verso subsequently used at a later point in the MS.*

294.13	was occupying] *originally* 'occupied'; 'was' *interlined and* 'cupying' *interlined above canceled* 'cupied'.
294.14	was] *originally* 'we'; 'as' *written over* 'e'.
295 title	CHAPTER 30] *the MS reads* 'Chap. 30.'; '30.' *follows canceled* '26.'
295.2	poorly fed;] *follows canceled* 'often hun'.
295.2	herding] *follows canceled* 'and'.
295.4	quite] *written over* 'w'.
295.7	for] *interlined above canceled* 'to'.
295.9	misgivings] *the terminal* 's' *possibly added.*
295.10	embarrassments departed] *originally* 'embarrassment and'; 'embarrassment' *expanded to* 'embarrassments', *and* 'departed' *written over* 'and'.
295.11	mine to] *followed by what appears to be canceled* 'ne'.
295.13	Grey] *followed by a canceled comma and dash.*
295.14	dismissed] *follows canceled* 'ordere'.
295.15	them, with] *followed by canceled* 'a'.
295.15	familiarly] *interlined; written over* 'long'.
295.16	lofty] *follows an unrecovered cancellation of two letters.*
295.17	hand,] *the comma possibly mended from a period.*
295.21	officers] *follows canceled* 'officers'.
296.3	distant] *originally* 'distance'; 't' *written over* 'c' *and* 'e' *canceled.*
296.8	called] *followed by canceled* 'him,—the late'.
296.11	four] *interlined above canceled* 'five'.
296.11	trebled] *interlined to replace canceled* 'increased'.
296.16	an earl, or] *follows canceled* 'a duke'; 'or' *interlined following a canceled interlined dash.*
296.16	duke,] *followed by a canceled dash.*
296.16	make] *follows canceled* 'shrivel'.
296.18	course in] *originally followed by* 'stopping the burning of certain sorts of'; 'stopping the' *canceled at the bottom of the MS page;* 'burning . . . of' *written on an MS page which was apparently abandoned and its verso subsequently used at a later point in the MS.*
296.19	otherwise] *followed by canceled* 'be imprison'.
297.1	prisons] *the terminal* 's' *written over* 'e'.
297.4	thieves and robbers] *interlined above canceled* 'criminals'.
297.4	executioner,*] *the asterisk interlined and the footnote added at the bottom of the MS page; see entry at 297 note.*

297.6	beseech] *interlined above canceled* 'beg'.
297.6	take away] *follows canceled* 'give her'.
297.12	lost] *interlined.*
297.12	prince,] *the comma mended from a period.*
297.12	return and] *followed by canceled* 'rehabilitation and'.
297 note	*Hume's England.] *added to the bottom of the MS page.*
298.1	almost] *interlined.*
298.12	mournful] *follows canceled* 'faces'.
298.17	solemn] *written over* 'c'.
298.18	hungry and thirsty,] *interlined.*
298.19	worn] *follows canceled* 'and'.
298.19–20	and clothed . . . was] *added on the verso of the MS page with instructions to turn over, replacing canceled* 'was one of a' *on the recto.*
298.21	with] *follows canceled* 'g'.
298.21	certain] *interlined above canceled* 'the'.
298.22	Westminster Abbey,] *originally* 'Westminster, a'; *the comma and* 'a' *canceled and* 'Abbey,' *interlined.*
299 title	CHAPTER 31] *the MS reads* 'Chap. 31.'; '31.' *follows canceled* '27.'
299.11	gush] *interlined following canceled* 'jet'.
299.11	smoke;] *followed by canceled* 'the'.
299.13	flame-jets] *originally* 'flames'; 's' *canceled and* '-jets' *added.*
299.14	again,] *written over an ampersand.*
299.15	Tower] *followed by canceled* 'was'.
299.17	vapor] *interlined above canceled* 'smoke'.
299.18	mountain-peak] 'peak' *written over* 'su'.
300.1	prancing] *interlined above canceled* 'great'.
300.2	his "uncle,"] *interlined.*
300.4–5	burnished] *interlined above canceled* 'shining'.
300.5	Protector] *originally* 'protector'; 'P' *written over* 'p'.
300.6	vassals] *follows canceled* 'glittering'.
300.8	breasts;] 'breasts' *followed by a squeezed-in and canceled comma and a canceled caret with no interlineation.*
300.10–15	Also . . . parliament.] 'Also . . . Parliament.' *added on the verso of the MS page with instructions to turn over; emended.*
300.13	at that time,] *interlined.*
300.14	possessing] *interlined above canceled* 'holding'.
300.14	possesses] *interlined without a caret above canceled* 'holds'.

300.15   holding . . . parliament.] *interlined to replace canceled* 'marching through the city of London with flags flying and drums unmuffled without asking permission of the municipal authorities.'

301.19   his heart] 'his' *mended from* 'he'.

301.21   Presently,] *followed by canceled* 'at a'.

301.24   his pride] *follows canceled* 'his heart'.

301.27   derided] *follows canceled* 'despised'.

302.1   Eagle] *written over* 'e'.

302.30   loyal] *originally* 'royal'; 'l' *written over* 'r'.

302.33   Whithersoever] *originally* 'Where'; 'er' *mended to* 'ith' *and* 'rsoever' *added.*

302.37   great] *interlined above canceled* 'great'.

302.37   triumphal] *follows canceled* 'grand'.

303.6   the splendor] 'the' *originally* 'this'; *the* 'e' *mended from* 'i' *and the* 's' *canceled.*

303.8–9   "And . . . Canty.] *squeezed in at the bottom of the MS page.*

303.11   his senses swam] *originally* 'he was'; 'he' *mended to* 'his' *and* 'senses swam' *interlined above canceled* 'was'.

304.4   sickening] *interlined above canceled* 'deadly'.

304.5–7   and up . . . habit!] *added on the verso of the MS page with instructions to turn over.*

304.6   old] *interlined above canceled* 'unconscious gesture'.

304.8   past] *interlined above canceled* 'through'.

304.9   with] *interlined above canceled* 'was'.

304.10   The same] *follows canceled* 'In the'; 'same' *interlined above canceled* 'next'.

304.11   King's Guard] *originally* 'king's guard'; 'k' *and* 'g' *underlined three times.*

304.11   snatched] *interlined above canceled* 'tore'.

305.2   arm.] *followed by canceled* 'Tom Canty was affecting to laugh; but'.

305.2–3   falling from] *interlined above canceled* 'on'.

305.6   she seemed] *interlined above canceled* 'she looked'.

305.18   shining] *interlined to replace interlined and canceled* 'lordly' *which in turn replaced canceled* 'glittering'.

305.30   woman!"] *the bottom quarter of the page torn off following this word; ink marks along the torn edge indicate that the inscription continued on the missing part of the page without a paragraph break.*

305.33   secret treacheries] *interlined to replace canceled* 'wrongs he'.

306.1   gladness] *interlined above canceled* 'joy'.

306.1   changed] *follows canceled* 'faded'.

306.5   bent] *follows canceled* 'uncov'.

306.9   these] *originally* 'the'; 'se' *added*.

306.10   disperse] *interlined above canceled* 'banish'.

306.12   retired] 'ir' *written over* 'u' *of* 'retu'.

306.13   few] *interlined above canceled* 'no'.

307.3   sharp annoyance,] *interlined above canceled* 'irritation,'.

307.4   pauper!—] *followed by canceled closing quotation marks; the exclamation point possibly added.*

307.7   the duke,] *interlined above canceled* 'him,'.

307.9   Protector,] *interlined above canceled* 'duke,'.

309 title   CHAPTER 32] *the MS reads* 'Chap. 32'; '32' *follows canceled* '28.'

309.12   ceased] 'now' *interlined preceding* 'ceased' *and then canceled.*

310.2   occupies] *written over* 'is'.

310.6   so it] 'it' *interlined.*

310.10–11   extinguished,] *followed by canceled* 'and a soft gray tint suffuses the great spaces,'.

310.17   an official] 'official' *follows canceled* 'grea'; 'n' *of* 'an' *added.*

310.17   satins] *preceded by a canceled caret with no interlineation.*

311.5   frosted] *follows canceled* 'roped'.

311.8   troublous] *follows canceled* 'heavy'.

311.12   jeweled] *interlined above canceled* 'shining'.

311.13   comes;] *the semicolon apparently mended from a comma.*

311.13   excitement] *interlined above canceled* 'perturbation'.

311.14   the hair] *follows canceled* 'for every lady's hair'.

311.17   array] *follows canceled* 'of'.

311.18   also] *interlined.*

311.23   electric] *follows canceled* 'thrill'.

311.25–26   marching . . . ambassadors,] *interlined.*

311.36   delay] *follows canceled* 'da'.

311.37   robes] *follows canceled* 'and splendid'.

312.2   with] *follows canceled* 'f'.

312.6   coigns] *follows canceled* 'points of'.

312.7   complete] *the semicolon possibly mended from a comma.*

312.14   platform] *follows canceled* 'royal'.

312.16   places;] *followed by canceled* 'next'.

312.26   Canty,] *followed by canceled* 'bearing the Coronation sword, and'.

312.35–36   swept the Abbey ... welcomed,] 'swept' *follows canceled* 'rose and'; 'Abbey' *interlined below canceled* 'Cathedral'; 'swept ... welcomed,' *squeezed in to replace a passage which was revised and then canceled. The canceled passage is reproduced below. The superior numbers refer to Mark Twain's revisions, which are listed following the passage.*

'rolled and reverberated through the vast spaces of the cathedral;[1] and[2] whilst this[3] still continued,'

1. cathedral;] *followed by canceled* 'and in'.
2. and] *interlined.*
3. this] *interlined above canceled* 'it'.

312.37   audience] *follows canceled* 'rapt'.

313.5   out] *followed by a canceled comma and canceled* 'over Tom Canty's'.

313.6–8   instant ... individual] *added on the verso of the MS page with instructions to turn over; replaces* 'instant every hand in one' *canceled on the recto.*

313.9   head,—] *the dash interlined.*

313.10   A deep] *Mark Twain originally started a new MS page with the words* 'At this' *which he canceled; he then turned the page upside-down and began it again with* 'A deep'.

313.10   hush ... Abbey.] *interlined above canceled* 'silence fell upon the vast assemblage.'; 'Abbey.' *interlined above canceled* 'cathedral.'

313.11   intruded] *follows canceled* 'stepped'.

313.12   in ... multitude,] *interlined.*

313.12   appeared,] *follows canceled* 'appeared in the great central aisle, in'; 'central' *interlined.*

313.21   in ... voice—] *added following a canceled dash.*

313.24   in a bewildered way] *interlined.*

313.28   himself] *followed by a canceled dash.*

313.38–314.1 he had ... beginning;] *Mark Twain apparently considered canceling these words; he made marks before and after the sequence of words but then canceled the marks.*

314.2   ran] *followed by canceled* 'to meet him'.

314.6   sternly] *interlined.*

314.9   retreated] *second* 're' *possibly written over* 'ir' *of* 'retir'.

314.12   perplexity,] *follows canceled* 'profound'.

314.13	with grave respectfulness—] *interlined to replace the revised, then canceled, passage* 'not reverently, but with a manner which might be said to lie between respect and deference—'; 'but' *follows canceled* 'but'; 'lie' *interlined above canceled* 'be'; 'respect' *follows canceled* 'reserve'.
315.4	true] *followed by a canceled comma.*
315.4	our lord] *interlined.*
315.7	Protector] *follows canceled* 'Lord'.
315.8–9	—but . . . direction] *interlined.*
315.10	sweeping] *follows canceled* 'drifting'.
315.12–13	so fateful a] 'so' *follows* 'a' *canceled in pencil;* 'a' *after* 'fateful' *added in pencil.*
315.15	this—] *followed by canceled closing quotation marks.*
315.17	lieth] *possibly mended from* 'is'.
315.18	answer!] *followed by canceled closing quotation marks.*
315.19	hang] *originally* 'hangs'; 's' *canceled.*
315.21	shot] *follows canceled* 'flashed from one to another of them in the form of approving glances.'
315.24	this forlorn] *follows canceled* 'if'; *followed by canceled* 'lad'.
315.30	confusion.] *followed by canceled* 'But it was'.
315.34–35	command] *written over* 'w'.
315.38	corner remotest from] *originally* 'corner furthest from'; 'furthest' *canceled and* 'remotest' *interlined above it;* 'remotest from' *canceled and then rewritten.*
316.2	will] *interlined above canceled* 'shall'.
316.7–8	without . . . mistake,] *interlined.*
316.9	peer] *followed by canceled* 'him'.
317.6	gorgeous] *interlined.*
317.10	movement] *followed by canceled* 'which had this'.
317.11	little, in the present case,] *the comma after* 'little' *added and* 'in . . . case,' *interlined.*
317.11	glittering] *interlined.*
317.13	new-comer.] *followed by canceled* 'If the new-comer had had a handkerchief, then,'.
317.14	during] *follows canceled* 'a season'.
317.22	assemblage] *mended from* 'assemblance'.
317.37	off] *interlined above canceled* 'back'.
317.38	perils his life!"] *interlined above canceled* 'shall die!"'.
318.8	Canty,] *followed by canceled* 'spr'.
318.17	knowledge.] *followed by canceled closing quotation marks.*

318.18   last,] *followed by canceled* 'last'.

318.19   punish] *interlined above canceled* 'chastise'.

318.22   fixed] *interlined above canceled* 'bent'.

318.23   among] *follows canceled* 'for'.

319.13   be,] *followed by canceled* 'lost,'; *the comma following* 'be' *probably added.*

319.14   bring] *followed by the canceled interlineation* 'the latest minutes of'.

320.2   officials] *follows canceled* 'courtiers'.

320.10   here it is,] *followed by canceled* 'I have scarce used it since; to write withal'; 'to write withal' *apparently canceled earlier and the semicolon apparently added.*

320.11   yet even] *interlined.*

320.11   the fingers are so stiff.] *interlined to replace canceled* 'but must content myself with a clumsy scrawl with the other.'

320.13   you call the Seal] *interlined.*

320.15   to hide . . . of—"] *squeezed in following a canceled dash and canceled closing quotation marks.*

320.21   it were] *interlined.*

320.22   dumb!] *followed by canceled closing quotation marks.*

320.24   assemblage] *follows canceled* 'vast'.

320.29   Time] *follows canceled* 'Time'.

320.33   Then such a] *interlined above canceled* 'A mighty'.

320.35   crash] *follows canceled* 'deafening'.

320.37   all] *followed by canceled* 'the'.

320.38   centre] *follows canceled* 'mi'.

321.1   great] *interlined to replace canceled* 'robed and coroneted great'.

321.4   give] *followed by canceled* 'me'.

321.6   The Lord . . . up—] *squeezed in.*

321.9   But] *follows canceled* 'He'.

322.1   his grace] *follows canceled* 'the'.

322.5   Seal] *written over* 's'.

322.9   your majesty."] *interlined above canceled* 'my liege." '

322.14   the Great Seal of England?"] *squeezed in following canceled* 'it?" '.

322.25   Then] *follows canceled* 'The king, and Tom, and certain officials, disappeared, now, for a time, and when they reappeared, no one discovered any change—yet the boys had exchanged raiment in the meantime.'

323 *title*	CHAPTER 33] *the MS reads* 'Chap. 33'; '33' *interlined above canceled* '29.'
323.1	enough] *followed by canceled* 'when he'.
323.2	out of it.] *followed by canceled* 'He was not rich when he drifted into that riot'.
323.3	at all] *interlined.*
323.6	task] *interlined above canceled* 'work'.
323.6	way, but] *followed by canceled* 'thought out the matter and arranged', *which is followed by canceled* 'set himself to'.
323.10–11	when homeless and forsaken,] *interlined.*
323.11	Whereabouts] *follows canceled* 'What'.
324.1	His] *originally* 'Hig'; 's' *written over* 'g'.
324.2	even] *follows canceled* 'also'.
324.6	the centre of] *interlined.*
324.7	sure; and] *followed by canceled* 'he would'.
324.17	miscalculation] *interlined above canceled* 'mistake'.
324.21	tolerably] *interlined above canceled* 'very'.
324.24	parting] *follows canceled* 'pawning'.
324.30	windings] *followed by a canceled comma and canceled* 'all the way to'.
324.31	drifted] *followed by canceled* 'about'.
324.37	rural] *interlined above canceled* 'country'.
325.9	wasted] *followed by canceled* 'to m'.
325.10	would] *followed by canceled* 'not seek out'.
326.1	him,] *the comma apparently mended from a period.*
326.3	ass] *follows canceled* 'ass'.
326.5	should make] *interlined above canceled* 'hath made'.
326.6	wasteful] *follows canceled* 'need'.
326.8	turned] *originally* 'chanced to turn'; 'chanced to' *canceled and* 'ed' *interlined after* 'turn'.
326.9	generally] *interlined.*
326.16	answered,] *follows canceled* 'said,'.
326.21	"I] *follows canceled* ' "R'.
326.24	"the king] *follows canceled opening quotation marks and an unrecovered canceled letter.*
326.26	Sir-Odds-and-Ends,] *interlined above canceled* 'one,'.
326.26	So he] *originally* 'He'; 'So' *interlined and* 'H' *not reduced to* 'h'.
326.29	a recess] *follows canceled* 'a vaulted alley-way'.
326.33	forth.] *followed by canceled* 'Hendon did'; 'Hendon' *followed by a caret with no interlineation.*

326.34   arrested] *followed by what is either a canceled comma or a canceled period.*

326.36   roughly] *interlined following canceled* 'angrily'.

328.5–6   and return his sword to him] *interlined.*

328.8   An'] *the apostrophe possibly added.*

328.11   arrived] *follows canceled* 'at'.

328.12   with another bow,] *interlined; the preceding comma probably added.*

328.14   through] *followed by canceled* 'a s'.

328.14–17   lined . . . turned,)] *added on the verso of the MS page with instructions to turn over.*

328.18   broad] *interlined above canceled* 'stately'.

328.20–21   reminded . . . off,] *interlined.*

328.25   away,] *followed by canceled* 'but with his face turned asi'.

328.32   He stood] *follows canceled* 'And it'.

328.35   Kingdom] *originally* 'kingdom'; 'k' *underlined three times.*

328.38   around] *follows canceled* 'ab'.

329.2   "But these] *originally* '"These'; 'But' *interlined following the opening quotation marks and* 'T' *not reduced to* 't'.

329.3   verily] *interlined.*

329.9   for—who . . . riddle?"] *originally* 'for?" '; '—who . . . riddle?' *interlined; two question marks inadvertently left standing.*

329.13   a rough] 'a' *written over an ampersand.*

329.17   attracted] *followed by canceled* 'his'.

329.20   stupefied.] *interlined to replace canceled* 'stunned with astonishment.'; 'stunned' *follows canceled* 'stunn'.

330.6   for we have] *originally* 'we having'; 'for' *interlined and* 'having' *altered to* 'have'.

330.6   ordained that] *followed by canceled* 'while the crown endures the head of his house shall have and hold the right to sit in the presence of the kings of England. Disturb him not." '

330.8   henceforth,] *followed by canceled* 'so'.

330.13   torpid bewilderment.] *interlined to replace canceled* 'stupefaction.'

331.13   The late . . . away.] *squeezed in;* 'late' *follows canceled* 'command'.

331.16   quaintly but richly] *interlined above canceled* 'richly'; 'but' *follows an unrecovered cancellation of one or two letters.*

331.17   between] *follows canceled* 'the'.

332.2   learned] *followed by canceled* 'thy'.

332.10	place in] *followed by canceled* 'the'.
332.21	news.*] *the asterisk and the following footnote added later.*
332 note	33] *followed by canceled* 'in'.
333.2	Miles] *followed by a canceled comma.*
333.4	the] *written over* 'a'.
333.11	brother] *interlined; follows canceled* 'Miles' *which was interlined above canceled* 'brother'.
333.14	died; and] 'and' *interlined following canceled* 'and the supposition is that'.
333.15–16	There were . . . Hall.] *squeezed in.*
334.2	Baptist] *interlined in pencil above canceled* 'Quaker'.
334.3	punished] *followed by canceled* 'all who were concerned in'.
334.6–7	a remnant . . . weaver;] *originally* 'the blanket;'; 'a' *interlined above canceled* 'the', *and* 'remnant . . . weaver;' *interlined above canceled* 'blanket;'.
334.8	forest] *follows canceled* 'pres'.
334.9	him] *followed by a canceled caret with no interlineation.*
334.10	pig, and] *followed by the canceled interlineation* 'in time'.
334.10–11	he had . . . and become] *originally* 'he became'; 'had . . . and' *interlined without a caret and* 'became' *mended to* 'become'.
334.12–22	As long . . . his heart.] *added on the verso of the MS page with instructions to turn over.*
334.14	midnight] 'mid' *interlined.*
334.15	hurrying] *interlined.*
334.33	assert] *follows canceled* 'm'.
335.9	great] *written over* 's'.
335.10	gilded] *interlined above canceled* 'splendid'.
335.11	urged that] *followed by canceled* 'the laws he'.
335.14	and] *interlined above canceled* 'and'.
335.15	of] *interlined following canceled* 'about'.
335.17	a] *interlined.*
335.18	times.] *the period added; followed by a canceled semicolon and canceled* 'and in the course of it efforts were made to modify the cruelty of the criminal laws, and with considerable success.'
335.18	keep] *follows canceled* 'rem'.
337.1	Note 1] '1' *follows what appears to be canceled* '7'.
337.3	most] *interlined.*
337.3	regard] *followed by canceled* 't'.
337.12	children] *follows canceled* 'young'.

337.23   [Henry VIII]] *the MS reads* '[Henry VIII.]' *(emended); the brackets mended from parentheses; a superscript* 's' *following* 'VIII.' *canceled.*

337.27   Hume's] *the MS reads* 'Hume's' *(emended); interlined above canceled* 'Froude's'.

337.27   vol. iii. p. 314.] *the MS reads* 'vol. III., p. 314.' *(emended); possibly added later.*

338.1   Note 5.] *originally* 'Note 4.'; '5.' *interlined following canceled* '4'; *two periods inadvertently left standing.*

338.25   reign by] 'by' *interlined above canceled* 'with', *then canceled, then interlined again.*

338.38–   But ... p. 339.] *added on the verso of the MS page with in-*
339.11   *structions to turn over.*

338.38   [the Protector,]] *the brackets apparently added later; follows canceled* '[Hertford'.

338.38   offence] *originally* 'offense'; *the* 'c' *written over* 's'.

339.1   mitigated,] *follows canceled* 'abated,'.

339.9   people.] *followed by canceled* '—Ibid, vol. iii, p. 339.'

339.17   Hamburg,] *originally* 'Hamburgh'; *the* 'h' *canceled and the comma added.*

339.35   Notes to Chapter 23.—Page] *originally* 'Note 10. Page'; '11.' *interlined above canceled* '10.', *then canceled;* 'Page' *canceled;* 's' *added to* 'Note', *and* 'to Chapter 23. Page' *added. The dash added in this edition for uniformity. See the textual introduction, page 416.*

340.13   offence] *originally* 'offense'; *the* 'c' *written over* 's'.

340.19–20   SCHOOL, "the ... World."] ' "the ... World." ' *added later; the comma mended from a period.*

340.22–23   institution] *follows canceled* 'church'; *followed by canceled* 'of a hospital'.

340.33   children.] *followed by canceled* '[The king richly endowed some other'.

340.33   charities at] 'at' *interlined above canceled* 'of'.

340.38   Papistry.—] *followed by canceled* 'J. Heneage Jesse's'.

341.30   1845.] *followed by canceled* '—Ibid.'

341.36   Hunt.] *originally* 'Hunt.—Ibid.'; 'Ibid.' *canceled; the dash inadvertently left standing; emended.*

342.4   *who imagine*] *interlined.*

342.5   *and inhumanity*] 'and' *interlined.*

342.5–6   *in reality*] *interlined.*

342.8   *Blue-Law*] *interlined.*

342.8   *all by itself,*] *interlined above canceled* 'all by itself,'.

342.9   *a century*] *follows canceled* 'near'.

342.10   *English*] *interlined.*

342.10   *side of it.*] *followed by canceled* 'These facts'.

342.14–note   *death!* These ... too. ... p. 11.*] *the asterisk,* 'These ... too.', *and the following footnote apparently added later.*

Word Division in This Volume

The following compound words that could be rendered either solid or with a hyphen are hyphenated at the end of a line in this volume. For purposes of quotation each is listed here with its correct form.

55.15–16	cook-shop		173.19–20	under-sheriff
82.3–4	Over-study		175.37–38	hare-brained
86.13–14	o'erwrought		210.7–8	semi-consciousness
90.16–17	straightway		222.4–5	noonday
92.4–5	straightway		235.20–21	overtake
126.27–28	horse-pond		239.20–21	quarter-staff
158.23–24	truss-point		243.17–18	over-gently
166.10–11	overwrought		260.16–17	gateway
			288.12–13	undermined

The text of this book is set in Continental, a typeface adapted for photocomposition from the Linotype font Trump Mediaeval, which was designed in 1954 for the Weber typefoundry by Georg Trump, a renowned German artist and typographer. Continental has been praised for the reserve and distinction of its light, clean characters. For display matter and headings, two closely related fonts were chosen to coordinate well with the text type: Weiss italic (a slightly inclined font with swash capitals) and Weiss Initials Series I (an elegant all-capital font). Both were designed by Emil Rudolf Weiss in 1931 for the Bauer typefoundry. The paper used is P & S offset laid regular, manufactured by P. H. Glatfelter Company. It is an acid-free paper of assured longevity which combines high opacity, for legibility and attractive illustrations, with low weight, for comfortable handling. The book was composed by Advanced Typesetting Services of California on Harris Fototronic equipment, printed by Publishers Press, and bound by Mountain States Bindery.